BROKEN WINGS

BROKEN WINGS

JOHN DOUGLAS
AND
MARK OLSHAKER

A LISA DREW BOOK

POCKET BOOKS

NEW YORK   LONDON   TORONTO   SYDNEY   SINGAPORE

POCKET BOOKS, a division of Simon & Schuster Inc.
1230 Avenue of the Americas, New York, NY 10020

ISBN: 0-671-02391-8

First Pocket Books hardcover printing November 1999

10 9 8 7 6 5 4 3 2

Printed in the U.S.A.

For
Carolyn and Pam
with all our love

There will be time, there will be time
To prepare a face to meet the faces that you meet;
There will be time to murder and create,
And time for all the works and days of hands
That lift and drop a question on your plate.

—T. S. ELIOT
"The Love Song of J. Alfred Prufrock"

AUTHOR'S NOTE

This novel has its origins in an idea John Douglas had and tried to implement during his years in the FBI. He proposed what he referred to as a "flying squad"—a multi-agency team of experts and specialists who would be prepared to fly immediately to the site of a major case, process the scene, and manage the case through to the arrest of the suspect. For a variety of reasons, John's proposal never came to realization. So it is gratifying for us, at long last, to see it realized in fiction. And for that, we have a number of people to thank.

It is rare these days to have a good editor, and by that I mean someone a writer can depend on for clear-cut vision, for an understanding of what that writer is trying to say and ideas on how to help achieve that goal, and for emotional support and sustenance along the way. We are extremely fortunate to have not just one, but three such individuals in our corner. Our longtime friend Lisa Drew of Scribner–Lisa Drew Books and our newer friend Jason Kaufman of Pocket Books are the best of the best, and we are tremendously grateful to both of them for everything. They are our champions and head up the Douglas-Olshaker personal flying squad. As if that weren't enough, Richard Marek, one of the living legends of publishing, came riding in like Shane (or the Lone Ranger, take your pick) just when we needed him. We're tremendously grateful and appreciative of Dick for leading us those final miles.

Other critical members of that team include our agent, manager, and confidant, Jay Acton, whose quarter century of friendship and encouragement has made all the difference to me; our assistant, Ann

Hennigan, who is my continual sounding board and who has become my literary alter ego; Lisa's assistant editor, Jake Klisivitch, and Jason's editorial assistant, Ben Kaplan. And of course: Carolyn, who, in addition to being my beloved wife and partner, first line editor, critic, and everything else, is also our general counsel and operating officer.

Special Agent Jana Monroe, as she has before, graciously gave us insight and guidance from her triple perspective of mindhunter, former homicide detective, and woman in a traditionally male field. Two other close friends have been equally gracious, generous, and supportive: John Weisman and James Grady are both outstanding and talented novelists, and their input, ideas, and influence extend throughout the book.

Special thanks to Doug Oliver and Lockheed Martin Aeronautical Systems, and to Senior Master Sergeant Buddy Bates and Brigadier General David Beasley of the Maryland Air National Guard for all of their help on the C-130 airplane that is the Broken Wings' mobile lab.

I want to stress that except when real names are used, all characters in this novel are completely fictitious and are not based on anyone. Any similarities are purely coincidental and unintended. Yet though this is a work of fiction, it is based on the truths and insights John has gained during more than two decades as one of the world's leading mindhunters, and I want to close here by thanking him for teaching, guiding, and sharing it all with me.

—*Mark Olshaker*
August 1999

BROKEN WINGS

PROLOGUE

Through the glass wall of the bedroom he gazed out over the bay for what he knew would be the last time. So beautiful from up here. So peaceful and ordered.

Almost directly below, white sailboats bobbed gently as the bay waters lapped into the marina. Scanning the middle distance from left to right, his eyes lit first on the wooded haven of Angel Island where he and Madeline had walked so many times, then the barren ruins of Alcatraz, which held their own drama for him. They reminded him of the glorious days when his organization had been responsible for providing the place with most of its more prominent residents. And beyond that, of course, that magnificent skyline. He couldn't quite see the Golden Gate Bridge from this vantage point, but that exquisite monument to the harmony between man and nature always held a prime place in his mind's image of this most magical location. He had always known this was the place he wanted to die, and, if he had any control over that event, this was the final image he wanted before his eyes.

He would leave no note, but that, as his colleagues knew, was not unusual. He knew he would leave a legacy, and that was far more important. He'd lived a full, productive, useful life, and there would be much sorrow and regret that he was gone. Of course, there would be relief and rejoicing among some, but that's just the way it was. If you live an important enough life, there are always going to be people who hate you. He had never worried about those people in life; why should he worry about them as he contemplated his own death?

Were there regrets? Sure there were, he admitted to himself. He would miss Madeline, in spite of everything. He would very much miss Jason and hoped he might come to understand. But there was nothing to do about that now. We all live our destiny. The decision had already been made. Events had taken over, had taken on a momentum of their own. In fact, he relaxed, if that was possible, knowing there were no more choices, no more decisions remaining of any kind. It made no sense to fear death.

Had his own actions led to this moment? he asked himself. Well, to a certain extent, he supposed. But that really didn't matter anymore, did it? It was too late to change the past: choices and decisions he had long ago made and lived by, and he would now die by. And there was another truism he'd learned from firsthand observation: none of us are without sin.

Still the detached observer, he saw the barrel of the revolver move up toward his eyes and felt his left index finger close around the trigger. Once the trigger was fully squeezed, he wondered idly, would he actually hear the sound of the muzzle blast, or would the bullet cancel all sensations before the sound even caught up? He had spent his professional life pursuing mysteries, and now he was on the verge of the greatest mystery of all.

SEVEN DAYS EARLIER . . .

My name is Jake Donovan. I see into the minds of psychopaths, sometimes into their souls.

No, I'm not a psychic, though I dearly wish I were. I'm not a psychiatrist or a priest, since my interest in redemption is limited and my belief in rehabilitation virtually nonexistent. It is because I am a profiler, the FBI's pioneer in that arcane discipline. I have come by my insights through experience, natural gift, and the study of the work of the leading experts in their own disciplines, whom I have sought out in their final places of residence—the maximum-security penitentiaries and death rows throughout the United States and the world.

Profiling was why I now found myself here, on direct orders from Mount Olympus, otherwise known as the Seventh Floor of the Hoover Building, in this remote forest of west-central Wyoming, almost midway between the Bighorn and Wind River mountain ranges. The area took its name from the stream, called Owl Creek, that served as the line of demarcation between us and them. I could see it from the sniper position on a high ridge above our campground, protected from return fire by dense foliage. Just below where I was standing, the spotter of a two-man sniper-spotter pair from the HRT—the Hostage Rescue Team out of Quantico—attired in woodland camo, maintained an intense gaze through eight-power Steiner binoculars down at the ramshackle ranch house that served as the focal point of the enemy camp.

The siege was in its eleventh day, without any sign of resolution. Beyond the creek, some fifteen or twenty militia/survivalists were holed up in a small compound that included the ranch house, a stable, and a barn. Their leader was Gene Claude Sickenger, owner of the compound and self-proclaimed commander in chief of the Wyoming Defenders. On our side of the creek was an ever-growing contingent of local, state, and national law enforcement officers, increasingly dominated by a detachment well familiar to the others and going by such appellations as Big Brother, the Five-Hundred-Pound Gorilla, the Stealer of Thunder, the Sucker of All Air Out of Rooms, or, simply, the Federal Bureau of Investigation. My employer.

An outer perimeter kept the encamped media at bay. Their participation could only complicate the issue.

I'd been on scene the previous four days, living in one of the campers that looked like the back lot of a particularly seedy carnival, tripling on a bunk with two guys from the Hostage Rescue Team on the midnight-to-eight and eight-to-four watches. Only Roger Greene, the SAC—special agent in charge—brought in from the Denver Field Office, the nearest large field office, to be the on-site chieftain, got choppered to a motel at night. And since I, dispatched from headquarters, could do no better than further complicate his already stress-laden life, Greene felt no obligation to make me feel comfortable or wanted.

Life is tough enough, I kept thinking. *And I am too fucking old to be living like this.* The big, macho HRT guys might get off on this back-to-nature movement, but as far as I was concerned, showering with a hose and crapping in a Porta-John gets old real fast. Toni practically had to threaten me with loss of visitation to get me to Eric's father-son Scout sleep-away.

All in all, I was no happier being here than Roger Greene was to have me. I was already freaky about the fact that the longer I was here, the more I was neglecting all my other bread-and-butter cases, cases whose outcome I might be able to affect. I had a set of dead prostitutes somewhere up in the north woods, three missing schoolgirls in Georgia, a serial poisoner in Florida, two entire families slaughtered in Idaho with similar signature elements, and a guy in New York City who claimed to be the original Zodiac killer from San Francisco. But when the director of the FBI, the Honorable Judge Thomas Jefferson Boyd, tells you to drop everything and get your butt out to Wyoming, you go. I was trying to keep up as best I could by phone and laptop with Peter Sutherland, my primary relief. But I didn't have the materials, the staff, or the concentration span here, and I was terrified people were going to die as a result of my lack of hands-on attention.

Roger Greene held court and counsel in an RV specially outfitted as a mobile command center. He even had an indoor john. When I went over there for the ten-o'clock status meeting that morning, Greene was sitting behind the desk, in front of an ordnance map of the area, already in heavy conversation with Gordon Abel, my opposite number on the tactical side. Not a good sign. Abel was the HRT's ASAC (pronounced *a-sack*, for assistant special agent in charge), and theoretically we were equals, but it was only a theory, since Abel commanded thirty-five special ops agents on-site, while I was here representing the behavioral side by myself. The abstraction of the organization chart quickly gives way to the reality of the field.

"Good, you're here, Jake," Greene declared. "Gordon and I were just talking."

"I could have been here for the beginning if you'd told me we were meeting earlier," I said.

Greene responded with a look one gets from severe indigestion. It is not an uncommon expression among SACs and it covers a wide variety of situations.

"Anyway, we both agree we've taken this reactive phase past the point of being productive."

"Productive?" I repeated, dreading the implication.

"We're not accomplishing anything," Abel clarified. "They've got plenty of food, plenty of supplies stockpiled, and they can sit here till hell freezes over if we let them."

"If we cut these creeps a pass," Greene went on. "you can bet we're going to be repeating this all over the damn place."

"A pass to do what?" I asked. "Gordon just said it: they're not going anywhere."

"That's just the point. The longer they resist our demands to surrender, the more ineffectual we look. These people are wanted for multiple counts of federal bank robbery, extortion, weapons charges."

"But not, so far, murder." The dread rose.

"Don't put that past them," warned Abel.

"Believe me, Gordon, I don't. But why make them into murderers? I'm not even convinced this siege was necessary. Sickenger wasn't exactly a recluse. He could have been picked up and arrested on any of his trips into town before the barricade situation even began."

"That was before I was called in," Greene said dismissively. "So it's ancient history. Let's just deal with the problem at hand."

"That's what I'm trying to do." I fought to tamp down the anger.

The SAC rose and swept his arm in the direction of the bulletproof window as he spoke. "This isn't the Louie Freeh era any longer where we're going to sit out the Montana Freemen for months and commit manpower and budget to an open-ended proposition. Director Boyd's slogan is 'zero tolerance,' and he's going to want to see some results. We've exhausted every peaceful option without accomplishing a god-damned thing. I'm giving Gordon the go-ahead to launch a raid tonight."

I struggled to contain the twisting knot in the center of my gut, already radiating out to either side. "Excuse me, sir, but you haven't exhausted *any* peaceful option."

Greene's head suddenly seemed to snap back. "Excuse *me!*" SACs are not accustomed to insubordination. But he wasn't my SAC, and damned if I was going to roll over so these guys could show Thomas Boyd how big his raganias were.

"These people don't accept the authority of the United States government," I said. "They've declared themselves a provisional power."

"All the more reason to cut 'em off at the knees," said Abel. "You can't reason with them."

"Yes, you can! If we deal with them the way they perceive themselves, if we approach them and offer to negotiate, one sovereign power to another, they'll realize they're being treated with respect, that they're going to get their message out. That's what they really want: to be taken seriously. I think I could get them to surrender and face trial with the expectation of making their political statement. They're contained and isolated here, but they've got radio and television. Let's go proactive and use that. We can get out of this without bloodshed. Unless we insist on backing them into a corner."

"If you negotiate with these guys, you're just legitimizing them," Abel protested, his jaw working defiantly, hard enough that his mandible was outlined against his cheek.

"No more so than getting a child killer to confess by offering a face-saving scenario. It's a means toward an end. These are deeply paranoid types—look at how they're worried about the United Nations coming in and taking away their guns. With a paranoid subject, you've got to downplay the show of force. It just feeds into his paranoid construct. It's the same with a paranoid group."

Abel sneered. "Or maybe you've been cooped up here long enough that you've developed the Stockholm syndrome. Maybe you've started identifying with these folks."

"Okay, you can stuff it now, Gordon." I started toward him, but Greene held up his hand like a traffic cop. "How do you know what's going on in their heads?"

"I have a pretty good idea," I said. "We don't know if Sickenger's glad or sorry he's in this. But let's apply some common sense. The one thing we can count on is that he wants to get out of it with dignity. It's very simple: we can either give that to him, or withhold it."

Greene drummed his fingers on the desk. "How long would these 'negotiations' take."

"I can't tell you that right now. Let's see if they'll let me into their compound. If I can deal with Sickenger face-to-face—"

But the SAC cut me off with a flick of his wrist. "I'm not risking a hostage situation. Especially not one as high-profile as you."

"I'm willing to take that chance."

"Well, I'm not."

Abel had the assurance to once again weigh in. "You may be the Bureau's media poster boy." He turned to Greene as if I were no longer in the room. "You know they call him the Mindhunter, 'the FBI's modern-day Sherlock Holmes.' "

"What's that got to do with anything?" I snapped.

"Exactly nothing," Abel snapped back. "An armed standoff is a different kind of animal."

"Then why did the director send me here?"

Abel grunted. "You'd have to ask him that. Maybe that touchy-feely stuff works with your serial killers and rapists, but you're not gonna sweet-talk this guy into giving up. If you were Sickenger and had your choice of calling all the shots and having the world's media focused on you, or surrendering and spending the next fifteen or twenty years in a ten-by-twelve-foot cell, which would you pick?"

"So you're saying our only course is to go in and kill everyone?"

"No," Abel responded with exaggerated patience, as if trying to get a point across to a contrary two-year-old. "We're dealing with a poisonous snake. And if you can cut off the head of the snake, the rest of the fucker isn't going to give you a whole lot of trouble."

"Absolutely wrong!" I shot back at him, though I knew I was overplaying my hand. "I assume you've both read my assessment. We're not dealing with apocalyptic, suicidal types like David Koresh and the

Branch Davidians at Waco. Yes, Sickenger is a paranoid opportunist. But don't think that means his followers are all gofers. He's recruited expert shots, people capable of making bombs. We know they're willing to commit armed robbery. You go in and kill Sickenger, it's just going to piss off the rest of them and make them take revenge, just like your men would do if Sickenger whacked you."

Abel seemed to recoil, then quickly caught himself. He eyed me warily, as a lion eyes an impala. "When was the last time you actually used your gun in the line of duty?"

The question surprised me. "A while. Detroit, probably. When I was a backup on the SWAT team." When I came out of the coma after the Black Diamond case, I was left with a tremor in my right hand and wrist, which, among other effects, made my shots tend to pull to the right whenever I fired. In the culture of the Bureau, that made me a "broken wing." And though they make a big deal over the dedication and sacrifices made by all those who carry the badge, we all know what happens to broken wings in nature. The Federal Bureau of Investigation is no less a survival of the fittest.

I'd desperately wanted this discourse to avoid degenerating into a pissing match. Now it had become about me rather than what I had to say. And that, I knew, was the one way to get out of this mess without a bloodbath.

I focused my attention squarely on Greene. "I've been a hostage negotiator."

"And a very effective one, from what I understand," Greene noted.

"I'll know when, and if, it's time to quit. But it's not now! Each of these situations has its own natural evolution."

"Point taken," he continued, the embodiment of conciliation. "But this isn't your typical hostage standoff that drags on for sixteen or twenty hours. We've been here eleven days and we're not making any progress. Jake, I appreciate what your saying. But if these people are perceived to be jerking federal authorities around, every two-bit survivalist or militia leader is going to have to prove himself by thumbing his nose at the FBI. I can tell you this is the thinking at headquarters. We should just thank God there aren't any hostages or children to worry about."

There was a knock on the RV door, then it opened. A large black man in his late thirties stepped in, six-two or -three, broad and solid, dressed in the standard HRT assault uniform of black T-shirt and utility vest and black cargo pants with large flap pockets on each leg.

"Good," said Greene. "Jake, you know Trevor Malone . . ."

We nodded to each other. Malone was the real thing of which the Gordon Abels of the world would always be pretenders. As soon as I saw Malone I knew that Gordon Abel, the administrators, the forces of career, of public image, of budget, of judicious allocation of personnel, had won the day.

"Not only is Trevor as good as anyone in tactical ops, he's an expert on the militia-survivalist movement."

Abel could now afford to turn diplomatic. "I think the consensus is this has gone on long enough," he told Malone for my benefit. "Under current conditions, we can't justify this stalemate any longer."

Malone said nothing. I tried to read his eyes.

Greene asked him, "What have you worked out?"

With a graceful economy of motion, Trevor Malone moved to the ordnance map. Greene moved aside to accommodate him.

"We'll stage the raid just before dawn, which means we'll begin at oh five fifty hours. This gives us the optimal conditions of darkness, most of the targets will be asleep and disoriented. The first thing they'll hear is a chopper overhead, and while their attention is distracted upward, we'll move in on all three buildings simultaneously, setting off flashbangs as we breach the doors and/or windows with Avon rounds and/or Foamex, depending on the individual situation. I'll be leading the strike on the ranch house."

"That all sounds good to me," Greene declared. "Gentlemen, I guess that about takes care of it."

It hit me with the same impact as it does every time I get a call that they've found another kid's body: the battle had been lost, and there wasn't a goddamned thing I could do about it.

o

Behind the semicircle of campers, trailers, and Porta-Johns was a small clearing. That afternoon, I sat cross-legged on the ground in my grimy khakis, as far away from the toilets as I could, and punished the keys on my IBM laptop, pounded the hell out of those little plastic squares in anger and frustration. It had all come down to this. I had lost the bureaucratic war and I was responding with the defeated bureaucrat's ultimate weapon: the memo.

I sat there, tapping away, marshaling every bit of reasoning, logic, history, analysis, anything. I had a feeling about this one, and the feeling wasn't good. I'm from Montana, where things are a lot more basic than in most of the rest of the country. A blizzard can roar suddenly out of the north with killer fury upon the unsuspecting. So you develop an instinct for the sudden and violent.

When I finished, I sent the file through the portable printer they had in the state-police trailer. It came to twenty-two pages. Then I strode back to the command post and dropped it on the desk. Roger Greene was sitting behind the desk, talking into the receiver of one of the three telephones. He looked up and cupped the mouthpiece.

"Please read this before you make your final decision," I said tersely. We held eye contact for a long moment, the gulf between us unbridgeable.

◦

I was alone in the camper, lying on the bunk and contemplating the quiet and the stillness and the dark. At times like this when the inner gnawing began in earnest, I yearned to have my family around me—Ali and Eric, even Toni. It was my own damn fault I'd let her realize she could get along without me, and these were the moments—quiet and dark and alone—when I replayed, over and over, all the blown and ill-conceived moves we'd both made over the years.

An explosion jolted me to my feet. I was aware of commotion and confusion around me, of screams and shouts, a chopper buzzing overhead.

I pulled on some jeans and a T-shirt and raced outside. I could hear gunfire from the direction of the Defenders' compound. Stumbling in the dark, I scrambled up the hill toward the upper sniper post, hoping that from there I could figure out what was happening. I knocked into thin trees, and brambles tore at my legs. Rocks skittered out from under my feet.

Finally I reached the position above the snipers. "What the hell's going on?" I asked the spotter, a guy named Tom Yamaguchi.

"Point man stepped on a booby trap on the porch, probably a trip wire."

"Fuck!" It was just the kind of thing I'd been terrified about. "Who started shooting?"

He shrugged. "Your guess's good's mine." He handed me a radio ear-piece and a pair of ITT night-vision binoculars. All the while, the sniper Jeff Lanier held his rigid prone position, monitoring the action from his own earpiece, peering intently through the twelve-power Nikon scope of his Remington 700 BDL, and searching for a "cold shot," should need and opportunity coincide.

I trained my binoculars on the front of the ranch house. Two other agents in helmets and night-vision goggles, holding up polycarbonate shields, were using their other arms to pull away the downed point man, or what was left of him. I didn't know what had been in that booby trap—plastique, black powder, a couple of grenades, or a stick of dynamite—and it didn't matter. Events had taken over. The whole thing now had an ugly inevitability as agents behind them laid down a withering barrage of covering fire to suppress the shots coming from inside the house and stable.

Trevor Malone and his team fixed gas masks in place. Together with the black helmets and goggles, these made the men look like giant insects, or invading aliens from a sci-fi horror movie. Without waiting for the bullets to stop, Malone raised his left arm and signaled his group forward, up the steps of the ranch house, retracing the fatal path of the point man. The guy had guts, I had to say, epitomizing navy SEAL legend Roy Boehm's universal two-word definition of good leadership: "Follow me!"

"On the front porch," I heard him report over the radio. I saw the team member beside him set off a tear-gas charge and lob it through the window. The whoosh crackled as static in the background. It had apparently been decided beforehand that they wouldn't clear the house with gas cartridges lobbed in from outside. Greene had ruled out chancing another Waco-type fire.

Defenders began trickling out of the house, all carrying rifles.

"Lay down your arms!" Malone ordered through the amplifier built into his mask. A few of the men raised their hands above their heads, dropping their rifles. A few more seemed to hesitate, from what I could see, and Malone's men immediately intercepted them.

"Where's Sickenger?" Malone asked the Defender closest to him. Either there wasn't any answer or I couldn't hear it through his helmet mike.

But it didn't matter, because within another moment Gene Claude Sickenger himself emerged from the house, dressed in green combat fatigues and carrying a scope-mounted rifle.

"Mr. Sickenger! Put down your gun!"

Sickenger's head darted from side to side, as if he was evaluating his options.

"Put it down! Now!" Malone had his Steyr assault rifle trained right on Sickenger. He had to know that in any head-to-head shoot-out, he was going to die.

He whipped around, shouldering his rifle. But instead of pointing it at any of the raiders, he aimed it up at about a seventy-five-degree angle.

"Fuck!" yelled Tom Yamaguchi into his microphone. "Trevor, he's going for the chopper."

Muzzle fire erupted from Malone's rifle. Almost simultaneously, Sickenger collapsed on the wooden porch floor in a heap, as if the bones had suddenly been removed from his legs.

A single .308-caliber, Federal, 168-grain, match-boat-tail slug entered Sickenger's head precisely, in the tiny region just above the upper lip but below the base of the nose. Malone would have known that to assure an instantaneous cessation of motor activity, he'd have to penetrate the medulla oblongata—the lowest section of the brain stem—and had keyed on the most direct and foolproof route.

What I now fervently hoped but did not expect, what Roger Greene and Gordon Abel expected and counted on, was that with their leader dead and their cause lost, the rest of the Defenders would fold.

Please God, let me be wrong!

For a moment I wasn't sure. But then it was like one of those nightmares where you know what's going to happen but you're powerless to prevent or stop it. Through the night-vision lenses I saw four more men emerge from the ranch house—each carrying a handgun, rifle, or shotgun—just where Sickenger had come from. Tears were streaming down their red faces. Malone's team fixed their weapons in firing position in case the men resisted. Just beyond where Tom Yamaguchi stood, his partner Jeff Lanier tensed, following the action through his rifle scope.

Then in one fluid motion, without having to communicate with each other, all four gunmen instantly turned on the raider closest to them. It showed planning, organization, a determination that if their leader was taken, they would go down fighting, making a statement for the world to hear.

God help us, I was right. Another FBI agent had just died in front of me. I felt sick. Lives were being wasted!

"Ron Pearl's down!" Yamaguchi shouted into his mouthpiece.

Before he had finished the sentence, Malone and the two other agents with him had mowed down all four of the Defenders. From the same door, two more ATF members emerged and reported, "Building secure."

"My God," said Yamaguchi quietly. Lanier eased up slightly on the trigger.

The final toll was two agents and six members of the Wyoming Defenders dead, including Gene Claude Sickenger. One of the four Defenders who had opened fire on Ronald Pearl survived his wounds, but two other Defenders were killed while aiming at the raiding team breaching the stable. The lone Defender in the barn was also wounded, though expected to recover.

But I didn't think I ever could.

∘

The firestorm of public and media reaction was immediate. By Sunday, it dominated debate on the public-affairs talk shows. Had FBI agents provoked the attack? Had they made killers out of cheap thugs and elevated them to the level of martyrs? Had the agents been arrogant and overconfident? Had they cold-bloodedly assassinated Gene Claude Sickenger because he and his kind had become annoying? Had nothing been learned from Ruby Ridge or Waco?

Amidst the outrage, the allegations, the conflicting charges, Attorney General James Maxwell Hewitt called an after-action evaluation conference in his conference room at Justice for Monday morning. Director Boyd, SAC Roger Greene, and ASAC Gordon Abel attended. Neither Trevor Malone nor I was invited.

When I asked my SAC, Neil Burke, a decent guy who was directed to attend the meeting, why we weren't there, he informed me that "it wouldn't be a productive use" of our time.

2

"Whoever fights monsters should see to it that in the process he does not become a monster. And when you look into an abyss, the abyss also looks into you."

Thus spake Friedrich Wilhelm Nietzsche, and it had become the guiding principle of the behavioral sciences at Quantico.

I'd been staring into that abyss for the four days since I'd returned from Owl Creek, and now I sensed that abyss was about to stare right back into me.

When I was ushered into Thomas Boyd's inner office on the Seventh Floor of the J. Edgar Hoover Building in downtown Washington, I was surprised to find myself alone in the cavernous room. It meant that whatever was to take place between us was intended for no other ears. That could cut good or bad.

I guessed bad. My prime of evidence was that I'd not heard word one about the previous day's after-action conference. I'd been given no official report, and none of the participants had sought me out. Plenty of media people had called me, but I made myself unavailable.

I studied the memorabilia on Boyd's walls for a few minutes, then drifted over to the floor-to-ceiling corner windows and gazed out onto Pennsylvania Avenue. It was after three and traffic was already heavy. It wouldn't be long before the early rush would begin, turning 95 South into a parking lot from here to Richmond, and the hour trip south to Quantico would be more than doubled. Rather than trying to make it back to the Academy, I'd probably just go home instead.

A side door opened and in came the Honorable Thomas Jefferson Boyd, most recently judge for the U.S. Ninth Circuit Court of Appeals in San Francisco and the current tenant of this office. Dressed in a conservative gray suit, he was tall and almost regal in bearing, a distinguished late forties with hair just starting to go gray on the sides, and the kind of slim, sober, and commanding countenance that wows Capitol Hill committee chairmen and reassures a public gripped by crisis. At least until Owl Creek.

"Mr. Donovan. Thank you for coming." Boyd had been a special agent for a few years himself, an interregnum between Stanford Law and appointment as an assistant U.S. attorney for the Southern District of New York, so he felt no need for titles within the Bureau. Still, that "Mr." had an ominous tone to it.

He didn't offer me his hand. He didn't offer me a seat and remained standing himself, proceeding directly to the point:

"Were you in the service?"

"Navy." It had seemed the easiest way to get out of Montana.

"Then you know what a cluster fuck is."

"I'm familiar with the term."

He leaned back against his massive walnut desk and folded his arms over his chest. "Because that's what we've got here."

"Excuse me, Judge Boyd?"

He picked up a sheaf of papers from the desk surface and started to read:

" 'Over and over, our studies show that the greatest fear for a woman is being attacked. But the greatest fear for a man is being humiliated. Like an animal cornered in a laboratory cage, it is when a man feels he has no options or meaningful choices that he is at his most dangerous.' "

He looked up at me. "Do you recognize this?"

"It's the assessment I wrote for Roger Greene the afternoon before the raid."

"And a very thoughtful and well-reasoned document it is. And therein lies the problem. Not the source of the cluster fuck, to be sure, but definitely an accelerant."

"I'm not sure I'm following you."

"Then let me net it out and save us both some time." He pushed off from the side of the desk and stood almost rigidly in front of me as he spoke. "The attorney general asked why you weren't at the after-action conference yesterday."

"I would have been happy to be there."

"Not the point, I'm afraid."

"With due respect, Judge Boyd, what is?"

"When I add up the score of this organization's performance at these high-profile, confrontational events in the years before my own tenure began, I'd have to say that Ruby Ridge gave us a black eye. The other eye was blackened the following year at Waco. We acquitted ourselves reasonably well with the World Trade Center and the Oklahoma City bombings, and our capture of Amir Kasi in Pakistan was a tour de force. But the Unabomber case dragged on far too long. Our investigation of the TWA Flight 800 crash was superb, but we derived little credit from that since it turned out not to be an act of terrorism. And we looked like fools with Richard Jewell and the Atlanta Olympic Park bombing."

He folded his hands over his chest. "The point I'm making is, given this decidedly mixed tally, we cannot afford another challenge to public confidence. For us to weather this one, the entire federal justice establishment must be perceived to be reading from the same sheet of music. We needed to contain this, Jake. Which is what I was attempting to do."

I was getting tired of standing. I shifted my weight from one foot to the other. "And how do I fit into this?"

Boyd raised one finger in the air. "Ah, yes, the heart of the matter." He pointed out the window to the upper reaches of the gray, neoclassic Justice Department building across the street where the meeting had taken place. "I thought I had explained to Attorney General Hewitt the reasons for the unfortunate outcome, that these were ruthless offenders who had stated an express disregard for the laws of the land. That no matter how long the siege had been allowed to continue, the outcome could have been expected to be fundamentally the same."

"I can't agree with that. It's what I told Roger Greene—"

Boyd held up his hand to silence me. "It was at that point, when I thought we were emerging from the meeting with a single, unified statement for public and media consumption, that Hewitt whispered something to one of the henchmen sitting next to him. Then he said, in that gratingly mellifluous Deep South accent of his, 'I do believe y'all're attempting to blow smoke up my hindquarters.' "

Boyd picked up my assessment again and this time waved it at me. "Then the aide handed him a copy of this and he held it in front of him, just as I'm doing now, as if he were playing the trump card in one of those bridge tournaments he's so fond of. 'Apparently there was a dissenting opinion which you've said nuthin' about.'

"I tried to explain to him that this opinion had been taken into account in the final decision, but that other tactical analyses and considerations had outweighed it."

The statement didn't seem to warrant a response. So Boyd went on, "It is far from a secret that the attorney general and I do not always agree. He is a creature of the new administration, while I am a vestige of the previous one."

An understatement. Boyd had been the last president's final major appointment—after the American voters, in their collective wisdom, had decided not to return him to office—rammed down the throat of a reluctant Senate in the wake of the school shootings and renewed drug wars. As a prosecutor in New York and then as a judge on the federal bench, Boyd had developed a solid reputation as a rock-ribbed, hard-ass law-and-order man whose watchwords, as Roger Greene had said, were "zero tolerance." Like his predecessor, Judge Louie Freeh, Boyd had been a special agent, so he was able to hit the deck running. In his first few months in office, he'd already taken off after the Italian and Russian Mobs, the drug runners, the militia movement, the religious right's gay-baiting, the gun lobby, pornography, and the entertainment industry's promulgation of sex and violence. All the while, he still had the moral energy to preach family values.

In other words, in his six-odd months in office, he'd managed to tick off just about everyone. And it was well-known that if the president and the attorney general could figure any way to blast him out of the Bureau before his ten-year appointment was up, they would do it. As it was, a barely civil standoff existed between the Justice Department and its most important agency, as hostile as it had been back in the days of Robert Kennedy and the seemingly immortal J. Edgar Hoover.

Boyd tossed my report back on the desk, then spun around accusingly. "So you can appreciate how Hewitt was able to use your assessment as a club to beat us to death. We need to let the public know that the deaths at Owl Creek were an inevitable consequence of Gene Claude Sickenger's initial decisions and actions. In law we call this the proximate cause, and I do firmly believe it is true here. And yet with your assessment, the water is muddied and Hewitt's going to be able to say that the FBI doesn't know what it's doing, that there's internal dissension. It'll give him the ammunition he's been looking for to start squawking about putting the Bureau under new management, personally selected by the new administration. Do you know how sanctimonious that son of a bitch is going to be standing next to me at those agents' funerals?"

"Judge Boyd," I protested, "it was you who sent me to Owl Creek."

"Exactly right, because I'd been told you're the best at what you do, and I wanted the field commander to have the benefit of the best input from all sides."

"I'll tell you the same thing I tell local cops and detectives: I didn't ask to be there, but as long as I am, I'm going to give you my opinion as forcefully as I can. If I think I'm right and that being right will save lives, I'm going to do everything I can to see that's it done my way, and if it isn't, I'm not going to be a very gracious loser."

"But like a lot of people who are the best at what they do, you believe that you alone are the custodian of the received truth."

Thomas Becket did fine until his friend the king made him archbishop of Canterbury. He didn't particularly want the job, but as long as he had it, he was determined to do it right. That's what got him into difficulty. That was what we profilers call the "precipitating stressor" that led to the murder in the cathedral.

My gut tightened. "Judge Boyd, are you blaming me for what happened at Owl Creek?"

"I'm neither stupid nor naive, Mr. Donovan," Boyd said as he moved around behind the expansive walnut desk. "Neither are you. What happened at Owl Creek happened. Nothing can be done to change it, and I mourn the loss of two fine men, as I'm sure you do. It is the aftermath, the perception, the managing of that perception, that concerns me now. I have the integrity of the entire organization to think of. Like a surgeon, if I can save the body as a whole by removing diseased tissue, that is what I have to do."

"Is that what I am—diseased tissue?"

He didn't bother responding, but declared, "I've never believed in letting anyone else do my dirty work for me; that's cowardly. So I'll ask you point-blank, Mr. Donovan. Were you the one who sent your assessment to Jim Hewitt?"

"You're damn right I did," I declared, seeing nothing further to be gained from pulling punches or doing the bureaucratic moon walk. "Somebody had to set the record straight."

"Then you're out of here. Your career in the FBI is over."

I felt as if the air had just been punched out of my lungs.

"Do you have any idea of the damage you've done?"

"No," I said stiffly. "I don't believe that I do."

"Then let me spell it out. Armed with your report, Hewitt's going to absolve himself and the administration and let the Bureau hang out to dry."

And so the Bureau, in turn, will hang Jake Donovan out to dry. In fact, if they play the Washington leak and innuendo game well enough, they might be able to blame the entire mess on him.

Or so I thought. But as the clarity of the moment descended upon me, I realized it didn't matter what I said now. *Res ipsa loquitur.* My deeds spoke for themselves.

When I'd regrouped, I said, "This wasn't a leak. I didn't pass it out to the press. I gave my opinion to my ultimate boss."

"Your *opinion*," Boyd repeated for emphasis. "And your ultimate boss is staring you in the face. That's how the Bureau works, you know that."

My survival instinct kicked in. "If you're as concerned with perceptions as you say, I don't think firing me for giving the attorney general legitimate information is going to play very well."

"You may be right. A media darling like yourself would know about such matters. Don't they call you the Mindhunter?"

I didn't take the bait. I knew Boyd didn't appreciate individual agents standing out any more than Hoover had.

"Well, maybe this one will play a little better." Boyd picked up a blue manila file that I now realized had been lying on the desk all along. As he brought it in front of him, I could see that it was marked DONOVAN, J., with a white stick-on label. I should have snooped in it before he came in.

The director made a show of scanning the contents. "I'm looking at your last two firearms qualifications. You failed both of them."

Another punch between my lungs. "I never use my gun in my work. I don't even carry it most of the time."

"Nevertheless, that remains a critical part of the job description of special agent. You never know when you'll have to deploy your weapon. And if you had to, you could be endangering yourself, your fellow agents and law enforcement officers, and the public."

"Why wasn't my shooting ability an issue until now?"

"It's been a crowded agenda since I took office, as I'm sure you can imagine. Individual personnel matters often take time. I've finally been able to turn my attention to this one."

"You know damn well why I can't shoot straight any longer. I went into a coma for over a week while working the Black Diamond case."

Boyd regarded me dispassionately. "Viral encephalitis, I believe."

"Brought on by the stress of overwork. That's what the doctors said. I had more than a hundred and fifty active cases going and I couldn't get headquarters to give me any of the manpower or resources I needed."

"No one denies the sacrifices you've made for the Bureau, Mr. Donovan, nor your heroic championing of behavioral science. But rules are rules."

"I damn near died at Black Diamond!"

"As of this moment, you are officially relieved of your duties as special agent and chief of the Profiling and Serial Crimes Unit. SAC Neil Burke is prepared to accept your weapon and credentials."

I felt like tearing his distinguished, well-coiffed, razor-trimmed head off. *This is my life!* I wanted to shout out.

But of course, I didn't. I merely stood there with my hands shaking, desperately trying to suppress the urge that, even in my excitement, I realized would have long-term consequences far exceeding any short-term satisfactions. And then, for some reason, it occurred to me to wonder if a calf, herded into increasingly narrow chutes at the stockyard, ever experienced a moment of insight—the sudden cessation of ignorance, we called it in my unit—in which he saw his unpromising fate laid out before him, as I did right now. I wondered if he ever understood that his little existence was merely a component of a far larger enterprise, and that no matter what he did, or how he'd lived his life, none of that would matter, that inevitably, in the end, he'd be ruled by forces beyond his control or comprehension.

"Please be assured that you'll retire on disability with your full pension and health and life insurance benefits, even though you're far from the full twenty-five years. I understand a retirement function has been set up at Quantico on Friday. I trust you'll be there."

3

Now perhaps in the great cosmic logic of things, I actually fell about midway between the aforementioned calf and St. Thomas. But you'll excuse me and understand if I was suddenly feeling every inch a martyr.

How could they do this to me? And it wasn't just me, I kept protesting to the cosmic logic. What happens to all of my open cases, the kidnappings and the disappearances, the serial rapists and the pattern killers? What happens to all the victims, the dead, the maimed, the survivors, all the ones to whom I've sworn a personal and sacred commitment? But I knew the answer. As Thomas Boyd himself had suggested, I was neither stupid nor naive.

Save your sympathy, Donovan, the cosmos aren't interested. And yes, you are good, but so are the people you've prepared to take over for you. Peter Sutherland can certainly do the job. Katie McManus will be back in a couple of weeks. Craig Alcorn looks promising. The mission will go on, even if you won't. Moses didn't get to the promised land, either, old man.

For the next several days, I didn't go out, I didn't read the papers, I didn't even watch television. The reporters and pundits and "experts" could churn all they wanted about Owl Creek—it was no longer my problem. If it brought down the FBI, or the whole Department of Justice for that matter, I didn't care. The only thing I did feel obligated to do at some point soon was go over my case files with Peter Sutherland, since, as my primary relief, he'd be the one to take over the unit. He was one of the few from Quantico who'd called to express his outrage over what had happened to me. And I could tell, playing his telephone message back several times to analyze the psycholinguistic content, that he really meant it, even though he was the one person who'd actually benefit and get a promotion as the direct result of my being canned.

But before I thought about getting Peter up to speed or doing anything else of either a practical or altruistic nature, I still had several bottles of pretty good Scotch to go through.

So what are you going to do with the rest of your life? my superego kept demanding of my ego.

Well, there's another full bottle of Glenfiddich we really should try to finish before facing the retirement dinner, my id replied.

I tried to ignore the mail, but one piece intrigued me. It was a written invitation, hand-delivered to my house: "Mrs. Millicent De Vries wishes to discuss with you a matter of mutual interest. Please indicate a convenient time and a car will be sent for you." That was all.

I knew about Millicent De Vries, a saga with just the requisite hint of intrigue and scandal. She was the widow of Fletcher De Vries—former ambassador to Switzerland—and heir to the Shipley Pharmaceuticals fortune, which Fletcher had taken over from Millicent's father, and which had ultimately bought him the ambassadorship. They had lived the European good life—London, Paris, Gstaad, Monte Carlo—amid persistent rumors that they both had connections to the international intelligence and counterintelligence communities. Millicent was said to have passionately loved Fletcher, a handsome and well-spoken Yalie, and was devastated when he disappeared in a boating accident somewhere between Monaco, from where he'd set out that morning, and St.-Tropez, where he'd announced he was heading. The rented fishing cruiser was never found, but during the inquest, the owner of the boat testified he was positive that a merry and extremely comely young redhead clad only in the briefest of yellow bikinis had boarded with Fletcher. Not a sight to be forgotten by a warm-blooded Frenchman, he assured the panel. Whatever her private doubt or pain, Millicent continued to cherish and venerate his memory. She established the Fletcher De Vries Family Foundation to keep bright his flame.

Which is where I come into the story, at least indirectly.

The foundation's stated goals had something to do with fostering understanding of human behavior in its various forms. Under that guise, though I always suspected it had more to do with Mr. De Vries's interest in counterintelligence and things mysterious, they had bought the helicopters the FBI uses at Quantico, then leased them to the Bureau for a nominal fee. I'd met her a few times at the Academy when she'd come down to take a tour and have lunch with Neil Burke, or to join the director in the auditorium for some ceremony or other. But I really didn't know her beyond saying hello, so my interest was sufficiently piqued by her note to make an effort to sober up, at least temporarily. Could it be that Attorney General Hewitt, whom I had notably not heard from since my encounter with Boyd, had chosen one of his highly positioned friends to send me a private message? Or, as I always warned my people against, was I reading too much into this?

Only one way to find out. I called and accepted.

The next morning, my doorbell rang at eight. A middle-aged man in a dark suit was standing there in front of a midnight blue Rolls-Royce Phantom limousine parked in my driveway. He introduced himself as Frederick and said little else as we drove more than an hour north to Washington.

Mrs. De Vries's home was a Tudor mansion in the Massachusetts Avenue Heights section of Northwest D.C., just across a dense valley of parkland from Embassy Row. It could easily have been transplanted from both the English countryside and the nineteenth century.

Frederick escorted me through the carved mahogany front doors, and into the entrance hall with its cathedral ceiling and broad, curving staircase. I half-expected suits of armor standing against the walls. He led me past a huge dining hall, into a room he referred to as "the study." It featured another vaulted ceiling and a huge carved stone fireplace at one end. Most of the wall space in the room was taken up with floor-to-ceiling cases of leather-bound books interrupted by an occasional leaded-glass window or Renaissance painting.

A door on the other side of the room opened and Mrs. De Vries came in. She was in her late fifties, not more than five-two or -three, neither overweight nor elegantly thin. Her face was pleasant and open, with none of the obvious nods to vanity you might expect from someone of her age and social position—no signs of a face-lift, heavy makeup, hair tinting or streaking. In fact, her hair was mostly gray and styled in a "sensible" cut. Her clothes appeared to be expensive and well made, but hardly fashionable. If anything, they were beyond fashion.

"Good to see you, Jake." She extended her hand as if we were old friends. She'd evidently noticed me eyeing one of the paintings. "Rubens. Do you have much background in art?"

"Just what I remember from working a heist from the Isabelle Gardner Museum in Boston several years ago."

"I remember that one. But haven't you also written in relation to understanding serial killers that, 'If you want to understand the artist, you have to look at the art, and the crime itself is what these perpetrators consider their art'?"

"Yes, I guess I did say that." But how—and why—in hell did she know that? The inner alarm suddenly went off. Was this a setup of some kind?

"Interesting analogy." She motioned me to one of two overstuffed leather club chairs flanking the fireplace. She took the other. I said nothing, waiting for her to indicate the agenda.

She picked up a manila file folder from the top of a stack of art books piled on the antique wooden table beside her. "This is a proposal you wrote a number of years ago, entitled, 'The Flying Squad.' "

I felt a sudden jab in the pit of my stomach. "May I ask how you got that?"

For the first time she showed an indication of an actual smile. "I could tell you, but then I'd have to kill you. Isn't that how the expression goes?"

"Something like that. It's just that you don't exactly fit my profile of the killer type."

A little more of a smile. "You'd do well not to underestimate me."

I was quickly learning not to.

She put on a pair of gold-framed reading glasses. "You propose here the establishment of a team of law enforcement professionals: a profiler-investigator, an evidence specialist, a weapons and tactics specialist, a pathologist–medical examiner, a forensic anthropologist, a laboratory technician, sketch artist, et cetera, et cetera . . . all of whom would be organized to fly to the scene of a major crime within a matter of hours and deal with the case"—here she read—" 'while it is in its most manageable phase.' "

She lay the folder in her lap and looked up at me. "Very impressive. Well thought-out. I can see why they call you the Mindhunter. Why was this never implemented?"

I had the feeling she already knew, that she was toying with me. "Too many fiefdoms, nobody willing to share any precious budget dollars, nobody willing to risk blame if it blew up."

"My husband and I operated in the government bureaucracy. I have not lost faith in institutions, but it has made me what an attorney friend refers to as a mature skeptic."

I shifted uncomfortably. "If I may ask, Mrs. De Vries, what exactly is the purpose of this meeting?"

She lifted the folder from her lap and set it back on the stack of books, then leaned toward me with body language that told me it was time to negotiate—about what, I had no idea.

"I think there's real merit to your proposal," she said. "I'd like you to consider implementing it."

"Excuse me?"

"Now that you've retired from the FBI, I'm suggesting that we set up this flying squad you proposed."

"You, Mrs. De Vries?"

"Salaries, support, equipment, logistics. Whatever you care to specify . . . within reason, of course. You recruit and qualify the personnel, I'll take care of everything else."

What was going on here? A bored rich lady's game? A high-ticket version of cops and robbers? "I'm not sure I understand," I said, "or maybe I'm not sure you understand."

She regarded me with a patient, indulgent look. "What doesn't either one of us understand?"

Through the wavy distortions of the leaded-glass window I could see a carefully tended garden with a rock waterfall and pond, manicured lawn, and perfectly clipped hedgerows. This was all on land that terraced down to the park.

I took a moment trying to find the best phrasing for my question, but finally decided on the direct approach. "Why would you possibly need a flying squad?"

"As I said, I think your proposal has real merit and I'm in a position to be able to make it happen."

"Umm, if you'll forgive my saying so, no one is that altruistic. Everyone acts in his own self-interest. Even charitable contributions are made in self-interest."

She continued smiling. "What are you saying?"

"Only that I'd feel better if we could get your particular self-interest in this out on the table."

Silence hung in the air between us. Finally, she pursed her lips, as if carefully considering her words, then said, "I assume the name J. P. Napoleon is not unfamiliar to you."

Again it was as though she'd put my fingers in a live electrical socket. "I'm familiar with the name."

For the last several years I have been trying to profile an individual known as J. P. Napoleon. All that was known of him was that he headed an organization once called Empire International Arms Company, though later streamlined simply to Empire International when they broadened out into other businesses. Whether he called the company Empire because his name was Napoleon or called himself Napoleon because his company was called Empire, we didn't know. It might even have been he was a Sherlock Holmes fan and wanted to be the real-life incarnation of Professor Moriarty, whom Holmes referred to as "the Napoleon of crime."

Empire had multiple headquarters—Grand Cayman, Channel Islands, Monaco—all invulnerable to us, Interpol, or anyone else. We had indirect evidence, though we couldn't prove it, that Napoleon's influence reached down to the most basic level of organized crime on the local level, rivaling La Cosa Nostra, the Russian Mob in New York, the Jamaican and West Indian groups and the Chinese, Mexican and black gangs on the West Coast. So far, he'd remained elusive, untouchable. No one knew what he looked like or how old he was. I even had suspicions at one point that Napoleon might actually be a woman. But we really knew little about him, other than that he was ultimately responsible for a lot of bad news.

My contribution—if you want to call it that since, so far, it hadn't led to any arrests or prosecutions—was figuring out a pattern to the tips that were coming in to the DEA, our sister agency at Quantico. These became particularly significant around major drug shipments. In virtually every case, the seized goods coincided with a shipment to a similar geographical destination of another large horde that the DEA didn't find. Putting a couple of things together, what this told us was that Napoleon was enhancing the value of his own product by eliminating the competitor's. And just as importantly, he apparently had the intelligence organization always to know what his rivals were up to.

Empire, so far as we could tell, was just the tip of the iceberg—the legal tip. Napoleon ran a vertical monopoly in large urban areas, from the drug distribution, to supplying the weapons, to loaning out the cash that allowed "ordinary" people to participate in the commerce he created. The profits were plowed into a number of "legitimate businesses," which, in turn, made him more and more money. Everything was done through so many levels that it could only be traced to this mythic individual through inference.

Mrs. De Vries removed her reading glasses, clearing them with a wave of her head. "I suspect you are aware that most of my wealth derives from Shipley Pharmaceuticals. In the past year you may have read about the tender offer."

"I may have," I said offhandedly.

"It was what is euphemistically referred to as a hostile takeover. Perhaps not hostile in the sense that you see hostility, Mr. Donovan. There was no murder, no torture, no rape—at least not in the literal sense. But this company that was created by my grandfather, A. Phillip Shipley, that was built up and nurtured by my father and then my husband, Fletcher, I now have reason to believe, is being controlled by . . ."

"J. P. Napoleon?"

"Yes, J. P. Napoleon. In any event, it was taken over by Empire International. They seemed to have a profound inside knowledge of the critical workings and corporate strategies. It was as if, like the Greeks in the Trojan Horse, they had defeated us from inside."

"Napoleon has an incredible intelligence organization," I said.

"Think of it: the most formidable purveyor of illicit drugs into the United States now has a major drug company as his personal toy. With his newfound capacity, I am given to understand he has been able to begin offering chemical and biological warfare products to his terrorist and rogue-nation clients."

We had heard through various intelligence sources that Napoleon intended to fill the void left by the notorious Russian Biopreparat after the crumbling of the Soviet Union, but so far, there'd been no verification.

Now Mrs. De Vries rose to her feet, as if the vehemence of her thoughts couldn't be delivered in so passive a position as seated. "That company and all the good it did, all of the millions of ailing, afflicted people it helped to treat and to cure, that company was a monument to my grandfather, to my father, as well as to my husband, may they rest in peace. And it sickens me to see that monument sullied and perverted. If you undertake this flying squad, you may take on any case in which you think you might do some good. In return, I ask only that you also use your talents and resources to continue your efforts in trying to bring down this Napoleon."

So that's what this was all about—a personal vendetta by a rich, powerful woman against an even richer, more powerful man who'd kidnapped her "baby" and was now turning it against her. Even in my booze-clouded, self-pitying state of martyrdom, I knew that being a rich widow's mercenary, or even worse, her plaything, always at her beck and call, was not the kind of new job I was looking for.

"I don't think I'd be able to help you much," I said.

"You couldn't, or you wouldn't want to?"

"Thank you for your generous offer."

Once more, she smiled indulgently. "Should I take this to be a turn-down then?"

I hesitated. How often does someone come out of the blue and offer to bankroll you in a new business? This would let me keep doing what I loved, what I'd worked so hard for. Or was it just making a game of all that?

"A turndown with tremendous gratitude," I finally forced myself to say.

She nodded slightly. "Well, then. That concludes our business. But what is it the detectives say—'If you think of anything else, here's my card,' although I'm afraid I don't actually have a card."

Glancing around the house on my way out with Frederick, I conclud-ed that this might be the only thing she didn't have. And with what she did have, she was willing to let me write my own ticket. Was I nuts?

4

Going to the retirement luncheon at Quantico (that's right, at such short notice they couldn't get enough people together for a dinner) was like attending my own funeral. I'd never heard so many nice things proclaimed about me. Maybe they had gotten said back when I was in the hospital in Seattle years ago during the Black Diamond case, but I was in a coma then.

The affair was held in the atrium of the Jefferson Building. Antonia showed up and was seated next to me, along with our children, Ali and Eric. Toni expressed surprise, even shock, when I told her about my swift and unexpected separation from the Bureau. But though she felt badly for me, I could tell she wasn't exactly displeased. She felt that the more I gave, the less I was getting back, and I was never able to convince her otherwise. As a rule, I wouldn't try to convince a psychologist of anything, but when she occupies a unique position in your life, you sometimes have to make exceptions. Here, she was her usual gracious self, with the manner that always made people figure I must be the jerk and the separation must have all been my fault.

Peter Sutherland had appointed himself master of ceremonies. But as it turned out, that was the only appointment he got. Because that was another shock I'd got when I'd shown up this day.

He'd greeted me at the front doors of the Jefferson Building, and before I could even say hello, he came right to the point.

"I didn't get it."

"What?"

"I'm not unit chief. Ted Novello is."

"I can't believe it!"

"Well, believe it. And be afraid. Be very afraid."

Theodore Novello, whose name I hadn't even known at this time last year, had become famous within the Bureau. He knew Thomas Boyd through Boyd's younger brother, Horace, with whom Ted had gone to law school. When he graduated, Tom encouraged Ted to join the Bureau and got him assigned to the Miami Field Office, where Tom was already an agent. When Boyd left to become a federal prosecutor, Ted followed along, and when Boyd was then appointed to the federal bench, Ted once again followed as his majordomo. Then, when Judge Boyd was named director of the FBI, he got Ted reinstated as a special agent and assigned him to headquarters.

My God! All the pieces of the nightmare were coming together. "That fucker's never written a profile," I spluttered, "and I don't think he'd be able to connect serial crimes if they were rammed up his ass together."

"Doesn't matter. He's the director's choice, and that's all she wrote."

"Neil Burke's got to be pissed off."

"Mucho pissed off. But Neil's a good soldier who understands the chain of command."

"I can't believe it. Doesn't anyone have any integrity? Doesn't anyone give a shit what happens to the unit? If this organization's going to be run on cronyism . . ." I just kept shaking my head.

Peter was one guy who was willing to stand up for me, as he made clear by what he said at the luncheon. "Every one of us owes Jake Donovan a tremendous debt. When he was just a rookie instructor for the FBI's National Academy, rather than be embarrassed standing up in front of a class of old-fart police officers and detectives, this young special agent spent his spare time during road schools visiting the penitentiaries where the actual offenders were. He interviewed them. He learned *why* they did it, *how* it made them feel, and *what* they were thinking about at the time. Soon Jake's exploits were being imitated in novels, TV shows, and movies. But there's a critical difference between Jake and all those pretenders and wanna-bes . . ."

None's been living on a government salary? I said to myself.

". . . Jake Donovan is *the real thing!*"

Jake Donovan was *the real thing until the middle of the afternoon on Tuesday.*

Director Boyd showed up; I'll give him that. He even got up to say a few words, after an effusive introduction from Ted Novello, the gist of which was, Judge Thomas Jefferson Boyd being appointed to head up the Federal Bureau of Investigation at this critical juncture was probably the greatest event in the history of the world since the sixth day of creation when God Almighty in His infinite wisdom came up with J. Edgar Hoover and the rest of mankind. Boyd was certainly the best thing ever to happen to Ted.

Boyd gripped the sides of the lectern as if he owned it and drilled the audience with his riveting gaze. "There are three words on the FBI crest: "*Fidelity. Bravery. Integrity.* F-B-I. And I can assure you that they weren't chosen cavalierly or capriciously. They were chosen because those three words represent ideals—ideals which are fundamental to the character and performance of every special agent issued a badge and creds bearing those initials. And when we look at Jake Donovan and his life in the Bureau, we find all three ideals in generous measure."

So it's too bad he overplayed his hand. But, hey, that's life in the big leagues.

"The dictionary defines *fidelity* as faithfulness to obligations, duties, or observances. Jake was not only always faithful to his Bureau obligations and duties, he created new ones for himself. Profiling, and criminal investigative analysis as we know it today, would not exist had it not been for Jake's vision and determination." Boyd gave this a moment to sink in before going on.

Then go on he did, at great length, and with no shortage of polysyllabic, red-white-and-blue language about bravery and integrity, to herald me as the most astonishing special agent ever to carry a badge. Such a shame a guy like that is retiring, I thought.

Was this the same guy who'd reamed me a new one in his office just three days ago? I think once you get to a certain level of management or leadership, the concept of irony must abandon you completely.

Boyd made his way from the podium and turned purposefully to pass my table. He made a show of clapping me warmly on the shoulder, then turned to Toni, gave her his hand, then ceremonially waved to Ali and Eric. "Good to see you all." Then back to me: "Sorry I can't stay; I'm off to San Francisco to address the Chiefs of Police association."

Without a hint of subtlety, Ted Novello came over to me just as Boyd had, as if to underscore the close relationship between them. "Sorry I can't stay either, Jake, but I'm traveling with the director. Take care now."

"I'll do that, Ted," I said. "Have a good trip." *And make sure you have the director's ass completely licked in time for his presentation.*

Most of the rest of the affair was predictable. I was presented with plaques from other law enforcement agencies I'd dealt with: DEA, ATF, Secret Service, and FAA. Seven or eight police agencies gave me testimonials—NY and LAPD, RCMP, Scotland Yard, Interpol. In my garage I already had a box full of plaques that had hung on the walls of my office.

I thought we were about to break up when Peter came back to the front of the room and announced, "And finally, ladies and gentlemen, we are honored to have a special guest with us today!"

The lights went down, a scratchy recording of "La Marseillaise" sounded, then in from the corridor, three men—all from my unit—wheeled in a shopping cart disguised with painted brown paper to look (vaguely) like a horse-drawn carriage. Riding in the cart and wearing a blue bicorne hat and a blue frock coat with red sash, his hand stuck characteristically into a white waistcoat, was Special Agent Craig Alcorn, the newest member of the unit, whom I'd brought in from the Milwaukee Field Office. I suspect his lack of seniority explained how he happened to pull this particular honor.

"Jake," Peter declared with a flourish, "may I present to you His Excellency, the Emperor Napoleon Bonaparte!"

Awkwardly, Craig climbed out of the shopping cart and strode majestically over to my table. "I keep twying to get een touch wiss you, Agent Do-no-veen, but you neverre retourne my calls!"

"I've been busy," I replied. The audience whooped it up.

Well, now my humiliation was complete. I tried to paste a glazed smile on my face as I died on the inside. Is this what my career added up to—making fun of a ruthless, deadly UNSUB (for unknown subject) I'd never been able to adequately profile and would now never have the opportunity to bring to justice? I was relieved Mrs. De Vries wasn't here to see this. And even though my kids were, I hoped it went over their heads.

When Craig climbed back into his shopping-cart carriage, that seemed to be the signal the luncheon was over. The people who were there because they needed to be quickly filed out, while the ones who genuinely wanted to be there hung around to greet me.

One of those was Special Agent Kathleen McManus, stunning as always and dressed to kill in a short, tight black silk number made even sexier by the slit up one thigh. Even in this age of politically correct overkill, Katie's legs were famous throughout the Bureau, which—there's that irony creeping in again—was one of the reasons I was surprised to see her here.

"I'm surprised to see you here," as it happened, was precisely what I said to her.

She came over and kissed both me and Toni, then gave me a swat of athletic camaraderie on the butt, which I could see Toni picked right up on. Though our relationship was as professional colleagues, it did make me uneasy for Toni to witness this kind of familiarity. But Katie was like that with a lot of us. Being shy, reserved, or inhibited were not among the criticisms frequently leveled at her.

"Aren't you still 'on the bricks'?" I asked.

"Uh-huh." Katie lowered her large, mischievous blue eyes in a rather convincing interpretation of the penitent schoolgirl, then gave herself away with a wide, dimple-revealing grin.

"I came for you," she said as she swept her long, tawny hair from her shoulder. "The fu—" She stopped herself when she noticed the kids, then pulled me aside and whispered, "the *fucked* have to show solidarity against the *fuck-ers*. But I've got to admit, it's kind of creepy here under these circumstances."

Katie had been given forty-five days' suspension without pay for "insubordination," which was one of the reasons the unit was shorthanded. Her crime: agreeing to pose for a calendar sponsored by No Nonsense panty hose of professional, action-oriented, and, needless to say, great-looking women. Katie was October—swerving around to nail some unseen bad guy with her Sig, captured just at the instant of muzzle flash, her short skirt flying up to reveal those gorgeous, nylon-encased gams. Proceeds from the sale of the calendar were to benefit various charities. Her ultimate sin was doing this without first seeking permission.

Personally, I thought the calendar was a boost for Bureau morale, at a time when we desperately needed one. Thomas Jefferson Boyd did not exactly inspire mirth any more than Louie Freeh had. I thought the photos of Katie "in action" would be a good recruiting device—for both male and female agents.

"I've still got to get you to autograph my copy of the calendar," I teased her. "Just don't cover up anything important with your signature."

"What is their problem?" she mused out loud. "It's not like I exactly enriched myself or anything. I specified the Police Memorial Fund as my charity. And it's not like I posed in a leather halter with the FBI crest tattooed across my left butt cheek." She glanced around the room at all the straitlaced Bureau types in suits. "How would that have been— *Fidelity, Bravery, Integrity,* right across my bare ass!"

I briefly contemplated that enticing possibility. But actually, the FBI would have frowned on this as well, it being a violation of regs to use the crest, on one's left butt cheek or elsewhere, without permission. On the other hand, they would have admired the permanent expression of loyalty it represented.

She swept a strand of light brown hair out of her eyes. "I swear, I've had it with all this bullshit. It wouldn't take much for me to take a hike, especially now." She put her arms around me and pulled me in for a tight hug. "Oh, Jake, I can't believe this. I don't want to lose you!" There was a momentary pause during which I tried to interpret this remark for its maximum libidinous potential, until, with her head still resting on my shoulder, she added, "None of us do."

Craig Alcorn came back, now out of his Napoleon getup and once again in the special agent's standard dark suit and white shirt. "Some of us are knocking off work early in honor of the occasion. Thought we'd take you over to The Major's and get you shit-faced. Whatayou say?"

"Best offer I've had all day" is what I said.

Peter Sutherland came over to pay his respects to the recently deceased.

"You coming with us to The Major's?" I asked.

"I'd love to," he replied, "but I've got to catch a plane for L.A. in about an hour and from there on to Hawaii. I'm doing a road school and homicide consultation in Honolulu."

"Sure, I understand. You still have a job."

He smiled and clapped me good-naturedly on the shoulder. That shoulder was beginning to hurt from all of my colleagues' good nature.

"How 'bout you, Katie?"

"Sure. I've got no place to go. I'll meet you outside in front."

Toni said she had to run or she wouldn't have time to drop off the kids before her four-o'clock. "I'm glad I could be here today," she said in her mature and responsible tone, giving me a peck on the cheek. "Give your dad a hug and a kiss," she directed Ali and Eric.

They dutifully obeyed, and I, in turn, wrapped both kids in my arms and squeezed them tight. One thing my job has done is to make it impossible for me take my children for granted or forget how much I love them. Too many times in my life I've been places—a park, a wooded stream, even a church parking lot—and I've flashed back to similar sites where I've watched the body of a boy or girl the same age as mine being pulled out and put in the ME's wagon. And each and every one of those times, I'd feel a trickle of ice-cold sweat make its way down my spine as I wondered how in the name of God an adult could willfully do this to a child.

"Be careful, kids," I said as I released my grasp.

The kids ran on ahead with Katie, whom they'd always liked. Eric, in fact, seemed to be developing his first prepubescent crush on her. He was the one who had the calendar up on the wall of his room, perpetually opened to October, and I'm sure he would have been thrilled with an invitation from her to go drinking at The Major's.

Toni lingered back a moment. "We've had our differences about the Bureau, Jake, but I would be very sad if you thought I was taking any satisfaction in this." She smiled. "In fact, I'd have to say I'm genuinely proud of you."

I took her hands in mine. "You always did go for the broken wings, didn't you? I guess that's why you went into the profession you did."

We'd met when I was just getting started as an instructor at the FBI Academy and she was a grad student in psychology at the University of Virginia, not too far away in Charlottesville. But as time went by, I realized I couldn't explain, couldn't bring home, couldn't share, even with my psychologist wife. Because while she was spending her days dealing with the unhappy and neurotically normal, I was residing in a world of psychopaths, men who hurt and killed for the sheer satisfaction and exhilaration of it all. Toni wanted to understand her disturbed subjects so she could help them to more fulfilling lives. I wanted to understand my disturbed subjects so I could hunt them down and put them away forever or, even better, help arrange a date with their local gas chamber, electric chair, or lethal-injection gurney. That was the difference between Toni and me.

Or at least the most manifest difference. I recalled a conversation we had had just before I'd gone out to Black Diamond—from which I'd come home strapped to a stretcher in an air ambulance.

"Don't you see what this job's doing to you, Jake? You can't turn it off. I heard a professional-football coach interviewed on TV. He said that when he won, he was euphoric for an hour, then he'd start stressing about the next game. But when he lost, he was despondent for a week, until he could play another game and begin the process all over again. You're the same way. When you nail an UNSUB or get word of a conviction, you're happy and peaceful for a few minutes. Then you get a call telling you the body of another kid's been found and you go into an instant depression. The only thing that can bring you out of it is going to work on another active case. How long do you think you can keep up with this 'hair of the dog' treatment?"

"As long as I have to," I replied sullenly.

"You mean, until you've personally eliminated murder and rape from the world? Good luck, but I can't wait around to pick up the pieces. It isn't fair to me, and it isn't fair to Ali and Eric."

But even that hadn't delivered the final death blow to our relationship. Actually, it was far more insidious, and far more banal, than anything I could have foreseen with all of my fancy profiling skills. After years of suffering through my constant traveling, of mourning all the time and energy my cases stole from our life together, of missing me and compensating and making do, suddenly, there came a day when she realized that she was doing all right without me. From there followed the revelation that she no longer needed me, and from there, that I had become unnecessary and irrelevant to her life.

But that was all behind us now, replaced by a bittersweet acceptance of who and what we each were and would likely remain.

"Let's get together sometime soon," she said.

"We'll do that," I replied, and went to join Craig and the rest of the group. I liked to think Toni and I still loved each other, or loved each other again, but we seemed to do it better at a distance.

5

I came to consciousness gradually, not through words or pictures, just a rhythmic pounding, like a tribal drum. As I floated up through the next level of wakefulness, the pounding grew stronger, more insistent. One more level and I realized it was my front door that was making all the noise, or rather, someone beating that door into submission.

I extended my wrist in front of me and tried to focus on my watch dial. Two twenty-eight. Since it was light out, it had to be 2:28 in the afternoon. The dim recollection of margaritas and the company of close friends and former associates after the retirement ceremony was starting to fit into a pattern. Welcome tequila sunrise!

Still the pounding continued, and now I became aware of a faint but rhythmic "Mr. Donovan . . . Mr. Donovan . . ."

"Okay," I rasped. I got up and staggered in the direction of the front door, all the time trying to effect the transition back to this world.

I opened the door and the pounding ceased. On the other side was Joe Ripley, one of Neil Burke's clerks.

"What's this about?" I asked groggily.

"Don't you answer your phone, Mr. Donovan?"

"Not when I'm unconscious."

Undaunted—FBI clerks are seldom daunted—he explained, "I've been instructed by SAC Burke to bring you back to Quantico."

"Excuse me, but if I remember correctly, I retired yesterday."

"All I know is that when you didn't answer your phone, Mr. Burke told me to come and get you."

Ah, so they've realized they can't run the place without you, Dono-
van. And if I thought that, I concluded I must still be significantly
drunk. But I was too weary and hungover to protest. "Let me just brush
my teeth and change clothes."

"No time," Ripley informed me without apology.

∘

Dozens of paranoid thoughts danced through my foggy mind as we
walked into the lobby of the Jefferson Building. Gloria at the front desk
smiled and buzzed me through the thick glass security door on the left.
But before I could go through, Ripley handed me a laminated visitor's
tag. "I've already cleared you," he said efficiently.

I kept forgetting I was no longer in Kansas.

We walked down the long, glass-walled corridor, then turned the cor-
ner into another glass tube that led to the Administration Building.
Silently, Ripley steered me down the suite corridor to Neil Burke's office.
"Wait here," he instructed.

I stood alone in the SAC's expansive digs with its panoramic window onto the green, parklike setting and the rolling, wooded Virginia
hills beyond. You could profile a lot about the differences between the
two of us simply from the evidence of our respective offices. Mine had
been Hollywood Central: photos, logo caps, even a director's chair,
from all the shows I'd been on and movies I'd consulted for. Then there
were all the artifacts I'd accumulated during my years of criminal investigative analysis around the world—police patches and badges, a
British bobby's hat and French gendarme's cap, billy clubs and batons,
the plaques and testimonials. Then there was the long, blue chiffon
dress hanging on my coatrack. It had been presented to me by the unit
after I'd been quoted on *60 Minutes* as saying if they ever found me
behind my desk in a blue chiffon dress and smoking a cigar, they'd
know I'd finally cracked.

Burke's office, by contrast, much larger than mine and unlike the
one I'd occupied, had actual windows out onto the real world, was taste-
fully, one might even say severely, decorated. There was all the FBI
memorabilia—a large, 3-D, enamel Bureau crest on the wall next to the
signed photo of J. Edgar Hoover—not in a dress—that all the old guys
had. Then there was a bookshelf of walnut matching his immaculately
clean desk on which were neatly arranged binders of FBI regs and case
reports. But where I had my shrine to Jake Donovan, maven of the

media, Burke had a flag in a glass case, action photographs, and a framed citation in testimony to his winning of the Navy Cross as a marine second lieutenant in Vietnam.

As I stood there reading of his fearlessness in the face of death, I had a revelation of sorts. Yes, this man is a natural leader, and I'm sure his bravery had saved many lives. But you can take fearlessness and heroism too far. I don't say Burke's one of those, but if you follow someone like I'm talking about without questioning him, you have to be suicidal. Those are the kinds of heroes who get the rest of us killed. I've got to tell you, I've seen a lot of dead bodies, many of them gruesomely tortured and murdered. Was in the navy myself and I've been in a couple of firefights as a street agent where I had to stare into the face of death. And each time, I was scared shitless. That doesn't mean I ran or didn't acquit myself as I should have. But anyone who's not scared shitless, who laughs at death, that's the kind I worry about.

Neil Burke came in from a side door followed by his henchman Harry Gillette, ASAC of the Critical Incident Response Group, looking no more or less grim than usual. Gillette had been my nemesis practically since I'd arrived at Quantico and seemed to live by the maxim that anything that got in the way of rules and bureaucracy had to be crushed as quickly as possible. He was the one who had engineered Katie's suspension after I had (unwisely, it turned out) laughed off his exhortation that as her unit chief I should be the one to "discipline her severely." When I'd related this to Katie, she'd suggested that I put her over my knee, which to me was not without its appeal. But that, apparently, was not the sort of discipline Harry had in mind. The guy has the sense of humor and zest for living of a Swiss banker on Prozac.

To my surprise, he and Burke were accompanied by a large black man in his fifties with steely gray hair whom I immediately recognized as Deputy Director Orlando Ravan, known by reputation as Ravan the Raven. I never knew where the nickname came from, whether it had to do with his color or something else more bureaucratically sinister. He had started as a clerk during the Hoover days and pushed and pushed until he became one of the first black special agents. Now he was the highest career man in the Bureau.

"How're you doing, Jake," Burke greeted me. "Sorry I had to duck out so early from your retirement celebration yesterday."

The apology didn't seem to call for a response.

"You know Orlando Ravan."

"Sure. How are you, Deputy Director?"

"Acting Director," Burke corrected me.

"What are you talking about?"

Burke hesitated, glanced at the other two men, and spoke tensely. "Mr. Ravan automatically became acting director this morning upon the death of Thomas Boyd."

6

It came as a physical jolt. Then it was as if I'd just gone into some sort of fugue state. "What did you just say, Neil?"

Each horrifying possibility raced through my mind. Car accident? Heart attack? Boyd was a runner and prided himself on his physical conditioning. Accident? Suicide? Murder? *My God!*

"Judge Boyd flew out to San Francisco yesterday afternoon. Today he was scheduled to address the International Association of Chiefs of Police at the Fairmont Hotel. He and his wife still own a house across the bay in the Sausalito hills from the days when he was on the federal bench out there. It's where Mrs. Boyd's family is from and they planned to retire there after he left the Bureau. It's where he likes to stay when he's in the area. At approximately nine twenty-five P.M., Pacific daylight time, a next-door neighbor heard a loud noise that she says sounded like a gunshot. She went over and knocked on the door. There was no answer. Since the house is empty most of the time, the Boyds had given her a key, which she went back to her own house to find and then let herself in. What the neighbor saw when she entered was Thomas Boyd on the floor of the master bedroom in a pool of blood. She said he was holding a gun in his hand. She ran out frantically and went back to her own house where she called 911, which dispatched an ambulance and Sausalito PD. They both arrived a few minutes later, and once the EMS squad leader determined the subject was dead—I don't gather it was too difficult—he relinquished control to the PD, which began processing the scene as well as calling in the

Marin County Sheriff's Department. As soon as the identity of the decedent was officially established, the San Francisco Field Office was contacted. They immediately located Douglas Steinberg, the SAC, as well as the head of the director's security detail, Sean Hennigan. It was Steinberg who called me.

"Sheriff's detectives identified the weapon as a Smith & Wesson Model 66 revolver with a two-and-a-half-inch barrel, Boyd's personal service piece. Indication is that he shot himself once in the mouth and the bullet exited the back of his skull behind his right ear."

"That's right, he was left-handed," I said idly. But my head kept spinning, as if on some deep level of psychological wish-fulfillment, I had caused this death as retribution for what he'd done to me.

Get a grip, Donovan.

"There were no other bullets in the cylinder."

"Jesus," I said, "he was at my retirement lunch yesterday."

"By the way," said Ravan, "I'm sorry I couldn't be there myself."

"It's okay," I said absently. I turned to Burke. "I'm very sorry." Before Boyd had left the Bureau to become a prosecutor in Dade County, he and Burke had been agents together in the Miami Field Office. "Boyd and Burke" had made a reputation as a successful team. And even though Boyd had shoved Ted Novello down his throat as new chief of the Profiling and Serial Crimes Unit, Burke and the director were known to be friends.

"Thanks," the SAC said.

"Weren't there any bodyguards around?" I asked, trying feebly to make some sense of the incomprehensible. "You just mentioned this guy, Hennigan."

"The director hated that kind of thing," Ravan said. "He thought it cramped his personal style and made the wrong impression on the outside world. I argued with him all the time—this is no secret—but he still cut way back on his security detail. When he was at home, either in Washington or California, he'd only let them pick him up and drop him off. It particularly bothered me since he wouldn't let any bodyguards along on his long-distance runs. Why don't we all sit down."

But before I could, Burke added, "Jake, there's something else about the scene you need to know. On the bed detectives found a nine-by-twelve-inch brown manila envelope—no address or writing on it."

"Anything in it?"

"No. But in the tub of the adjoining bathroom they found what apparently had been a series of four-by-six-inch photographs which some-one, presumably the director, had attempted to destroy by burning. Only a small part of one of the photos was still intact, and from that, they can't tell anything."

Burke took a seat behind his desk. It was a high judge's or execu-tive's type chair. Ravan took the other visitor's seat. My old nemesis Harry Gillette insinuated himself into a standing position about two steps behind Burke, looming there as if he were a tough guy.

"Blackmail?" I asked.

"That would be speculating in advance of the evidence, but, yes, that is very definitely what we're concerned about."

This was incredible—even the suggestion that Boyd could possibly be blackmailed. He was as rock-ribbed and traditional American fam-ily values as you could get. When he was appointed, he talked about how it wasn't law enforcement but the family that was going to have to bring down the violent-crime rate. At his swearing-in speech, flanked by Madeline and their son Jason, he quoted the legendary Tennessee prosecutor Henry "Hank" Williams, saying, "The federal government spends billions of dollars to fight crime, and they have to. But the only real answer is for mommas and daddies to raise their kids right."

Despite our manifest differences, that's the kind of guy Thomas Jeffer-son Boyd was . . . or appeared to have been. This wouldn't be the first time someone in Washington turned out to be a something in something else's clothing, a leader who preached to others to do as he said, not as he did.

"We think this may have been an attempt to neutralize the director's effectiveness," Harry Gillette stated helpfully. It was the first time he had spoken during this meeting.

"You know, you may be right, Harry," I offered.

"Don't start baiting him," Burke warned me.

"Does the press know?"

"No one knows yet," Burke said. "There is an absolute embargo on all information, and we've got an agent baby-sitting the neighbor. The Chiefs of Police were notified that Boyd was suddenly taken ill and wouldn't be able to attend the meeting. Steinberg of the San Francisco Field Office and the senior resident agent from San Rafael have been brought on, and they're liaising with Sausalito PD, Marin Sheriff's, and California State Police. Ted Novello, who accompanied the director on this trip, is pretty broken up, as I'm sure you can imagine."

You bet I can.

"And the president has been informed."

It seemed that someone was being left out of this discussion. "What about Mrs. Boyd?"

"Of course, but as little as possible."

What struck me as the most obvious question of all just hung in the air unanswered.

"Umm, if I remember correctly, and I admit you don't have me at my best, I retired yesterday."

All three men stared silently at me.

Are they shitting me? I sprung to my feet. "Wait a minute. Are you suggesting . . ."

"Suggesting what, Jake?" Gillette said.

"That I'm a suspect?"

"Should we be?"

"Don't kid a kidder. I came up with those interrogation techniques you're using."

"You had the motive."

"And you're giving me another one!" I lunged at the sorry son of a bitch and came up with a hunk of lapel in each hand. A look of abject terror flashed through his sagging eyes as I realized that, like so many who send others out to do the tough and dangerous jobs that they will later claim overall credit for, Harry was a physical coward.

I felt Neil Burke's powerful hands wrap around my shoulders and pull me back, but I sensed the effort was more obligatory than earnest. He had a responsibility to protect his ASAC from having a former employee beat the shit out of him.

Upon his release from my grasp, Harry coughed a few times, shook his head to regain his composure, then glared daggers at me.

"Are you saying you don't think it was a suicide provoked by blackmail? Well, I can account for my whereabouts. In fact, *you* can account for my whereabouts."

Gillette smiled thinly, though he was still shaking and rubbing his chest. "We're not saying you offed him with your own two hands. You'd be far too smart for that."

"Are you guys fucking serious?" I demanded. "Because if you are . . ."

Burke stood and put up his hand in a peace offering. "Hold it, Jake. Sit down. Let's not get all bent out of shape here."

"You get me up out of a sound drunken stupor, bring me here and accuse me of murdering the director of the FBI—that tends to bend my shape."

"No one's accusing you of anything. Fact is, we need you."

I responded with nothing but a look of total perplexity.

Ravan took over. "Let's net it out here." FBI officials liked to net things out. "When this gets out in the next several hours, it's going to be the messiest situation the Bureau has ever had to face. If it turns out to be the suicide it appears, we've got a huge scandal on our hands. If it turns out to be something else, then it's even worse."

"No argument there," I agreed grimly. "But I still don't see why I'm here."

"For one, you're as good as any criminal investigative analyst we have . . . uh . . . had. But just as important, anything we do as far as internal investigation of this case is going to be suspect. You remember the Uncle Remus story about the tar baby?"

"I think I saw the Disney movie when I was a kid."

"We've got a lot of questions to deal with here, and every one of them is a tar baby: the more you touch it, the stickier it gets. I don't want another Vince Foster situation, where a high public official kills himself but people don't believe it; Washington couldn't take that. Faith in government institutions is low enough. People are still speculating about J. Edgar Hoover's secret life. And I don't want another JonBenet Ramsey case where everything is compromised in the beginning so then no one believes anything from the get-go."

I stood up again, took a couple of paces toward the window, then stopped and turned, looking right at the acting director. "So you're saying you want me to investigate this case?"

"That's right," Burke confirmed. "It was Orlando's idea, and I concur in it completely."

"I understand no one's better on crime-scene staging than you," Ravan elaborated. "You'll report directly to me. We want you to undertake an independent investigation. We don't want anyone to think this thing is wired. Before we declare that the Bureau is confident this was a suicide, I want you to be able to confirm that."

"Oh, sure, no problem," I responded. "Tom Boyd just destroyed my career. I'd be happy to work in his behalf. You guys should know you can always depend on me."

"Sarcasm isn't called for," Gillette said solemnly.

I turned to him. "What? I would think even you would recognize that sarcasm is the only thing that's called for."

I stood to go but Ravan put up his hand to stop me. "That's a reasonable reaction, I don't deny it. I'd feel exactly the same. But please try to think of the larger issues involved."

"You mean like the fact that except for Peter Sutherland, no one in the Bureau came to my defense?"

"I mean that for you to have dedicated as much of your life and energy and passion to your work as you have, what this organization means and stands for must mean something to you. And when it's threatened, as it definitely is right now, I find it hard to believe that you wouldn't put aside personal grudges to be able to do something truly important."

I considered this appeal a moment, then continued toward the door. "Let Harry do it. He's as loyal and true-blue as anyone. My profile is that he even sleeps in FBI jammies."

"Okay, Donovan—" the red-faced Gillette started in. But Neil Burke put out a hand to silence him.

"Harry can't do it. We all know that. He couldn't do it if you wrote him a fucking step-by-step manual."

Gillette looked at his boss as if he'd just been slapped.

"Harry's a paper-pusher," Burke continued. "You're the man who can do this, who can save our asses for us after we didn't save yours. I can't believe there's no appeal in that for a guy like you."

Old Neil knew the buttons to push, I had to say that for him. A thousand conflicting thoughts raced through my addled and grudge-bearing brain. This wasn't my problem; Judge Boyd, rest his soul, had seen to that. But here they were, calling me in as the conquering hero. Vindication, so soon after my debasement and degradation. Maybe there is a God after all. How could I turn that down? Or were they just setting me up as the fall guy? Maybe Harry wasn't just blowing smoke. Maybe they really did think I had something to do with it.

"What about expenses, personnel?"

"We'll do what we can with the director's discretionary fund," said Ravan. "I'll put the General Counsel's Office onto seeing whether it's legal for you to be paid in addition to your pension."

"I'm not asking for money for myself," I said. "But what if I need extra people?"

"We'll do our best. As you can appreciate, we're working this out as we go along."

"How much authority will I have?"

"Take what you need. We'll cut back if we have to."

You live long enough, you hear everything. The acting director was actually telling me to be completely independent. *Okay*, I said to myself, *so suppose I do go along with this and at least see where it's headed . . .*

I crossed my arms over my chest. "So?"

Neil Burke took over. "We want you to fly out to San Francisco immediately. The body has been removed for preliminary forensic workup, but other than that, the crime scene is still intact."

"When's the next flight?"

"Right now. Mr. Ravan's arranged for the director's plane to come back and fly you out."

Burke must have noticed a frustrated look on my face because he stopped for a moment. "Is something wrong, Jake?"

"No," I said, turning to Burke. "But you remember that proposal for a flying squad I made a couple of years ago?"

"Yes, of course," he said stiffly.

"Well, I can't help but imagine how perfect that would be for this particular situation."

"Yes, well . . ."

I let it hang in the air, driving my point home like a knife blade. When it was in as deep as I wanted it, I said, "Okay, well, I'll just go home and change."

"There isn't time," Ravan responded, retaking the tactical position. "I'm holding off informing anyone else until I get word from you on the scene, but every minute makes the situation more delicate. I've had Mr. Gillette look up your sizes. A change of clothing will be available for you on the plane."

I suspected there was another motive for not telling Mrs. Boyd more than they had to right away. Tom and Madeline Boyd were deeply religious, and their faith forbid tampering with the body. Once she was brought fully into the situation, she'd likely refuse permission for any further postmortem examination, let alone a full autopsy. They'd have to get whatever they could from the preliminary forensic analysis.

Ravan pulled a business card from his case, scrawled a number on the back, then handed it to me. "I can be reached at this number any time of day or night."

○

Quantico had suddenly taken on a surreal quality as Neil Burke himself escorted me out of the office and back down the corridor, while Harry Gillette was dispatched to go buy me a toothbrush and a shaving kit at the base exchange next to the cafeteria in the Jefferson Building.

We met up at the entrance to the gun-cleaning room, across the hall from the armory. Clearly unhappy in his new role of personal shopper, Harry was holding a plastic bag full of stuff, which he wordlessly and unceremoniously handed to me.

"Thanks, Harry."

Still he said nothing, so, obnoxious SOB that I am, I decided to press the issue. "You don't really like me, Harry, do you?"

"Don't start with me," he replied wearily.

"No, really. I don't give a fuck if you do or not, but if we're going to be working together again, I just thought we ought to establish a realistic footing."

He gave me one of those *Okay, fella, you asked for it!* looks. "Let's just say I don't like your style."

"Oh, my style, is it?"

"I don't like the way you're always mugging for the media. I don't like your attitude toward authority—"

"Oh, well, if that's all it is."

"I don't like your fancy Italian suits. I don't like your James Bond car—"

"Whoa, Harry, hold it right there! James Bond drove a 1964 Aston Martin DB5. Mine is a 1962 DB4 Series 3."

"What's the damn difference, Donovan?"

"Well, the headlights for one. And then under the hood . . ."

He turned and walked away in disgust.

The car was waiting at the loading dock near the outdoor firing range, which meant taking a circuitous route through the Investigative Support Unit's windowless warren of offices several floors down from the cafeteria level.

I got a clutch in my throat as we approached what until the day before yesterday had been my office. I hadn't expected to be back here so soon. I thought I'd have more time to prepare myself emotionally.

But when we got up close, all feelings of wistfulness and melancholy instantly evaporated.

My nameplate had been removed from the wall next to the door and another had replaced it. Ted Novello had already moved in; his books and case reports filled the shelves, his memorabilia adorned the walls, and his shiny new blue FBI windbreaker hung where my favorite dress used to be.

The office looked like the fucker had been there for years.

7

As the Gulfstream II climbed from the Quantico airstrip and banked sharply to the right, I could see the entire FBI Academy laid out below me. From this lofty perspective it looked so substantial, so orderly, so organized: a collection of ten or eleven red-brick and glass buildings, three of them high-rise blocks, nestled into the woods like some high-tech industrial park. How could a regular airline passenger, gazing down on the complex from such a height without knowing what it was, possibly imagine, possibly comprehend, the chaos and disorder of the human mind so carefully accounted for, studied, processed, within those confines? How many thousands of linear feet of files, crammed in metal cabinets or stacked in long rows in subbasements, attested to the incredible, unbelievable, monstrous things human beings were capable of doing to one another? But those of us who worked there didn't need those tons of paper to know or understand this. We carried it with us, a semiconscious overlay, informing everything we were and did.

It was just me and the two pilots. Before we took off, one of them asked me if I wanted anything to drink, and when I said no, they closed the cockpit door but told me just to come forward if I wanted anything during the flight. After that, I was alone with my thoughts, and the communications console the director used to remain in contact while he was in the air. The plane was a flying living room of expansive and well-padded seats and sofas done up in soothing neutral colors. In fact the only thing that jarred the peaceful and relaxing atmosphere was the prominent FBI crest on the forward bulkhead.

The last time I recalled anyone from our division on the director's plane was back when a young female stenographer from the San Antonio Field Office was raped and murdered in her garden apartment. You can't mess around with the FBI that way, even with the support staff. So Director William Webster, one of the Bureau's real champions, had Special Agents Roy Hazelwood and Jim Wright—two of the best and sharpest of Quantico's criminal investigative analysts—get their tails down to the scene and crack the case, immediately. They arrived in Texas late in the afternoon and went directly to the crime scene.

The scene told them a lot. Based on the physical setting and the victimology, they became convinced that the murder was actually a sexual assault gone bad, committed by a type we refer to as an anger retaliatory rapist. The way to get him, Roy and Jim advised the police, was to go proactive: to publish relevant portions of the profile that would allow someone who knew the UNSUB to recognize his pre- and postoffense behavior. That's just what the police did, and the media picked up on it, including an article in the *San Antonio Express-News*. The drift was that the UNSUB would have confided his crime to a close acquaintance or associate, and in the FBI agents' opinion, that person would now be in grave danger.

Within hours of the publication, the offender's armed-robbery partner turned him in. And what did Hazelwood and Wright get for their troubles? Tickets home in the crowded coach class of the next scheduled commercial flight.

I had no illusions as to why I was now being chauffeured across country at taxpayer expense. I was the coal-mine canary, hung out front to make sure there's no danger to the cautious people holding the cage away from themselves on a long pole. If there was anyone, or anything, to be lured out, I would do it for them; this canary was also walking point, drawing fire. And then, of course, there is the corporate wisdom basic to any bureaucracy that holds that bringing someone on from outside for a risky job is often the best move. If he or she does well, all credit and glory accrue to the organization. In the event of a fuckup, there's someone convenient to blame who has no stake, no protectors, and can't bring anyone else down with him.

When the plane leveled off, I went to the head and brushed my teeth. Then I peeled off the suit I'd been wearing for two days and opened the plastic bag of clothing that had thoughtfully been put aboard for me. The problem was that the only "real" clothing—as opposed to sweatshirts and running togs and the like—that the Academy's exchange sold was what new agents and police fellows wore for training: an ensemble of khaki slacks and either a blue-and-gray (FBI) or red-and-gray (non-FBI students) jersey embroidered "FBI Academy." Not exactly the desired look for showing up at a crime scene. The one nice thing is that this is purposely a comfortable outfit. Unfortunately, Harry, in his infinite resentment, had neglected to include the accompanying white socks and running shoes, so I'd still be wearing my black, cap-toe oxfords when we landed. And maybe I could pick up some new underwear when we got there.

We landed at San Francisco International and taxied out of the way of the commercial jets and onto the tarmac in front of the corporate aviation terminal. As the copilot came out to lower the stairs, a cream-colored, unmarked Ford Crown Vic pulled up next to the jet. A man in his early thirties in a dark blue suit and shiny white shirt opened the door.

"Mr. Donovan?" he said, extending his hand. "Special Agent Bill Gaylord, San Francisco Field Office. Hope the flight was okay."

The young-and-eager type. You can spot them half a city block away. "It wasn't crowded," I said.

We took 101 north into the city. One of the benefits of my career is that I've been all over the world at Bureau expense, so I've seen many of the great cities and tourist attractions. The flip side is that now I associate each of those cities—London, Paris, Rome, Barcelona, Sydney, etc., etc.—with some grisly crime or series of crimes. Not too far from where we were right now, I'd worked the case of a serial rapist-murderer in Golden Gate Park. The press had dubbed him the Park Pervert. After surveying the crime scenes and body dump sites, I told the task force I thought the profile would be pretty standard and therefore not terribly helpful. The most "usable" characteristic, I thought, was that the killer had a speech impediment.

"You can tell the asshole's got a speech impediment just by looking at the scene?" one detective said. "You a fuckin' psychic?"

The attack sites were all secluded, with little chance of the offender being witnessed, which meant he should have been able to "take his time" with each victim, enticing her with some kind of verbal ruse or con to get her guard down—perhaps a lost hiker asking for directions. Yet the attacks were all blitz style; he must have rendered his victims unconscious or nearly so before they were more than marginally aware of his presence. This type of behavior suggested that even with the seclusion and the essentially nonthreatening locale, the offender didn't feel confident enough to engage these women in even casual conversation. And this, in turn, suggested something about his person or appearance he was self-conscious about. The most likely possibility would be a physical disability or prominent scarring. But if that were the case, I would have expected someone to have taken note of him in the area around one of the murders. So the next possibility was a speech impediment: something not visually apparent but manifest as soon as he opened his mouth. He wouldn't be able to lure or entice his victims. If he wanted to rape them, he'd have to neutralize them right away. It's all a matter of looking objectively at the evidence, filtering it through your experience, and letting it tell you something.

I was convinced the UNSUB was a local guy because of his knowledge of the most secluded areas. We found a pair of eyeglasses at one of the scenes. I advised the cops to ask local establishments if any of their recent customers had an obvious speech impediment. One optical shop on Geary Street recalled such a customer. The records on his order matched the frame type. He was brought in for questioning, but spoke perfectly well until we accused him of rape and murder. Then his stuttering became uncontrollable. His DNA matched a semen sample from the scene, he was tried and convicted, and I hope he never gets out.

○

Thomas Boyd's house was a cedar-and-stone bungalow style tucked on a steep, wooded Sausalito hillside with a spectacular view overlooking the bay and the city of San Francisco beyond. You could just make out the crumbling roofline of Alcatraz in the middle distance. I knew all of this because Ted Novello met me at the front door and escorted me around the redwood walkway on the side of the house that connected with the wide deck in the back. The entire rear of the house was glass, affording this same view from practically any room.

"I'm sorry about this," I said. I really was. I suspected Ted's ultimate career hopes included following the director from the Bureau to some high-priced law firm where, riding Boyd's coattails, Ted would start making piles of money. All those elaborate plans down the toilet.

He nodded at my expression of sympathy. "Thanks for coming."

"What can you tell me?"

"No sign of forced entry, no obvious indication of a struggle. No obvious defense wounds, no foreign blood or tissue under the fingernails, and no other bodily injuries than the fatal one."

"Any farewell note?"

"No. They've looked all over the house."

Not a surprise. Contrary to what most people think, suicide notes are not that common. In fact, we've broken several homicides staged to look like suicides because of what the inexperienced killers *thought* a note was supposed to sound like.

"You knew the director better than I did," I said. "Was he the kind of guy who would kill himself?"

Ted shrugged, and the glib operator I knew was gone. "I don't know what to tell you, Jake. I never would have thought of something like this."

From the rear deck, we stepped through the sliding glass door, past the drawn floor-to-ceiling curtains, and into the bedroom. "This sliding door was found unlocked," Ted explained, "but the neighbor says this wasn't unusual when the Boyds were home. Not much violent crime in this area, mostly B and E's when no one is home. People in the neighborhood knew this was the director's house, so it was low-risk. The curtains, by the way, were open when police arrived. They closed them for security."

"Oh, fuck!" I said.

In sharp contrast to the peaceful, isolated atmosphere outside the house, inside the place was crawling with cops and other officials. At first glance I recognized uniforms for the local police, county sheriff, state police, and even a guy from California Highway Patrol. I assumed the other suits were Bureau. They all must have parked their cars on the next street so as not to attract attention. I felt somewhat self-conscious in my Academy duds, as if I were the only one who came dressed up to what turned out not to be a costume party.

"What the hell are all these people doing here?" I demanded.

No one answered.

A uniform came over with a clipboard and asked me to autograph a sign-in sheet: name, date and time, agency/department affiliation. A large number of names were already listed. This was distressingly typical for a high-profile case, even one that was supposed to be need-to-know at this point.

But it could turn any investigation to shit. Any usable hair and fiber or other trace evidence had probably been obliterated or corrupted by now. According to the theory of transfer, the most basic principle of crime-scene investigation, no one enters or exits a room without leaving something, and taking something with him. The wool, sisal-style carpet was such a tight weave that it wasn't much good for capturing footprint impressions, but whatever subtle ones might have been there would be long gone by now. What was the point of bringing me out here, I wondered, if there was no crime scene left to process?

"What's everyone doing here?" I repeated loudly.

A guy in a suit made his way through the crowd. "You have a problem here, Mr. Donovan?" he said sarcastically. He wore an ID on a chain around his neck that identified him as Lieutenant Anthony Mervis of the Sausalito PD.

"Well, matter of fact, yes, I do. Strikes me this scene is out of control."

"No," he replied as if talking to a simple child. "In fact, I'm *in control* here, seeing as how we got a questionable death occurring on our patch of real estate."

"Ah, but the decedent happened to be a federal officer on official duty. That's the essence of the thing, you see, which is why I'd like everyone else the fuck out of here."

He stuck his face in mine. "Look, I don't know who invited you, Jake . . ."

I felt the heat rising from the back of my neck. Christ, it was like being back in Boyd's office, or all the other places where I'd uttered variations on the classic *I didn't ask to be here. Your people asked me to come. I can get back on the plane and fly back to Quantico. No skin off my ass.* It's a fact that local departments aren't always what they should be, and it's a fact that the FBI has been famous over the years for swooping in and stealing the glory. Sometimes it's hard to remember we're all supposed to be on the same side.

Ted quickly grabbed me by the arm and pulled me aside. "Come on, Jake, we've got to work with these folks. Calm down."

He introduced me to Douglas Steinberg, SAC of the San Francisco Field Office. "Jake, how are you? How was your flight?" he greeted me grimly. No one was saying anything about the strange circumstances of my being here so I had to assume orders had been passed down from on high.

As Steinberg led Ted and me down a hallway, I stopped and pointed up toward the ceiling. "That's a surveillance camera."

"Right," Ted confirmed. "It was installed in the house when Tom was appointed."

So why were we going through this stupid drill? "Then the case is solved."

Ted shook his head. "Afraid not. It was never used. Tom wouldn't let anyone in to maintain or service it. He said the time he was here he wanted to be private."

Judge Boyd, you're still giving me grief. We went into the bedroom and Steinberg signaled a Sausalito uniform to come over. "This is Charlie Allenson, who was first on scene." Allenson gave me the rundown.

Depending on the angle of entry and exit, the spatter patterns of gunshot wounds to the head can be more or less contained, but, particularly if it's a contact wound, there's going to be a lot of blood and gore. The shape of Boyd's upper body was fuzzily outlined in blood where he'd fallen back on the bed. Most of it was now dried and soaked into the sheets and mattress, but some was still stickily wet, and bits of bone and charred tissue residue were adhering to it.

The only other sign of anything amiss was a lamp that appeared to have fallen off the night table and shattered when it hit the floor. It must have hit pretty hard, because I could detect tiny fragments over part of the bed. The largest remaining pieces suggested that it had been a frosted-white globe about eight or so inches in diameter, which had rested on a three-prong wooden base. Though the bulb had also been broken by the fall, the base was intact.

Other than the large red blotch approximately in the center of the bed, and the shattered lamp, the room looked strangely normal and lived-in. A pair of slippers were on the floor, a robe was draped over a wooden valet, a pair of open reading glasses rested on top of a book entitled *Journey into Darkness* on the night table. And that magnificent view of San Francisco Bay was still visible through the drawn, semisheer drapes. But I wondered how many subtle details and indicators had already been lost.

I checked out the bathroom where the photos had been burned. The only other significant feature was a bottle of Absolut vodka, about three-fourths full, on the counter next to the sink. Beside it was a plastic bathroom cup. I leaned over and sniffed. It still smelled of booze. A man contemplating suicide might well lower his inhibitions and resistance through alcohol. I could imagine him with the bottle in one hand, confronting himself in the bathroom mirror, trying to decide if he could go through with this as the vodka took effect.

"Did the director drink?" I asked Ted.

"Hardly ever. I've seen him take a sip of something for toasts; that's about it."

"Then where did the bottle come from?"

"He and Madeline kept it around for company. We checked downstairs; there's a bottle of Scotch, a bottle of bourbon, and a couple of liqueurs."

I went back to the bedroom. Ted introduced James Grady from the San Francisco Field Office Evidence Response Team. Unfortunately, just like Ted and his guys, they'd arrived after the locals.

Grady was a tall, well-built guy, with intense and penetrating eyes that seemed to contradict the easy casualness of his manner. He had short but shaggy blond hair and his shirt was coming out of his pants. From his pocket he produced a set of Polaroids, which would have to do until the standard scene photos were developed. Boyd was lying on his back on the bed. He was wearing khakis and a black, knit polo shirt bearing the FBI crest. In the close-up of Boyd's head, there was some obvious stippling—or pinpoint hemorrhaging—on the cheeks, chin, and neck, caused when tiny fragments of burned powder from the gun's muzzle blast are driven into the skin at close range. You try to remain objective when you view a death scene, thinking of it as a puzzle—the most basic homicide investigation textbook will tell you that—but I've always found it difficult to do. It's hard to get your mind away from the simple truth that death represents the biggest mystery of all. And it's a mystery that, in the end, each one of us is going to have to face.

"You've recovered the round?" I asked Grady.

"The locals recovered it but we managed to grab it back, saying we needed it for FBI Lab analysis." I was glad Grady was on the ball. "It passed through Mr. Boyd's skull, exiting in the back, came to a stop, and deformed when it embedded in the oak headboard."

The preliminary forensic findings confirmed the impressions at the scene. Powder and paraffin tests came out the way they were supposed to, Boyd's prints appeared where they should have, such as on the bathroom cup and vodka bottle, and didn't appear where they shouldn't. All in all, except for the fact that a distinguished man had died in this room, it was a relatively "ordinary" scene.

I stood looking directly at the spot where Grady figured Boyd had been sitting. What kept running through my mind was how all this dried blood all over the middle of this king bed had been circulating around inside Boyd's vessels and arteries when I'd seen him yesterday. Now, the blood and the body were no longer the Thomas Boyd who had until yesterday wielded so much power, who had single-handedly wrecked my career. Now it was evidence in an equivocal death investigation, and here I was, investigating. *Is there irony up in heaven, Judge Boyd, or wherever you are?*

TV shows or movies often portray 'profilers' visiting a crime scene, getting a constipated look on their faces, then going into a kind of trance and imagining exactly what happened between victim and perpetrator. That's an easy and dramatic way to show the analytical process of profiling, but unfortunately, it's got nothing to do with the truth.

Sure, you want to get a feeling for the place, and sure, what I do is based on hunches. It's an art as well as a science. But just like with an actor or a painter, the hunches and the art are based on a lot of experience and the assimilation of a lot of data. If I have a "vision" that an UNSUB has a speech impediment, it's not because I'm psychic; it's because I know from experience and research what certain behavioral indicators mean. When people tell me I have a God-given gift, my response is always Big Fucking Deal. I mean, come on—being able to think like a killer is the minimum requirement to get to work in my unit.

The most likely scenario I saw in front of me was that Boyd was sitting on the edge of the bed, placed the gun in his mouth, and when it fired, fell backward against the bed. There was some minor spatter, but most of the blood was confined to a central spot. The force of the impact must have been transferred from the bed to the night table, which was touching it, causing the lamp to topple over and crash.

I positioned myself on the far side of the bed so I could consider the final moments of Boyd's life from his perspective. While I've never gotten a psychic image of what happened at a crime scene, I think it's important that you put yourself in the mind of the victim and try to imagine and understand what she or he was experiencing at the moment of death. In the case of a homicide, you have to understand the transaction between the victim and the attacker before you can really know what happened and why. In the case of a suicide, you have to figure out what ultimately made him pull that trigger or down those pills or put that ligature around his neck or turn on the car in the closed garage.

I considered the instance at hand. Honor would be important to a guy who held himself out as a poster boy for family values. A highly admired and respected admiral—the navy chief of staff—killed himself over something as trivial as a misunderstanding over which battle ribbons he was entitled to wear on his uniform.

Taking into account what Grady said about where Boyd was at the moment of death, then the last thing he beheld before he swallowed the gun barrel was that glorious view of the bay. This was a potentially significant piece of behavioral evidence. Often in suicide attempts intended to be successful—as opposed to those merely meant as a cry for help or attention—victims choose a location that has some deep sentimental significance or choose as their last view the image they want to take into the next world. That's why jumpers off the Golden Gate Bridge almost invariably choose the bay side rather than the ocean side. In this case, I could even imagine him using the view to test himself: Seeing all this, do you really want to go through with it? If the answer is yes, then it's a pretty deliberate decision. The open curtains were another clue. Someone killing someone else has plenty to hide. A man killing himself may not be as concerned. I thought it was unlikely anyone staging a murder to look like a suicide would have been aware of these elements, so I considered it a strong piece of evidence that the suicide was genuine.

Ted came back holding a cell phone. "When you're ready," he said, taking me aside, "the acting director would like to talk to you." He led me out of the room, into the hallway and downstairs to the lower level. There was a combination den/study, with an equally magnificent view of the bay.

Ted closed the door behind us, then punched a long series of numbers into the cell phone. After a brief pause, he said, "Novello. . . . Yes, that's right. Thank you. . . . Yes, sir, I have him here." To me he said, "This is a secure line."

He handed me the phone. The voice at the other end said, "Jake? Orlando Ravan here. What can you tell me?"

There's an interesting phenomenon when anyone from my unit shows up at a crime scene: we're expected to perform magic—not only give the UNSUB's profile, describe his habits and pre- and postoffense behavior, but just about come up with a name, address, and phone number. Sometimes, depending on the indicators we find, we can actually do this. Most of the time, we can't.

No sense complaining about the fucked-up scene, I decided. So I reported, "There are three possibilities in every case like this one: suicide, homicide, and accidental death. Within those three, you can further break it down into suicides staged to look like homicides, such as to collect insurance money, and homicides staged to look like suicides. The most likely here is that it was a genuine suicide, and then your crime is blackmail. Still, we can't be sure it's suicide yet because we haven't fit the pieces together. I'd need to have all the forensic reports, go into victimology, that sort of thing. If it's not a suicide, it could be an accidental death, but I don't think so. There's no gun-cleaning paraphernalia on the scene, accidental deaths from head shots usually go into the forehead or temple rather than the mouth because of the way the subject would be looking at the gun, plus Judge Boyd would be too sophisticated to pop himself accidentally.

"But if it's not one of the first two possibilities, then it's a carefully staged murder. And if that's the case, then the UNSUB—or UNSUBs— is an organized, criminally sophisticated individual in his thirties or forties—"

"How do you know that?"

"Because the crime would be too sophisticated for a beginner. He'd have to have enough maturity and experience to think it all through, right down to the nuances. Any older than late forties, he probably wouldn't have the physical dexterity that'd be required."

"Fair enough," Ravan allowed.

"Whoever it was, he'd either have a personal vendetta against Mr. Boyd or is involved in a larger, organized criminal enterprise which believes it has a need or desire to have the director of the FBI eliminated. In any case, he would know a fair amount about staging a crime scene."

I once did a case with the Centers for Disease Control trying to figure out whether an unexplained cluster of seemingly natural deaths was, in fact, a product-tampering or some other willful homicide. An expression in epidemiology states, "When you hear hoofbeats, think of horses, not zebras." In other words, rule out the common things before you start conjuring up the exotic stuff.

"So where do we go from here?" Ravan asked.

"I guess that depends on you, Mr. Ravan."

He hesitated for a moment. "I can provide you with basic support— telephone, copying, that sort of thing. But I can't make you 'official,' and so I can't allocate manpower without raising all the red flags I don't want raised. I'm sorry, Jake. I know I'm asking a lot, and I know how you might feel about us now, but please consider the good of the Bureau, maybe even the survival of the Bureau as the effective organization we all want it to be."

I hate appeals to conscience and higher good; they're always justifications for why you should do something you don't want to do, in a way you don't think it can be done. Besides, the FBI wasn't exactly my favorite organization at that moment.

There was a long, pregnant pause, so pregnant it was about to give birth. Finally, Ravan said, "So can we count on you to stay with this and see it through, Jake?"

"Sure," I said at last, milking the moment. "The Bureau can always count on me."

"Good."

"Yeah," I said.

We went out the way we had gone in—through the glass doors onto the deck and around the side of the house to the front. Before we even got there, I sensed something was wrong, and when we turned the corner, I saw what it was. While it would be an overstatement to say that all hell had broken loose, a fairly large contingent of media were now waiting to pounce: a pack of TV and press reporters, a bunch of cars, and even two or three remote trucks, the first wave of what promised to be a full-scale assault.

Oh, shit! Someone may have picked up the police call on the scanner before the blackout was imposed.

A reporter I'd never seen before stuck a microphone in my face. "Agent Donovan, why are you here at Director Boyd's house?" The other reporters closed ranks behind him.

"Why are you here?" I asked, on the theory that the best way to avoid a question was to ask a different question.

"We've heard reports that Judge Boyd is dead."

"I really don't know anything more substantive than you do," I said. That wasn't completely true. I knew that Thomas Boyd was dead, which really was the most substantive issue at hand.

"Are you here to investigate Thomas Boyd's death?"

"I retired from the Bureau yesterday."

"And is it coincidental that you show up today at the West Coast home of the man who fired you?"

"Who told you I was fired?"

"Come on, Jake, you know we have sources."

"Well, I was paying a courtesy call," I replied. And it was time to get out of Dodge.

Before we were even out of earshot, the reporter and his cameraman were already taping a stand-up: "... the legendary profiler, who was wearing an FBI Academy shirt despite stating that he officially retired from the Bureau yesterday, would not confirm the report that FBI director Thomas Boyd is dead, but neither did he deny it. Now, Jake Donovan has a reputation for playing it straight with the media, so ..."

It came as no big surprise when we got to San Francisco International that instead of driving to the corporate terminal, Gaylord pulled up in front of the United Airlines entrance and handed me a government travel voucher. Even though I'm not psychic, I had that feeling I wouldn't be going back on the director's Gulfstream.

Before I got on the plane, I ran into a gift shop and bought a 49ers sweatshirt, then ducked into the men's room and changed into it, balling up my Academy jersey and putting it into the bag. If the Boyd story was already breaking, I didn't want to be a walking billboard.

I flew back to Dulles on a loaded 757 red-eye, trying to get some sleep, squeezed in next to a friendly but decidedly overweight middle American and in back of the obligatory mother with screaming baby. It was like I'd never left the Bureau.

8

I grew up in Broadus, Montana, the intersection of U.S. 212 and State Route 59—a small-town flatlands kid from the southeastern corner of the state, always running toward a horizon I could never seem to reach. Montana is a place of primal experience and sensation, still a habitat of nature and still a frontier, where the difference between the quick and the dead is the ability to react instinctually.

One summer I worked as a lifeguard at a public swimming pool, where I learned to size up, on an instantaneous and barely conscious level, who was in trouble and who needed my immediate reaction. This was in the days after the oil strike, and for several years now our little town had been inundated with roughnecks and drillers. These strangers signaled prosperity, but also the possibility of danger, as surely as those storms I mentioned that blew suddenly out of the north. Montanans have always been wary of outsiders. The first two digits of your license plate indicate which of the fifty-six counties you're from, so people instantly know whether you belong or not.

Anyway, I hired on as a roughneck myself during the summer in high school. It was tough, physically exhausting work. It is also scary, dangerous work, and don't let anyone tell you otherwise, with the roar of the equipment so loud you can't hear someone yell "Duck!" from ten feet away. If you're going to make it in that environment, you develop a sense about your physical surroundings. I made good money, I faced the dangers and the physical challenge, I felt like a man among men. But I also grasped that, man or not, you go into the wrong bar on a Friday night, you could get the shit kicked out of you. So I learned to read people. Those are the skills—the lifeguard's sense of physical distress, the roughneck's sense of danger, the adventurous young man's sense of who is safe and who will kick your ass—all further honed by four years in the navy, that served me well once I joined the Bureau. Long before I thought much about Fidelity, Bravery, and Integrity, I knew that, to get by, you needed Information, Awareness, and Guts.

There are few situations, I've found, in which this formula does not apply. It certainly applied to the one I now found myself in . . . that the entire Bureau found itself in. They needed more information, and that's why they'd brought me in. If I was able to give it to them, though, it remained an open question as to whether they would have the awareness and the guts to know what to do with it.

Though they may not have consciously admitted it, I was sure Orlando Ravan and his people would have been happier, if that's the right word, if I'd told him I was convinced Judge Boyd had been murdered, and that it had to have been a complex conspiracy among sophisticated antidemocratic elements set on destabilizing the American government. The fact is, people are drawn to conspiracy theories. They make a world that is often horrible and difficult to endure seem somehow comprehensible, the random intended, the chaotic, in a certain sense, ordered. So while it might not at first seem so, conspiracy theories are comforting, reassuring.

I could understand this. As a teenager and young adult I was convinced, like most of my generation, that President John Kennedy's assassination had been the result of an elaborate and highly sinister conspiracy—possibly headed by Castro, more likely by the Mafia, who didn't like the way he was threatening to crack down on organized crime, possibly even by secret forces within the American intelligence establishment itself. For my generation, the Kennedy assassination was what the Roswell, New Mexico, UFO theories have become to the current group of young people: prima facie evidence of a government unwilling to trust its citizenry with the cold, hard truth.

Only after I was already in the Bureau and had begun my research on assassin personalities and methodologies and acquired the analytical and investigative skills to examine the case on my own did I begin to waver. I won't take the time here to fully convince you why I came to believe that Lee Harvey Oswald was the lone gunman that November day in Dallas, but let me just say that the more I studied him, the more he fit the classic assassin personality I'd seen and interviewed so many times, and the more I learned about conspiracy, the more I realized the impossibility of keeping secrets. Even with the Jimmy Hoffa murder—always held up as an example of how at least one organization, the Mob, can keep secrets—we have a pretty good idea of who did it, and why. It's just a lot easier for most of us to deal with the notion that dreams were destroyed and history was changed by a sophisticated group of evil men than by a single obsessive, disenfranchised loser trying to get back at society for ignoring him. We want our villains to be worthy of our hatred and fear.

○

The plane got into Dulles a little after six in the morning. When the airport limo got to Quantico and the Academy front gate, I could see that security had already been tightened. A long line of cars in the visitor's queue were waiting for clearance. I told the driver to pull into the staff lane, then I rolled down the back window so the guard in the gatehouse could recognize me. He waved me through, apparently not focusing on that I was no longer on active status and therefore technically no more authorized to be there than the limousine driver.

My silver birch Aston Martin DB4 was waiting in the staff parking lot. The fuel gauge was reading almost a quarter of a tank, but all of northern Virginia is such a constipated glut of traffic that you never know when and where you can get stuck. So I figured I'd better fill up before heading up north.

I pulled onto Hoover Road, drove past the guard station, then turned onto the long, winding road through the section of the marine base on the west side of 95. A training platoon of sweaty grunts in dirty BDUs were jogging in patrol formation with their rifles held out in front of them, while behind them, the air was filled with the blasts of automatic weapons fire from the outdoor range I was passing.

A tan pickup truck behind me was close on my tail, a Ford F-150, I thought. It looked like two guys in there, but the windshield was tinted so I couldn't be sure. I wanted to let them know I was impatient myself cruising along at thirty-five. The twisty, hilly roads through the marine base, between the FBI Academy and 95, just called out for an Aston Martin to be driven as nature, and David Brown, intended. But many of us who'd been around Quantico for long knew from bitter experience that the MPs with jurisdiction over these roads loved their power to give out speeding tickets. Out in the real world, when we get stopped for speeding and happen to flash our creds while getting our driver's license out, more often than not we'll get cut some significant slack—something like "Have a good day and watch that speed." Not these guys. I'd be damned if I was going to risk a $50 ticket just because the guys behind me wanted to tear ass. They were probably Southern or Midwestern sheriffs in for the National Academy session. They weren't from Virginia, because there was no front license plate on the truck.

I thought they'd peel out when we got to the 95 access ramps, but they were still tailgating me until I turned into an Exxon station on Route 1 near the marine base's main entrance. I could hear tires screech as they were finally able to maneuver around me and get on their way.

Back on Route 1, I switched on the radio. As I suspected when I'd seen the encampment outside Boyd's house, the news services had geared up into their "high intrigue" mode. They had little hard news, but the best guess of "FBI watchers" and "usually reliable sources" was that the FBI director was dead. At this level, I gave it between three and five more hours before the shit really hit the fan.

I could have doubled back toward the Academy road and picked up 95 there, but it seemed easier to just head north on Route 1 until I reached the next crossover. Past this stand of gas stations, fast-food places, and strip shopping centers is a garden complex of off-base housing for married personnel, and beyond that, an undeveloped, uninhabited stretch of trees and greenery before the unrelenting tawdry commercial strip picks up again.

In this stretch, I became aware of a pickup truck following close behind. In the glare of the sun I couldn't be certain, but it sure looked like the one that had been tailgating me out of the Academy grounds. And this time it was pissing me off because this was a two-lane road and if they wanted to pass me, they could.

Without warning, the truck banged into my rear bumper.

I couldn't believe it! Do you have any idea what it cost to replace a bumper on a 1962 Aston Martin?

What the hell was going on? This felt like a fairly typical highway rape/abduction MO. The offender causes a minor accident, then when both parties get out of their cars to examine the damage, he grabs her. But that made no sense. They could see who I was. Were they targeting me?

I'd picked up my car several years ago in England, so it's right-hand drive. So I yelled out the window, "Watch it!" With the tinted wind-shield, I couldn't see if I was getting any reaction.

I started up again slowly, but rather than shift lanes, the pickup stayed right on my ass. Then it bumped me again.

Maybe my tired nerves got the best of me, but I stopped my car to make sure I blocked the pickup, slammed the door as I got out, and marched back to where it was now parked. I was ready to reach through the window and grab someone.

But I didn't have to. Before I got to it, the cab doors opened on either side and three large guys in camouflage fatigues lumbered out. They were remarkably similar-looking. All three were wearing Vietnam-era boonie hats, mirror sunglasses held on with Velcro straps, and the kind of combat boots we used to call shit-kickers when I was in the service.

Profiling expert that I am, I was instantly able to analyze the situation from a behavioral and victimological perspective and concluded that I was in some serious shit. Don't try this at home, folks; I'm a trained professional. But it was too late to back down or run, so I reasoned that offense was the best—and that's a relative term here—defense.

"What the hell do you think you're doing!" I yelled, pointing my outstretched hand and arm menacingly in front of me.

"What the hell you think *you're* doin'?" the guy from the driver's side shot back at me with kind of a nondescript Midwestern accent.

Glancing back at myself in those three pairs of mirrored lenses, able to make out little of the three faces behind them, and noting the strutting pomposity with which they wore their fatigues, I concluded I had little hope of reasoning with them. There would be no dialogue on the merits and justifications of our relative positions.

I knew I was correct when the driver kicked me in the groin with the shiny toe of his combat boot.

I buckled to the pavement, clutching myself and gasping in pain. I was so frigging mad and so charged up by the pain in my balls that I jerked up and lashed out at the guy with both fists. Before I could land a punch, one of his two confederates came at me on my blind side and cocked me upside my head.

I staggered and saw stars, but didn't go down. The third guy sent his boot into the back of my knee, and this time I hit the asphalt, leading with the back of my head. I heard a crack, which sounded all the less pleasant coming, as it did, from the inside. The three of them crowded around and started kicking. I balled up into a defensive mode, but it wasn't much protection. One guy concentrated on my gut, another went for my back, and the third directed himself to my thighs and butt. An objective slice of my brain registered that these three looked like they were practiced at this sort of thing.

I hated the idea of letting them beat the shit out of me without getting off a single punch. It was a matter of pride. The part of my consciousness floating above the scene strongly suggested that if I didn't quickly get proactive here, I had a strong chance of becoming a dead man . . . or at the very least a crippled man, and in ways I particularly did not want to be crippled. It certainly was no accident that this was happening on the one section of Route 1 around here that wasn't built up and so didn't have any walking traffic.

I had no more than one shot. As they continued kicking me, I got back up to my knees, figuring they'd like this chance to knock me down again. Ducking my head, I worked my way in close to the leader's body. None of them had pulled out any weapons, so I was actually better off closer in than at swinging or kicking distance. I was running out of energy, could hardly breathe, and my face and shirt were moist with blood.

I timed the one blow I hoped I could get off. I leaned back from the waist, going to maximum leverage without losing my balance, pulled back my right arm, then sent my right fist directly into the left lens of his mirrored sunglasses.

I could feel the lens crack and my knuckles shred on the sharp edges. More importantly, I heard the gratifying howl of agony as they embedded in my attacker's eye. This time it was he who staggered backward, blood streaming down his face.

"God damn!"

The two others backed off, as if being able to do this to one of them, I'd be able to do it to all of them.

"Let's get the fuck out of here!" one of them suggested, and grabbed hold of their leader. Just to make sure I knew they still controlled the situation, he gave me another jolting kick that knocked me back to the ground.

As he was being helped backward, the leader spat out at me, "Stay away, Donovan! Leave it alone. This isn't your fight!" Then the three of them were back in the cab, the doors slammed simultaneously, and the truck lurched into gear and jerked around my Aston Martin and sped off.

Stay away! This isn't your fight! What the hell was that supposed to mean? What isn't my fight—Owl Creek? The Boyd investigation? The Bureau in general? What?

I hurt like hell. I had a couple of gashes on my head, my gut was throbbing, I could hardly feel my legs, and my hand was bleeding from bashing it through the sunglass lens. I walked toward the tree line to heave.

Then I made my way back to the Aston Martin, opened the door, fell onto the seat, and closed my eyes.

I was awakened by rapping on the passenger-side window. It was a cop, a Prince William County cop. I'd forgotten I was still blocking a lane of traffic. I leaned over and opened the passenger door.

"What happened to you?" he asked, some revulsion at the sight of me showing in his expression.

"I'm just trying to figure that out."

"Are you able to move your car off the roadway?"

"I think so."

After I moved the car, he came back over to my window. "Now, tell me who you are and what happened."

So I told him as much as I knew, which only took about two and a half minutes. When I told him who I was—or, more specifically, who I had been until a couple of days ago—he seemed to treat me more seriously.

"Sir, I'm going to radio to have another officer come and drive your car to the station. You get in the car with me and I'm going to take you to the emergency room and get you checked out. Is that okay with you?"

That was fine with me.

In the emergency room of Prince William Hospital in Manassas, they examined me right away, probably not so much because I looked like I might be dying but because I was brought in by a uniformed cop. I needed some stitches across the knuckles of my right hand and a couple more on the left side of my forehead, and the rest of my body was a map of what they called "large and extensive contusions." But miraculously, I thought, nothing seemed to be broken. They gave me a tetanus shot just to be safe and some painkillers that didn't seem to be strong enough.

After they'd cleaned me up, I gave a formal statement to a detective by the name of Bill Gross, who seemed to know his way around. I have to tell you that it felt strange after all the thousands of consultations I've done with detectives around the United States and the world to be talking to one this time as the victim of a crime. He sat on one of those uncomfortable orange plastic chairs while I sat on the exam-room bed, trying to clear my head of the pounding.

"You say you didn't recognize any of these folk," stated Detective Gross. He scribbled notes on a yellow legal pad as he spoke to me.

"That's right, except that I think they were the same ones who were tailgating me as I came out of the Academy."

"And yet they called you by name. Think they'd been surveilling you?"

"I don't know. But I've been on TV a lot in the last eighteen hours or so. I guess they might have recognized me from that."

Gross lifted his eyes briefly. "About Thomas Boyd?"

I nodded. He sort of half-sniffed, half-snorted at this. "Figures." He scanned his yellow pad. "And you didn't catch a plate."

"There wasn't any in front. I never got a look at the back of the vehicle."

"And as far as physical description . . ."

"Just what I've told you. They were dressed like three guys playing soldier, with the hats and glasses. I have to assume they were purposely trying to conceal their identities. You've gotten no other reports about them?"

"Uh-uh, though as I'm sure you appreciate, three guys in BDUs and sunglasses around here, between the marine base and Fort Belvoir, ain't exactly likely to arouse suspicion." Gross folded over the pages of his legal pad, signifying that the interview was over. "Pleasure to meet a colleague as distinguished as you," he said, rising and extending his hand. "Sorry it had to be under these circumstances. We'll be checking hospitals and doctors' offices in case your man shows up to get his eye taken care of, but I wouldn't count on it."

"No, me neither."

"Anything comes up, we'll be in touch." I had the feeling I wouldn't be hearing from him soon. "By the way, I don't think you ought to drive. Can you have your wife pick you up?"

"I'm not married." Well, technically I still was, but the last thing I wanted to do was call Toni and get her all upset. More than that, I wanted to keep this from Ali and Eric if I could.

"We'll get you a ride," Gross offered.

"That's okay. I think I can have someone get me."

9

I was the first one to teach the introductory profiling course to new agents at Quantico.

In one case I liked to use, I would show the class a slide of a buxom blonde with a bouffy, trailer-trash hairdo posing playmate-of-the-month-style in front of a gaudily decorated Christmas tree. We saw her from the side, except her face, which was turned toward the camera. Her knees were bent, her ass stuck out suggestively, and her arms swept back like the winged figure on Mrs. De Vries's Rolls-Royce. She had on a Santa Claus cap, a sheer red nightie, and nothing else except for a broad, seductive smile. The setting was a warm, cozy living room, and wrapped presents were around the base of the tree.

This visual always secured the immediate attention of the male agents, and the faces of the female agents generally indicated their first reaction was either offense or puzzlement at my choice of graphics. A few of them seemed to be mentally matching themselves up with Santa's cheap but shapely helper.

Once the class had gotten an eyeful, I would then take the slide off the screen and say, "Okay, from looking at this picture, would you have reason to suspect that any crime was being committed or that you needed to pursue the evidence any further?"

This was usually met by a sea of perplexed faces, especially among the men. Indecent exposure? No, it couldn't be that; this was obviously a private home. Were the presents stolen? No reason to think so. Maybe the woman and whoever took the picture had broken into this house.

But people break into houses to steal things, not to pose for cheesy calendars. Maybe Donovan is just jerking our chain.

Then one time a new female agent raised her hand. She was a former homicide detective from California named Kathleen Cromwell, very attractive—a knockout, actually: that rare combination of beautiful and cute with large, inquisitive, and mischievous eyes, high cheekbones, and a slightly upturned Midwestern-cheerleader nose that reminded me of my sister, Nell.

"A child is being sexually exploited," she stated.

The men in the class looked at her and I could sense them saying, "What's this bitch's agenda?"

"Very good," I declared. "You got it!" I put the slide back on the screen and cautioned, "Forget about the woman in the nightie. What else do you see?"

And then, of course, all the rest of them saw it: a tiny bare foot and lower leg just entering into the lower right corner of the frame. The foot and leg of a little child. Everyone had been so preoccupied by the woman, including the photographer, that they'd all missed it.

Immediately, the questions presented themselves. Who was this child (who turned out to be a little boy)? Why was he placed in the presence of a mostly naked woman in a sexually provocative pose? Did he belong to those two people—the woman and the photographer? Did they even have children?

All of those questions were answered by the case materials. The couple were not married. They lived together and baby-sat for this little boy in their own home while his parents who lived down the block were at work. No one suspected them of sexual abuse of children until the woman was showing off the stack of naughty photos to her girlfriends and one of them, who happened to be a psychiatric social worker, noticed the incidental information in the corner of one of the twenty-four prints and called the county's Bureau of Child Welfare. If not for her, the life of this child and who knew how many others might have been very different. I always stress how it's important to look at the big picture, then take a couple of steps back to make sure you're not missing anything important around the edges. This is what radiologists studying X-ray films refer to as a "corner finding."

Kathleen Cromwell, I soon learned, went by Katie in all but the most formal situations. From then on, I followed her Bureau career, and when the time was right and she'd had some seasoning in the field, I requested her for my unit. By then she'd married Rob McManus, another special agent whom she met when they were both assigned to the Milwaukee Field Office. When Katie joined the profiling unit, Rob went to the inspection staff at headquarters. I have to admit that I never thought much of Rob McManus—it was the only time I really questioned Katie's judgment. My impressions were confirmed when he abruptly left her for a doe-eyed clerk he'd met and shared the enticements of South Beach with during an inspection trip to Miami. She followed him back to Virginia, and when I finally met her at the Christmas party, she was indeed a cutie, but hardly a match in any way for the woman he'd dumped. I tried to help Katie through this bleak period. When Toni and I split, she began returning the favor.

∘

She arrived at the emergency room about an hour after I got there, swept through the curtain, took a look at me, and declared, "You're a mess! What happened to you?" She was wearing leather sandals, a white T-shirt, and tight, faded jeans.

"Why don't you just read my police statement?" I said disgustedly.

"How many did you tangle with?"

"Three. But they started it. And you should see what I did to them."

She gave me that look, an equal mixture of love, concern, pride, and disapproval, that mothers reserve for their little boys who've just been pounded by the schoolyard bully.

"I'm sure." She registered my red and gold jersey. "Since when are you a Forty-niners fan?"

"I was trying to go undercover."

"Good thing I'm not working now, huh?" she said as we left in her green Mazda Miata.

"How much longer is your suspension?" I asked.

"Ten working days. Unless I decide to quit first. I hate to give those bastards the satisfaction of 'taking me back.' I mean, I'm a former homicide detective, I deal with the worst that human beings do to each other, I'm trained to be able to kill in the line of duty, and it's like they're saying to me, 'If you can be a good girl now, we'll let you out of your room.' "

As she vented, she kept speeding up, impatiently tailgating cars in front, taking turns with a downshift instead of the brakes.

"Kathleen!" I protested.

"When one of my parents called me that, I knew I was really in for it."

"We're both going to be in for it if you don't slow down."

Instead, she downshifted around a sharp turn and said with a wide, dimple-revealing grin, "Don't you trust me, Jake? Besides, I know most of the cops out here."

"What about coroners?"

She insisted on taking me back to her house instead of my place. Inside, she stuck out her hand, took hold of my chin, and with her arm extended, studied the bandaged wounds on my face the way she might have studied a corpse back in her days as a homicide detective.

"This one's oozing through," she said, looking at the cut on my forehead. "We're going to have to change the dressing. All right, let me see the rest of the damage."

"You mean, strip down?"

"For the time being, take off your shirt."

For a variety of reasons, I did as I was told.

"There's another one that needs changing," she said, touching a bandage on my side, just above my waist, and making me wince. She took my right wrist. "Let me see that hand." She looked at it a moment before pronouncing it satisfactory. "You go sit in the living room; I'll be right back."

She came back a few minutes later carrying bandages, scissors, tape, and gauze . . . and a thermometer. "Put this in your mouth," she ordered as she shoved it between my teeth.

"Wha's zis for?"

"If any of the wounds become infected, you could get a fever."

"I won't have one yet."

"Baseline reading. We've got to follow up several times a day and make sure you don't run into problems."

"*We?*"

"You live alone, and you're not going to remember to do this for yourself. Now, behave yourself; keep the thermometer under your tongue and stop talking or I'll put it somewhere else."

"Yes, ma'am!"

"I'm serious."

But what was she serious about, I wondered. There was so much bravado and swagger with Katie that it was often hard to know who exactly was the person just below the surface.

Slowly and deliberately, she peeled off the bandage near the bottom of my rib cage. "Owww!" I yelped, trying not to bite through the glass thermometer.

Without halting the procedure she said, "What did I tell you about talking?"

"Tha' hurt!"

A faint but clearly discernible smile crossed her lips, as if my momentary pain and her control might just trigger the hint of a turn-on. "Try to be brave, Jake," she cooed with a soothing tone one might reserve for a pet cat.

With an undeniable sensuousness, her fingertips explored the surface of my wounded flesh. "They really did a number on you," she sighed, then tore off two strips of tape to redress the ragged cut. I winced under the pressure but determined to show no pain.

After what she claimed was only three minutes, she removed the thermometer and examined it. "Okay. Right on the money; that's a good sign. And you can put your shirt back on."

"I could use a drink."

"I'll see what I've got." She sauntered out into the kitchen, then came back carrying a bottle of Johnnie Walker Black and two glasses with ice. She poured, handed me one, then plunked down in the easy chair facing me. Using one foot on the other, she slipped off her leather sandals. "Cheers." She took a swallow and then immediately shifted into detective mode. "I take it you do not coincidentally happen to be wearing a San Francisco Forty-niners shirt."

"That is correct." I took a swig of the Scotch. "I bought it at SFO so as not to have to be seen in the Academy jersey in which I happened to be attired."

"And would said appearance at SFO happen to be in some way connected to the reported demise of the Honorable Judge Boyd."

"It would indeed. And I might add that those reports are, in fact, accurate, if you didn't already know."

The ice cubes clinked in her glass. "Did he kill himself?"

"I thought so when I got on the plane. Now I'm not so sure." I gave her a quick overview of what I knew, concluding with the burned photos in the bathtub.

"You think Boyd had some action going on the side?"

"I don't know. It sure seems out of character. If he did, then the question is, Who found out and how?"

"Just like, Who are those guys who attacked you and how did they know your name?"

"Probably saw me on TV from San Francisco."

"And they were trying to scare you off?"

"Presumably. And I thought they were pretty convincing. So be a profiler, Katie. What does this suggest to you?"

"Three guys in crisp, neat combat fatigues, boonie hats, and mirror sunglasses? First of all, they don't want to stand out like bank robbers but they don't want to be personally identified, either."

"Right."

"They probably weren't real military. But the way they pounded you into the ground was certainly for real."

"And for them to know who I was, and, presumably, follow me, means they had to have done some surveillance. Even if they didn't know that I, specifically, was going to be at Quantico, they were still sur-veilling. Maybe because of Owl Creek. Despite what really happened there, I'm one of the ones they'd blame."

We both sat, silently nursing our drinks for several moments. Katie had tucked her feet up under her in one of those contortions women make look easy that men can never do.

"Tell you who I wouldn't want to be right around now," she com-mented.

"Who's that?"

"Ted Novello. Without Boyd as his patron saint and protector, the man could be dead meat. I've heard that Ravan the Raven doesn't count himself among Ted's greatest fans."

"It'll be interesting," I said.

"And what the president does now that he can appoint his own man."

Aside from all their other differences, it was no secret that the cur-rent chief executive considered Boyd's obsession with organized crime a waste of resources, and his unwillingness to fold on the right-wing cult/militia issues to be waving a red flag in front of a lot of conservative voters.

"It's going to be a mess for a while," I commented.

She held her drink with both hands in her lap and contemplated the glass. "I swear, this really may be a good time to get the hell out."

"You don't mean that."

"I do! It wouldn't take much for me to walk away. And I'll tell you something: that should go for you, too."

"What are you talking about?"

"Those thugs were right about one thing. This isn't your fight. I certainly wouldn't have wished anything like this on Judge Boyd, but we're not the ones who should have to be feeling particularly kindly to him. And you said yourself, the Bureau just wants a fall guy if their own investigation heads south. This is a no-winner, Jake. Walk away from it."

"I can't."

She stood up and put one hand on her hip. "Why the hell not? It's that stupid male ego thing."

"No, not this time. You ever see the Hitchcock movie *The Man Who Knew Too Much?* It came out in the 1950s."

"Well, I didn't. I wasn't even a twinkle."

"Hitchcock was a cult when I was in college. Anyway, it's got the basic plotline of almost all thrillers: an innocent man stumbles on a piece of information that makes him dangerous to certain bad guys, so dangerous that they're trying to kill him to keep that information from being revealed. The man doesn't know much, just enough to be in danger. But to make himself safe and be able to thwart the bad guys, he has to know more. That's the situation I might be in. So I can't leave this alone."

The phone rang. Katie stretched out across the easy chair to reach it. "Yeah, that's right. . . . Yeah, he is. Just a second." She covered the mouthpiece. "It's for you. Orlando Ravan."

I stood up and took the phone from her. "How'd you know where I was?"

Ravan laughed sardonically. "We're the FBI. I just heard about what happened to you."

"News gets around fast." *And do you now think you own me, finding me and jerking my chain whenever the mood strikes you?*

"Are you all right?" He sounded more like a general taking stock of his troop situation after a battle than someone genuinely concerned with a colleague. Maybe I was being unfair.

"I'll live."

"When I asked you to take on this assignment, I had no idea you'd become the subject of personal attack."

"And so quickly, too!"

"Unfortunately, I can't guarantee your safety. I don't know what's going on any more than you do. But needless to say, the Bureau will do everything it can to solve this crime and bring the perpetrators to justice. Do you want to back out?"

"I'm afraid we've gone beyond that point. But here's what I want: I want a reinstatement of my federal officer's right to carry a firearm across state lines. That would make me feel a little more secure."

"I'll see what I can do."

"You're the director of the FBI, Mr. Ravan."

There was a brief pause and I detected a sigh. "I'll take care of it." Then another, longer pause. "Some new evidence has been brought to my attention."

That phrase *new evidence* always makes me nervous. It usually meant there had been a screwup at the scene, which was certainly a believable possibility here. "What kind of evidence?"

"I'd prefer that you come here in person. Tomorrow morning, about ten."

10

Katie had a small, book-crammed den that doubled as an office, cluttered as if she had shoved all the messiness of her life into this room. I sat at her desk, then scrounged the drawer for a notepad. I checked my phone answering machine at home. It was flooded, but only a couple of messages were significant: one from Toni stressed that she was serious about getting together for that drink and saying how proud she was at the farewell luncheon. I wondered how proud she'd be, knowing how bravely I'd endured getting the shit kicked out of me.

A number of messages were from reporters—*Washington Post, New York Times*, CNN, as well as producers from the TV interview shows. The supermarket tabloids had all called.

The other notable message was from Peter Sutherland: "Jake, I'm at the airport in Honolulu. I've just heard about Boyd, and they've called all of us in the unit back to Quantico. It's all incredible, isn't it? There's a rumor floating around that you've been called in to run a parallel investigation, but I'm not sure I've got all the facts straight. Anyway, I'd like to talk to you when I get back. I have a feeling things are going to get pretty weird, especially with Ted and all, if you know what I mean."

Peter was my one ally left at Quantico and I did want to talk to him about it all. But I also knew that as soon as Pete found out what had happened to me with the soldier boy pretenders, he'd want to track them down himself and exact revenge.

The plain fact of the matter was, despite the nice things Neil Burke was now saying about me at Harry Gillette's expense, despite the vague support Orlando Ravan was now offering me, despite that my replacement, Ted Novello, was now a man without a country, I knew that except for Peter, I could really count on no one in the Bureau. If Boyd had been murdered instead of killing himself—still a long shot—then there was one key reason Ravan had asked me to undertake an independent investigation. I mean, the entire concept of "independent" is totally alien to FBI culture. So for Ravan to call on me for that, he had to believe, or at least suspect, that there could be involvement from inside the Bureau. Therefore, it seemed inescapable to me, if I was going to pursue this investigation—and keep myself alive in the process—that I'd need real help and real resources. And the only ones I could count on would have to come from outside.

So I made my call. I went through several layers of gatekeepers before I heard, "This is Millicent De Vries. How are you, Jake?"

"I guess I'm okay," I lied. "I know you must be busy, Mrs. De Vries . . ."

"Not too busy for you."

"Okay, well, anyway, are you still interested in the Flying Squad idea?"

There was a slight pause on her end, but I couldn't tell if it was one of surprise or merely her subtly controlling the situation. "Are you?"

"Ah, yes. Yes, I am." I'd never had any trepidation about going into a firefight back when I was a street agent. I'd never felt any fear or foreboding interviewing the most depraved serial killers for our sexual-homicide study. I'd never had any problems interrogating suspects in the most grisly murders. Why did I find this kindly and impeccably mannered older woman so intimidating? The only reason I could think of was that, unlike with the violent criminals I'd faced, I wasn't sure I knew what Millicent De Vries's real agenda was.

"I'd feel better if you understood some of the background."

"Very well," she said indulgently.

I told her about the unexpected call to investigate Director Boyd's death, about the quick trip out to San Francisco, the attack as I drove home from Quantico, my reasoning about why this had to be pursued. At the end of the narrative, she simply said, "Fine. If you'll stop by my house tomorrow, I'll have the details organized for you."

No, I really couldn't profile her or figure her out. She reminded me of Miss Havisham from *Great Expectations*, this eccentric rich woman living in a mansion amidst the decaying remnants of her past. And as I sat here on the phone with her, I envisioned her in her sunroom, tending her orchids like Nero Wolfe, as she interpreted and directed the actions of unseen others. I wasn't sure if either of these images had any validity. But I didn't have the luxury of waiting until I knew. She was the one lifeline I had. Orlando Ravan was offering me encouragement and vague support, but who knew what that meant? With her offer, I wasn't as dependent on the Bureau. I could call my own shots.

I had one more call to make. I knew Trevor Malone lived somewhere in the northern-Virginia suburbs.

As the phone rang, I tried to remember his wife's name. Trevor and I didn't know each other well. The Hostage Rescue Team had a separate building out behind the ranges, but we nodded when we saw each other in the cafeteria or the exchange, and the families came to Bureau picnics and other functions at the Academy. But the few minutes in the command post at Owl Creek was probably the most time we'd spent together.

Sure enough, a female voice did answer, and in a quiet panic, I pulled the name Valerie out of my semiconscious reserves.

I told her who it was. She didn't seem to be all that taken with the fact. I couldn't blame her. But when I asked for Trevor, she agreed to tell him I was on the line.

"What's this all about?" he said as I heard the receiver picked up. It wasn't exactly a challenging or unfriendly tone, but a definite wariness was in the voice.

"Hi, Trevor. I'm glad I got you in. I first want to tell you how sorry I am you got axed."

"I guess you're the one person I can accept that from," he responded plainly. "Sorry about you, too." I felt a rapport and closeness with Malone I'd never experienced before. Rumor had it that Roger Greene was being reassigned to a smaller field office or resident agency, and it had been announced that Gordon Abel was going on extended leave with pay. But as usual, it was the operational people, the troops in the trenches, who paid the price for the generals' decisions.

"I need to talk to you," I said.

"About Owl Creek?"

"Well, about . . . events surrounding Owl Creek."

"I've gotten a lawyer, Jake. I assume you have, too. We probably shouldn't be comparing stories."

Unfortunately, I can't guarantee your safety. Orlando Ravan's warning kept echoing through my head.

"That's not what I'm talking about," I assured Malone. "This is more like matters of life and death—mine."

I could sense his tone change even before he said anything. Trevor Malone had seen enough of matters of life and death in his various careers to take the phrase seriously. "What can I do for you, Jake?"

"I'd like to meet with you. How about tomorrow afternoon? I'll come to your house."

I went back to the living room where Katie was still sitting on the stuffed leather chair. She looked up.

"Take care of business?"

"I will tomorrow," I said. "In the meantime, I think I'll go home and rest up. Mind giving me a lift?"

"I don't think that's such a good idea. I don't think you ought to be staying alone."

"I'm a big boy. I can take care of myself."

"I think you ought to stay here." I must have reacted visibly because she gave me a look. "What's wrong? You afraid I'll attack you during the night?"

"Actually, I'm afraid you won't."

She flashed her mischievous grin. "Another demonstration of the famous Donovan proactive technique?"

"You know that only works hunting bad guys."

"I'm not sure. I haven't quite figured you out yet."

I could have said the same thing to her.

11

I slept like a rock that night, all of the tensions of the past several days finally draining out of me, at least in sleep. The dreams I've had so often since Black Diamond were mercifully absent. When they brought me comatose to the hospital back there, while they were cutting me with scalpels and sticking me with needles and shoving some kind of tube or probe up or down every orifice of my body, I became convinced I was in hell, being tortured by all the killers and rapists and child molesters I'd put away in my career. Since then, I've lived in that same place many nights, the only variation being which of the monsters and which of their tortures I've documented in real life is featured.

In the morning, when I ventured into the kitchen, Katie was standing at the counter barefoot with her hair pulled back into a ponytail, wearing running shorts and an Academy T-shirt that looked as if it had been designed for her. Around its edges was the damp shadow of perspiration not completely dried. Beads of moisture were also along her hairline. While I slept, she'd been out running.

She had put out coffee, milk, juice, and cereal and was cutting up fruit and placing it in a large bowl. I was impressed at how organized she was this early in the morning.

"You do all this for me?" I asked.

"No. For me. I do it every morning. You just happen to be here." What we had proved in our criminology study really is true across the board: women and men really are hardwired differently. In all my years, I'd never made a dinner this elaborate just for myself, much less a breakfast.

She glanced at my own ensemble. "Still rooting for those Forty-niners, I see."

"No choice until I get home and rustle up some clothes." I sat at the small, round butcher-block table.

She transferred the fruit bowl to the table along with the milk and juice. "Don't eat anything yet!"

"Huh?"

She left but quickly returned with the thermometer.

"Katie!"

"If your temperature's normal this time, we can stop. Now open your mouth."

She sat across from me as she waited for the results. We stared at each other for what seemed like several minutes. She didn't say anything and I was afraid to, based on her previous day's threat.

"It has to be three minutes already," I finally muttered through clenched teeth.

"Okay." She pulled the thin glass shaft out of my mouth, glanced down as she positioned it into the light. "Okay, you're clean."

"Good. I'm going to need a car, so could you drive me to get mine?"

"Take the Miata. I'm not going anywhere today. I'm going to stay in my room and think about how I can be a better, more obedient girl who doesn't give my mother or Harry Gillette any trouble."

I could feel an unpleasant twinge in my lower back as I twisted myself into Katie's Miata. She may still be as limber as a gymnast, I thought, but I'm too old for this.

The FBI had wisely ended the news blackout. Through Orlando Ravan, they'd released a statement saying simply that Thomas Boyd had died as the result of an apparent suicide while alone at his home in Sausalito, and that a rigorous investigation was now under way. When I switched on the car radio, it was all I could get. It had been announced that burial would be in California after a private funeral today. Later this week, there would be a memorial service in Washington where the president would speak.

My first stop was my own house, where I made a quick status check and then changed into something more appropriate: the standard agent uniform of black suit, white shirt, and bold tie. I even put the small gold Bureau-badge lapel pin on my jacket to show there were no hard feelings.

I took the Fourteenth Street Bridge into Washington, cutting over to Pennsylvania Avenue and then to the Hoover Building where I'd see if I could find a meter. I felt a little squeamish going into D.C. unarmed, now that I was only licensed to carry a gun in Virginia and Ravan hadn't gotten me my federal officer privileges back yet. It's not that I expected any trouble in the neighborhoods I'd be driving through. But when you're used to having a gun on your belt—not to mention, just being beaten up—it just generally affects the way you approach any situation. Besides, the way the laws are in the capital city of the free world, the most anyone can be guaranteed for murder one is twenty years. So when you're a lawman and you don't have faith in the justice system in a given jurisdiction, that can make you squeamish, too.

Since Thomas Boyd became FBI director, procedures at headquarters had changed noticeably. You no longer walked in through the front door, which was closed off, but through a makeshift security office squeezed in next to the vehicle entrance on the Eleventh Street side. There, two rent-a-cops looked at IDs and put you through a metal detector and your possessions through an X-ray machine. That I'd spent all those years in the Bureau meant nothing. Nor did that I was going to see the acting director. The only thing that meant anything was that I said I was the same guy whose name appeared on my driver's license and that the photo approximately matched my actual face, and that my name was on a list of expected visitors.

Inside the small lobby there was another wait while one of the three receptionists behind the counter and glass shield called to get someone to come down and escort me. This time I actually had to surrender my driver's license in exchange for a visitor's badge.

I also noticed the display on the wall behind the reception desk. Normally, there were three large color photographs: the president, the attorney general, and the director of the FBI. Boyd's photo had already been removed, and none had gone up to replace it. The empty space on the wall only served to emphasize the gap in our knowledge and understanding of his death. Nothing would really be secure until we could close that gap.

I was ushered into Orlando Ravan's office—his old office, not the director's. Unlike Ted Novello, taking over like that wouldn't have been Ravan's style. Inside I was met with the Father, Son, and Holy Ghost trinity of Ravan, Neil Burke, and Harry Gillette. Ravan and Burke, as usual, were somewhere between serious and grim.

Ravan slid a manila envelope across the desk to me. "I think it will speak for itself," he said.

I opened it and slid out a clear plastic evidence envelope containing a grainy black-and-white, four-by-six-inch glossy. I held it up and positioned it to eliminate glare. It showed Director Thomas Boyd in sexual congress with a woman who was clearly not Mrs. Madeline Boyd.

My own reaction surprised me. I wanted to be shocked at this stripping away of one of the things I still esteemed Judge Boyd for, to be unable to believe my eyes that Mr. Family Values had, as Katie had suggested, some action going on the side. But I was afraid my capacity for disappointment at the divergence between public depictions and private truths had been all but exhausted.

I looked up and asked, "Where did this come from?"

Neil Burke answered, not Ravan. "When Sean Hennigan, the head of the director's security detail out there, got to Boyd's house, he did an immediate reconnaissance of the premises to make sure there was nothing lying around that could be deemed sensitive."

Well, he hit the sensitive jackpot on this one, I thought.

"Under the bed on which Judge Boyd lay, Hennigan found the photograph you now hold in your hands. Presumably, it is from the set the director burned in the bathroom. It must have been dropped or slipped out from the others and gone unnoticed when the rest of the pack was carried into the bathroom. Hennigan removed it from the scene before the local team arrived and brought it to us."

"Does anyone else know about this?" I asked.

"Not as far as we know," said Ravan.

"At least there's one thing the locals won't be able to leak out. Are we absolutely certain this photo is real?"

"It appears to be legitimate," said Burke, "but that will have to be confirmed."

I looked down again at the picture. The quality wasn't the best, but you could plainly see Boyd and an unidentified woman engaged in sex and reasonably nimble sex at that. The woman's back was flat against the wall, her legs wrapped around Boyd's torso, and she was being supported by his raised right leg. One of her arms was around his neck. Her skirt was bunched up around her waist, and her black panties lay on the floor beneath her. Boyd, wearing a tie and dress shirt, had his trousers opened and slightly lowered and had managed to enter her while balancing both of them on his left foot. Pretty athletic for a guy his age.

"Do any of you recognize the woman?" I asked.

"Nope. Never saw her before," said Burke.

"What about Ted Novello? He was pretty close to the director. Has he seen this?"

"Harry showed it to him." Gillette nodded, as if to make sure I understood his crucial role in the investigation. "But he didn't recognize her, either."

I looked across to Ravan. "You didn't know, or had no reason to suspect, that he was having an affair?"

"No, certainly not."

"But this clearly puts the blackmail theory into some perspective," Burke added.

"Yeah, I guess it does," I had to agree. Though something about it still troubled me. Maybe it just didn't fit my profile of the late director who'd fired me.

12

At Millicent De Vries's house, I ditched Katie's car on the circular drive, got out, and rang the bell. Frederick himself answered right away, as if he knew exactly when I'd show up.

"How are you, sir?" he said. "Mrs. De Vries will be with you directly." He led me into the study, and soon the lady of the house appeared and right behind her a large man in a dark suit a lot more expensive than mine. I wondered if he was a bodyguard.

"This is Michael Sanders," she said, "my attorney, my trusted adviser, and my good friend."

We quickly exchanged how-do-you-dos. From the top of the desk Sanders produced a blue file folder, opened it, and spread out papers. "You'll see that all of the key points for the organization of the Flying Squad should be laid out here," he explained. "You'll notice that the term of employment is open-ended. Mrs. De Vries tells me this was at your insistence. You'll also notice that your monthly compensation has been left blank so that you can fill in your own number."

"I don't think that's such a good idea," I said. I'd spent my entire career being told exactly how much the government was prepared to pay me, then how much they were going to snatch back for taxes.

"This item was at Mrs. De Vries's insistence," Sanders said as he glanced over to her.

She smiled. "I meant it when I said, 'Write your own ticket.' "

"Well, how about a thousand in expense money for right now," I said, "and then let's see if I earn anything more."

"Give him ten," she said to Sanders, and I had a feeling a check would be in the mail before dinnertime. "How quickly can you put your team together?"

"I don't know," I said. "But I hope it'll be soon."

"You let me know when you have." She turned to Sanders. "Michael, I'm sure Jake doesn't want to waste any more time here than he has to, so . . ."

"Yes, of course," said the attorney. "Mr. Donovan, all we need is your signature and social security number and I think we're ready to roll."

I asked, "Should I take this to my own lawyer before I sign?"

He smiled pleasantly. "If you wish, then by all means." He proffered a business card. It was thick and engraved. "Have him call me whenever he likes."

Of course, if I was going to take this to my own lawyer, I'd first have to get my own lawyer, because unlike Trevor Malone, I didn't have one. And what the hell? I was more interested in staying alive and well than in the fine points of something I wasn't doing for money, anyway.

"That's okay," I said. "Just show me where to sign."

"Very good," said Mrs. De Vries. "American Express and Visa cards will be delivered to you within a few days. In the meantime, should you need additional money, simply call Michael and he'll take care of it. He'll also send you some simplified expense-report forms which you are to complete at your leisure, though monthly would be preferable. Anything else?" We looked at each other. "Good."

Then the three of us shook hands and Frederick was showing me out of the house. A flood of relief washed over me—not the kind you get when something difficult and risky is successfully completed, but the kind you get when you realize you've finally made the decision that effectively cuts off all other options, so you've got to move forward, whether you want to or not. I suppose it was the relief Caesar must have felt once he'd crossed the Rubicon, or Eisenhower once he'd committed the troops to Normandy. It was the relief of apprehension transformed, for better or worse, into action.

My next stop was back in Virginia. Trevor and Valerie Malone lived in the Mount Vernon section of Alexandria, and like Toni and me, they had two children—a boy and a girl. The girl, Tracy, was about Ali's age. I couldn't remember the boy's name.

Whereas Old Town has trendy and tightly congested row houses, Mount Vernon has solid, traditional single-family homes, and the Malones' was no exception. When these houses were built, it would have been unheard of for a black family to occupy one of them. But now, even in the Old Dominion, capital of the Confederacy, the times, they've been a'changin'. Trevor hadn't struck me as a terribly humorous fellow, so I was quite amused when I saw the white-faced lawn jockey at the entrance to his driveway.

Valerie answered the door and did a double take as soon as she saw my face.

"It's a long story," I said, "but I'm okay now."

Gracefully, she didn't pursue it, only said, "Hello, Jake. Trevor's waiting for you." She's a beautiful, stylish woman around my age, an elementary-school special-ed teacher, and I could feel those suspicious, disapproving teacher eyes bearing down on me.

"Just don't make this more painful than it already is," she said, then seemed to soften. "I'm sorry. You're the last person I should be complaining to."

I offered a faint smile. "We'll both get by. We're survivors, Trevor and I. At least, I hope we are."

"Some would call you both dinosaurs, with your sense of honor and duty. That doesn't seem to mean much anymore."

Trevor was waiting for me in a paneled den at the back of the house. He was wearing a pair of black fatigue pants with the large cargo pockets that the Hostage Rescue Team trains in. His white polo shirt had "HRT—Quantico" embroidered on the breast.

Unlike Valerie, he actually cracked a wry smile when he registered my face. "You look like hell, Donovan! At least Boyd only fired me."

I smiled. "I certainly wouldn't mess with an HRT guy."

The room had been converted from a porch. One wall was covered with Trevor's various FBI awards and mementos.

"Coffee, a Coke or anything?" he asked.

"No, I'm fine, thanks."

"How 'bout a shot of bourbon?"

I smiled. "Maybe later."

He indicated two loungers set at an angle for optimum viewing of the projection TV in the corner. I took off my suit jacket before I sat down.

"We may not have looked at what was happening at Owl Creek the same way," I said. "The behavioral and the tactical seldom do. But I just want you to know, in case you don't, that I was up in the sniper position with Yamaguchi and Lanier. I had a headset and I watched it through night-vision binoculars. What you did was not only the right thing, you were a hero. In my book, you saved the lives in the chopper."

He sighed. "The rules of engagement were very clear. Sickenger was carrying an AR-15 outfitted with a .37-millimeter smoke-grenade launcher, and if he'd gotten off a shot, that chopper would have exploded in the sky. This business about us assassinating him—I can't believe anyone falls for that horseshit."

I told him about my run-in with the militia types just outside of Quantico; that that was where my temporary facial realignment had occurred. I gave him as much background on my assignment from Ravan the Raven as he'd need to set it all in context. "I know that long before Owl Creek you'd become an expert on the militia-survivalist movement. What do you think?"

"I've faced these guys a long time. For months after the Ruby Ridge hearings, they would wait for any of us at the main road out of the Academy, even ones like me who weren't there. They'd be dressed in BDUs, just like your guys."

"Would they threaten you?"

"Not overtly. They must have known better than to try anything. That would have bought them a one-way ticket to hell."

My eyes traveled from the Browning hunting rifle mounted on the wall to the framed poster from his Airborne Ranger days: "Mess with the Best, Die like the Rest."

"Sometimes they'd follow me all the way home. It's a favorite tactic of theirs. They were trying to provoke me, but I always waited for them to make the first move. After a while, they got tired of it and left me alone. But sure, it could be the same guys, or the same kind of guys."

"You think they could be involved in Boyd's death?"

"Certainly within the range of possibility." Trevor stood up and walked over to the wet bar. "Jack Daniel's?" I'm not sure how he'd decided it was time for a drink, but he was right.

"I'll take some Scotch if you have it."

"I have it. I'm like the guys we're talking about: don't want to get caught short when the revolution comes. Rocks?"

I nodded. Trevor prepared the two glasses as he talked. "I read that analysis you did. You were right. With these guys, everything's symbolic. That's why Oklahoma City happened on the anniversary of Waco. The worst thing for them is not to be taken seriously. That may be why they decided to go after you."

"Now that Sickenger's dead, is there anyone we can key on?"

"Richard Royce is the commandant of the Wyoming Defenders. But that might not mean too much. Despite all their political rhetoric, they're pretty much anarchists."

"Could they have assassinated Boyd?" I asked, taking the drink he extended.

"They could've tried to take me out since I was the one who actually fired the shot. But I'm not a big enough fish for them. The FBI symbolizes government oppression to them, and Boyd symbolized the FBI. They could have been making the statement that they were taking their own revenge—judging the Bureau guilty and executing its director."

"Are you saying they blackmailed him and led him to suicide, or they out-and-out killed him?"

"Could be either."

"Then why wouldn't they make it an obvious assassination? Hate groups usually make their murders highly symbolic. Why would they leave the ambiguity?"

Trevor sat back in the lounge chair and pushed himself all the way into a recline. "I don't know. Maybe it was cowardice. Maybe it was stupidity. Maybe something else. Maybe their playing games and beating you up was part of it."

I turned so I could face him. "What are you going to do? I heard something about the D.C. Police."

"I have some buddies there from the service. Said they could get me a job piloting their chopper on a contract basis. It'll keep me occupied and keep up my flying skills. I can also shoot on their range."

I held his gaze. "How'd you like to work with me?"

His heavy eyebrows raised spontaneously. "Last I heard, you were out of a job."

"Trevor, I need you. Your skills and mine will complement each other perfectly. And we've both got something to prove."

"What the hell are you talking about?"

And so I told him.

∘

When I got back to Katie's house, she'd changed into a sleeveless white tee and worn, faded jeans. She looked great, sitting at the desk in the den paying bills, a pen in her right hand as her left twisted a strand of hair intricately between two fingers.

"Well, you cleaned up rather nicely," she said, eyeing my fed threads. "How'd it go?"

"Okay. How 'bout yourself?"

"I hate this," she said, putting her feet up on the edge of the desk and tipping the chair back on its rear legs. "Especially when I don't have any pay coming in."

"I may be able to help you out," I said.

"Thanks, but no loans. I still have my pride."

I sat on the edge of the desk facing her. "I'm talking about a job."

13

I'm not like the detectives you read about or see on TV. I'm not a recovering alcoholic. I don't use a 7 percent cocaine solution to relieve depression or boredom. I don't play championship-level chess, raise orchids, race cars, or sky dive.

When I stop to consider the defining moments of my life—going to school for the first time, losing my virginity with Cindy Marshall on the carnival grounds after closing time the summer after tenth grade, joining the Bureau, getting married, having kids, being made chief of the profiling unit, nearly dying during Black Diamond, separating from Toni—none of them seems to give that capsulized nugget of insight that we look for when we're studying behavior.

I can't say I always wanted to be a profiler, since when I was growing up, the term didn't even exist. But I did want to be a G-man; that is, after I realized I'd never be playing second base for the Yankees. If you couldn't be a pro athlete, that seemed about as cool as anything I could come up with. They got to use guns and catch bad guys and rescue innocent people, which is pretty much why a lot of us went into law enforcement. And in my case, I knew it was something that would get me away from the flatlands of Montana, which motivation was my prime reason for joining the navy. There were no oceans in southeastern Montana, so no matter where the navy sent me, it would be somewhere else. I'd always gotten along okay with my folks, and I loved my little sister, Nell, who became the cutest cheerleader at Broadus High, went on to marry the handsome cocaptain of the football team (it's true!), and still lives with him and their four beautiful kids in Montana. But I knew instinctively from early on that I wasn't like the rest of my family. I always seemed to think about, to perceive, more things in heaven and earth than were dreamt of in their philosophy.

When I got out of the navy, most of which time I spent home-ported in San Diego, I still had it in my head to get away from my roots. New York City seemed as far from Broadus as you could get, so with my GI Bill, money I'd saved from roughnecking, and a partial scholarship based primarily on a letter of recommendation from former senator Iron Mike Mansfield, I enrolled in John Jay College in Manhattan with the idea that a degree in criminal justice might help get me into the FBI.

People often ask me why I do what I do, why I'm willing to spend so much of my time staring into the abyss. Actually, it started out simply enough. Right out of new-agents training, I was posted to the New York Field Office since I already knew my way around there. On a rainy Super Bowl Sunday, several of us had just rounded up a bunch of high-ticket bookmakers in a sting operation. I had one of them, a charming and good-looking guy in his thirties, in the back of the car. I asked him why someone with that much going for him would get involved with this illegal shit.

"You just don't get it, do you?" he said. Apparently, I didn't. It was starting to rain harder now. With his cuffed hands he pointed at the side window. "You see those two raindrops? I'll bet you the one on the left reaches the bottom of the glass before the one on the right. We don't need the Super Bowl. All we need is two little raindrops. You can't stop us, no matter what you do. It's what we are."

This brief encounter was like a bolt out of the blue, that instant cessation of ignorance we talk about. Suddenly, it all became crystal clear.

It's what we are. It dawned on me then that if a way could be found to analyze a crime from inside the perpetrator's mind based on the behavioral clues he left, then we might be able to construct a complete description of the UNSUB that could help police start looking for the right type of individual. Profiling wasn't the ultimate answer, but it could be a critical part of the team, a new kind of team I outlined later in my ill-fated Flying Squad proposal.

∘

Now I had to put the rest of the team together on my own. That was the topic of conversation as Katie and I drove in her Miata out to the slope of Mount Weather.

She'd submitted her resignation from the FBI, effective immediately. I wondered how sorry they'd be to see her go. They probably didn't even realize what they were losing.

She and Trevor were a good start and would make the nucleus of the team. They'd also complement each other talent-wise and emotionally. But they were both from the operational side, as I was. Between us, we could handle crime scene, investigation, behavioral analysis, and weapons and tactics. And Trevor was also a pilot, which was a bonus. What we still needed were the scientific/technical people. At minimum, I wanted a lab guy and a medical-examiner type. In a perfect world, I'd want a forensic anthropologist, but there aren't too many of those, and most had secure jobs in museums or universities, so they tended not to turn up at the last minute. It would be great to have a bug man—an entomologist—though at the moment I couldn't see how that specialty would impact on this case. But you never know, which is one of the key reasons for the Flying Squad in the first place: have everybody ready for when you suddenly find you need them. A computer whiz would be another high priority, but we didn't have time for all the front-end setup that would require, so for the time being, we'd have to rely on basic programs and Katie's computer skills. If we could go deeper with a wider array of talents, fine, but with time the commodity in shortest supply at the moment, it was more important just to get going.

Katie seemed to have appointed herself my activities director while I was staying under her roof, which is how we happened to find ourselves at Ground Zero, John Weisman's secluded estate in the Virginia woods of Mount Weather, a little over a mile from a secret government installation well-known to those of us in federal law enforcement. Weisman was a former journalist who had become an internationally popular novelist with strong ties to the counterintelligence community. He maintained a fifty-yard combat firing range on his property where his friends and associates often came to shoot. I'd known John going back to my days as a street agent in Detroit when he had the cop beat at the *Free Press*, and I found him to be a straight shooter—both literally and metaphorically. I'd introduced him and his wife Katie during the mopey period after Rob dumped her, and the three of them had gotten on splendidly. Weisman was on some secret trip out of the country, but he'd given Katie permission to use the range anytime she wanted. Since neither one of us wanted to be spotted on any of the FBI ranges, this was a welcome offer.

Among Katie's several reputations within the Bureau, one of them was as a crack shot. One time when she was with the Miami Field Office, her squad was working a joint undercover op with DEA, and Katie stopped a female suspect by shooting the high heel off one of her shoes while she was trying to escape. Bureau policy on the use of deadly force, drummed into us since the first day of new-agents training, is that FBI agents shoot to kill, not to wound, slow down, or stop, that the only motivation for firing your weapon at another human being is because you have made the determination that your life or the lives of others are in jeopardy if you do not attempt to kill that individual.

But this was something of a special case. The woman, her boyfriend, and several cronies were attempting to flee from a raid at the garden apartment building where they were surprised while cutting and preparing cocaine, and to keep agents from shooting at her while she shot at them, she grabbed her two-year-old daughter in one arm and used her as a shield. Any of the agents was easily capable of dropping a moving target at fifty yards or more, but no one was willing to take the chance of hitting the little girl.

In her flight, the suspect ran from a paved area outside the apartment building onto a patch of lawn. As soon as she did, Katie blew away the heel of her right shoe with a clean shot. The suspect tumbled, letting go of the toddler, who fell relatively harmlessly onto the soft grass. Other agents immediately swarmed, scooped up the stunned and crying child, and neutralized the mother. Ordinarily, taking a shot like that could have gotten the shooter a letter of censure or worse, but Katie's quick evaluation and action in saving an innocent life was so obvious and the incident became such a media favorite that she actually got a letter of commendation instead.

Since the ostensible reason I'd been retired from the Bureau was my physical limitations, Katie had decided it would be good for me to get my confidence back with my gun, which was why we were out here so bright and early this morning.

"If you're going operational again, you've got to keep up your skills," she explained. "Your life could depend on it. So could mine."

She walked the length of the range and sprayed fresh paint on the five Por-ta Target center-mass plates, then took a magazine from the pocket of her canvas shooting vest and rammed it into her Heckler & Koch USP. She put on ear protectors, spread her feet, locked her elbows, and squeezed off five shots in rapid succession.

Her shots sounded like an alarm clock as they impacted the quarter-inch-thick steel plate. A look of cool satisfaction came over her face. She quickly turned her body, shifting her attention to a different target, and fired the remaining five rounds, all with equal precision.

"Nice going," I said as we pulled down our ear protectors.

"Thanks," she said, glowing.

After that display, I wasn't thrilled by having to perform in front of her. My personal weapon was a Smith & Wesson Airweight .38 snub-nose Special with a shrouded hammer. I liked that feature because it meant I could carry it in my coat pocket when it was cold without worrying about the hammer snagging on anything. At the moment, it was in the pocket of my own shooting vest rather than in a belt holster, and I made a mental note to change this sloppy habit.

I stepped up to the line, adjusted my ear protectors, assumed the stance, and sighted down the short barrel toward the same target Katie had chosen. I couldn't get comfortable with the sight picture; the target seemed to move away from the front sight, and I kept moving the sight to compensate. We call that "chasing the X-ring." Maybe the sight was a little off. Maybe it was the tremor in my right hand and wrist.

I fired off all five rounds in quick single-action succession. One missed completely, the other four pinged around the outer edge—all on the right side.

"Well, the good news is he would have dropped his gun . . . if he was left-handed," Katie commented. "And there's no question, that shot over there would have ripped the sucker's earlobe off. That'd make him easy to identify if he got away from you."

"Shit!" I exclaimed. "Same thing keeps happening."

Katie stared at the target a moment. "You were taught originally with the Weaver stance, weren't you?"

"Yeah."

"You're probably not completely comfortable with isosceles."

"Maybe not." Though I knew that wasn't the problem.

"You're applying too much pressure laterally with the ball of your left hand in an effort to stabilize your sight picture, your thumb pressure is too strong, and you're flinching slightly in anticipation of the recoil, not a lot, but just enough to throw you off."

She practically radiated raw sexual energy on the firing range. I felt myself go hard and wondered if she was experiencing a corresponding sensation. God, she was something.

"So let me ask you, strictly from a research perspective," I said. "Is shooting like that a turn-on for a woman?"

She blushed slightly, then caught herself with her enigmatic kitten-with-a-whip smile. "No, Jake. I stick out my chest, spread my legs, and do something I do better than almost any man, which gives me the power of life and death. Strictly routine, all in a day's work. But just in case, I used to bring along spare underwear when I thought I might be shooting someone in the line of duty."

"If you could only get over your shyness . . . ," I lamented.

She dropped the mag out of the pistol butt. "You brought up the subject, mister. Is it a turn-on for you?"

"It used to be."

"Then we'll have to get it back." The statement stirred in me an irrational sense of delight, an emotion so foreign since long before my separation that I hardly recognized it at first. I waited a moment to see if she would make a move to go along with her words, but when she didn't, I tried to put them on hold for later, hoping a little fearfully that the sensation would keep.

We walked back to the hood of her car where we'd spread out our equipment. I opened the barrel and shook the spent shells into my palm. Katie leaned up against the Miata's front fender and crossed her arms. "So who else are you thinking of?"

"Well, Dominic Sanchez, for one."

"The name rings a bell."

"Used to be ME in Detroit where I was a street agent after New York. He taught me how to interpret autopsy protocols and use postmortem evidence. He was the one who really showed me how much you can learn from a body."

"Yeah, I had a guy like that in California when I was on the police force. Said I was his favorite living person at work."

"Dom's like that, too," I mused. "Much more comfortable with the dead. I used to consult with him on some of the unit's toughest forensic stuff."

"That's why I know the name. What's he doing now?"

I shook my head sadly. "Kind of nothing, last I heard. After his wife died, he started hitting the bottle pretty hard."

"A shame. But he sounds perfect if he's off the sauce. Who else?"

"Well, we'll need a lab person."

"Anyone in mind?"

"I was hoping you might. The only ones I can think of work for the Bureau."

Her eyes brightened. "What about Jerry Carruthers?"

I brightened, too. I didn't know why I hadn't come up with that name on my own. Gerald Carruthers had been a fixture for years at the FBI Lab in Washington, a Ph.D. biochemist by training who was regarded as one of the last of the true generalists, having spent the early part of his career at the Armed Forces Institute of Pathology at Walter Reed Army Hospital in Washington. A lot of our training in the FBI comes from AFIP, and after a while, the Bureau must have gotten tired of their people telling them how good Jerry Carruthers was, because they made him an offer to move across town that he apparently couldn't refuse. He earned a national reputation, which was another reason I was surprised I hadn't thought of his name until Katie mentioned it.

But then there came a time when he got too conscientious about his job, at least too conscientious for the powers that be. When the lab started having problems with quality control, chain of evidence, reliability—all the things people looked to the FBI Laboratories for as the foremost forensic-analysis facility in the world—Jerry was one of the folks who didn't think those problems ought to be swept under the rug. The only way a scientific establishment could maintain its integrity, he later testified before a congressional hearing, was to plainly state the facts as observed and let the chips fall where they may. The Bureau brass didn't see it quite that way, and Jerry was one of the first chips to fall.

"And he's also a sketch artist," I noted. A pretty unusual combination of talents.

As I remembered, Jerry had never married, so he'd have the freedom to move around, which was another major plus.

Katie unloaded another mag into another of the targets. Then I shot again—with no better results.

"I can see we have to work through this," she said, the bright promise still lush in her voice.

At least that's the way I interpreted it.

14

When we got back to Katie's house, I had no trouble tracking down Dominic Sanchez. He still lived where he had when I'd been in Detroit all those years before.

"It's so good to hear from you," he said, and I could tell he meant it. He still retained his patrician Cuban accent. "You're not in town, are you?"

"No, I'm calling from Virginia."

I could hear a shift in his voice. "Is everything all right? Toni's okay?"

"Toni's fine, but we've been apart for a while. You know how it is in this business."

"I do," he confirmed sadly. "Perhaps you heard I lost Marguerite."

"I did, Dom. I'm very, very sorry."

"It's been lonely since then, I have to tell you." They didn't have any children. "Perhaps you also heard I had to retire."

"Yeah."

"Life's incredible, is it not? All those thousands of dead bodies I did all that time, and I felt like I had a personal relationship with every single one of them. Then the one live person I really cared about died, and I went to pieces." I could hear him sigh on the other end of the line. "They say that in a case of a long illness, you do some of your grieving ahead of time so that when the end finally comes, you're already partway there."

"I've heard that," I said.

"Not in my case. Marge was there one minute and then the next, she wasn't." He paused. "But I'm sure you didn't call to hear me bewail my fate."

I just said, "Well, actually, the reason I called was to offer you a job."

"What sort of job?" I could sense his wary excitement.

"Kind of as a consultant on major cases—like what you did for me at Quantico, only there'd be more on-scene work."

There was a long pause, so long, in fact, that I finally broke the silence. "What do you say? Is it something you might be interested in? Shall I go on?"

"I appreciate what you're trying to do here; I do, really," he said at last. "But don't ever feel you have to pay me back."

"That's not it," I insisted. And it wasn't. For one thing, there was no way I could pay him back for all the small and large kindnesses, for all the touching concern, for all the demands on me to be as good as I could be, for being a man a jaded young street agent could look up to. For another, in my present state I was much too selfish and focused even to think about giving any charity.

"I just want the best," I said.

"I've got a decent pension from the city and that's really all I need to get by. I would never want to finish out my career being taken on as a rehabilitation project."

"Dom, you know me well enough to know I don't even believe in rehabilitation. I need you, that's why I'm calling."

"You know I had a drinking problem, but I've taken care of it. It was related to Marguerite's death."

"If you say you have, that's good enough for me."

"What exactly do you have in mind, Jake?"

I told him about the Flying Squad and our first case. I explained that I needed a medical examiner I could trust, who could interpret bodies, wounds, fluids, the way Trevor Malone interpreted broken branches and marks on the ground when tracking a deadly fugitive, the way Katie or I interpreted behavioral clues at a crime scene. And I knew this was something Dominic Sanchez could do, because he was the one who had showed me that it could be done. "I don't know exactly what the pay will be," I said, "but it'll be enough to make your time worthwhile."

"I don't care about the pay," he replied. "I never cared about the pay; none of us would be in this business if we did."

"That's great, Dom. I can't wait to see you."

∘

It took a while to track down Jerry Carruthers, but I finally got the info from a contact I still had at AFIP. Jerry was up at Harvard, handling lab sections for undergraduate courses in the chemistry department. What a fucking waste, I thought: one of the most talented men in the field reduced to wiping snotty undergraduate noses, taking a job a dull grad student could easily fill.

I didn't really know Jerry Carruthers the way I knew the others I'd approached, so I decided I'd better do it in person. I took an early-morning US Air flight from Dulles and then grabbed a cab at Logan for the ride into Cambridge. Before I left, I'd gotten the class schedule from the chemistry department.

Summer-school classes had just begun, so there was an air of ease about the campus that I'd always found took itself oh so seriously. Every time I'd come up here to lecture at the college or law school, I took pleasure in commanding the attention of an academic establishment that would never have had me as a student.

I found the room and spied the guy I presumed was Jerry Carruthers up at the lab bench at the front of the room. He was either early-to-midfifties, or if he was still in his forties, the years hadn't been all that kind. He was heavyset, the kind that looks as if he doesn't believe in physical exercise. His curly, gray hair was thinning, he wore thick glasses, and he seemed just the slightest bit confused, even though this was his own classroom. I waited until all of the students had funneled out.

"Dr. Carruthers?" I said. He looked up at me, startled. "I'm Jake Donovan."

"Yes, of course, Jake, I remember you." He was neither pleased nor displeased to have me there, just perplexed that I'd turn up in this setting. "Are you here now, too?"

"As a teacher, you mean? No, not exactly my style."

"I didn't think so," he said as if confirming his own hypothesis. "I knew you wouldn't leave the Bureau."

"Well, I have, actually."

"Oh?"

"Is there somewhere we could go for coffee or something?"

"I guess so." Jerry shrugged, as if it had never occurred to him people sometimes did that sort of thing.

o

"So let me get this straight," Jerry Carruthers said after I'd explained my mission. We were seated across from each other at a small table at Au Bon Pain back on Mass. Ave. "You want to make me part of this 'Dirty Dozen' group?"

"Well, 'Dirty Five' to begin with," I said, "though I might have come up 'Magnificent Seven.' "

"And we go all over the country and solve crimes?"

"Ah . . . yeah. That's pretty much it, I guess."

"Who's backing this? Not the Bureau, I assume."

"Millicent De Vries is her name. She has a foundation."

"She ran Shipley Pharmaceuticals after her father."

"Actually it was her husband, Fletcher, I understand."

"No, it was Millicent," Jerry said with knowing authority. "Fletcher was never more than a figurehead. Very smart woman."

"You know her, then?"

"Met her once, sometime after Fletcher died. I was recruited to come work for Shipley. They brought me up to Connecticut to meet everyone and invited me to lunch with her. She was very charming, very convincing. I was going to take the job."

"Why didn't you?"

"The company got bought out, suddenly and kind of mysteriously. Rumor was that the new owners had something to do with Empire International—you know, J. P. Napoleon's company. I didn't want anything to do with that."

I got a momentary twinge every time Napoleon's name came up. "Does it surprise you that Mrs. De Vries would be backing the Flying Squad?" I asked.

"Nothing about Millicent De Vries would surprise me."

"So you'll come on board?"

"Why not?" he replied matter-of-factly.

"Great. I'd like you to start right away."

"Okay." He shrugged. "All they have to do is open a box here and another graduate student pops out. It won't be hard to replace me."

"We've already made arrangements for temporary apartments for Dom Sanchez and you near Tysons Corner."

"Fine," he replied casually, as if where he happened to live was of no more consequence to him than how much the compensation would be was to Dominic.

"Oh, there's just one thing," he said as I was paying the check.

"What's that?"

"I'm scared to death of flying."

Of course! I said to myself. *It would have been too easy and straight-forward to get a lab expert for the fucking Flying Squad who actually enjoyed flying.* "We'll figure out something," I said hopefully.

∘

On the flight home, I had an entire row to myself. I thumbed through the in-flight magazine, then *Black Enterprise* and *Golf Digest*, the only two publications that for some inscrutable reason are always available on every American-flag carrier. But although I don't play golf and had no money to invest in any enterprise, black or white, I couldn't numb my mind to the point of relaxation.

Where was all this heading? How did Millicent De Vries, Trevor Malone, Dominic Sanchez, Jerry Carruthers, and of course Katie McManus fit into this new and unknown direction my life was taking? How did the late Judge Thomas Jefferson Boyd fit into it? In every way I could think of, I owed my new status to the actions of a dead man.

15

I still hadn't been back to pick up my Aston Martin, so I drove Katie's Miata to Mrs. Madeline Boyd's house in Chevy Chase. Orlando Ravan had gotten her to agree to see me.

The house was an impressive wood-frame colonial on a side street just off Connecticut Avenue, an easy walk from the Chevy Chase Country Club, where I knew the Boyds were members. An agent was planted in a car outside, to whom I identified myself, but Mrs. Boyd answered the door herself when I rapped the brass knocker held in the jaws of a brass lion.

"I hope this time's convenient for you," she said. "I had my regular tennis game at the club. Please don't think me insensitive for not canceling it. I find the physical exertion helps deal with the stress."

"I quite understand," I said.

Madeline Boyd was probably in her late thirties, with no attempt at flashiness or glamour. Her wavy, light brown hair was cut to just above her shoulders so as to require the least amount of care and fussing, and on her square, suntanned face I detected only lipstick and rouge. She was dressed in a white, short-sleeved blouse, khakis, and sneakers that could have come out of an L.L. Bean catalog. Her face and arms showed the effects of years spent out of doors, sailing and on tennis courts and golf courses. But it was a tight and athletic body, so far as I could make out, and I thought her attractive. In my job, not only do you come into contact with the lowest of the low, you also see regular people at their worst, when their lives are unraveling and coming apart. Some women are at their most beautiful and poignant in moments of greatest sadness or grief. I guess this is one of those secrets that painters and detectives share.

Madeline Boyd's pleasant but noncommittal smile told me she was accustomed to greeting her husband's professional contacts, people she probably had little knowledge of, or interest in. I told her how deeply sorry I was for her loss.

"It's a nice day," she said, as if in reply. "Why don't we sit on the back porch."

She led me through a house that was traditionally furnished, but not grandly or with any of the pretense I'd often seen from people used to living their lives on so high a level. I was accustomed to going into houses like this and knowing right where to look for the first-floor den with an expensive, antique-looking desk and power wall of photos, memorabilia, and other citations attesting to the owner's prominence. I saw no such display here. Instead there was an informal TV room with a banged-up leather sofa, standard TV, and rubber chew toys and other random evidence of multiple dogs.

Outside, we went over to two old redwood deck chairs covered with those green pads most people don't bother taking in during the winter. I brushed off some fairly ancient bird shit and unbuttoned my suit coat before I sat down.

"I'm sorry I have to put you through this," I began, but she cut me off with a wave of her hand. I noticed she wore a plain, narrow gold wedding band, but no engagement ring or other jewelry.

"My husband was a lawyer, an FBI agent, a judge, and then director, so I appreciate the need for investigation. I doubt you can ask me anything the other Bureau agents haven't already come up with. Let's just make this as easy as we can on both of us."

"Fine," I said. "Then let's begin with the obvious. Was there any reason why your husband would commit suicide, and at this particular time?"

She sighed. "Yes, well . . . that is the question, isn't it? I've been going over that in my mind ever since." She looked at me with cool, serious eyes. "There was a lot of tension in our relationship and in our marriage. It's not the kind of thing we thought ought to be broadcast, but we considered separating."

"How seriously?"

"Seriously enough that we were occupying separate bedrooms. But we didn't think that one of us leaving would be the right thing to do for Jason at this point."

"He's . . . ten?"

"Eleven."

"How's he doing?"

"He misses his father." The statement was like an iceberg: most of it remained below the surface. "We made several attempts to—how shall I say it?—normalize relations between us. The final results were not yet in when . . . this happened."

"Was your husband despondent over this? I mean, despondent enough to . . ."

"To kill himself? I've never known him to be that vulnerable to anything, or anyone. The thing about Tom, he was so emotionally self-contained and so self-assured that I wouldn't think his relations with anyone else, including me, would be enough to . . . cause what happened. That probably contributed to some of the differences and tension between us. But then, I suppose you'd have to say that maybe I didn't know Tom as well as I thought I did. So if he were going to kill himself, he would have done it the way he did—alone and far away." She glanced idly at her hands. "I don't know how much of an answer that is."

How much of an answer did I expect? One of the great dark secrets of my profession is that though a trained, talented, and experienced observer can see into the mind of a psychopath, whose range of genuine interests is limited, the minds of the rest of us remain infinitely subtle and obscure.

"Were there any communications in the days or weeks before Judge Boyd died that gave you any sense he might have been planning to take his own life?"

She pondered the question. "Not that I can think of. I've been trying to figure out if anything I might have done could have been a factor. But no, I haven't a clue."

"Did you talk to him while he was in Sausalito?"

"No, we spoke before he left and everything seemed normal. He did leave a message on our voice mail for Jason."

"Which said?"

"That he was sorry he couldn't be there for his Little League game that afternoon, but he promised he'd be back for the next one. That would have been Friday." For the first time, her composure showed cracks.

Regardless of the subtleties of his mind, I couldn't imagine a man as stuck on duty and character as Boyd making a promise like that to an eleven-year-old that he didn't intend to honor. Unless, of course, he hadn't known about the blackmail when he made the call. It depended on whether that packet of photographs was in his briefcase when he arrived at his Sausalito house, or whether someone had visited him there and brought them with him. And with the scene compromised, we might never know that detail.

"Did Judge Boyd leave a will?" She nodded. "And might I know the terms, specifically with regard to you and Jason?"

"I don't know. I haven't seen it, though I assume we are the prime beneficiaries. My husband was very private on personal matters and his will is in the office safe of his attorney, Irwin Altschuler. Irwin's hiking in Nepal and can't be reached."

"I'm sure the FBI could find him," I suggested.

"I suspect they could. But Tom wouldn't have wanted to make such a scene. And since nothing really depends on it as far as we're concerned, it seemed we could all wait until Irwin returned to probate the will. He hasn't had a vacation in years from what I understand, and I know Tom wouldn't want to be the one to ruin it for him."

I made a note to myself to check on the terms once Altschuler returned. If there were any unusual bequests or instructions, that could be a useful clue.

I leaned forward. "Mrs. Boyd, do you have any suspicion that your husband did not commit suicide? It doesn't have to be a rational reason. But does any gut instinct tell you anything one way or another?"

Madeline Boyd rose and moved to the rear of the porch, where she placed her hands on the white railing, as if contemplating the rosebushes in her garden. "Selfishly, I'd like you to be able to prove he didn't kill himself," she confessed. "It would make me feel less guilty. And of course, if he did kill himself, I don't think his life insurance will pay."

On the other hand, if he was murdered, then most insurance companies consider that an accidental death and pay double. But that did not make Madeline Boyd a suspect. It was just something to file in the back of the mind.

"I'd like to know for sure that I had nothing to do with what Tom did," she continued. "It's just that . . ." She rubbed one thumb over the other and I could see tears welling in her eyes. "I just can't imagine Tom being murdered, either. None of this . . . None of this makes any sense. Unless you can make some out of it."

"I'm trying," I said. "But so far, I'm as baffled as you." Now came the toughest part. "Mrs. Boyd, has anyone mentioned the possibility that your husband was being blackmailed?"

This stopped her short. She blinked several times and then the mistiness was gone from her eyes. "What are you talking about?"

I told her about the photographs, or rather the one photograph we had and the other burned ones whose corners matched the background of the intact one. "I have a copy of the photo with me," I said, "and I'd like you to take a look at it if you don't mind."

"No!" She'd gone suddenly tense, as if these photos were evidence of the secret fear she'd always harbored. "I've tried to be cooperative with you, but this is where I draw the line." My heart broke for her, and I was afraid she would lose control, which I sensed was something she desperately wanted to avoid. "This is not something I need to see."

I've always stressed to the folks in my unit that profiling the victims and their families is equally as important as profiling the UNSUB, and with the information I'd had to go on about Madeline, I'd anticipated this possibility.

"I understand how you feel," I sympathized. I reached into my inside jacket pocket and brought out a second photo I'd had made up. This one was a close-up of the head of the unidentified blond woman in the picture with Boyd. "Could I just get you to look at this one, then?"

Her hand trembling, she took the picture from me and scrutinized it for several seconds.

"Have you ever seen this woman before, Mrs. Boyd? Does she look at all familiar?"

Now the tears began to fall. "I've never seen her. I'm sure of it."

16

The plane was bigger than I remembered from my navy days—a fat, gawky-looking affair with a pug nose, thick, high-mounted wing supporting four forward-thrust engine pods with stubby black propellers, and vertical stabilizer at the rear out of all proportion to the rest of the fuselage. It was painted a dark brownish green with no markings other than the tail numbers. I suspected it was supposed to look like a generic National Guard–type transport, the kind of plane everyone is familiar with and no one notices.

We'd all met on the tarmac behind the private-aviation terminal at Dulles Airport. I had finally had Katie take me to get my car since she couldn't fit four people into her Miata. The Aston Martin is pretty tight in the back, so we picked up my other vehicle, which was a hunter green Land Rover 110. Despite my masochistic penchant for English cars, this one was at least outfitted with left-hand drive. We picked up Dominic Sanchez and Jerry Carruthers at the Oakwood temporary apartments at Tysons Corner and then headed out Route 7 to the Dulles Access Road.

When we got to the airport and found the meeting point, Trevor Malone was—not surprisingly—already there, dressed in black cargo pants and a khaki hunting vest over an olive drab T-shirt that showed off his chest and arm definition. He was leaning against the back of his truck, a shiny, two-tone forest green and gray Ford F-150 pickup with chrome brush bar and winch, running boards, floodlights above the cab, aluminum utility bins built into the cargo area, and a trailer hitch in the back—the full hunting rig.

I introduced Dom. Jerry had met the others, so it was kind of a reunion. As soon as Katie saw Trevor's truck she grimaced.

"What's wrong?" Trevor asked.

"I don't like hunting," she replied.

He was prepared as a sniper must always be. "We're all hunters in our business."

"Yeah, but we only hunt people, and only bad people. You kill innocent animals for recreation."

"Ah, Katie, is that a leather belt I see adorning your shapely hips? Are those Reeboks on your athletic feet made of leather? And last time I saw you in the Academy cafeteria, I don't recall you limiting yourself to vegetables."

It was time to exert some leadership. "Okay, guys, let's not be going there."

She protested, "You can't expect me not to react when—"

"Do I have to separate you two for the rest of the trip?"

Millicent De Vries's dark blue Rolls pulled up a few feet from the plane. The chauffeur jumped out and opened the door.

"How nice to see you again," she said, extending her hand as she walked toward me, every bit the ambassador's wife. "Ah, I see that the team's assembled."

I made the introductions. "I'm very sorry about what happened to you and Jake because of Owl Creek," she told Trevor. "You deserve nothing but the gratitude of the nation. Disgusting business."

"Thanks," Trevor said, obviously surprised.

The plane's crew entry door opened, up on the port side near the cockpit, unfolding into a stairway. A man and a woman in gray air force flight suits bundled onto the pavement. The man was tall and dirty blond, with an infectious grin that proclaimed how much he liked what he did. His counterpart was tall for a woman, well-built and trim, also with dirty blond hair. In fact, they could be brother and sister.

"Hi, Scott Kenworthy," the guy said.

"This is your pilot," Mrs. De Vries took over, "and this is Patricia O'Connor, your copilot."

"Call me Trish."

"In addition to Scott and Trish, you have a ground crew on twenty-four-hour standby," said Mrs. De Vries.

Handshakes and greetings were exchanged. The uniforms weren't really air force—neither one of them had a full set of insignias—but air force surplus. No doubt another attempt to look generic.

Kenworthy made a special point of going over to Trevor. "Mr. Malone, I understand you're a flier, too." Trevor nodded. "It'll be a pleasure sharing the cockpit with you." Kenworthy had one of those indeterminate Southern accents, full of syrup most of the time, but I bet it could quickly assume a kick-ass tone when it wanted to.

"Thanks, I look forward to it," Trevor replied.

"Scott, why don't you tell us about your airplane?" our hostess suggested.

"Actually, it's your airplane, Mrs. De Vries, but I'd be happy to."

He stood near the forward landing gear and slapped the side of the plane affectionately. "This here is a Lockheed C-130H Hercules, the best and most versatile medium-transport flying machine ever to take to the air. It's been in production more than forty years in various forms, and there's upward of two thousand of them operating around the globe. It can land on dirt or loose gravel and can take off in only eight hundred feet. They landed one of these on a carrier once and didn't even have to deploy the dragline."

He pointed back over his shoulder. "Power is supplied by those four Allison T56-A-15 turboprops, which each deliver forty-five hundred shaft horsepower. Now, if you all'd like to follow me up the stairs here and into the Herky Bird itself as we call it . . ."

He led us up into the cockpit. "You might be curious to know that this particular plane began life with the First Special Ops Wing of the air force's Sixteenth Special Operations Squadron at Hurlburt Field, Florida. It was later sold as surplus and found its way to a prominent Colombian drug cartel, which retrofitted the latest Doppler radar and evasive equipment into the nose radome for low-altitude flying, and upgraded the cockpit with the avionics package and full GPS system from the new C-130 Model J design. This allowed for a two-man flight crew instead of four. The plane was seized by the Drug Enforcement Administration and . . ." For the first time his narrative began to falter.

"And it was placed on loan to my foundation," Mrs. De Vries helped him along. It made sense. With the helicopter deal she'd worked out with Quantico, they'd be only too eager to return any favor she wanted.

I noticed that all labels and instructions in the plane were in both English and Spanish.

"But it's aft of the cockpit that the real interesting reconfiguration was done," Scott commented, leading us through the door in the bulk-head. I recalled what a versatile design the C-130 was. In addition to their basic use as troop and equipment carriers, the planes had been outfitted as hospitals, weather reconnaissance craft, air-refueling tankers, firefighters, mobile command posts, spy planes, AWACSs, al-most anything.

On the other side of the bulkhead, what is normally the Spartan, bare-metal forward troop bay had been transformed into an executive-passenger compartment for about eight or ten, something like the cabin of the FBI director's Gulfstream, only plusher. Behind it was a confer-ence room with a polished wooden, barrel-shaped table and six chairs.

"This VIP module was designed to meet the needs of foreign chiefs of state, senior government officials, and their staffs with the utmost in convenience and comfort," Scott said.

These drug runners like to fly in style, I thought. Here, too, there were bilingual signs. I could imagine some gorgeous flight attendant coming on the PA in mellifluous Spanish: "Ladies and gentlemen, we are approaching a remote jungle clearing in the dead of night to pick up four hundred kilos of fine, uncut heroin, so please return your seat backs and tray tables to their upright and locked position and keep your seat belts fastened for the duration of the flight. *Muchas gracias.*"

Trish took over. "You'll see on the console there we have a computer and high-speed fax modem with the same state-of-the-art encryption technology as we do for voice."

Tucked into a compartment in the back of each lavishly upholstered leather seat was a plastic-wrapped package. "What's this for?" I asked.

"It's called a parachute," said Trevor. "It's for jumping out of planes without going splat at the other end."

"I understand that," I confirmed, "and I don't like it."

"You never know when you might have to perform a high-altitude/low-opening insertion, particularly at night."

I told Trevor of my nearly ironclad policy of not jumping out of per-fectly good airplanes, a policy I had originally formulated while in the navy and had refined in the years since.

"You're not a wimp, are you, Jake?"

If I were somewhat less secure than I am, I would have taken the time to elucidate the difference between the analytical and tactical per-sonalities, and that neither one was necessarily a wimp, but that each merely externalizes emotions in divergent ways.

"No," I said. "What might initially be mistaken for wimpiness actually suggests that I'm not a suicidal nutcase like you and the rest of your HRT friends." I hadn't planned on giving him the preliminary personality profile so soon, but in this business, you grab your opportunities where you find them.

Trevor grinned sardonically. "I see what I'm going to have to put up with here," he declared. Mrs. De Vries just smiled as if she were hosting a U.N. party for children from around the world.

To the rear of the conference room was a short corridor space with a well-appointed head and shower on one side and an area for stowing cabin luggage on the other. As I recalled from my navy days, the standard toilet facilities on the C-130 consisted of a metal funnel with a connection to the outside for number one and a plastic bucket bolted to the fuselage wall in the back for number two. This was luxury.

"Here's the really good part," Scott Kenworthy said.

Aft of the conference room the narrow corridor took a jog to the right. It led to the back of the plane and another cabin, which, as soon as Scott opened the door, appeared as a gleaming array of stainless steel. To me, it looked like an operating room. A wheeled gurney was fixed in place by floor brackets, and large surgical-style lamps were attached to armatures on the ceiling. Dominic Sanchez beamed and I realized it was actually a flying forensic lab.

"How did you get this done so fast?" he asked in amazement.

"The job was partly done already," Trish related. "We didn't have to do any structural work or move any bulkheads. The previous owners had this installed as a drug-processing lab, based on the standard airlift intensive-care module. And as you can see, they spared no expense. All we had to do was replace some of it with equipment more suited to what you guys are going to be needing."

"I've always wanted something like this," said Dom.

"And I've always wanted a brand new Aston Martin," I said. "I'm glad one of us is fulfilled." But I had to admit, I loved this plane, too. I'd never seen anything this cool in the navy or the Bureau. It was like having my own little Air Force One. I just wanted to play with it all.

Dominic slowly paced around the bright room, taking inventory. "Downdraft necropsy table—first-rate! Multiuse dissecting sink with built-in emergency station, elevating laminar-flow hood. I love it."

"And Dr. Carruthers will be pleased with the laser-imaging system, trace-metal detector, and scopes," Scott added.

"Is that what I think it is?" Trevor asked, pointing to the Mobile-Mort refrigerator against one wall.

"As an FBI agent, I'm sure you realize how quickly bodies go bad at room temperature," Dominic responded.

"I'll make 'em dead, you deal with them after that, Doc."

"Good," I said. "Then we all understand what each of us is here to do!"

Scott jumped in. "And the entire system can be powered by a gas-turbine auxiliary-power unit whenever it's not operating on the bird's main power. Once under way on a mission, we're not dependent on any other service support except for fuel."

"The entire array is modular, so you can rearrange or replace as needed," added Trish.

I couldn't imagine how much this was all costing our benefactress. Was it that personally important to her to get J. P. Napoleon? The issue of what else might be going on with her still nagged at me.

Next stop on the tour was a small but efficiently designed galley. There was a walk-in storage locker for supplies and provisions and next to that a place to stow personal gear and equipment. Beyond that was the cargo bay, where once heavy armor had been carried and paratroops deployed, and more recently, vastly profitable illegal drugs had been flown into the country.

"One more feature," Scott said, pointing. "You'll notice the dropped ceiling here in the cargo bay. That's because above it are eight bunks, arranged in two facing rows of four each, so we can all sleep on the plane in relative comfort, either on long trips or overnight deployments."

The floor of the C-130's tail section lowers into a ramp for tanks, troops, and heavy armament. We all walked down the ramp and back out onto the tarmac, where Frederick handed Mrs. De Vries a bottle of 1990 Dom Pérignon.

"I brought this along to christen the plane," she explained. "All we have to do is come up with a name."

Katie and I exchanged a glance. "I think there's only one logical choice," she stated.

"And that would be . . . ?"

"The Broken Wing!"

"Umm, could you explain the meaning?" Jerry asked nervously.

"Jerry, be cool, man," said Trevor, slapping his hands against his new colleague's shoulders. "Got to get a grip."

"It'll be lucky," said Katie.

"Then so it shall be," Mrs. De Vries declared. "Scott, let me know where."

The pilot escorted her back toward the nose of the plane. We formed a semicircle around her as she swung the bottle back and smashed it on the side of the fuselage. I watched the expensive white foam trickle down to the pavement.

17

From the way the president spoke about Thomas Boyd at the memorial service, you would have thought they'd been best buddies rather than known political antagonists. But that's Washington.

The service was held at the Justice Department auditorium, and for official Washington, it was the place to be. The room was overflowing. CNN and C-SPAN covered it live. Despite Ravan's pains to contain the situation, not since Vince Foster's death had Washington seen such a paroxysm of ghoulish fascination regarding a suicide. By some stroke of luck or uncharacteristically efficient security, the blackmail aspect had not surfaced publicly. Sure, there was a lot of speculation that Boyd had been murdered, just as there had been in the Foster case. But like the Foster case, it was mainly confined to the traditional conspiracy theorists and those who could grind their own particular political axes by proving that some sinister group (a) was out to get Boyd or (b) had reason to shut him up because of what he knew.

The theme of most of the speakers, from the president to the attorney general and on to Orlando Ravan, was duty, patriotism, and sacrifice. Kind of like Boyd's fidelity, bravery, and integrity speech at my affair. But I had no problem with that. It's what Boyd was all about.

I went for two reasons. One was simply to pay my respects. After all, whatever our differences, Thomas Boyd had been my boss, and though I hated the bureaucratic crap, there's still no organization I would rather have been associated with. And second, you go to funerals and memorial services of people who died unnatural or equivocal deaths to see who shows up, and whether that tells you anything.

I ran into Peter Sutherland just as the crowd was breaking up, or rather, he ran into me, grabbing my arm before I actually saw him. "I heard about you getting beat up. You don't look as bad as I thought."

"I'm glad I could pleasantly surprise someone."

He pulled me aside and whispered, almost conspiratorially, "Have you heard the latest?"

"I don't think so," I said. "What are you talking about?"

"Ted's out!"

"He's out of the Bureau?"

"No, he's out as your successor." Then, as if to let this sink in, he restated, "He's out as chief of the Profiling and Serial Crimes Unit. He's been kicked upstairs to section chief for Building Security. Instead of hunting serial killers, he checks to make sure everyone shows their passes."

I felt a sudden surge of sinister joy that immediately made me feel guilty. "When did this happen?"

"Official word came down yesterday. Ravan the Raven acts in mysterious ways, but he acts quickly. Almost makes up for losing Katie after losing you."

Wait a minute. Why was I feeling guilty? Ted had no right to the job in the first place. He was plainly unqualified, merely a crony of the director's . . . "And who . . . ?"

"That's the best part!" Peter positively glowed. "I'm the new acting unit chief of ISU."

"Maybe there is a God after all." And maybe the universe, after an inexplicable perturbation, was starting to make some sense again. At least I wanted to take this as a sign.

"Ravan called me into his office and said it was up to whoever became the new director to appoint the permanent chief, but as far as he was concerned, I was his choice as long as he was in charge. By the time I got back to Quantico, Ted's nameplate was off the door and mine was on it."

"I am thrilled for you," I said. Peter was the absolute natural choice. I'd selected and trained him myself for the unit, he was a terrific profiler, and he had excellent rapport with the local police agencies, which are our lifeline to doing effective work. If I couldn't head the unit anymore, Peter was the one I wanted. All that time Ted had spent with the kneepads strapped on had paid off, but with Boyd dead, so were his prospects.

Just then, that same divine providence I had just been invoking sent Ted our way.

"Ted. Congratulations on your promotion," I greeted him.

"Thanks," he replied without enthusiasm. "I would have just as soon stayed where I was."

"I can sympathize," I said sincerely. "But I guess we all have to do our part, whatever the Bureau thinks is best."

He smiled. "I've never known you to be such an organization man, Jake."

"It's easy once you're out of the organization."

He changed the subject. "Come up with anything in your investigation yet?"

I shook my head.

"Well, good seeing you again," he said, and walked away. His ignoring of Peter had been blatant, which Pete noted with a triumphal expression.

"Ravan told me to give you whatever assistance you need," Peter said. "I'm to act as your liaison."

"Perfect."

There was a gauntlet of reporters before I could make it out of the building. The news media had now turned their attention from the event of Judge Boyd's death, to the why of it. To get to the bottom of that, they were trying to sift through every inch of his personal history.

One guy stuck a mike in my face and said, "Sources inside the FBI tell us you're working on the case independently for the FBI. What have you been able to learn about why a man with the power, prestige, and respect that Judge Boyd enjoyed would take his own life?"

"We all have our demons," I said as Peter and I pushed our way out to the street.

18

I organized the first meeting of my broken wings as if I were back in the unit leading the weekly case-consultation conference. The venue was Katie's living room; her house seemed the most central location. I didn't dress up, but I did wear my blue ISU polo shirt to establish a semiprofessional tone. Katie had on black, pleated slacks with a black, sleeveless shirt and a silver and turquoise necklace that set off the shiny buckle of her flattering belt—the "basic black" theme clearly being another interpretation of her theory of "power dressing." She had such a sense of herself in so many ways, and as I stole a glance in her direction, I felt proud of how far she'd come.

Trevor, as usual, was garbed as if he were still on the Hostage Rescue Team and could be called out at any moment. God knew what he had in that heavy canvas haversack he always carried. Jerry Carruthers was attired in a dark, rumpled suit that nicely complemented his pale, rumpled body. Dominic Sanchez, his sartorial opposite, was jacketless, but sported a crisp white shirt with contrasting blue collar and cuffs and a subdued red tie. You could tell that everything with Dom was a matter of pride.

"I'm honored to have you all aboard," I began. "When I used to do this in the unit, we called it a psychological autopsy. Before we can go any further with this case, we have to do just what the press has been doing—only more seriously. We have to conduct a *This Is Your Life* on Thomas Boyd."

What I didn't have to say was that we all knew we were really competing with the FBI itself. And Trevor, Katie, and I were all determined to show that despite our small numbers and limited resources, we could make something happen while a huge bureaucracy sputtered. At least that was the collective fantasy.

We had what Harry Gillette assured me was a full duplicate file of crime-scene materials, medical-examiner protocols, and follow-up reports—the same things we would have requested from any local department when I was at Quantico. It was all spread out on Katie's coffee table. But we didn't have what by now would be an endless stack of FD-302s—the reporting form agents use for any interview or investigative leads, which would already have been transferred to computer by the Major Case Management Team. We couldn't possibly keep up with all of that or sift through all the garbage to try to find the few nuggets of useful information. If this was the kind of case that was going to be solved by throwing sheer numbers of man-hours at it, then we weren't going to be the ones who would crack it. But if it turned out to be the kind that hinged on the critical bit of inspiration, that sudden cessation of ignorance, then we had as good a shot as anyone. The FBI had the power of numbers going for it, but as anyone who's ever worked for a large organization can attest, that same power would also be working against it.

"First, let me bring you up to speed on what I've found out about his domestic life." I related what Madeline had told me: how they were living separate lives under the same roof, how they'd made a few disappointing attempts at rapprochement, and how at the time of his death, she really didn't know how things would turn out between them.

"But does someone who's trying to work things out with his wife suddenly up and kill himself?" Dom asked.

"Good question," I said. I looked to the others. "Ideas?"

"With someone like Boyd, the whole issue is going to be control," said Katie. I agreed with that. "As long as he felt in control of his life, I don't believe he'd kill himself. It comes down to whether this blackmail threat was enough to make him feel permanently out of control."

"And whether this was the only incident," added Jerry.

"That's right," Trevor said, "because if it wasn't the only one, then he'd have to know what could happen at any time."

I put on my list to check with Peter on the Bureau's own investigation into the identity of the blackmailer.

"He just didn't seem the type," Katie commented.

Trevor seemed to sneer. "Those are the ones who can't handle it, if and when the shit hits the fan."

"And you're speaking from experience, Trev?"

"I'm just saying I wouldn't get myself involved in anything I didn't think I could handle. You always have to consider the contingencies. That's what keeps people in my field alive."

Trevor was famous for his contingencies. Since he was out of town a good deal during his time with HRT, he'd insisted that his wife, Valerie, be prepared for any emergency. For most suburbanites, that meant knowing where the breaker box and all the cutoff switches were and having the presence of mind to dial 911 at the first hint of trouble. But for Trevor, this meant drilling her on being able to roll out of bed and grab the loaded .357 magnum from the night-table drawer in one fluid motion, ready for use.

We went over the implications of suicide. I told them about Boyd's message to his son and how it gnawed at me. I could empathize only too well with that part of Boyd's personal life—fidelity to the Bureau at odds with family loyalties. You miss enough baseball games, enough school plays, enough bedtime stories, disappointing your kid and yourself, that when you make a promise to be at the next one, you keep it.

"And there's another way he'd be letting his family down by killing himself." I mentioned the insurance policy.

"I don't think a guy like that would cheat his wife and son out of the insurance money by blowing his brains out," Jerry agreed.

"He *cheated on* his wife," Katie said dryly. "Whether he would also *cheat* her is an open question."

"Depends on what else was going on in his head at the time," said Trevor.

"And isn't there already a fair amount of family money on her side?" Katie said.

"I think you're right," I said. "Why don't you check into that?"

After an unexplained airplane crash, in investigating the possibility of a bomb or sabotage, we review all possible victimology, going over each passenger to determine if he or she could have been the target. Here, we knew the target. So the critical determination was figuring out who might want to target him, and why. I folded over a page of my legal pad. "Okay, now who might want Judge Boyd dead?"

"Almost anyone," Dominic suggested. "The militias who wanted to avenge Owl Creek, the organized crime elements he was coming down so heavily upon, anyone who thought he had a better idea how to run the FBI."

"And his arrest of Yuri Variyinko, the crime boss in Brooklyn, had to piss off the Russian Mob," said Trevor. "Boyd wanted to make an example of him. The Russkies are just foolhardy enough to decide to make an example out of the FBI director."

"Okay, that makes sense. Who else stands to gain by Boyd's death or disgrace?" I prompted. "Who could've had a grudge against him?"

"Are we talking inside or outside the Bureau?" Katie asked.

"Either, from as much as we know at this point, anyway."

"Well, starting with inside," she began, "how about Peter Sutherland?"

"Come on," I said, "let's not waste time."

"I'm serious," she persisted. "Who was it who always taught us to consider all the possibilities before limiting any of them? He's the only one who's gained so far from Boyd's death."

"You're correct in principle," I allowed. "Peter might have had a motive, just as I might have."

"Exactly!" Katie said triumphantly.

"Except for the fact that he's alibied by his trip to Hawaii." Then I had another thought. "What about Ted Novello? He was right there in the same city with Boyd."

"But why him?" Jerry wanted to know. "From what you say, he had the most to lose from Boyd's death. You guys even joked about him needing key-man insurance on Boyd."

I turned to my disciple. "What would you say to that, McManus? What kind of scenario could you come up with?"

"Well," she considered, "maybe he gets tired of everyone saying how he owes all his current success to Boyd's patronage, so he decides to get rid of him and prove that he's his own man."

Trevor nodded. "Ted's enough of a weasel to make it legit. In fact, maybe he's been a mole all along."

"For who?" Jerry asked.

"I don't know. Maybe the president."

"That would be clever," commented Katie.

"Maybe it's not the prez himself. Maybe it's one of his minions, like in Watergate. They tapped someone known to be close to Boyd, he's been supplying them with intelligence on the Bureau. Then they set up

Ted to kill Boyd, since he can get close to him alone without arousing suspicion."

"What's in it for Ted?" I inquired.

"Maybe he gets appointed the new director. It's perfect, if you think about it. Everyone thinks the president's appointing Boyd's boy for continuity and all that shit, when in reality, he's got his own operative running the most sensitive and critical agency in government."

It was far-fetched, but farer-fetched things have come to pass.

"Well," said Jerry, "what about the bodyguard—the first FBI agent on scene?"

Katie's lips formed an endearing pout as she considered the problem. "There was no sign of forced entry. But though the front door was locked, the door to the terrace wasn't. So it's theoretically possible that Boyd actually let someone in through the front door, or someone just walked in from the back and surprised him."

Trevor shuffled through the set of crime-scene photos until he found the one he was looking for. "Or that the terrace door was locked but that an intruder let himself out that way. If you look at this photo, you can see that this door can't be locked from the outside."

Jerry said, "If someone came in through the back, he'd have to know the Boyds' habits pretty well."

"Or have been surveilling him," Trevor suggested.

"Only an insider wouldn't assume that the director of the FBI would be heavily guarded in his own home," said Katie.

I asked Trevor, "You have something for us on the bullet?"

"Yeah. I talked to the guy at the FBI Lab. It's a good thing our man out there was able to get the round. It's the one break we caught at the scene. It severely deformed as it passed through Boyd's skull and brain and then smacked into the headboard, but it looks to have been one of those old lead, round-nosed bullets, nothing the Bureau's used for years. It had to have come from some outside source."

"Is there any reason Boyd would have acquired ammunition outside the Bureau?"

"I can't think of any. Even if he were contemplating suicide, there'd be nothing to hide since he had a registered firearm and therefore legitimate reason to have ammo."

"Who uses this particular type of round?"

"I know one group who does," Trevor said somberly. "The Wyoming Defenders."

What! My gut clutched. "Are you sure?"

"I examined their guns myself. Including Sickenger's."

What could this mean? Was Boyd secretly in league with them? No, that was too absurd. But . . .

"Where would Boyd get that kind of bullet?" I asked.

Trevor shook his head. "No idea."

"It has to mean something," said Katie. "It's too much of a coincidence."

"I've learned that there's no such thing as too much of a coincidence in a death investigation," I responded. "Anything's possible, because we've all seen it. But I agree with you, it's too unlikely. Trev, I guess you'll want to follow up on that angle. See if we can make a connection between the Wyoming Defenders and the guys who tried to take me out."

"Sure," he said. "But we're all just spinning our wheels until we know if this is a suicide or a murder. What does the MEs report say?"

Dominic had been scanning it as we talked. " 'Death apparently due to self-inflicted gunshot wound.' "

"What's your evaluation?" I asked.

"No red flags to indicate otherwise," Dom said. "The postmortem close-ups of the entry wound and the medical examiner's drawings are certainly consistent with this type of injury, but when the gun is that close, it's often hard to tell for sure. Trevor, does it work for you?"

Trevor started drawing a diagram on his legal pad. "Like you, Dominic, it's going to be hard for me to tell. The trajectory of the bullet after it leaves the body is largely going to be determined by the deflection and deformation it goes through passing through the hard palate, the brain, and then the base of the skull, and there's a lot of variables in that pathway. Let's put it this way: the round ended up where you'd expect it to be, and in the shape you'd expect it to be in if the subject swallowed his own gun and then squeezed the trigger."

Dom pulled out another sheet from the file. "I don't know how closely you've looked through all this, Jake, but there's a copy of a confidential intra-agency note here. It says that in deference to Mrs. Boyd's stated wishes, a complete autopsy would not be performed, but that they were satisfied with the conclusions of the postmortem exam and tox tests as they were performed in Sausalito."

I desperately needed something concrete. "Is there anything in the postmortem evidence that could tell us definitely whether Boyd pulled the trigger himself?"

"The residue on his hands suggested he did," said Jerry.

"Yeah, but is there anything more definitive?"

All eyes turned to Dominic. "Without the body, I'm not sure how much help I can be. I mean . . . in point of fact . . . the dead body is so important as evidence that the term *corpus delicti* refers not only to the corpse itself. It represents the 'body of the case.' "

"Should we petition for a disinterment?" asked Katie.

"Mrs. Boyd would never agree to that," I said. "We'd have to go to court."

"Where we'd almost certainly lose," added Dom.

Trevor said, "Then let's dig him up ourselves." He looked around to me and the others.

Katie's look said, *You can't be serious!*

But I was already thinking, *Dig him up! What an interesting idea! And it's something our friends in the Bureau could never get away with.* What a minute, what was I saying?

"Why not?" Trevor verbalized.

Katie bored in on him with large, disapproving eyes. "Well, for one thing, it's called grave robbing."

"We'll put it back after Dominic's finished with it and we've taken some pictures," Trevor offered reasonably.

See, that's what I like about a group like this—nothing's impossible. And this is the kind of thing I meant when I said there are certain things a bureaucracy is good at, and certain things they're not. If you wanted to sift through thousands of forms and reports, well, then, you'd want that bureaucracy. But if, say, you wanted to steal a body without a lot of people knowing about it, why then, of course, you'd come to us.

19

"In a real dark night of the soul it is always three o'clock in the morning, day after day."

F. Scott Fitzgerald's statement was seared in my memory. It applied to so many situations I saw in my own life and all the unfortunate lives with which mine intersected.

It was about three o'clock in the morning, or 2:43 to be exact, by the green numerals from my clock radio that hung in the darkness. I was lying awake, as I often seemed to be at this time of the night: mentally prioritizing my list of worries. Whatever was the most serious worry floated to the top of the list, followed by four or five other good, solid ones after that. If, for any reason, I managed as I was lying there to figure out a way to solve or otherwise dispense with the top worry, then number two would rise up to take its place, creating a concern and anxiety equal to that which had been devoted to its predecessor. At the moment, the prime worry had to do with personal safety. Not only mine—an FBI agent gets used to that—but the safety of my family and those close to me, and that's something none of us ever gets used to.

It wasn't just passive worry, either. I used to try to educate my kids, drill them, every chance I got. One time, when Ali was eight, I took her to a fair set up in a park not far from where we lived. We were just passing the pony ride when I pointed to a slight, potbellied guy in shorts with glasses and a floppy hat. A camera was around his neck. "Ali, you see that guy over there?"

"What guy?"

"That guy right over there. You see him? You see how he's looking at those kids on the ponies? This is the kind of thing I've been telling you about."

"Daddy, be quiet!" she whispered.

"No, Alexandra. Turn around and look at him. See the way he's acting? You see the way he's staring at that little girl getting off the pony?"

"Daddy, everyone's gonna be looking at us!" At that age, this is one of the worst fates imaginable.

"Let's play detective," I suggested. "Let's tail him. See the way he's taking pictures of those girls? You think they're his? I don't think so."

She apparently understood, because a year later she was in town when she spotted this same guy on the street. He still had his camera, and this time he was taking her picture. She quickly ducked into a drugstore and sought out a woman paying at the counter. She'd never seen this woman before, but started talking to her. She glanced over her shoulder and noted that Mr. Creepo had seen this, must have figured the woman was Ali's mother, and had moved along. Creepo wasn't the kind of guy who was going to snatch a kid off the street—he would be too retiring and cowardly for that. He'd be able to get off just fantasizing with his photos and swapping kiddie porn on the Internet. But if the situation arose where he could get a kid alone—say in an alley or if she came to his house by herself trick-or-treating or selling Girl Scout cookies—then his fantasies could suddenly evolve into action. I was proud of Ali that day. She was aware of her surroundings, she used her head, and she took a proactive approach to a potentially threatening situation.

But you know they're still kids and that they're not going to remember to be little profilers twenty-four hours a day, and that no matter what you do, no matter how much you warn, how much you lecture, how much you punish or how much you reward, no matter how strict you are or how permissive and indulgent, you can't watch over or protect them twenty-four hours a day.

When the phone rang, I thought maybe I'd lapsed into sleep and this was part of a dream. But after about three rings, I became convinced I was still awake and the phone was calling me for real. "Hello?"

The voice at the other end was an urgent whisper. "It's Toni."

Suddenly, I was bolt-upright awake. "Toni, what is it!"

"I'm in the closet on the cell phone. I think someone's broken into the house."

Oh, God. I felt a wave of nausea and the cold sweat between the shoulder blades. Oh, God, the moment when the dread comes true.

"Where are the kids?"

"I've got them in here with me."

"Okay," I said, triaging my thoughts. I felt vulnerable, powerless, and the sudden need to move. "Did you call the police?"

"Yes."

"I'll be right over."

I darted outside, saw the two cars, opted for the Land Rover; it was newer and less temperamental than the Aston Martin. I climbed in and gunned the engine. On the straightaways I got it up to ninety, but then slowed down when the road got a little curvy. I wouldn't be much good to anyone if I wiped out on the way over. All the time my heart was pounding. *If I can't even help my own family, I'm worthless.* As I drove, I cataloged the possibilities. No cash, jewelry, or drugs were in the house, so this wasn't a professional burglary. That was bad news, because those types don't generally injure their victims if they don't have to. An opportunistic break-in could have any result, depending on whether the burglars felt threatened and panicked in a confrontation. The worst possibility of all, and the one I was trying unsuccessfully to keep suppressed, was an offender or offenders who had broken in for the express purpose of sexual and physical assault.

And what if it was related to Boyd? Or, worse still, the guys in the pickup truck? That could mean anything, none of it good.

I couldn't face any of those possibilities other than to vow that if I caught whoever it was, I'd kill him myself. You threaten my family, you take your life in your hands. Those are the rules.

I didn't see any cop cars in front of the house—a bad sign. I moved quickly but stealthily up to the front door, extracting my gun from my vest pocket. I held it high in my right hand as I tried the brass door handle with my left. Locked. Whoever the intruder was, he hadn't entered this way.

I raced around back. There was a rear door to the farm-style kitchen. The gate in the backyard fence was open and . . . as soon as I reached it, I realized the kitchen door was, too. *Get a grip!* I kept telling myself. I had to control this shaking. *Focus on the mission. Nothing else matters. Nothing else can help. Use your training.*

But I couldn't stop shaking.

There are two ways to enter premises that have been broken into.

One is slowly, noticing everything along the way, gathering evidence and making sure not to compromise the crime scene.

But not when lives are at stake. Especially these lives.

My gun out in front of me in a two-handed grip, using moonlight and the spill from the streetlights as illumination, I stepped into the room. In police parlance, this exercise is known as clearing or sweeping.

Where the hell were the cops?

I went through the door that led to the front hall and front door, with the dining room on one side and the living room on the other. I stopped before each doorframe, before every window, every opening into another room, each time ready to jump out and fire at the intruder. I heard no sounds that suggested another human being. It was too dark to notice whether anything had been taken or disturbed.

Once I'd convinced myself the downstairs was clear, I made my way up the stairs, which are often the most dangerous place. If the intruder came from around the corner and fired, I had nowhere to hide. I got to the upstairs landing and quickly glanced in both directions. Nothing.

Without consciously analyzing my choice, I went first to Eric's room, bursting in with my weapon in front of me. There was no sound in response, so I flicked on the light switch. Again, nothing. Everything seemed to be in place, and by that I mean the total tornado that a nine-year-old boy's domain usually is.

I raced over to Ali's room, swept the entire space, then turned on the light. Everything seemed to be okay: the array of CDs and stuffed animals all lined up the way she insisted upon. Dresser looked untouched. Quickly, I crossed over to her closet and opened the door. All of the shirts, dresses, shoes, boxes, and whatnot appeared in order.

In spite of myself I flashed on the Brauer case in Omaha. Assailant herded the twin seven-year-old girls into their mother's bedroom—father out of town, intruders had to know—raped them in front of the bound and already raped Mrs. Brauer before slitting all three throats. From the crime scene, I was convinced the UNSUB knew them well and had recently been in the house. I used that to get the son of a bitch.

But the Brauers were still dead.

Where were my children? And where the hell were the cops?

I took a quick, deep breath, then charged down the short hallway to Toni's bedroom. The door was closed. Had she closed it after she brought the children in, or had someone else closed it?

Here goes.

I kicked the door open and jumped into the doorframe ready to fire. What I saw in front of me were only the dim outlines of a slept-in bed. But from the walk-in closet I heard what sounded like whimpering. I crossed to the door and flung it open, there to find my ex-wife and two children huddled together, terrified.

Thank you, God!

"Oh, Jake!" Toni practically collapsed into my arms. Ali and Eric grabbed me around the waist from either side. I was still holding my gun aloft.

"Are you all okay?"

She nodded.

"It's all right," I said, trying to comfort them. They were trembling. "Whoever was here is gone now."

"Who was it, Daddy?" asked Eric.

"I don't know, Son. Did anyone hear anything?"

"No voices," Ali offered.

I put my gun back in my vest pocket. "You wait here. I want to go lock the back door."

"It was open, then?" said Toni.

"Oh, yes."

She shuddered.

I cleared the entire house again, including the basement, this time with all the lights on. Someone had definitely been here. The deadbolt lock on the kitchen door had been opened—not jimmied, not shot off or otherwise destroyed. Opened. That was a pretty good trick. Various small pieces of furniture had been knocked out of the way as the intruder stumbled around in the dark. That was what Toni and the kids had heard. But as far as I could tell, nothing was taken. That someone had gone to some trouble to gain entry and then hadn't taken anything of value . . .

It wasn't what was in the house, it was who was in the house.

"Did you make any noise when you heard him?" I asked when I'd returned from my surveillance.

"No," they all confirmed.

"I ran out to get both kids as soon as I heard the noise," Toni explained.

"Did he come into the bedroom while you were in the closet?"

"I don't think so," she said. "But I'm not sure. Kids, go get your pillows. You sleep with Mommy the rest of the night."

"I'll sleep in Ali's room," I said.

Toni smiled gratefully. "Thanks."

She held herself together long enough for Ali and Eric to go back to their rooms, then came apart.

"Toni, Toni, it's okay now," I comforted, taking her in my arms.

"No . . . no, it isn't," she protested through her sobs.

I smoothed her hair. "You're all safe now."

She shook her head from side to side, as if she couldn't get the words out. "It's not that," she said finally.

"Then what is it?"

She just kept shaking her head next to my shoulder.

"I'll do the same thing with you that you always did with the kids: 'Try to tell me exactly what it is that's bothering you. Because if you can describe it, then we can deal with it. What exactly is the terrible thing you're thinking about?' "

"It's . . . it's that . . . I . . . I had to call you tonight."

"And that was exactly the right thing."

Tears still streamed down her face. "You . . . you don't understand. I called because I knew the FBI man would come over with his gun and take care of it."

"Of course," I soothed.

She pulled her head back and looked me straight in the eyes. "Oh, Jake, don't you see?" she said hoarsely. "I needed the part of you that I hate."

"Toni, listen—"

I was interrupted by a shriek from Ali's room. I grabbed for my gun and raced in that direction, the moment stretching out into infinite parts. I bolted through the door and landed with a two-hand grip on my gun. The last joint on my index finger was already twitching.

"Freeze! FBI!"

Ali looked up from her bed where she was sitting and shrieked again.

When I realized she was unharmed, I lowered the revolver. Toni and Eric were standing behind me in the hallway just beyond the door. I sat on the bed with Ali, took her tightly by the shoulders. "What is it, honey?"

Sobs racked her. I wrapped my arms around her tight enough to feel her lungs heaving in and out. She gestured behind her. I moved her shaking body to the side so I could see.

On her pillow lay her *X-Files* Barbie and Ken dolls, sent to me after

I'd consulted with the producers about a serial killer episode they were developing. The two dolls were dressed in dark gray suits with FBI credentials, and even though Ali had evolved past the Barbie stage, she displayed these because they represented Daddy's career.

And now, someone had not only moved them from their place of honor in my daughter's bedroom, but had decapitated each of them. Barbie's golden-tressed head had been tucked into the crook of Ken's bent arm, just as his head balanced in hers.

∘

Two uniformed police officers finally arrived. I'd already started to berate them when they told me, annoyed themselves, that they'd been sent to the wrong place. It turned out Toni had given the 911 operator the address of the house where we'd lived together. I decided not to read in anything emotionally significant, but it made me even more nervous. It meant that as smart and levelheaded and resourceful as my ex-wife was, when it came to such a crisis, my family was just as vulnerable as I'd always feared.

Early in the morning, while the kids were still asleep in Toni's bed, she and I had our serious discussion in the kitchen.

"This was aimed at me, not you," I said. "But there's no way of knowing how far they're willing to go to make their point. I think it'd be better if you took the kids and went away someplace safe for a while."

"But I've got work, Jake. I'd have to cancel appointments. We'd have to pick up our entire lives."

"It wouldn't be for very long."

"How do you know that?"

"Because someone's trying to scare me off. And doing a pretty damn good job of it, I might add, and—"

"You're sure that's what it is?"

"Nothing of significance was taken, you said so yourself. But the scene on Ali's bed was symbolic. Here's the deal, Toni: If this case is going to be solved, if there even is a case to solve, it's going to happen pretty quickly, or not at all. If someone's trying to scare me off, it's because they think I know something. If I crack the case, then I neutralize whoever's doing this. If I don't, believe me, they'll leave me alone and fade into the woodwork. So I only need a couple of weeks. If nothing breaks by then, come on back and I'm confident you'll all be safe. Just give me that long. For your and the kids' safety, and my own peace of mind. How about your sister and brother-in-law's vacation place in Wisconsin, somewhere we can control the variables. I've got good police contacts up there."

"I don't know."

"The kids are on summer vacation. They're not going to miss any school."

"It's just not all that easy."

I stepped over to her and took both of her hands, directing her gaze right into mine. "I rely on you and trust your advice in your field—with me, the kids, all of it. This is my field, I know what I'm talking about, and you have to trust me."

She finally agreed.

I met with Peter Sutherland in my old office at Quantico, only now it was his new office. File by file, I went over my active cases with Peter, explaining my analyses, strategies, recommendations to local police. Many of these he was already familiar with because we'd gone over them in our regular Monday-morning unit-wide consultation meetings. This was where the torch really got passed.

Most of Peter's stuff was still in boxes piled up around the periphery. The only thing he'd already made a point of putting on the wall was a photo of the profiling group taken in the old "glory days," shortly after Pete came on board—while Ted was still safely ensconced in the Miami Field Office. I was in the center and the shot included some of the real legends of the unit before they had retired or moved on to other positions—people such as Jim Wright, Jud Ray, Roy Hazelwood, Jana Monroe, Greg Cooper, Gregg McCrary, Bill Hagmaier, and Steve Mardigian. Everyone looked so happy and confident back then.

"Your ghost still haunts this place," Peter commented. He had relinquished his position behind the large mahogany desk, out of deference to my sensibilities, I suppose, and taken the visitor's chair adjoining the sofa I was sitting on.

I grinned. "I don't know how to take that."

I told him about what had happened at Toni's house.

"Jesus! This is serious."

"Damn right it's serious. When you rush into your daughter's bedroom with your weapon drawn, it's serious."

"No, I mean, whoever pulled that off is a pro. This is either an expert lockpicker or someone with a master set of skeleton keys. This is someone with resources."

"So what are you saying?"

"I'm not sure. Maybe I'm saying, give it up. It's not worth the risk to you or your family. Let the Bureau handle it. This is your friend talking, Jake, not your FBI liaison. You said it yourself, if you crack this, the Bureau takes the glory. If you don't, you get the shit."

I sighed. "I wish it were that simple." I gave him my *Man Who Knew Too Much* theory, and he couldn't argue with the logic.

"So where have you sent Toni and the kids?" he asked. "I'll try to get them full surveillance."

"It's probably better if we leave the Bureau out of this until we figure out what's going on."

He gave me a skeptical look. "I think you're taking an awful lot of this on yourself. But I'm not going to argue with you. If you change your mind, I can help."

"I appreciate that. I'll let you know." I wasn't going to compromise my friendship or my professional relationship with Peter by getting him involved with protecting my family.

"Okay, then," he said in a tone of grave finality, "so where do we go with this thing?"

"What has the Bureau got on the possible blackmailer?"

"Not much, so far as I can tell. No witness account of anyone knocking on the door or otherwise entering the house in the time before the gun went off. That doesn't necessarily mean no one was there; it just means no one saw anything suspicious or unusual, which would weigh against a forcible entry."

"Agreed."

"My guess would be that Boyd had the photos in his briefcase when he got there, so the point of contact was probably somewhere around headquarters in Washington or home in Maryland."

"Can I assume that our guys went through all the trash receptacles in the Sausalito house and the cans outside?"

"According to the report I've got, you can indeed."

"And they didn't find a mailing envelope?"

"They did not."

This was just one more way of limiting when and where the compromising photographs arrived. If there were no one besides Boyd in the house and no envelope with canceled stamps, then Peter was probably right that Boyd had the photos with him when he arrived . . . which, though probably incidental, also probably meant that he had them at my retirement luncheon.

"Any word yet on the woman in the photograph?" I asked.

Peter shook his head. "They're going through every photo collection and database they've got, and it's gone out on the wire to every agency in the country. They're interviewing people close to Boyd, but they're trying to be discreet about it—at least as discreet as this bureaucracy of thundering elephants knows how to be."

We brought each other up-to-date on our respective pieces of the investigation. I told him Dominic Sanchez's conclusion that the way the postmortem was conducted, he felt he would need to see the body himself to come to any strong conclusions about suicide versus homicide and asked if anything in any of the reports Peter had seen might speak to this issue.

"Not a thing," he said. "In fact, when I saw the postmortem stuff, I thought it was all rather sketchy, especially when you consider who the subject was."

Peter had brought up a little-realized but common phenomenon. As events surrounding President Kennedy's assassination had shown, and as it's been reconfirmed many times since, the prominence of the subject, and the public consequences of a screwup, have little to do with how good a crime-scene or postmortem investigation is carried out. You'd think, for instance, in a case that promised to be as obviously high profile as the murder of O. J. Simpson's ex-wife and her friend Ron Goldman that every procedural *i* would be dotted and *t* crossed. But the more prominent the victim, the more people were likely to compromise the scene, and here we had the compounded problems of mixed jurisdiction between the locals and the feds, the fact that the postmortem was done by whoever was available at the moment, and a wife who didn't want a complete autopsy, but rather a quick, private burial.

Peter sifted through the file folders on the coffee table in front of us. It looked like the same material I'd been given. "There's a lot of things that just fall off the cliff," he said. "Unless they're withholding stuff from us guys in the trenches."

"You think that's possible?"

"Anything's possible around here. Is it likely? I don't know. How do we know what everyone's agenda is?" He was right again. When something like this happens at the top of an organization, people who didn't even know they had agendas suddenly start figuring out where their own best interests lie.

"Trevor Malone wants to go in one night and dig the guy up for Dominic to examine."

"You're joking!" Peter exclaimed.

"I don't think Trevor is much of a jokester. I bet if I gave him the go-ahead, he'd do it."

"You're not going to."

"Peter," I said in a tone of mock admonition, "that would be illegal."

"Anyway, just don't get caught," he said conspiratorially. Then he shifted back to his professional tone. "Let me go over the profile we've come up with on the possible blackmailer."

This was in some ways the toughest kind of profile to construct, since there was no direct behavioral evidence of this individual's existence; it was only implied by the existence of the photographs. And as far as motive, you had as many possibilities as a doctor has for diagnoses when the patient presents with "flulike symptoms."

I listened silently as he laid it out, just as I'd taught him to do at a case consultation meeting for a local string of murders none of us would ever had heard of till then.

". . . Organized and sophisticated, with resources to be able to take and develop those pictures . . . have to assume at least one other person is working with him, since this kind of photographic ambush would be very difficult for one person to pull off on his own."

"Motive?"

"That's the hardest part. The most obvious one would be money. Boyd certainly wanted to avoid disclosure and so could be considered a good target for blackmail. But though he was a celebrity of sorts, unlike a businessman he didn't have the ability to come up with a whole lot of cash, certainly not without his wife's knowledge or cooperation, which he couldn't exactly ask for."

"No, he certainly couldn't." But would that lead him to take his own life? It was so tantalizing, so frustrating, trying to figure out what was going on in that mind in those last crucial seconds.

"So that's why we keep coming back to the political. Did some group the FBI's after compromise Boyd to get him to call off an investigation or something?"

"I know," I said. "I've been thinking the same way."

"Could be the Mafia, the Russian Mob, drug cartels . . . With what happened to you and what Trevor says about the bullet, I think the militia groups have to stay at the top of the list unless or until we can rule them out."

There was a knock on the door and Peter's secretary, Jacqui—my former secretary Jacqui—came in, carrying what looked like an airtel, the standard communication document between FBI offices.

"Sorry to interrupt you guys, but the New York Field Office is looking for Jake."

We both looked at each other. "How come?" Peter asked.

She studied the airtel a moment. "An NYPD homicide detective, Paul . . . let me try to get this right . . . Paul Sochaczewski." Her pronunciation was a noble try. "He contacted them and specifically said he wanted to get in touch with Jake."

"He was in the National Academy a couple of years ago," I said. "Jacqui, it's pronounced Sock-a-chef-ski." But what the hell would he want with me? Maybe he hadn't heard that I'd left the Bureau. Did he know I was working on the Boyd case?

"Oh, sure. I can see that."

"Or something close to it. A very sharp guy. He really got into profiling."

"When did the airtel come in?" Peter asked.

"This morning. It says right here: June sixteenth."

He turned to me. "Any idea what this is all about?"

I shrugged. "Haven't talked to him since he was at Quantico."

"Shall I try to get him on the phone for you?" Jacqui asked.

"Sure. Let's see what he wants."

A few moments later, Jacqui had him on the line.

Peter started to get up. "Do you want some privacy?"

"No, I'll just take it here, if that's all right."

I made my way back to the desk and sat down. It was strange sitting there again. "This is Jake Donovan."

"I don't know if you'll remember me or not."

"Of course I do, Paul. How're things going in Gotham?"

"No rest for the weary. I hope you don't mind: I called your former office because I didn't know where else to reach you."

"And you got me. I hope I don't get a reputation as one of those old geezers who just can't stay away."

"Lucky break. We haven't been in contact since I took the National

Academy classes, but I want you to know I've followed your career since then and I always thought you were a real stand-up guy." He paused. "But listen, the news says you're chasing down the Boyd situation for the Bureau even though you're retired. That true?"

"I guess it is."

"Okay, then. I caught a case last night and I got something here I think you ought to see."

"What sort of something?"

"I'd rather we do this face-to-face if it's all the same."

I get a specific feeling when a case gives its first indication of coming together, and I was getting it now—my pulse sped up, my breathing grew shallower, somehow I felt my brain get more focused. If you could've taken a galvanic skin response, I think you'd have found something akin to what a lion must feel stalking prey.

I glanced over at Peter, who seemed to be following the conversation from hearing my end of it. "Ah . . . sure, Paul, if that's what you think is best. And in that case, I'd like to bring the rest of my team along, if you think this may be something important."

"I do. When could you get here by?"

"How's tomorrow morning?"

"Tomorrow morning's okay. I'll try to hold the scene intact until then. I'll meet you."

"I think it'll be at Kennedy," I said.

"La Guardia'd be a lot easier into the city. Which airline you coming in on?"

I hesitated. "Actually, we've got our own plane. But it's not the kind La Guardia's set up to handle."

"No shit! You must be traveling in the right circles."

"We're about to find out."

I hung up and stood.

"A lead?"

"I don't know," I said. "Let's hope so."

∘

I was impressed by how well the system worked the first time. I called Scott Kenworthy on his mobile phone and told him I wanted *The Broken Wing* ready to go to New York first thing in the morning. When we all got to Dulles, he and Trish O'Connor were in the cockpit.

"Ready when you are, chief!" he greeted me, far too chipper for this hour of the morning. "Flight plan's been filed and approved, we're fueled up and ready to rock and roll."

"Thanks," I said. "But I'd appreciate it if we could keep the rocking and rolling to a minimum until I'm fully awake."

"We'll keep it smooth as a greased pig for you." Another image that didn't set all that well at this hour. "That's what we're here for." He turned to Trish. "Ready, O'Connor?"

"Ready."

I wore a dark, Bureau-style, tailored suit, which made me feel as if I were back in harness. Dominic was attired in a spiffy gray sport jacket, crisp white shirt, and sleek black slacks, the creases perfect. Trevor was in his SWAT getup—black cargo pants, polo shirt, and khaki utility vest. Katie was in jeans and a jean jacket and carried a suit bag with her.

Everyone climbed in behind, except for Jerry, who was hanging back on the tarmac. I made my way back down the stairway and out to where he was standing, regarding the plane with some manifest skepticism.

"What's the problem, Jerry?"

He didn't take his eyes off *The Broken Wing*. "It's just that, I, uh, thought I'd be able to see my way clear to going up in this thing when the time came."

"Well, the time has come, Jerry."

"I know that. And it's just, uh, I don't know if I can."

Well, I could try reasoning with him. I'm supposed to be good at that. "You're handpicked for this team. You're critically important to the mission."

"I know that, and I don't want to let down any of the others. But it's this phobia, you see."

Trevor came over to where we were negotiating. "What's going on?"

"We're trying to work out Jerry's fear of flying," I said.

"I could take the train and meet you," he offered.

"That might take care of today," I said. "But what happens if we have to go farther away, or even overseas?"

"Well, we could cross that bridge when we came to it," Jerry said hopefully.

"Or we could cross it now and be done with it," said Trevor. "You know, some of us have had the same kind of problem you're having, Jerry."

His eyes grew wide. "Really?"

"Yeah. First time we had to jump out of one of these suckers into a hostile-fire zone, some of the guys just couldn't bring themselves to do it."

"So what happened?"

"The jump master, he was a pretty smart guy and he understood a lot about psychology. He unholstered his service piece and said, 'You can jump with your chute, or you can jump without your chute; it doesn't make a rat's ass of difference to me which way you choose. But you all volunteered to serve in this outfit, and the one for-sure thing is that one way or another, we are all going out this door.' And you know something, they all went."

Jerry was getting noticeably nervous. "So what exactly are you saying, Trevor?"

"I'm saying that you can climb aboard this plane, or I can carry you aboard this plane; it doesn't make a rat's ass of difference to me which way you choose. But you volunteered to serve in this outfit, and the one for-sure thing is that one way or another, you're getting on board so we go wheels up and get on with our mission."

Jerry looked to me. I tried to keep my face impassive. "He has a point."

"Ah, okay." Jerry headed tentatively for the stairs.

The first mission of the Broken Wings was under way.

21

Though Jerry still looked a little green around the gills as he gripped the arms of his upholstered seat, the flight was pleasant. That is, until somewhere over New Jersey when we heard an ear-piercing screech, followed by a high-pitched squeal, both emanating from behind the rear bulkhead.

Trevor and I bolted up and raced toward it, through the door at the rear of the passenger cabin.

Just as we got there, the sign on the lavatory door was shifting from OCUPADO to LIBRE. The door flew open, and Katie burst out, still screeching, struggling to pull up her jeans, a look of terror on her face I'd never seen before.

And practically at the same instant, something else producing an equal amount of racket sprang out of the lav or, more accurately, sprang from the general direction of Katie's head. It was kind of like a scene out of the movie *Alien.*

Instinctively, I went for Katie, wrapping my arms around her and trying to pull her out of harm's way. Just as instinctively, Trevor went for whatever was attacking her, lunging for it and grabbing with both hands. We collided and all ended up on the floor in a heap. Katie was trembling. She'd managed to wrestle up her panties into a position of relative modesty. Though my eyes lingered, this was unfortunately neither the time nor the place to pursue any possibilities.

By now Jerry and Dominic had made their way back, too, and beheld the scene with wide-eyed confusion. Jerry seemed momentarily to have forgotten his own problems, specifically that he was about twenty-five thousand feet higher above sea level than he preferred.

"Oh, Jesus," Katie exclaimed, one hand on her chest while she caught her breath. "It's a cat!" It had no collar or tags.

Trevor released his tight grip on the medium-sized, grayish brown, shaggy-coated beast, which hissed at him unpleasantly.

"It jumped on my head as I was sitting on the john. I don't know where it came from." Katie made it the rest of the way to her feet. "Excuse me," she said as she finished finessing her jeans over her butt to their full and upright position and snapped them in front. Dominic and Jerry looked away discreetly. Trevor and I didn't.

"Good thing my pants were down," she whispered to me. "Otherwise, I really would need that change of underwear." She struck a philosophical pose. "And I guess it could have been worse. I often wear thongs with my jeans."

"My loss." She punched me on the arm—gently enough to let me know she was just kidding around, forcefully enough to let me know she could pack a wallop when she wanted to. I'd always marveled at Katie's spunk and resiliency.

She reached out, took the cat from Trevor, and started stroking down the raised fur on the back of its neck. "Hey, how are you, sweetie?" she purred.

Scott must have heard the commotion from the cockpit, because he suddenly appeared and saw what had happened. "I do apologize, Ms. McManus," he said. "I have no idea how that got in here."

"You sure you didn't plant it?"

"Surveillance everywhere, even in the bathrooms," Jerry mused. "It's like going back to the days of J. Edgar Hoover."

Katie held the cat up in front of her. "That's what we'll call you: J. Edgar. That is, if you've got the right equipment."

"And what would that be?" Trevor inquired.

"Don't be crude. He's had enough trauma already, if he is a he." She presented it business side out to Dominic. "Doctor?"

Dom performed a cursory exam. "He."

"Then J. Edgar it is," Katie declared.

Trevor said, "Why would you bother to name it unless . . ."

"We're planning to keep it. Right here on the airplane. It'll be like our mascot."

Trevor grimaced. "I hate cats."

"I forgot, Trevor. You only like shooting animals." Katie cradled J. Edgar protectively in her arms and spoke to him soothingly. "Let's go see if we can find you some milk."

"Okay, folks," I announced. "Show's over. Nothing to see."

◦

Two unmarked NYPD cruisers met us outside the private-aviation terminal at JFK. One was driven by our host, who walked over to me.

"Paul Sochaczewski, Manhattan South Homicide Task Force," he said in a soft, low, serious voice. He was short and well built, with intense, dark eyes, kind of an olive complexion, a thick mustache and a close-cropped fringe of graying brown hair framing a dome bald except for some dark fuzz.

I introduced him around. He let his eyes linger a moment on Katie; most men do. On the plane she'd changed into one of her power suits—lavender silk blouse, blue-gray mini, and matching jacket that reached almost to the bottom of the very short skirt, specially tailored not to indicate the Gould & Goodrich leather paddle holster and extra magazine she wore at her waist. Sochaczewski took Katie, Trevor, and me in his car. The other driver took Jerry and Dominic back to their headquarters. I could feel the hunting responses beginning to surge inside me again.

"Sensitive or high-profile murders go to one of the homicide task forces," Sochaczewski explained as we headed onto the Van Wyck Expressway. "We operate out of the Thirteenth Precinct station house on East Twenty-first Street and handle anything from Fifty-ninth Street down. There's a Manhattan North force for everything above that."

He maneuvered expertly through the traffic. "We're heading down to the Tenth Precinct. Chelsea," Paul continued. "Kind of a mixed area. Apartments, some studios, shops. Very gay area. A little of everything. But as you'll see, as soon as I caught this one, I thought this was something you ought to see."

We ended up in front of a nondescript gray-faced brownstone walk-up on Eighteenth Street. Paul parked at the nearest fire hydrant and took us up to the fourth floor, the top one, and down a seedy hallway to where a uniform was standing in front of a door marked with yellow crime-scene tape. The cop was tall, well over six feet, handsome and youthful-looking, with brown hair and a lanky but athletic build. He opened the door.

"This is Bobby Acton," Paul explained. "One of the best uniforms on the job. We're grooming him for the homicide squad."

"I'll be looking forward to working with you," I said.

Sochaczewski brought us inside. The living room, full of old, functional furniture, betrayed nothing of the personality of the occupant other than that he wasn't terribly well-off. But the dining area had been set up with a desk and file cabinets and a fax machine and was cluttered with books and paper, a couple of computers. Starting to profile the apartment's occupant, I decided he didn't go out much, and when he did, it was mostly at night. That is, when he wasn't playing arcane computer games on the Internet with people whose personae he knew well and had never met. The small Pullman kitchen, though, was a surprise. I would have expected dirty dishes in the sink and on the drainboard, but it was clean. I opened the fridge, which was well stocked and neatly arranged.

"This guy is in some kind of lab business," I said.

"How do you know that?" Paul asked.

"He's some hotshot chemistry student who creates designer drugs, or he recuts and packages heroin or coke for the local Mob syndicate, or maybe he does something illegal with computers. He may even be a counterfeiter."

"What makes you think he works in a lab?"

"The rest of the place is pretty messy, but the kitchen isn't. He has a respect for cleanliness and order, but only where he thinks it really matters."

"And how do you know he's involved in something illegal?"

"Because he obviously got whacked, and Manhattan South Homicide's involved. Or you wouldn't be bringing us here."

He displayed a faint smile, which I was learning was a fairly demonstrative expression for Sochaczewski. "Let's go into the bedroom. That's where it happened."

I got a sudden flashback to the Boyd house in Sausalito. The bedroom was where *it* had happened there, too.

As soon as I saw the room, the similarities began multiplying in my mind. The single bed was covered with blood, which had stained the dingy white cotton-pile bedspread varying shades of brown and purple, depending on the density of the seepage at any given spot. I didn't see evidence the victim had been shot and recoiled, as Boyd had. The spatter pattern was pretty much confined to the bed itself, which suggested the killing had been up close and personal, and performed while the victim was already in a supine position.

Paul handed me a set of crime-scene photos, which I passed off in turn to Katie and Trevor. The victim was indeed lying flat on his back on the bed. A white male in his late twenties to early thirties, but it was difficult to tell for sure because of the disfigurement and mass of blood on the face. He was naked—only slightly overweight, but the soft, flaccid kind. Physical exercise was clearly not a priority. In high school, he would have been the one other kids snapped towels at in the locker room. His chest was stained with blood down to the sternum. Other than the neck and facial wounds, no distinguishing marks or characteristics could be seen except one: his left wrist sported a flashy gold Rolex with little diamonds for hour markers. This told us two things. Despite the dreary surroundings, this guy did something that made some bucks. And the motive had nothing to do with robbery.

I thought I knew what had happened, but I shuffled down through several more photos to be sure. The man's eyes had been gouged out of their sockets, leaving two dark, bloody pools and a mouth locked open in a grotesque rictus of agony.

"This wasn't the cause of death, was it?" I said.

"No," Paul replied. "If you look down two or three more shots, you'll see a close-up of a piano-wire garrote around the neck. It's pretty well embedded so it's hard to notice at first. Used to control during torture, then to kill after that."

"Sheesh," Katie murmured.

"His name was Louie Knox," Paul told us. "Thirty-six years of age when he met his untimely end."

"Do we have an established time of death?"

"Close as the ME can tell, about the middle of the afternoon, day before yesterday."

"This guy seems to be a nocturnal type," I said. "I wouldn't be surprised if he was sleeping when the intruders arrived. A daytime break-in also tells us they were professionals with a specific agenda." I glanced briefly around the room and met Trevor's gaze. "What's it look like to you? Mob-related?"

"Russian Mob," he confirmed. "They do the eyes."

"Their signature," said Paul. "We've seen some of this over around their hangouts in Brooklyn. This may be the first one in Manhattan, I'll have to check."

Trevor handed back the stack of photos.

"Now here's the most interesting part of our tour, ladies and gentle-men," the detective said as he guided us out into the shallow hallway and into what promised to be a second bedroom.

It turned out to be a photo darkroom. There were twin sinks and a built-in counter against the far wall, a small refrigerator, and a couple of tall cabinets. Dried prints and contact sheets hung on clips suspended from a wire near the ceiling. Others were stuck on a bulletin board.

"You were right about the lab," Katie said to me.

Sochaczewski pulled open a built-in cabinet, revealing an impressive array of cameras and accessories. "Leicas, Bronica, Hasselblad, this guy had some pretty fancy stuff. He must have gotten paid pretty fancy to afford it all."

The homicide detective slipped on a pair of latex gloves, then direct-ed us over to one contact sheet nearly covered by several others. "I prac-tically missed this among all the hundreds of sheets."

From his breast pocket he took out a magnifying square that angled out from a leather cover and handed it to me. With his gloved fingers, he held the other contact sheets out of the way so I could focus on the one he'd indicated. "I trust you'll find this as interesting as I did."

I played with the position of the magnifier until I got a sharp image, then scanned down the sheet.

"Ho-ly shit." I passed the magnifier to Katie. She had to lean her upper body forward and stand on tiptoe to get close enough to study the images.

"Ho-ly shit," she repeated, then handed the magnifier to Trevor. Being even taller than me, he didn't have to stretch.

"You ain't kidding," he said.

"You can appreciate why I didn't want to describe it to you on the phone; why I thought it was better for you to see it firsthand in the set-ting," said Paul.

"Yes," I agreed. "Who knows about this?"

"My partner, Phil Robbins, and I. It's gone into the report, but we still control the case file."

"Trev, let me have the lens back." I positioned myself in front of him and went over the rows of tiny black-and-white pictures one by one, building the sequence in my mind, to make sure I hadn't dreamed up or misinterpreted what I'd just seen.

But no, there wasn't any mistaking it. There, right before me, in a series of thirty-six images, sharper in this small format than in the print I'd seen, was the late director of the Federal Bureau of Investigation and the unknown woman, as they used to say, in flagrante delicto. In the beginning of the series he had on his trousers, shirt, and tie, and her medium-tone knit suit was still on and in place. The one I'd been shown in Orlando Ravan's office—with Boyd still in shirt and tie but with his trousers open, her still in her skirt but with it up around her waist, and jacket, shoes, and dark panties already shed onto the floor—must have come from right around the middle of the series. By the end, both participants were down to their birthday suits.

22

"Who is this guy Louie Knox?" I asked Paul Sochaczewski.

"We don't know too much about him," the homicide detective replied. "He's listed as a commercial photographer, and as you'll see in a minute, the next room here has been set up like a studio, so that part seems to be legit. But that doesn't seem to tell the whole story, does it? No priors recorded, at least none under this name. We're trying to find out now who might have known him and what circles he traveled in."

"He doesn't strike me as the kind working the weddings and bar-mitzvahs circuit," said Katie.

I turned to Paul and Trevor, who seemed to know about these things. "Do I assume that the eye-gouging is a technique reserved for informers?"

"Informers and people they want information from," Paul said, "which means there may be someone involved more important than Mr. Knox here."

"What else do we know?" I asked, taking another look around the apartment. "I didn't notice any signs of forced entry when we came in."

"No."

I thought of the back door to Toni's house. "What's wrong? Doesn't anyone break in anymore?"

"You have to assume that whoever did something this personal to Knox knew him," Trevor pointed out.

"The question," I said almost to myself, "is whether Knox took the photos or merely processed them for someone else."

"Possibly whoever did this to him," Katie offered.

Sochaczewski took us into the studio, a bare, white-walled room with a couple of lights on stands and a rod attached to the ceiling on which backdrops could be hung. Several pieces of tape stuck to the floor must have been used as spot markers for a job.

Katie and I each took another tour around the apartment, independently looking for the behavioral clues we'd later compare. A sleeveless T-shirt and a pair of striped boxer shorts had been found on the bedroom floor near the body, presumably what he was wearing when the intruder or intruders entered. They had been sent to the police lab for analysis. Stripping him naked was probably part of the interrogation scenario. That he hung around during the day in his underwear told me a lot about his personality—asocial, uninvolved with his appearance or self-image, task-oriented, likely to become absorbed in what he did.

I studied dust patterns on all of the surfaces to see if anything had recently been moved after some significant time in one place. I opened drawers and closets, looking for any women's clothing—either suggesting a female relationship or, if they were the right size, cross-dressing. There was nothing. I looked in the kitchen, bathroom medicine cabinet, and darkroom refrigerator for alcohol and drugs, either prescription or illicit. But other than a half-drunk bottle of house-brand Scotch and bottles of Halcion and Valium, the place was pretty clean and unenlightening. A calendar was up on the wall, but nothing was written on it. I suspected there must be a date book of some sort, but Sochaczewski said none had been found. It was probably taken by whoever killed Knox. The Rolex might not have been valuable to the killer or killers, but a diary or address book would be, either for what it told them or, more likely, because it would have given the police information.

Some paperback novels were in his dining room/office. The hardbacks had mostly to do with technical aspects of photography. Two books stood out for me. One was entitled *Successful Glamour Photography*. A blonde on the cover had on nothing but a sheer wet blouse, so I thumbed through it. In addition to many more shots more provocative than the one on the cover, there were serious chapters on film, lighting, color temperature, makeup, props, and other techniques of the trade.

The other book I examined was a large, plainly printed paperback without any pictures. It was called *How to Make Hidden Camera Photography Work for You.* While it was written from the perspective of a private detective who tailed errant spouses for divorce clients, my cursory reading suggested a virtual manual for blackmailers.

I handed the book to Trevor, who looked at the spine. "Independence Press. They're a survivalist publisher out of Idaho. They put out books on booby-trapping, bomb-making, poisoning, fake IDs, you name it—always with the disclaimer that it's for informational purposes only."

"Right." Was this a working manual for Knox, or was he looking to expand his business horizons?

Before we left the apartment I said to Paul, "You mentioned that you and your partner still control the case file?"

"That's right."

"Might we keep it that way?"

"In terms of who?"

"In terms of law enforcement agencies outside of your own; the FBI, for example." His silence made me feel a need to clarify. "Until we figure out the significance of what you've just shown us, and who's involved, I think this is the kind of thing we ought to hold pretty close, if you see what I mean."

"I do."

"And if you trust us to handle it."

"I wouldn't have called you if I didn't."

Officer Acton resealed the front door as we left. In the stairwell, Katie pulled me aside. "What was that all about?"

"What?"

"Asking Paul for a close hold on the case. Is it really because you're afraid of what the Bureau would do with it, or because you want an advantage in the competition?"

"Good question," I answered honestly. "I'll have to give it some thought when I have the chance."

But Katie's question continued to gnaw at me in the police cruiser heading back to the precinct house. Why wasn't I willing to share this new stuff with anyone at the Bureau? Did my unwillingness to cooperate rise to the level of obstruction of justice? My brief from the acting director of the FBI, I told myself, was to conduct an independent investigation, to stay untouched by anything that might be going on, or anyone who might be untrustworthy, within that organization. The only way I could fulfill that brief was to remain aloof and objective. If the Bureau got any of this on its own, fine. But at this point, withholding information, and even obstruction of justice, were academic subtleties that had little to do with the investigation—as little to do with it as the issue of whether I was also doing it to satisfy my ego. Still, I savored the secrecy. If my team was better than theirs, fuck 'em!

23

Katie stayed at the precinct to start investigating Louie Knox while Trevor went to take a nap. Mrs. De Vries kept a suite at the Waldorf Towers and had given us full use. Jerry was already there when Trevor arrived. Sochaczewski picked up Dominic Sanchez, then the three of us went over to the Medical Examiner's Office at Thirtieth Street and First Avenue, adjacent to NYU Medical Center.

Laurin Andrews was the pathologist on duty, and Dominic knew her; she'd taken courses from him years ago. By the time we got there, the body was already laid out on the steel table, ready for the autopsy, or "post" as we call it in the business. Out of respect, Dr. Andrews asked Dom to put on gloves and a lab coat for the procedure. Paul and I stood a couple of paces back on the other side.

By the time a corpse gets to the autopsy table, it's lost most of its human qualities. By that I mean that most of the emotion is gone for the observer, to be replaced by the exercise of putting the puzzle pieces together. Had I seen Louie Knox dead on his bed with his eyes gouged out, I would certainly have reacted with revulsion and horror. Now I was looking at a piece of evidence—a flabby, naked one. Even the gaping, black eyeless pools in the face assumed a clinical quality. The corpse just lay there, and if you've ever seen a body on an autopsy table, you understand the term *dead weight*.

Dr. Andrews adjusted the microphone into which she'd dictate her narrative, then she began with the standard description: "The body is that of a well-developed, well-nourished white male, sixty-seven inches in length and weighing one hundred seventy-four pounds. The deceased appears to be the stated age of thirty-six years. The body was in a state of full undress at the time of death. Both eyeballs have been excised from their sockets, but this appears to have been carried out post-mortem. There is a wire ligature around the neck, which has cut through the skin in places. There are no other obvious external wounds. External genitalia are unremarkable. I will begin by removing the ligature." She turned and picked up the Polaroid camera from the countertop and offered it to Dominic. "Would you do the honors, Dr. Sanchez?"

"Of course." He shot one photo of the neck, then another as Andrews snipped off the wire garrote and inserted it into a plastic evidence bag.

She then moved the head to hyperextend the neck, picked up a scalpel and pierced the tissue right below the center of the chin. "As the cause of death appears to be ligature strangulation, we will dispense with the usual Y-shaped incision and instead make a single, anterior midline cut, followed by a layerwise dissection so as to best appreciate the condition of the neck structures, including the laryngeal cartilages and hyoid bone."

"Very good," Dominic whispered proudly to his former pupil. She smiled back at him before continuing, delicately retracting the skin on either side of the slit she'd just cut.

"Could you stabilize the head a little?" she asked.

Dominic put down the camera, secured both sides of the jaw with his hands and pulled evenly to bring the neck into alignment. The corpse's left hand flopped over with the palm resting upward.

"Hold it just a minute!" I said.

The other three live participants turned to me. "Is anything wrong?" asked Andrews.

"No. Well, I'm . . . Look at the wrist. Dom, could you . . . ?"

Dominic took Knox's hand and held it up. "That's right. See there?" I said.

There was a tattoo on Knox's left wrist. It was all in one color—green—a complex design for something that small: a circle with sort of a Maltese cross flanked by a sword on one side and a quiver of arrows on the other, and a broken chain running diagonally from lower left to upper right. I'd missed it in the crime-scene photos since it had been covered by the Rolex.

"Could we get a picture of that?" I asked.

"Sure," said Dom.

I turned to Paul. "Ever seen that design?" He shook his head no.

It was like a new and unexpected turn in a mystery story, and like every clue, it opened up a new horizon of possibilities.

○

When I got to the suite at the Waldorf, Trevor still seemed to be sleeping; a regular rhythm of heavy breathing emanated from one of the two bedrooms. Since he always prided himself on his survival skills, this struck me as a good opportunity to test one of my people.

I stepped toward the bedroom, and when the regular breathing continued, I continued my approach. He must have been beat. He hadn't even bothered removing the bedspread. Then I lunged, going for Trevor's neck with both hands.

I'm not exactly sure what happened in the next second or so, but I suddenly found myself with my right arm behind my back in a hammerlock, staring down the barrel of a fifteen-shot Colt .45 semiautomatic, specially modified by the Les Baer Company.

"Oh, it's you," Trevor said matter-of-factly as he released the painful hold on my arm and removed the business end of the gun from my face.

"You weren't even sleeping, were you?" I said, trying to rub some circulation back into my right elbow.

He laughed.

"Now that I've got your attention, take a look at this." I removed the Polaroid from my jacket pocket and handed it to him. "It's on Louie Knox's wrist, under the watch."

Trevor stared at it. "It's the insignia of the Knights of Liberation."

"Who the hell are they?"

"A little-known fringe group. In fact, we don't think they even exist any longer."

"Then it's probably irrelevant," I sighed. "I thought maybe we were on to something."

"Maybe we are," Trevor replied. "It's the group Gene Claude Sickenger was in before he joined the Wyoming Defenders."

○

I got permission from Paul Sochaczewski to send Jerry over to Knox's apartment to see if he could collect any trace evidence that might further link Knox to any of the Western militia/survivalist groups. I didn't tell Paul exactly what I was after, just that I wanted another stab at the traces. The way this case was going down, I wanted to keep as much as I could compartmentalized. Since the NYPD team had already had their go at the place, Paul had no objection.

I went back to the Waldorf and tried to relax. When that didn't work, I decided to work on my expense reports for Mrs. De Vries accounting for what we'd spent so far. This was something I always hated doing in the Bureau, so I thought I'd try to get it out of the way.

It was around nine-thirty and Katie wasn't back yet. I was starting to get concerned. I could page her, but I didn't want her to think I was hovering or didn't trust her, so I decided to give it another half hour. It was a strange sensation; it felt like waiting for Ali to come home from her first party.

Finally Katie returned, and my first instinct was to scold her for making me worry. Was I projecting the daughter I couldn't hold and be with now, I mused, or was something else going on? I shouldn't say anything to her, I decided.

There was a triumphant look in her eyes as I opened the suite's door for her. I recognized the expression. It was the taste of blood, the indication of a successful hunt.

I ordered up room service and the five of us sat around the ornate dining room table, illuminated by a cut-glass chandelier.

"This Knox has cut quite a swath," Katie related. "I started out at One Police Plaza—Paul was great about smoothing the way. Knox's local rap sheet isn't particularly interesting—some shoplifting as a teen, then a couple of B and E's, some retailing of coke and pot, bippety-bop. Minor jail time. But then I went over to the FBI field office. And we've got him—" She stopped herself. "I guess it isn't *we* anymore, is it? Anyway, the Bureau has him altering passports and creating phony IDs, and I don't think they were for underage kids wanting to drink. There's also a note in the file of Secret Service liaison, so I get someone over there to access their records, and lo and behold, he's suspected of passing bad money."

"Any convictions?" Trevor asked.

"No. And they were never able to discover a printing plant." Finding the physical source of the counterfeit money is always the final step of a Secret Service investigation. Without that, no counterfeiting case is ever closed.

"Any military service?" I asked. Something about this guy told me he would have.

"He was in a photographic unit in the army. Got a general discharge after a little more than a year. That's like not honorable but not dishonorable, right?"

"Right," said Trevor. "He probably stayed in just long enough to learn what he wanted."

"Or else he met someone who could advance his career faster than Uncle Sam," I said.

"Is he the type who could have blackmailed or killed Boyd?" That from Jerry.

"He could fit the profile from what Katie's found out about his background," I said. "He could certainly have a grudge against the director of the FBI. But I doubt whether a guy like this could get close enough to him to blackmail him. Still, we've got a larger issue here. We can't build a case unless and until we know for sure what happened to the director. We can't even assimilate this Knox development until we make that determination."

I glanced around the room until my eyes fell on Dominic. "Can you do anything for me?"

"Not without looking at the body."

"If you'd been able to examine it in the first place?"

"I think there's more than a reasonably good chance I could." The statement was made with quiet confidence, but without any intellectual arrogance or bravado.

"What about now?"

"It would be more difficult, but I think to a trained observer such as myself, certain elements might make themselves clear."

"So you're telling me that if you could examine the body, even at this stage, you could tell if it was a suicide or homicide?"

"Nothing in medicine is guaranteed," Dom said, "even among the dead. But yes, I think there's a good chance."

I considered the implications of what I was about to authorize. "That being the case, that's what we've got to do."

"So what's next, O fearless leader?" Katie asked. "We staying here tonight?"

"No, we've done what we can at this end. It's time for the Mindhunters to fly again."

24

Instead of going right to the plane, I had the New York cops take us to the Hertz rental counter. I couldn't be sure we'd be able to get vehicular transportation where we were going, so I figured we'd better secure our own and take it with us. Mrs. De Vries would just have to eat the hefty drop-off charges, since I had no intention of taking the trouble to return it to JFK. I asked for a full-size Ford Crown Victoria because we could all squeeze into it, it could pass as an unmarked police car at a casual glance (we had a Kojak light for the top to make the illusion convincing), and I needed something with a really big trunk. I took out the full insurance.

It was nearly midnight by the time we got back to *The Broken Wing*, dropped the tail ramp, loaded the car, secured it to the cargo floor, and prepared for takeoff. Scott assured me that he and Trish were well rested and ready to fly. In this kind of assignment, you always assume you're going somewhere else at a moment's notice and so you take your rest when and where you can.

Trish had computed the flying time to San Francisco at about six hours, which would give the team some time to sleep in the tail-section bunks. All except Jerry, that is, who was too nervous to sleep, so I got him set up in the lab analyzing the samples he'd collected at the Knox scene.

Once we were airborne and the ABRÓCHENSE LOS CINTURÓNES sign went out, Katie announced she was going back to change into her comfy clothes and minister to J. Edgar. Meanwhile, I retrieved the best

BROKEN WINGS • 163

booze from the galley, then got Trevor and Dominic together in the main cabin.

As soon as my eyes met Dominic's, I realized my gaffe. His career had been ruined by alcohol, and I was putting it right in front of him.

"Don't worry," he said with a wave of his hand when he saw my discomfort. "I can be around it. No problem." Then, before I could protest that I'd put it away, he changed the subject with, "Is the purpose of this trip what I think it is?"

"And that would be?"

"To exhume Thomas Boyd's body for my perusal."

I gave him an expression that said, *What a good idea!*

"How do you plan to get away with this, if I might be so bold?"

"We have a couple of old sayings in the FBI," I replied. "One is that 'It is far better to ask forgiveness than permission.' The other is that 'Nothing succeeds like success.' If it doesn't work, or we don't get what we want, no one's going to know. The grave is still freshly dug. There won't be a lot of grass growing yet. Right, Trevor?"

"Sounds reasonable," he allowed.

"So what do you think?"

"If that's the mission, we'll do it."

"Do we have the equipment we need?"

"We can put something together," he assured me.

I made my way up to the cockpit with a computer printout from the set of national ordnance maps on CD and pointed out to Scott where the cemetery was. "I'd like to land as close as we can."

Scott studied the map. "There's a small landing strip we can use about five or six miles away. I'll just have to make sure we can get fuel. Or I can deadhead the bird out to someplace we can while you're working tomorrow."

"Good enough," I said. Things felt as if they were coming together.

Before heading for the bunks myself, I stopped in the lab to see how Jerry was making out.

"This is very interesting," he said. "There were only two sets of shoes in the apartment: a pair of waffle-soled work shoes and a pair of old sneakers. There wasn't anything significant on the sneakers, but take a look at this." He placed a slide under the microscope.

It didn't mean much to me, so I looked to Jerry for interpretation. "Dirt," he informed me.

"Dirt?"

"Right. But the cool thing is where it comes from."

"And that would be?"

"Not from New York or the surrounding area. We have numbers and codes we use to classify soils. This residue from Knox's shoes is a Western soil."

"Say, from Wyoming or Idaho?"

"Could be. Idaho more likely than Wyoming, but, yeah, either one. If I had the right reference materials, I could narrow it down even further."

"How do you know all this stuff about dirt?"

He beamed. "You're not the only trained professional."

"You're right," I replied. "I won't try this at home."

○

After landing, Katie, Trevor, and I drove to Flint Hill Cemetery, situated across the Marin Peninsula from Sausalito, near Muir Woods National Monument and Mount Tamalpais State Park. If you have to choose one place to have your mortal remains spend eternity, this is as good a spot as I can think of.

The cemetery was secluded by hills on one side and tall trees on the other, and it was as lovely as the surrounding countryside. Like season tickets to Washington Redskins football games, all the spots were already spoken for. And like the tickets, if you hadn't gotten your reservation in decades ago, you were out of luck. The reason Thomas Boyd was buried here, according to Katie's research, was because Madeline's family had owned a plot for generations.

It didn't take long to find the grave. We parked in front of the caretaker's cottage and told him an approximation of the truth: that we were FBI agents and wanted to pay our respects. He led us down a tree-lined path, around a small lake with a tiny island in the center, and over to a bluff that was dotted with gravestones. As the eye traveled down to flat land again, he indicated Boyd's final resting place. There was no gravestone yet, and as I'd hoped, the earth still appeared freshly turned.

"I'll leave you to your contemplation," the caretaker said. "I'll be here all day, till about four-thirty or five, if you need anything."

We thanked him and lingered in front of the grave until he was out of sight. A peaceful area, this little valley was hemmed in by wooded hills on either side.

"Okay, what do you think?" I asked Trevor.

"We can't get the car any closer than where we're parked, so we'll have to dig him up, open the coffin, put him in a body bag, and carry him back. That's a long way to hump a body. Maybe we ought to take Scott with us."

"No, it's not fair to involve him if this blows up," I said. "We agreed to the risks, he didn't."

"Then we'll need both Dominic and Jerry."

"Are we going to just leave the grave dug up while we've got him out of it?" Katie asked.

"No choice," Trevor concluded. "It would take too much time to fill it in and then dig it up again if we're going to have him back in the ground before sunrise."

"Think we can do it?"

"We have to," I said. I tried to suppress a sense of urgency, of barely suppressed hysteria. Without that body, we had nothing certain. With it, we had a chance to know what no one else could.

When we got back to *The Broken Wing*, I advised everyone to get some sleep, because it was going to be a long night. Dominic took it in stride when I informed him he'd be serving as both a ditchdigger and corpse carrier. Jerry, not surprisingly, was not as keen.

In the afternoon, Trevor drove to the nearest Home Depot to buy whatever equipment he didn't have on board: four shovels, rope, and some tools to get the casket open if it offered resistance. Body bags and other such esoterica we already had. He spent the evening hours in the cargo bay, staging the equipment we'd need and then loading it into the trunk of the car. It was a pretty tight fit. At eleven-thirty, when it was as dark as it was going to get, we Mindhunters embarked on our newly found occupation as grave robbers.

Trevor drove. We were all wearing dark clothing. He cut the head-lights before we got to the caretaker's cottage, which was now complete-ly dark. Good so far. He positioned the car out of sight on the grass on the side of the structure.

"Okay, you three wait here," he instructed. "Jake and I are going to surveil the site. If it's clear, I'll come back and lead the rest of you in with the equipment while Jake maintains a visual fix."

I'm sure I'm revealing no trade secret when I point out that a ceme-tery takes on an entirely different atmosphere at night. And even those of us used to dealing with dead bodies get the creeps, at least I do.

I was glad Trevor was with me, and I wasn't particularly relishing the time I'd have to keep watch while he went back for the others. We were wearing night-vision goggles, which were perfectly natural to Trevor, but for me cast everything into a disorienting, hazy, greenish yellow glow.

Once we got past the lake, we turned off the course we'd followed in the morning and began working our way up the side of a hill through some dense trees. Trevor was wearing combat boots, but all I had were sneakers; I hadn't thought of buying anything heavier when I had the chance during the day. With every couple of steps, I felt a rock or twig trying to pierce through the sole.

We moved agonizingly slowly, the way Trevor was trained. When I tried to hurry him along, he harshly whispered, "If one of us falls and twists an ankle, or someone happens to spot us, we're dead meat."

Finally, after some twenty minutes, we found ourselves on the crest of the hill. Trevor paced between the trees until he finally found a lookout spot he liked. He set down his pack, removed his goggles, then peered through an infrared scope until he could pick out the grave site. I watched as he moved the scope in ever-increasing circles until he'd taken in the entire area where we'd be operating. It was fascinating how smoothly and methodically he worked. I was mesmerized.

"Fuck!" he exclaimed.

This is not the kind of thing you want to hear at a time like this. "What is it?"

"We're not alone."

"Who the hell else would be here?"

"I don't know, but look." He aimed the scope for me.

Indeed, three figures in black SWAT clothing were camped out on the opposite ridge from us with an equally good view onto the grave.

"Cops."

And what they were doing there, I was equally sure, was surveilling the grave in case the UNSUB—be he killer or blackmailer—came back to unburden his conscience or otherwise communicate with the departed. It wasn't a common tactic, but it wasn't unique, either. Some of the more sophisticated departments used it with impressive effectiveness. I knew, because the tactic had originated from our prison interviews with serial killers. I'd been the one who came up with it.

25

"What do we do now?" Jerry asked once we were reassembled back at the car. I think he was the only one relieved that our plan had gone bust. I had to figure out something; this was our one shot.

I decided we should repair to accommodations more comfortable than the bunks in *The Broken Wing*. But not too much more comfortable—I didn't want us to get soft or call undue attention to ourselves. So we all checked in to the Motel 6 in Larkspur. Nothing too obvious about five unrelated adults checking in at four-thirty in the morning. True to their word, they kept the light on for us.

I was keyed up and couldn't sleep. I thought about calling Toni to see how the kids were, but I knew she would ask me where I was and what I was doing, and I knew I wouldn't be able to lie to her and didn't want to lay that burden of worry on her. I waited until it was morning on the East Coast and then I called Peter in his office at Quantico.

"How, and where, the hell are you?" he said.

"On the coast, trying to tie up some loose ends."

"Anything I can set up for you?"

"Not at this point." I couldn't tell him what we were doing, particularly after he'd responsibly warned me off during our meeting. I'd told him about the Knox discovery, but that for the moment we weren't going to share it formally with the FBI. This way, I'd have a way of testing Peter's loyalty—whether it was stronger to the Bureau or to our relationship. "Is the Bureau making any progress?" I asked.

"They've begun a comprehensive review of all potentially threatening correspondence to Boyd in the last two years, they're going over all the internal personnel records, they've filed about a million FD-302s, and so on and so forth. That answer your question?"

"I'm afraid it does. What about in the unit?"

"In the event there's a local element to the case, I've been advising California State Police and Marin County Sheriff's Office on some proactive techniques."

My fears had been confirmed. I knew just where this was leading. "Would they happen to include surveilling the grave site?"

"Yeah," he said almost defensively. "I figured it was worth a try. Is there a problem?" There was an awkward pause. "Jake, you weren't serious about digging him up, were you?"

"No, of course not."

"Though I don't know how much longer they'll be willing to put up the manpower if there aren't any results. In this case, it was a long shot anyway for anything to come of it."

Except screwing us up, I thought. But I couldn't tell Peter to have the surveillance pulled. After all, he was a federal law enforcement officer and I couldn't get him involved with interfering with an investigation, much less abetting a grave robbery.

"Have you made any more progress on the guy in New York?" he asked.

I told him about the soil residue that Jerry had traced to the West.

He digested the information. "Boyd didn't kill himself, did he?"

"I'm trying to figure that out even as we speak," I said. *And if I can't, I don't see how I'm going to be able to move on with my life, but that isn't your problem.*

"I can tell you, the prevailing feeling around here is that he did, but I don't believe it."

"If I find out, Pete, you'll be the first to know." *But how I'm hoping to find out, the less you know at this point, the better for both of us.*

Late morning, I got together with Trevor in his room and laid out the dilemma. "I've done enough grave-site surveillances to know that it's only a matter of time before the cops get tired of nothing happening, and they'll pull off the detail. Do we wait it out?"

Trevor was stretched out on the bed with his hands behind his head, as if there were no point expending physical energy until it was actually needed. I've noticed this trait a lot in tactical types. "The longer we go, the riskier it gets."

"I know. But what are our alternatives?"

"I could shoot them for you," he offered casually.

I was starting to feel that desperate. "But eventually you wouldn't feel good about yourself. I was kind of thinking of something a little less drastic. Couldn't we set up some kind of diversion?"

"We need them out of the way for quite a while. No matter how good our diversion was, we couldn't count on it for more than a few minutes. We need to figure out a way to neutralize them for as long as it takes us to do what we have to do. And that includes removing the body to the plane, examining it, then getting it back in the ground again."

"What about just putting them to sleep?" I suggested.

Trevor grinned. "Now why didn't I think of that?"

Within a couple of minutes I had Dominic and Jerry in on the meeting. "What about it?" I asked. "Trev says he can hit both of them from over a hundred yards with darts he has in his ammo kit if you can rig up the tranquilizing agent."

The two scientists looked at each other. "Something like MD99 or ketamine, a dissociative anesthetic that works on big game should do the trick," Jerry offered. "It's primarily a question of titrating dosage to relative body weight between the animals and the, uh, targets here."

"I'm not an anesthesiologist," said Dominic, "but I should think the safest way to do it . . . I assume you're interested in the safety of the subjects?"

I nodded. "Yes, of course. Has to be safe."

"Then I think we'd be wisest to use as small a dosage as possible just to bring them down and put them out, and then to inject them intramuscularly little by little."

"I agree," Jerry said, then turned to me. "Is this legal?"

"No, but it's for a good cause," I deadpanned. "So you guys can get what we need?"

"I believe so," said Dominic. "We'll just have to go to a veterinary-medicine supply house with some story." A smile crossed his narrow lips. "Then I think we can spruce it up with some things we've got on board."

I slapped my knees and rose. "Good, then. Same mission tonight, same time, but with a new twist."

○

I didn't want to be seen by the cemetery caretaker, so we didn't go back to reconnoiter, which would have made me feel more secure. But

Trevor and I did take a drive around the perimeter to see if we could figure out where the cop surveillance team kept its wheels. Sure enough, we
came upon a service road on the other side of the cemetery property.
This was actually good for us because it meant they had a fixed routine
and wouldn't likely stumble upon our car. Meanwhile, Dominic and
Jerry secured the drugs they needed for Trevor's darts.

Before we ventured out for the night's mission, Katie and I had a private dinner at a McDonald's close to the motel. Don't say I don't treat
my loyal troops to the best. The problem here, as in many places, is that
even something as simple and American as this fast-food restaurant can
dredge up chilling associations. At Quantico, I did postoffense analysis
on James Huberty, the guy who walked into the McDonald's down the
street from his home in San Ysidro, California, one July afternoon in
1984. Before his body was dragged out by SWAT team members a couple of hours later, twenty-one men, women, and children were dead and
another nineteen were injured. So I'm sure you can appreciate how every
time I take my kids to a fast-food place, I never fully relax, keeping one
eye on them and the other on the doors.

Katie broke my thought. "Are you sure you want to go through with
this?"

"I think we've got to."

"What if we're caught?"

"I'm hoping Ravan the Raven would bail us out."

"But there's no assurance of that."

"There isn't."

"Then let me ask you the question you always posed at our case consultations: Why?"

I wiped a glob of the Big Mac's special sauce from my lip. "I've been
thinking about it. What it comes down to is, for all our bitching and
griping about the Bureau, we all bought into the whole fidelity-bravery-
integrity thing, or we wouldn't have invested so much of ourselves in it.
And until the death of the director is resolved, the most important law
enforcement agency in the world is called into question. This is too vital
not to give it everything we've got. I almost feel like Bogart at the end of
Casablanca."

She looked at me skeptically.

"You know," I said, trying to curl my lip into the trademark sneer, " 'I'm
no good at being noble, but it doesn't take much to see that the problems of
three little people don't amount to a hill of beans in this crazy world.' "

She dipped a fry into the little ketchup cup as if she were stirring a cauldron. God she was beautiful, even doing something as simple as eating a French fry. "Jake, you didn't even like the guy."

"John Weisman once told me that Commander Roy Boehm, the guy who created the navy SEALs, said to President Kennedy, 'Sir, I didn't vote for you, but I'd die for you.' Am I making any sense?"

"Some."

"If our careers and everything we worked for in the unit are going to mean anything, this is where we're going to have to take our stand." I paused and took inventory of her expressive face. "Still making sense?"

She swallowed the fry in her mouth, leaned across the small table, and kissed me on the mouth. At that moment, I knew the taste of ketchup would take on a whole new association for me.

∘

Once it was dark enough, we followed the same mustering procedure and drove to the same staging area near the caretaker's cottage. Again, Trevor and I took the forward patrol, only this time he had one of his sniper rifles slung over his shoulder and an ammo pack attached to his belt. We achieved the same vantage point, at which time Trevor handed me his night-vision goggles and I traded him the infrared scope. He scanned across the little valley to locate our human prey. I was still having doubts that we could effectively neutralize two or three police officers without killing them, but I tried to suppress those doubts. We were committed now and doubt was a luxury I couldn't afford.

I'd considered leaving evidence at the scene to make it look as if science students from either Stanford or Berkeley had neutralized the cops as a prank. But our rule in the unit always was that the more behavior we see, the more evidence we had to work with. If the cops happened to think of consulting someone good, such as Peter Sutherland, he might just be able to figure it out. And that would be—how shall I say?—most embarrassing. So I just hoped that when they woke up, the sentries would be too confused to figure out what had happened. If we were lucky, no one would order tox screens, since Dominic's little drug cocktail included not only MD99, but also Rohipnol, which has been much abused in date rapes, but which would work for us in clouding the memory of the recipients.

Looking through the scope, Trevor finally whispered, "I don't see them."

"Maybe they've given up," I suggested hopefully.

"Maybe," he replied, unconvinced. He handed me the scope. "Here, you take a look. Make sure I'm not missing anything."

I took the scope and tried to imitate the circular observation pattern I'd seen him follow. Nothing.

"They're not here," I declared.

"I guess you're right." I could tell he didn't like it.

"Excuse me," I said, "but that's good, isn't it? This is what we call a positive development."

"Not necessarily." Where Trevor was trained, they not only study Sun Tzu on the art of war and analyze von Clausewitz on strategy, they also meditate upon Murphy on fuckups and take seriously his adage that anything that can go wrong will, and at the worst possible time. "This means we've got to carry out our mission *as if* those guys could come up on us at any moment," he explained. "That's gonna take a lot of effort and energy."

He still wanted me to maintain my forward observation position while he went back and brought the others and the equipment to the grave site, where I was then to join them. "Good luck," he said, clapping me on the shoulder. I watched him disappear into the thicket.

I didn't realize how shallow and nervous my breathing was until I finally spotted the others assembling at the grave and I took my first deep breath in twenty minutes and almost choked myself. I just hoped I remembered the route back down without Trevor to guide me.

I got there okay and was relieved to see that the earth on top of the grave still appeared freshly dug. We could get the casket out of the ground and then back in again without the site giving us away.

"All right," Trevor directed, "one person has to keep watch at all times, alternating between eyes and the scope. Dominic, you start, then we'll switch off to Jerry, then Katie. The rest of us will dig—two at a time for twenty minutes, then the other two."

"Why don't we all four dig at once?" asked Jerry. "It'd be a lot faster that way."

"We'd get in each other's way," Trevor responded. "And you four brainy, analytical types have no idea how hard it is to dig a hole—we've got to go down six feet." He was already turning over dirt with his own shovel. "Maybe Mao was right about sending the intellectuals into the rice fields."

The dirt was not yet compacted in the grave. If it had been, I knew, we'd have no chance of reaching the casket, removing it, analyzing it and returning it to the ground, freshly recovered, by morning. Still, ditchdigging is friggin' hard work, especially in the dark, especially when you're tired, especially when you're tense and on edge. After roughly an hour and a half of feverish work, we were down to the five-foot level, with Katie and me on the latest shift. About every ten minutes Trevor would demand of whoever was on watch whether he'd seen or heard anything. I wasn't surprised that the surveillance had been lifted, but it could have been a trick, so none of us relaxed, if that's the word. We all became so focused on the task that we almost forgot we were in a cemetery in the middle of the night.

Trevor offered Katie his powerful forearm and lifted her out of the ditch. Her face was smudged with dirt and dripping with sweat, but she hadn't uttered a peep of protest. Neither had Jerry.

Trevor jumped into the hole himself and shone his flashlight. "Should be any time now."

He'd rigged up a piece of canvas—attached to a rope—that lay flat on the ground, could be piled with dirt, and would then close up like a sack when hoisted from above. It proved to be an efficient way of removing fill from the ditch. But it seemed as if no matter how many of those sacks we filled and hoisted up, we weren't getting to the casket.

"Keep digging," Trevor ordered.

About five minutes later he put his hand on my shovel. "Stop for a minute."

"What is it?"

He didn't reply, but knelt down to the ditch floor, shone his light close to the surface, and clawed the earth with his hand. "Fuck!"

"What is it?" I repeated, my heart sinking fast.

He took my hand and pressed it down to the floor. "Feel where I put your hand. Try to grab some dirt with your fingers." I did as I was told. "Feels different, doesn't it?"

"Yeah," I said, and suddenly the implication hit me.

"From this point down, the earth hasn't been disturbed. This is as far down as the grave was dug. The coffin isn't here. Someone's beaten us to it!"

26

Okay, so Mr. Murphy was right. Expect the unexpected. But who—other than us—would want to dig up the director's body?

If another law enforcement official had gotten the same idea we had, vis-a-vis trying to determine the manner of death, then that would be known. And I could get the answer if I knew whom, and how, to ask. If, on the other hand, there were another set of grave robbers, with intentions even more nefarious than ours, then that would most likely not be known. And I was damned if I could figure out how to tell someone in authority that we'd discovered the empty grave.

Could Peter Sutherland have taken it upon himself to have an official exhumation conducted? It wouldn't be the first time we'd done something like that. Our recommendation that the body of a murder victim in Ohio be exhumed and examined had led to the arrest of her killer. But why wouldn't Peter have told me?

We got back to the Motel 6 earlier than we'd planned—there would still be several hours of darkness—and I suspect we tested the limits of the establishment's water heaters, all of us wanting to scrub away the caked-on graveyard dirt that represented our second night in a row of frustration. I hoped the troops weren't starting to lose faith in my leadership.

Once again, I waited until I could call the East Coast, only this time I figured I'd pressed my luck about as far as I could with Peter. I decided to call Orlando Ravan directly. It was time I reported in, anyway. I sat on the side of the bed in my T-shirt and shorts while I dialed the secure connection.

"Where are you?" he asked.

"California." No use lying when I didn't have to. I gave him a set of action reports that sounded good, but in effect, told him nothing. That was one of the great legacies of the Hoover days: the FBI had come up with all sorts of ways of marking progress against the war on crime while no progress was being made. This sleight of hand was later pulled off in Vietnam.

"Has there been anything more than I've seen on postmortem examination or tox reports?" I asked.

"No, and there isn't going to be anything, either."

What the hell was he talking about? Was he pulling me off the case? "With respect, Mr. Ravan, I'm concerned that if those reports remain incomplete, then whatever we come up with, the public isn't going to trust what you tell them."

"I agree with you, but I'm afraid it's out of my hands."

"Again, I don't mean to tell you how to do your job, but what about a court order to have the body disinterred? Unfortunately, the embalming will have precluded achieving some of the answers, but a full physical examination could still—"

He cut me off. "Believe me, I hear what you're saying, but that's all water under the bridge."

"I don't understand."

"Judge Boyd's body is being cremated."

"Cremated! I thought that sort of thing goes against their beliefs."

"It may go against *hers*," Ravan replied, "but apparently not *his*, according to the will."

"But . . ."

"When Judge Boyd died, his lawyer was mountain climbing in Nepal or something. He was the only one who had access to the will."

"I remember."

"Turns out, Judge Boyd didn't want to be buried in Madeline's family's plot. Turns out he didn't want to be buried at all. He wanted his ashes scattered at the Golden Gate, and Madeline respects those wishes enough to do it that way."

Okay, Peter, I thought, *you're off the hook.* "Ah . . . when is this going to happen?"

"This afternoon, I understand."

Mr. Murphy, leave me the fuck alone. "So they, uh, dug him up?"

"Yesterday morning, I think. Brought the body to a crematorium nearby."

That explained why the dirt was so easy to dig. And why California's finest were no longer there to greet us. "Has the cremation taken place yet?" My heart was in my mouth.

"You've got me. But forget about the court order. Madeline would be against it, and there's no institutional will here to go against her. It would be a PR mess."

"Okay, well, thanks. I'll keep in touch."

As soon as I hung up, I called each of the others, telling them to come to my room in five minutes. A more bedraggled bunch you'd be hard put to assemble. I think each of them had been asleep when I called.

"We have to make some quick decisions," I announced. "I hope it's not already too late." I filled them in on my conversation with Ravan.

"If we proceed further in this, I don't see how we can avoid direct confrontation," I said.

"What happens if we don't proceed?" asked Dominic.

"Then we're pretty much back where we started."

"And this'll be like the Kennedy assassination," Katie offered. "No one will ever know for sure what happened."

"I'm in," Dom declared.

"You know I'm in," said Trevor.

"Me, too," said Katie. "I think we've got to get the information, regardless of the risk."

The four of us turned to Jerry. "Oh, what the hell!" he announced. "How much worse can it get?"

"We'll soon find out," said Trevor dryly.

∘

We'd faced just about everything else in this investigation. Now we had to deal with one of the most formidable adversaries of all—coincidence. I can't tell you how many cases have been thwarted or gone off in entirely wrong directions either because a random, unrelated fact looked significant and got misinterpreted, or because something capricious and unpredictable just happened to neutralize a piece of well-planned proactive strategy. A rape-murder I consulted on in Brooklyn was thrown off course for months when police insisted my profile was wrong about the race of the UNSUB. I said it was a white male, while forensic findings indicated a black, based on a negroid pubic hair found in the victim's genital region. It turned out, after much digging, that she'd been transported to the morgue in a body bag that had previously been used for a black gunshot victim and had not been sufficiently cleaned. Then in the case of the Cincinnati Child Murders, I was convinced we could get the UNSUB to show up when we advertised the hiring of security guards for a citywide memorial concert. But nothing came of it and I took a lot of shit from the Cincinnati PD. When we finally did catch the killer, it turned out he'd been on the way to the hiring interviews but had gotten stuck in traffic.

There was no time for planning; we'd have to improvise as we went along. We raced back to *The Broken Wing* to pick up the gear we thought we'd need. Katie grabbed the phone book from my room and tracked down the local crematorium as we drove. Fortunately, there was only one, Starr Funeral and Cremation Services.

By the time we reached the plane, we each knew what we had to do. Katie was the fastest typist, so I had her crank out on the computer the document I hoped would seem to legitimize us. We turned around and raced back toward our target, which was due north in an industrial section of San Rafael. The success or failure of the mission, I knew, would hinge on our ability to make whomever we encountered cooperate without too much questioning.

I hadn't done anything like this since my younger days, when I was on the Detroit Field Office's SWAT team. And the emotional sensation was just the way I recalled it—all senses on alert and the continually prodding thought, *God, I hope we get there in time.*

I decided to put everyone in blue nylon FBI parkas and ball caps. Since we didn't have credentials, that would convey some sense of legitimacy.

Starr Funeral and Cremation Services was in a warehouse park that it shared with an automobile painting-and-body-repair business, a restaurant-equipment supplier, and a carpet wholesaler. Once inside the park, you had to take three turns to get to Starr, which was fine with me. I could just imagine the rental agent: "Tell you what, let's not put the crematorium out front."

We parked the Crown Vic on one side of the loading door. I'd decided that a large show of initial force and resolve was probably the best strategy, so I told everyone to come in with me. I hoped someone might think there were a lot more where these five had come from.

Inside was a small office manned by a gum-chewing woman in her early twenties, with about fifteen earrings in one ear and five or six in the other. Her short hair was purple streaked with orange, which I did not believe was her natural color. She made a sound signifying a sudden intake of air when she saw us all, looking tough in our blue jackets, and I was afraid she was going to swallow her gum.

"Can I, uh, help you?" she asked. Then, as a quick afterthought, since she'd clearly been well trained, "Are, uh, you all together?"

"Yes," I said quietly in a tone I use for interrogating suspects. "FBI. I'd like to speak to whoever is in charge on the premises. This is a matter of utmost urgency and importance."

"Uh, that'd be Mr. Dalrymple. He's in the, uh, casket room at the moment."

"Will you get him, please."

"Uh, sure. Sure." She looked only too eager to get out of the room and left through a door in the back.

About three minutes later a slightly built man in his fifties, in a black suit and ill-fitting toupee, came through the same door, with an expression on his face that said we'd already upset his day. "Harold Dalrymple," he said. "What can I do for you gentlemen . . . and lady."

"Mr. Dalrymple," I said, taking him by the arm and pulling him aside even though there was no one but us in the room to overhear, "we're from the FBI."

"Ah, yes, I can see that."

"And you are in custody of the mortal remains of former director Thomas Boyd."

"Yes, that's right."

Inwardly, the relief was making me almost giddy. It'd better not show. At least we'd gotten that part right. And we weren't too late. "This is a matter of the highest security and sensitivity." I produced the single-page document Katie had typed up and printed out on the plane. On some FBI letterhead that she'd had at home, it looked like an airtel. Actually, airtels are transmitted on plain paper, but I thought this would look more authentic to an outsider. I held it up for Dalrymple to read, but put it away before he had a chance to ask for it. It gave orders that we were to collect Judge Boyd's body from Starr and that they were to substitute other ashes for them to be scattered over the Golden Gate.

"But why?" Dalrymple spluttered.

"I'm afraid I can't go into that. Suffice it to say that this is related to an extremely important investigation." That part was true.

"Look, I just can't turn over a body that's been given to us to cre-mate," he protested. "This is all highly irregular. I'm going to have to make some calls."

"There isn't time for that," I insisted. "Mr. Dalrymple, I appreciate the awkwardness of this situation, but if you won't cooperate, we're au-thorized by Acting Director Orlando Ravan to use whatever force is re-quired. This has been signed off by the president." If Ravan the Raven had heard me talk like this, he would have had my raganias for break-fast tomorrow.

"It's probably too late anyway," Dalrymple said.

"What do you mean?"

He looked at his watch. "The cremation is scheduled for right now."

Fuck! No! I removed my Smith & Wesson Airweight from its holster and held it up. "I'm sorry to have to do it this way, but take us to Direc-tor Boyd's remains. Now!"

He flinched, as if he expected to be shot.

"Now, Mr. Dalrymple!" I pointed the gun at him. He turned hesitant-ly, still keeping one eye on me, and went back out the door he'd come in through. I followed just behind him, hurrying him along with my gun still drawn. The others came after us.

He led us down a hallway and into a large room with little in it other than a furnace at the far end. I guess you call it a furnace; it seems a lit-tle too grisly to call it an oven. A simple wooden casket was on a wheeled cart that two men, one black and one white, both in blue cover-alls and both in their mid-to-late twenties, were moving toward the fur-nace entrance. The end of the casket was about six inches from the furnace. We had gotten here just in time.

"Gentlemen, stop!" I ordered. They both turned around in surprise. "This is the FBI speaking. Step away from the casket, please."

They looked to Dalrymple for direction.

Trevor stepped forward and aimed his gun. "You heard the man, motherfuckers. Step away!"

They did.

"Now please leave the room, and don't come back until Dalrymple here gives you the all-clear. Understood? This is private government business."

"Yeah, man, understood," said the black one, who muttered as he got the hell out, "I don't get paid near enough to be doing this shit."

"You tell it, brother," the other one agreed.

I waited until they had left and Trevor had closed the door. "Is that him?" Dalrymple nodded. "Check it out!" I directed Dominic.

Trevor removed a hammer and a crowbar from his utility bag and pried open the lid of the casket. Dominic looked in, then he signaled me over.

I took a look. It was Boyd. Like most embalmed bodies, it looked more like a wax figure than the director himself, but not a bad job, all things considered. I forced myself to reach in and feel the neck, just to make sure this was an actual corpse. It was.

"Okay, close it up and wheel it out," I said. I still had my gun out, effectively preventing our host from interfering as the others rolled the casket back out the door. "Mr. Dalrymple, we're officially assuming custody of this body." I wanted to keep him here so he wouldn't see that we were putting it in a trunk.

"Now this part is very important," I emphasized. "You are not to tell anyone the circumstances of this transfer. You are to proceed with the scattering of the ashes as if this never happened."

"But we won't have the ashes!"

"Find some! You must have plenty around a place like this. Or have a company barbecue; I don't give a shit! I assume you know that Mrs. Boyd will be at the scattering ceremony." Another shot in the dark.

"Yes. Yes, of course."

"Are you certain you know the exact time of the ceremony?"

"Yes, of course. Four o'clock this afternoon."

"Good. You are to say nothing about this 'substitution' to anyone, and if you do, or if you give any indication as to what has happened, she will report that information."

"She knows?"

"Of course she knows. Do you think this would be done without her consent?"

"Well, I, I don't know."

"She will go along with the ceremony as if nothing is different. But she'll be observing closely. And if she reports anything negative about your conduct or actions, you're liable for prosecution for impeding the work of a federal law enforcement agency. Is that understood?" He said nothing. "Is that understood?"

"Uh, ah, yes."

"And we'll be surveilling so we'll know. Remember, not a word to anyone. Government security is at stake."

I left the room. By the time I got outside, the rest of the Mindhunters had transferred Boyd's remains into a body bag and wheeled the wooden casket and cart back through the front door. Everyone was wearing gloves, so there would be no fingerprints in case someone decided to try some analysis. Trevor slammed down the trunk lid, and we all piled in and sped back to *The Broken Wing*.

I thought it was best to load the car right up into the plane in case there were any witnesses to our caper. Once we did and Scott lifted the tail ramp back into position, we opened the trunk and carried the body bag into the lab. We lifted it onto the steel dissecting table where Dominic, already gloved and changed into a lab coat, removed the body.

Thomas Boyd was dressed in a dark blue suit, white shirt, and red tie. I wasn't sure, but I thought it was the same suit he was wearing the afternoon of my retirement luncheon. I didn't know if people were routinely cremated in dress-up clothes, or clothes at all, but I suppose this was kind of a special case, since he'd first been buried.

"I guess you can take your time, Doc," commented Trevor. "No hurry getting him back now."

Dominic and Jerry undressed the body, then we all pressed in tight around Dominic as he began the examination. Slowly, meticulously, he began with the feet, seemingly working his way up the legs inch by inch, making sure he missed nothing. He ran his gloved hands along the legs, then palpated the groin and abdomen.

"Nothing so far," he stated. He picked up first one hand and then the other, shining a penlight at each fingertip individually. "No defensive wounds. No petechial hemorrhaging. The postmortem report we read turns out to be accurate so far. But let's move on."

He examined the chest area, then asked Jerry to help him turn the body. "No evidence of drag or grab marks." This was significant because it meant the scene was probably not staged. In other words, where the body was found was most likely where it had fallen after the gunshot. In lieu of any evidence to the contrary, suicide was looking like the right explanation.

"Okay," Dominic said, "let's lay him back down again."

He combed his gloved fingers through the hair, studying them with a magnifying lens as he did so. "Hmm," he uttered. We all leaned in closer.

Come on! Tell me something!

Dominic peered intently at his magnified fingertips. "Tiny shards of glass. Frosted white, very thin, as if they've chipped off of something thicker."

"I think I can account for that," I said. "The force of the body recoil after the gunshot knocked a glass lamp globe off the night table. Some of the fragments landed on the bed."

"And some on the body, too," said Dominic.

"I'd like you to bag those samples," said Jerry.

That took several minutes, while the rest of us waited impatiently. After he thought he had all of them, Dominic positioned the head into a cranial support that hyperextended the neck, giving him good access to the mouth and teeth. He inserted a calibrated bite block between the teeth and twisted the tiny knob until the mouth was held open sufficiently wide. He picked up a retractor and an angled dental mirror as he began probing.

The only sound in the room was the faint scraping of the retractor against tooth enamel, or a click of the mirror against a tooth. Dominic picked up a fiber-optic magnifier and, contorting his body almost sideways, closed one eye and peered intently with the other.

Finally, when the rest of us couldn't hold our breath any longer, he said, "Get the camera. See here? It's very slight and easy to miss, but these front teeth are unquestionably chipped inward."

I knew you'd come up with something! I thought triumphantly.

"So?" said Katie.

"I'll need your handgun to demonstrate what I'm talking about."

Katie removed the bullets from her H&K USP and handed it butt-first to Dom. He moved over to the one chair in the lab and sat on the padded metal arm. "Jake, is this about the height of Boyd's bed?"

"Yeah, about," I confirmed.

Dom checked the chamber and stock again to make sure the weapon was unloaded, then grasped it in both hands and turned it so that it faced him. He inserted it into his open mouth, removing it again to comment.

"Follow me here. If I put this gun in my mouth myself, I'm going to close my lips around it and my upper teeth will rest against the top of the steel barrel. Then, if I willfully pull the trigger, the split second the bullet explodes out of the end of the barrel and into my brain, I'm going to release the tension of my grip, which means the gun is going to recoil, the force of which means it will tend to move backward and upward, away from the point of impact."

He shifted his grip slightly and continued. "But if the gun is being forced into my mouth by someone else, the barrel will still rest against my upper teeth, but the only force that's going to be neutralized as the gun is fired is the force of me trying to push it away from my mouth in defense, which will have the effect of increasing the force of the attacker trying to drive it in."

"So what does this mean in practical terms?" asked Katie.

"That if Boyd pulled the trigger himself, the bottom of his front teeth should be chipped outward, even if only slightly. If the gun was forced into his mouth, however, those same teeth should be chipped inward. And that, in fact, is the case here."

So that was it. An eerie calm descended upon me, as it often did at times like this. Going back to my navy days, it was like the brief quiet time in the eye of the hurricane, before the second onslaught begins. The calm quickly gave way to an almost inexpressible sadness as Dominic declared:

"Thomas Boyd was not holding the gun himself when it went off."

27

From atop the Marin headlands at Fort Baker, Trevor Malone watched through high-powered binoculars as Madeline, Jason Boyd, and a small group of family and close friends stood at the rocky breakwater at Fort Point on the San Francisco side. Together, mother and son opened a small urn and poured what they thought to be Thomas Boyd's ashes into the swirling waters of the bay. Then they turned solemnly and all walked back along the breakwater to the strip of parking spaces and into their cars. Despite what he'd experienced himself under Boyd's tenure at the Bureau, Trevor said he found the ritual strangely affecting. I found myself feeling the same way as he related it.

Our final action before departing the coast was returning the rental car to the nearest Hertz counter. I stood there stone-faced as the counter clerk glanced from the opening mileage number on the contract from the JFK location to the closing mileage figure I recorded. "Ah, sir, there must be some mistake," she pointed out. "The mileage differential is substantially less than the distance from New York to here."

"Life is full of mysteries," I commiserated. "I see it all the time in my business." Then I half-explained, "We didn't drive the whole way. Just send along the statement to the address on the contract." I left before she could interrogate me any further.

Back at the plane, Scott approached. "We're ready to take off, chief. Just one thing I was wondering. What do you want to do with the, uh . . ."

"The body?"

"Right. The, uh, body."

"I think we'll just have to hang on to it until we figure out what to do."

In the main cabin, Jerry was sitting with a clipboard resting on his knee. I glanced over his shoulder; he was completing a pencil sketch of Katie, which he must have begun in New York. She was seated on one of the Empire sofas in Mrs. De Vries's suite. The casual manner in which her arms lay along the back cushion and the graceful, sexy crossing of her endless legs under a short, tight skirt contrasted sharply with the formality of the furniture. She was laughing, as if reacting to something funny, and Jerry had captured her dimples and the impish delight of her expression just right.

Jerry looked up at me. "You like it?"

"I love it. It's Katie to a tee." In addition to his other skills, he really was an accomplished artist.

"It's easy when you know what a person looks like. When someone's trying to describe them, that's a little more of a challenge."

"Well, I think it's terrific."

After an awkward moment, Jerry said, "Would you like it?"

"Yes, very much."

"I'll just put in the finishing touches."

"Thanks, Jerry. Really."

I continued my way toward the back. Just before I reached the bulk-head door he said, "She's a great girl, Jake."

"I've always known that," I answered glibly, but wondered whether he was offering me advice.

In the conference room, Katie was curled up on the couch. I sat on the couch's arm and watched her sleep, still visualizing Jerry's sketch. It was frustrating in a way, because it showed so much about her that I felt but couldn't put into words. Maybe it could only be done with images as Jerry had done. Watching her like this, it reminded me of when I would come home late at night and steal into my kids' rooms and watch them, as I swelled with love, as if by standing sentinel over them, I could keep all potential harm at bay. I was surprised by my re-action. I guess I was so used to seeing her so competent, so efficient, so sexy, that it was strange to see her looking so innocent and sweet and vulnerable.

Before I could fully articulate it to myself, she sensed my presence, as anyone good with a gun will, opening her eyes and smiling contentedly.

Then she reached up and took my hand. I wasn't sure what this affecting gesture was about, maybe just to hold me there.

"How are you doing?" she said softly.

"Okay."

"What can I do for you?"

"Go back to sleep and let me keep watching you."

"That sounds boring," she said with a charming self-deprecation.

"Nothing about you is boring."

"Well, anyway, I'm awake now," she replied sassily, "so what's your second choice?"

"Okay, then, I'd like you to work your magic with the computer, scan your various sources, and see if you can get a home phone number for Richard Royce."

"The militia guy?"

I nodded. "The commandant of the Wyoming Defenders."

"You got it, boss man."

I made my way back up to the cockpit to tell Scott and Trish about a possibly altered flight plan.

I'd been thinking for some time—since I'd seen the wrist tattoo during the post on Louie Knox, to be specific—about how to approach Royce. Though I would not expect to rank exceptionally high on his list of favorite people, I decided the best approach might also be the most direct one.

When I got back to the conference room, Katie had the number. I dialed through. After four rings a male voice came on.

"Mr. Royce?"

"Who is this?" Instantly wary. I was already ready to confirm my profile of this guy as a paranoid asocial.

"Jake Donovan, Mr. Royce."

Dead silence. I took this as a sign I was talking to the guy I wanted.

"Mr. Royce, I'd like to come meet with you."

"What!" As if the very idea were preposterous. "Why should I meet with you?"

"Because if you give me the right answers, you may be able to save yourself and your organization a shitload of hassle."

"Is this about Boyd?"

"Yes, sir, it is. And I can tell you the government is about to come down hard on you. But I may be able to short-circuit that, unless, of course, you want to become a martyr like Mr. Sickenger."

I could tell from his change in breathing that I'd succeeded in getting to him. "Why should I trust you?" he demanded.

No good reason I could think of. So I responded, "Maybe you heard that I've retired from the FBI. It wasn't by my choice. I may be as pissed off as you are. Anyway, I'm not asking you to trust me. I'm asking you to meet me as an adversary in battle for what could be mutually beneficial."

"When do you want to do this?"

"I can be there in a couple of hours," I said casually.

I really liked this idea of having my own plane.

∘

Richard Royce lived on a small ranch outside of Sheridan, in the foothills of the Bighorn Mountains. We arranged to land at a community airstrip nearby, and he said someone would meet me there.

Trevor was nervous about this, and for good reason. "They're probably going to make you go somewhere, unarmed and alone," he predicted.

"Nothing I can do about that."

"No, but I want to keep track of you. I don't want to risk having you wear a wire in case they strip-search you." That was an enticing thought. He held up a tiny metal cylinder. "If you wear this, we'll at least be able to track you."

"You're not going to . . ."

Trevor grinned. "Shove it up your ass? Don't worry. Take off your shirt."

He positioned the tracer in my left armpit and covered it with a small bandage. "Okay, you can put your shirt back on. Even if they search you, they're not likely to notice this."

When we landed, a faded red Dodge pickup was waiting. "Be careful," Katie whispered, and put a concerned hand tenderly on my chest.

Two men in combat fatigues got out and waited for me to come down the stairway. "Mr. Donovan?" one of them said.

"That's right."

"Are you armed?"

"I'm carrying one handgun."

"May I have it, please? It will be returned to you later."

I handed him the Airweight, then the other man patted me down completely. I was grateful to forgo the strip search.

They put me in the pickup's cab between them, then blindfolded me. I felt like telling them I had no real interest in coming back here, anyway, thank you very much, but humor didn't seem to be their strong suit.

I was scared. I was alone and unarmed, a stranger in this strange land, in the company and control of two guys whose East Coast friends had beaten the shit out of me. I represented the enemy, and essentially, I was a prisoner of war. I felt the way I had when I'd gone into maximum-security prisons to interview serial killers and had first had to surrender my gun and sign a waiver of liability for my safety. Part of this waiver was an acknowledgment that if I was taken hostage, the prison would not negotiate for my safe return. But I thought the work I was doing then was important enough to take the risk, and I thought the same thing here.

We bounced along for about twenty minutes. When we stopped, they removed the blindfold and let me out in front of an aging, wooden-frame ranch house.

Richard Royce came out on the porch and looked me over. He was in his mid-to-late fifties, dressed in jeans and a jean jacket, with a hard, weather-beaten body. He didn't extend his hand, but merely turned and silently led me into the house.

We sat in the largest room, where there was a long bunkhouse table. He chose a spot in the middle and indicated for me to sit opposite him. The two militiamen sat at the two ends. I wondered if there was any intended symbolism in that the four of us formed a cross.

I described the beating I'd suffered and told him that some evidence connected the Defenders and other militia/survivalist groups to Thomas Boyd's death, then about the Knights of Liberation tattoo on Louis Knox's wrist. And I told him that if he could give me any reason not to suspect him or his group, then I might be able to short-circuit a full-scale investigation.

"I'm not afraid of the FBI," Royce assured me.

"I understand that, but if you can avoid another incident, why not try? So first of all, was it your people or anyone you know of who attacked me?"

"I didn't order it. Though I cannot say that your attackers were not people who sympathized with our movement. A great many Americans were outraged by what your organization did at Owl Creek, and before that, at Ruby Ridge, at Waco, and so many other stands of patriots. If some of them decided to use the FBI's own tactics against them, well, that is to be expected."

"Just for the record, I was against storming Mr. Sickenger's house."

"That is what I'm given to understand from reports in the media, though since the information came from Attorney General Hewitt, that hardly encourages confidence. Frankly, Mr. Donovan, once you agree to be a combatant, you can hardly expect your adversary to distinguish you from the rest of the enemy's position. I'd say you were fortunate to have escaped with your life. That's more than can be said for Gene."

I leaned forward and met his eyes directly, the way I would while interrogating a murder suspect. "Let's get down to it, then: Did you have anything to do with Thomas Boyd's death?"

Without looking away he said, "Were you in the service, Mr. Donovan?" *Same goddamned question Boyd had asked me.*

"I was in the navy."

"Did you ever see combat?"

"There was no combat to see while I served."

"I was a Green Beret in Vietnam. I killed the enemy whenever I could and they killed us whenever they could. That is the nature of war. And make no mistake, we're in a war even as we speak. We're fighting for our very survival as an independent nation. And if that freedom is to be preserved, it will be because of organizations such as the Wyoming Defenders and the Knights of Liberation."

Our eyes were still locked. "Answer my question, Mr. Royce." His two henchmen made a threatening move toward me, but I held my ground, trying to make my anger override my fear.

Royce leaned back in his chair, crossed his legs, and tented his fingers together. "Thomas Boyd was the equivalent of an enemy general. I respected him as such, and as such he represented a legitimate target. We didn't kill him. But as to whether any of our sympathizers did, that I do not know. Each man is responsible for his own choices, for defending that which he holds dear. Am I sorry to see him dead? No. Gene Sickenger was a personal friend of mine. I admired what he did and what he stood for."

It wasn't what he stood for, it was what he stood against, you self-righteous son of a bitch, I thought to myself. *Blacks, Jews, Catholics, liberals, foreigners, you name it—those were all the things he was against.* But when was the last time I sat across an interrogation table from anyone I liked or approved of. *Accept the fact, Donovan: the two of you would each be much happier if the other suddenly dropped dead.*

"But as I say," Royce continued with icy calm, "neither I, nor anyone with whom I am in contact, had anything to do with this action you describe."

"You Green Beret types kind of specialize in stealth kills, don't you?" I asked.

"That's right. A good Green Beret can steal into an enemy barracks at night, slit the throat of the soldier in every other bed, and then get out before the remaining ones wake up."

"So I guess what you're telling me is that if you killed Judge Boyd, or ordered him killed, we'd never know. It would just look like a suicide."

"Affirmative. But as I told you, I had nothing to do with it."

"But if you did, Mr. Royce, an effective soldier like yourself would deny it and we'd all be none the wiser."

"Also affirmative."

We both realized the interview was over. The two nameless henchmen put the blindfold back on, put me in the truck, and drove me back to where *The Broken Wing* was waiting.

28

When we were airborne, I headed back to the bunks to try to pay back on some of the sleep deprivation I'd been putting myself through, stopping in the lab, where Dominic was organizing his supplies. I pointed to the Mobile-Mort refrigeration unit. "He's gonna be all right in there, isn't he? I mean, you know, keeping him on the plane for the time being?"

"Don't worry, at the morgue we used to keep unclaimed bodies a lot longer than this. The only thing is, we're now fully booked. There's no room at the inn until you cancel this one's reservations."

I assured him I wouldn't be taking on any more such passengers.

I grabbed about two hours of sleep, and when I got up and walked toward the main cabin, I found Katie sitting in the conference room, her legs crossed under her, with the case materials spread out on the table. She was studying something intently with a high-power magnifier light. J. Edgar was sitting on the table next to her, apparently peering just as intently. A bowl of milk and another of some sort of cat-food glop sat on the table nearby.

"If we hit turbulence, that stuff's gonna go all over the place," I warned.

"Then I'll clean it up."

I came around the table to see what she was looking at. It was a duplicate we'd had made of the contact sheet from Louie Knox's apartment in New York.

"Getting excited?"

She glanced up at me. "I can hardly contain myself. Actually, I'm picking out the juiciest ones for you—trying to save you some time."

"She is pretty cute."

"Yeah, well, boys will be boys." She picked up the cat and tickled him under the chin. "Isn't that right, J. Edgar?"

The beast purred in agreement. Katie leaned back in the chair. "I was just thinking back to my new-agents training at Quantico."

"Is there a moral lurking somewhere in here?"

"I remember my profiling class, and the instructor who told us to look around the edges of the photograph to see what was really in it. And I remember that I was the only one in the class who looked beyond the blonde with the big boobs in front of the Christmas tree, to the little foot at the corner of the picture. I remember how proud I was when the instructor praised me in front of that entire class of men, and how from that moment on, my goal in the FBI was to work with him as a profiler in his behavioral unit at Quantico."

"Very touching. What are you getting at?"

"I'm not sure. Maybe I'm way off base on this, but there's something strange about these pictures."

"You mean other than the fact that the family-values director of the FBI is getting down and dirty with someone other than his lawfully wedded wife?"

"Something like that. Come over here and take a close look at the series. Tell me what you see."

I took the magnifier from her and focused on the final strip of the contact sheet, concentrating on finding the hidden Waldo in the picture. But nothing popped out at me, except that when seen in the altogether, the late director was in good physical condition. That didn't surprise me, however. He always wanted to set a good example for the troops.

"I give up," I said. "What am I supposed to be looking at?"

She wriggled in next to me so that we could share the magnifier. This close, she looked and smelled well scrubbed. She took my hand, as if she wanted to lead me down the path beside her. It had become so natural, so comfortable to be with her, yet at the same time I kept thinking . . .

"You're visualizing me naked, aren't you?" Katie said.

"Umm, uh . . . ," I replied cogently.

"You're imagining me in this series of pictures. I can see into men's minds, too, you know."

"You've learned from the best," I said, trying to wriggle off the point of her barb.

"Okay, get a grip. Now, did you notice in a couple of these frames you can see the woman is wearing a wedding ring?"

"I hadn't."

"Men never do."

Sure enough, Boyd's playmate wore a narrow wedding band. It was easy enough to miss in these small black-and-white photos, but I should have picked up on it.

"Don't you think it's odd he'd choose a married woman to do his diddling with?"

"I don't know," I said. "Maybe a little."

"Okay. Maybe not. I just thought it was strange. He's obviously selected a young looker for his fun. Why wouldn't he choose one who was unattached?"

"Maybe it was a 'legitimate' affair with someone he knew well. You know, a real—though extramarital—relationship."

"Fine. Then why haven't we been able to identify her? If he knew her, how come no one, including his wife, has ever seen her?"

"Good point," I said. It was typical of the analytical sophistication she brought to our case consultation meetings, almost as soon as she got to the unit.

"Even if it was a blackmail setup—you know, someone sent in to meet him and seduce him—don't you think whoever did it would figure they had a better chance of success if Boyd didn't think he was doing a married woman?"

"You're right, but I don't know where you're heading with this."

"Okay, then, let's keep going."

"You mean there's more I've missed? You're making me self-conscious."

"Look at her hands. You can see them well in this frame and in this series here."

"Okay. About five fingers on each one. Seems about right to me."

"You're such a man," Katie groaned. "No wonder the Bureau had its head up its ass all those years until it hired women agents. Now come on, look closely."

I squinted through the lens. "Maybe they look a little worn or wrinkled, like she's been doing some physical labor."

"Good for you! Jake gets the gold star. I just wouldn't figure a babe like that to have what my mom's generation used to call dishpan hands."

"That is odd." Katie had uncovered the "corner finding" and I had missed it. I was proud of her. At the same time, I felt a pang of alarm. Was I losing it, or was it just the stress?

"And another thing: look at her shoulders and forearms. Do you see how tanned or sunburned they look?"

I did, at least as much as I could tell from the magnification of this small black-and-white image.

"It doesn't conform to what the profile of a woman like this should be."

"How do you figure that?"

"I might expect her to be tanned all over if she spent a lot of time out in the sun. But she's not. There's no bikini lines. Her whole body is pale except for her shoulders, hands, and forearms. This is all pretty fuzzy, I know, but it just doesn't wash."

I'd worked with Katie long enough to set great store in her hunches. "We'll follow it up," I said. I shifted the contact sheet beneath the magnifier and went back to the beginning of the series.

"Don't tell me you're looking at her with clothes on. You'll ruin your image."

"Very funny. Something about that outfit looks familiar."

"If it does, you've got good taste. That's a St. John's knit she's wearing."

"Looks very familiar."

"Maybe Toni has one."

"I'd remember it," I said. "I'd at least remember the bill."

"Unless she bought it after you split." She stopped, suddenly self-conscious. "I'm sorry. I shouldn't bring up things like that."

"It's okay. You're talking about history."

"Yeah, but it's painful history, I'm sure."

"I'm over it. I think we both are. We're getting to a better place with each other."

"Do you miss her?"

I considered it a moment. "I miss something. I'm not exactly sure what. I miss not having the kids, of course. But it's . . . it's more than that."

"I think I know what you mean," Katie said, taking my hand again and squeezing it gently. "When Rob left, I felt this . . . emptiness. Not that I still loved him, because believe me, I didn't; that drained away immediately. But there was like an emptiness of love . . . a void. That's what hurt so much." Her eyes were misty. "You know. You helped me through it."

"I tried." We stared wordlessly at each other for several seconds. "Keep up the good work," I said, rising.

I left her alone in the conference room and proceeded through to the main cabin, that outfit the woman in the pictures was wearing embedded in my mind.

Trevor was the only other one in the cabin, reading a highbrow gun magazine. He raised his eyes as I sat across from him.

I settled back in the seat, tried to relax, and just stared out the window for a while.

Where the hell had I seen that suit before, and why did it seem so important to me?

There was the issue of Katie's problems with the inconsistencies in the profile of the unknown woman in the photographs.

I sensed Katie was onto something here. I just didn't know what.

I tried to clear my mind by thinking about Ali and Eric. The conversation about Toni was still fresh in my mind. That was the thing that really bothered me, I admitted to myself—Toni taking the children from me. That's the part that made me angry, that still made me angry. Whatever she thought about our relationship, she was a psychologist; she had to know what the separation would do to me.

Stop feeling sorry for yourself, Donovan. What about the kids? As always, they were the ones who bore the burden because two adult professionals couldn't get along.

Twelve-year-old Ali had said it best one night. It was about two months after the split and we were all having dinner together at a TGI Friday's after one of Eric's soccer matches. "You're a behavioral profiler who's always on TV," Ali said to me, then turned to Toni. "And you're a clinical psychologist. You should both be able to figure it out. Do what you have to do to get us all back together!" The tears in her large and winsome blue eyes set off her long shiny brown hair. "I wish I could spank you both and send you to your rooms until you learn how to behave toward each other."

Neither of the two professional parents knew what to say.

I tried to imagine where the kids were this very minute and what they were doing. But they weren't where they were "supposed" to be. Because of me, they'd been shuttled off to Wisconsin. I had no idea what their routine would be, where they'd go, whom they'd be with. It was so hard to envision. God, I missed them. It made me sad to think about.

Then inexplicably, my mind shifted and it hit me.

I bolted up and headed back to the conference room.

Katie looked up in surprise. "Back so soon?" she asked. J. Edgar only screeched.

"Can you pull up some photos on the computer for me?" She and Jerry had scanned all the significant case materials and digitized photos into the computer so we'd have a complete record in one place.

"Sure. What is it you want?"

"The Boyd memorial service. I told Ravan and Neil Burke I wanted pictures taken in case an UNSUB happened to show."

"And you think you know who it is?"

"No, but I want to see the shots."

Katie pressed some buttons, and within a few seconds we were into the memorial-service photo file. "Anything particular you're looking for?"

"Yeah. I want to see if we have anything with Mrs. Boyd."

"Mrs. Boyd?" Katie clicked through image after image. Unlike news photographs, which would have some center of interest—show some action taking place or a notable person speaking—these were mostly random crowd shots. Whenever you do this kind of photography, the hope is always that in analyzing them afterward, you'll notice something, maybe an expression on the face of one of the observers, that will give the perpetrator away. We've found this to be a particularly effective technique for suspected arsons, since the UNSUB firebug often shows up at the scene to admire his handiwork and get off on all of the public resources he's been able to marshal for his own gratification. A couple of times, we've actually spotted a masturbator in the photos—our arsonist. I wasn't expecting anything this overt when I requested the memorial-service pics.

"Wait! Back up," I instructed.

Katie clicked several images back till we came to a scene where everyone was beginning to leave the auditorium. I pointed to the screen. "I think that's her. Can you zoom in and blow up this portion of the picture?"

"Up to a point."

"We shouldn't have to go too far."

She clicked and dragged open a box around the area I'd pointed to and then blew it up so it occupied the entire screen.

"I knew it!" I said. "I *had* seen that suit before. Madeline Boyd was wearing it at the memorial service for her husband!"

Madeline Boyd, who wore a simple, narrow wedding band. Who looked as if she dressed straight out of an L.L. Bean catalog. Who was pretty but took little time with her appearance and spent much of her life out in the sun, causing her hands and shoulders to look "older" and more weathered than other less exposed parts of her body.

"Well, that sure ain't Mrs. Boyd's face on the contact sheet," Katie said.

"No, but I'll bet it's the rest of her." *You hit the bull's eye, Kathleen!* "And if it is, then Tom Boyd was having sex with his own wife in those photographs!"

"So they put someone else's head on Madeline's body." Katie grinned proudly.

"That's my working hypothesis."

"Wow." She shook her head slowly as she scrutinized the photo image. "No matter how hard I look, I don't see any cut line or anything."

"Photo enhancement is so good today that you probably wouldn't. Anyway, we don't even know what generation of photo that contact sheet actually was."

"It's amazing that whoever did this would go to all that effort and then leave us these clues, like an identifiable designer suit."

"Don't forget," I pointed out, "I don't think we were ever meant to see the rest of the series that showed any of those clues that clearly."

"Which means we were meant to see one of them: the one that slipped under the bed?"

"I'm beginning to have my suspicions."

"We've got to be sure we're right about this," Katie said, grabbing the contact-sheet copy off the table. "The outfit could be a coincidence, but I doubt it." She studied the early shots of the woman on the contact sheet, then quickly shifted her attention back to the blowup detail on the computer. "I have to admit it, you do have an eye for fashion."

"Go to the later ones in the series. Now that we know what we're looking for, let's see if we can pick up any other distinguishing characteristics."

We spent the next couple of minutes huddled side by side.

"Okay, here we go," Katie said at last. "Look here on this one. Just at the bottom of her backside."

"Where?"

"As we're looking at her, near the lower outside curve of the left buttock. I think it's a tiny birthmark."

"Sure it's not just a speck on the negative?" I asked.

"No. A speck would be bigger. And you can just about see it in this other image, where she's turning toward Boyd and away from the camera."

"Well, there's only one way to know for sure."

Katie frowned. "Are you serious?"

"Sure. Now the next challenge is figuring out a way to get to see Madeline Boyd naked."

29

"Why don't we just ask her?" Katie said.

"Huh?"

Katie had come forward to where I was sitting in the main cabin and plopped down in the seat across from me. "Why don't we just explain the situation to her, then ask her if she'll discreetly peel for us?"

"I don't think that's such a good idea," I said.

"Even if we tell her it's part of solving her husband's murder case?"

"First of all, if we tell her we're convinced it *is* a murder case, we've got to tell her how we know, and that involves informing her that we've got her husband on ice in the back room while she thinks she's spread him to the winds under the Golden Gate Bridge. And if that piece of information gets out before we've completed our investigation, we're dead meat. This is further compounded if we're wrong. And that is something we won't know with any confidence until we— or more likely, you—are afforded the opportunity to observe the naked posterior in question."

"I see your point," Katie conceded.

"And I don't feel comfortable taking her into our confidence on any of this. Remember, she wouldn't even agree to look at the photo found under the bed. I had to show her a close-up of the other woman's face and imply what was going on."

"Okay." Katie swung her legs over the armrest and dangled them in the aisle. "So the question remains: How're we gonna get her to flash us her derriere? And if you're thinking about a twosome, forget it."

"Let me make a few calls."

I had my strategy pretty well formulated when I walked back to the office/conference room. Now it was a question of seeing whether it had a chance of working. The phone system on the plane allowed me to dial through to anywhere on earth, just as if I'd been sitting in my former office.

I wasn't surprised that Millicent De Vries was home. She always seemed to be at home when I wanted to see or talk to her, almost as if she always knew where I was and what I was doing.

"What can I do for you?" she asked cheerily.

"Are you a member of Chevy Chase Country Club?"

"Yes."

I figured a woman in her position would be. Her late husband would certainly have done business or solidified contacts on those exclusive golf links. "Do you play tennis, Mrs. De Vries?"

"Occasionally."

"How'd you like a tennis partner this week?"

"You?"

"Much as I'd love to, no. Katie McManus."

"I don't think I'd offer her much of a game, but certainly. When do you . . . when does she want to play?"

"You can help us figure that out, too. Let me tell you what I had in mind."

○

Mrs. De Vries came through for us.

Having determined through her sources within the club Madeline Boyd's regular tennis schedule, Millicent and her new tennis opponent, Kathleen, arranged to appear in the women's locker room at the same time as Madeline. Katie had bought new whites for the occasion, figuring it wouldn't do to play in the shorts and T-shirt she normally wore.

I sat in Millicent De Vries's sunroom overlooking her terraced gardens and the densely wooded park beyond. The three of us were drinking white wine as she and Katie regaled me with their exploits. I could see that Mrs. De Vries enjoyed her new work as an undercover operative.

"I staked out the locker room ahead of time," Katie related, "surveilling for when Madeline Boyd came in and selected a locker. As soon as she did, I came down the aisle with my gym bag and selected a locker nearby. I kept glancing out of the corner of my eye hoping to catch a glimpse of the critical area. As expected, she didn't strip down beyond her underwear. But when she was in her bare feet, I managed to get close enough to peg her height in relation to mine."

This would be important in confirming the identity of the woman in the photograph since we'd computed the height from detailed measurements.

"Tell him how I played," Mrs. De Vries prompted.

"Very impressively," said Katie. "But you didn't seem to go much out of your way to return shots."

"It's undignified for a woman of my age to run too fast, even on the tennis court."

"But she really ran my glutes off," Katie added with admiration.

"Thank you, dear," said Mrs. De Vries. "That's very kind."

I waited impatiently for the badinage to stop.

"Madeline was playing with an athletic red-haired woman in her forties."

"Michele Green," Mrs. De Vries elaborated. "She's an editor, married to Sam Green."

"Oh, Sam Green," I said, still waiting for the one part that interested me.

"Anyway, as they finish and leave the court, we leave, too, and follow them into the locker room. I try to time the pace of my own undressing to roughly match Madeline's, so that we'll be ready to go to the showers at the same time. But as soon as Madeline gets down to her undies, she wraps a towel around herself and holds it under her arms while she pulls off her panties."

"I'm always amazed the way women can keep towels in place so effortlessly," I said. *So what fucking happened?* The episode had become fun and games to these two women, but my case was riding on what did, or did not, appear on a third woman's ass.

Kate flashed me a dirty look. "So I strip off my own skivvies, grab a towel, and pad over to the showers. At this point I'm starting to think this isn't going to work out. I even consider barging into Madeline's shower stall, pulling aside the curtain, then profusely apologizing for the 'mistake.' But that seemed pretty obvious, especially with the curtain closed and the sound of water running.

"So I'm down to my last trick. I'm in the adjoining shower stall from Madeline. I soap up and wash myself off as fast as I can so I can be ready as soon as she finishes her own shower. As soon as I hear the water stop and then the curtain pull open, I turn off my own shower and start drying off so I can follow her back to the lockers. I use the towel I'd wrapped myself in to dry my hair.

"Now the next part, we worked out very carefully."

"A surgical strike," Mrs. De Vries said with obvious delight.

"Mrs. De Vries, Millicent, now dressed in her street clothes, comes down the aisle as if she's waiting for me to get dressed. I'm nervously eyeing Mrs. Boyd, who's already reaching for her panties. Once they're on, ball game's over."

"Then I appear to notice Madeline," Mrs. De Vries recited. "She was still wrapped in her towel. 'Madeline, how are you?' I say. We exchange pleasantries and I tell her how sorry I was to hear about Tom. And I was, of course, as you well know. Such a . . . I don't know . . . such a horrible thing. I ask her how she's been holding up and if there is anything I can do for her."

There was something more than ingenuous delight at a social prank. Mrs. De Vries was sounding too slick, too practiced, as if she had experience in special ops. Still sticking with the Miss Havisham image, I had to add another level—Mata Hari, maybe.

"Millicent grabs her by the wrist and pulls her over to meet me," Katie said, taking up the narrative. "Anyway . . . May I have some more wine?"

"Certainly, dear." Mrs. De Vries poured Katie another glass.

"Anyway, Millicent pulls her over, saying, 'I'd like you to meet Katie McManus, who's just retired from the FBI.' I express my condolences and make out like this is a really awkward moment Millicent's gotten us into, which isn't hard since I'm standing there buck naked drying my hair."

"Katie has a lovely figure," said Mrs. De Vries. "And in the process of bringing the two of them together, I just 'happen' to catch the edge of the towel Madeline's wearing with my ring . . ."

A diamond about the size of New Hampshire.

". . . and it momentarily flaps off her hip."

"And that's when I get my peek," Katie announced triumphantly.

"And?" I was getting annoyed with her, the way I did when any of my agents wasted my time or didn't take things seriously.

"Right smack-dab near the bottom of her cheek! The birthmark in the picture. I've never had such an urge to literally kiss someone's ass."

"Fortunately, she was able to restrain herself," Mrs. De Vries added.

o

So we now had some idea of the what and the how. We still needed to learn more about the why and the who. Madeline Boyd was the one in the photograph, and therefore, that would not have been a means of blackmailing him. Why did someone go to so much trouble to set this up? Whoever it was, this wasn't an easy thing to do. Whomever we were looking for was someone with resources, connections, and power.

When I got home, I first called Toni to make sure she and the kids were okay. I talked to each of them. It was difficult; each one asked me when I could come home and when they could see me again. I didn't have an answer, so I could only say, "Soon, I hope. Soon." Eric asked after Katie and wanted me to give her his love. When I told her, I actually saw tears.

I tracked down Paul Sochaczewski at home in Manhattan.

I gave him the sanitized version of what we'd been doing since we'd left New York and how I was convinced that at least some of the important answers lay in the late Louie Knox's photographic collection. "Have you looked through everything he's got?" I asked.

"We've started to," Sochaczewski replied, "but there's thousands, tens of thousands of individual items in there, and it's just my partner and me."

"How would you feel if I brought my team in to look?"

"It's okay with me, if you want to put in the manpower."

The next day, I rallied the troops and told them we were flying back to New York. Jerry had worked up from his terror of flying all the way to intense dislike. Again, Sochaczewski picked us up at JFK and we drove straight to the Knox murder scene in Chelsea.

Since it was no longer fresh, it was no longer guarded, simply indicated by yellow crime-scene tape and a posted warning that the premises were under the control of the New York Police Department and trespass or violation was punishable by law.

"Just page me when you're ready to be picked up," the detective told us. "If I haven't heard from you in three days, I'll send in a new crime-scene team to document your skeletized remains."

"Okay," I said to my people. "It looks like there must be about fifty thousand strips of negatives, prints, and contact sheets here, and we've got to go through every last one of them. We're looking for the Boyd photos in their original state so we can figure out where they came from. Also, we need to find anything of this mystery woman."

"That's a lot of stuff," Jerry complained.

"It sure is. That's why we're all here. We can't trust anyone else. But if my theory's right, then we're going to find something that will connect Madeline Boyd to the contact sheet we've already seen."

"How do you want to do this?" Katie asked.

"Why don't you, Jerry, and Trevor take the darkroom. Dom and I will go through the office. Just in case we find something interesting, I want everyone to put on latex gloves. If anyone thinks they've come up with a strike, tell me right away."

The most tedious, and often the most critical, part of any criminal investigation is the methodical sifting through files of one sort or another. In many cases, when we do threat assessments or try to come up with bombing or sabotage subjects, this means combing through year after year of personnel records for a given company or organization, seeing if any clue suggests a particular individual is capable of, and has motive for, doing violence, at a particular time to a particular place or group. Sometimes it means going through the arrest records of every Peeping Tom or other sex offender within a certain geographical area, knowing that the UNSUB we're looking for is working within his own physical area of comfort, but that since this is his first major sex crime, the only rap sheet he's going to have will be for something the local police may regard as nothing more than a nuisance offense. Whatever the situation, the work is neither fun nor glamorous. It just happens to be necessary. And now we'd hit it in this case, and we couldn't pawn it off on the Bureau clerks or NYPD. We had to do it ourselves.

No one said anything for at least an hour. If it were simply random crimes we were looking for, this was a treasure trove. Knox had run a lucrative business providing phony passports. That alone would have been enough to earn him his bejeweled Rolex, even if he hadn't had all these other side ventures. In consideration of Paul Sochaczewski's kindness and discretion, we'd let all the credit for what we found go to him, and he could hand it over to the proper authorities for disposition. There were probably enough leads for everything from drug-running to terrorism to illegal flight to avoid prosecution.

Despite what Katie had learned from the Secret Service, we didn't find any counterfeit engravings or printing plates in the apartment. But that didn't surprise me. It would be unusual to have a plant set up in a small place like this, much less an apartment house where people are observed coming and going with great regularity. And a guy who was involved with this much unkosher activity wouldn't take a chance on having evidence for one unlawful business on the premises of another, especially as counterfeiting is a federal offense that the government regards with the utmost seriousness.

What made our task even more difficult was that Knox did a fair amount of legitimate studio photography, too. So we had to wade through file after file, contact sheet after contact sheet, of studio sessions with models of all shapes and sizes, in all manner of dress and undress. Normally, I would not have considered this a chore. But when you're trying to go through thousands of images in as little time as possible, it quickly stops mattering how interesting the subject matter or how beautiful the model is. If it isn't what you're looking for, it gets refiled real quick.

It was well into our third hour there when Katie called out, "Come in here a minute. I may have something."

She had a contact sheet in her hand. "Take a look at this."

I scanned from one frame to the next. It was a studio series of the same blonde from the Boyd sheet getting it on with another man. As in the first contact sheet we'd seen, both parties shed articles of clothing as the shots progressed.

Peering over Katie's shoulder, Trevor whistled. "That girl sure gets around."

"Look carefully at the whole series," said Katie.

I did. At the beginning, the man was in a dress shirt and tie and the blonde was wearing a knit skirt and top like the one we'd identified as Mrs. Boyd's. The set of images looked similar, actually, to the contact sheet with Boyd.

In fact, if I remembered correctly, they were identical.

I was suddenly aware of my heartbeat, the hot, prickly feeling of my skin, the sharpening of the senses. Hunting mode.

"Other than the substitution of the unknown male, the main difference," Katie pointed out, "is that this set is shot against a neutral gray studio backdrop."

And there was definitely no birthmark on the model's left buttock.

"As if they were trying to duplicate something they'd already seen," said Trevor.

I nodded. "Exactly. They're copying the positions, poses, and actions of the Boyd series." The theory was correct. Now we had a target. Now we had someone to look for and ask specific questions of.

"Why would they do that?" asked Jerry.

"Because they wanted to make it look realistic when they superimposed this woman's head on Madeline Boyd's body," Katie explained.

"I see."

"Keep looking," I directed.

One of the things profilers do is predict what they expect to find once they start looking. By that I mean they have to know what it is the investigator is going to find in the possession of a given subject based on the indicators noted at the crime scene. This is largely predicated on behavioral experience. A key application of this technique is in preparing affidavits in support of search warrants. For instance, let's say you're trying to convince a judge you have probable cause to search the home and van of a guy you believe to be a serial killer who picks up his prostitute victims on the side of the road, then rapes and sexually tortures them before casting their bodies out in the woods. In that instance, it's helpful if you can list ropes, hunting knives, cord, pliers, whips, needles, bondage pornography, Polaroid and/or video cameras, small tape recorders, etc., etc. Then the judge knows you know what you're looking for and are not on some fishing expedition. For other types of crimes or other personalities of offenders, you'd have other items on your lists.

Now, with Katie having found this piece of linking evidence, she and I could begin predicting what it was we were looking for next.

"If Knox was this meticulous about placing her in the same poses just so the facial expressions would look real, then there had to be a set of blowups of the original Boyd series for him to shoot from," I said.

"Yeah, but I'll bet he destroyed them as soon as the studio shoot was done," she responded.

"You're probably right, but there's bound to be something else around here that he would have kept, that wouldn't have been as directly incriminating. I don't know what exactly, but keep looking. We'll know it if we see it."

It wasn't too long afterward that Katie found it. She handed me a file folder with four eight-by-tens clipped together, four pictures of the same blonde: one facing front, one from behind, and one from each side. In each one she stood completely naked with her hands at her sides, staring expressionlessly ahead. She was standing against a wall marked off with a height chart, the kind you see in some pediatricians' offices, but this one went high enough to measure adults. The shot from behind showed that the woman was noticeably absent a birthmark near the bottom of either buttock.

"Did you find any other models in these poses?" I asked.

"No," Katie said. "But I'll bet he tested others."

"Do you want us to keep looking?" Trevor asked.

"No," I said. "I think we have what we need. Let's go find this woman."

30

But finding one individual who may be anywhere among the twenty-odd million people of the metropolitan area of New York, or may even have gone anywhere else in the world, is not a simple task. When Paul Sochaczewski picked us up, I asked him in the car if they'd had any luck.

"No," he said with obvious frustration. "Without saying why we were looking, we prepared ID packs which were distributed all across the city, along with be-on-lookout bulletins to each precinct. But when someone doesn't want to be found, as you know, Jake, it can be pretty damn hard to find them."

How well did I know, which is why I'd spent so much of my time in the Bureau working on fugitive assessments. Sometimes you hit it and you find them right away, literally within blocks of where you predict they're going to turn up. In a prominent Midwestern drug-tampering case in which seven people died, including two children, the only evidence of where the prime suspect had fled to was a letter to the editor that seemed to be from him, postmarked New York City. I told the task force they'd find him in New York before too long if they surveilled libraries that carried out-of-town newspapers, and that they should place special emphasis on the reading room of the main branch of the public library. Sure enough, that's where he was. My theory was that he would want to keep up with developments in the case on a level that only his local papers would cover.

Late that afternoon, as Katie and I grabbed a bite in a little coffee shop near Mrs. De Vries's suite, I netted it out. "NYPD can't find her.

We've got to go proactive. It might mean some exposure, and it might mean divulging more than we want to at this stage, but I think it's a risk we have to take."

"What did you have in mind?"

"Playing the basic psychological trump card—the one that gets right to the heart of nearly everyone's needs and fears, whether they turn out to be on our side of the law or the other one. If we could appeal to her own survival instinct, maybe she would bring herself in."

"Don't you think she might already be dead?" Katie asked.

"I'm betting not."

"Why wouldn't they have just killed her after the photo shoot? They proved they're willing to kill by what they did to Knox."

"He may have done something to get himself offed. And whoever killed him staged it to look like something else. For this woman to get involved the way she obviously did from those test photos you found, she couldn't have known exactly what she was getting into, so the bad guys might not consider her much of a risk. They'd be too smart to kill anyone they didn't really have to. NYPD is too good. There is much more of a chance they'd be found out that way."

Katie sighed. "Let's hope you're right. A lot's riding on it."

When we got back to Mrs. De Vries's suite, I called Trevor in. "Can we arrange with the phone company a totally secure line that is also wireless, so that one of us can have it with us at all times?"

"The digital technology is pretty hard to tap," he replied. "But if you want total security, we can have the incoming and outgoing signals scrambled and encrypted. The hardware isn't cheap, though."

"I think Mrs. De Vries will be willing to pay for it. How fast can you set this up?"

"By tomorrow."

"Good. Let's get on it."

I spent several hours on the phone, going through my address book for every media contact I'd ever had good luck with in the Bureau, calling in credits and favors I had bestowed on selected favorites of mine. Once I got to the right management level, most of them were pretty forthcoming. The Boyd story was still a big one, but there hadn't been much substantive to report, and the FBI itself was keeping quiet. *America's Most Wanted* offered to put me on the next show. I managed to get commitments from a couple of CNN programs, too, and I knew that before too long, we'd reach critical mass.

That evening, I called the team together.

"I think we've been making progress," Jerry offered. There were nods from the others.

"I agree," I said. "But there's something I don't like."

"Which is . . . ?"

"The investigation goes off in too many directions. Just about everyone who might have had a reason to hate the director and want him dead seems to have a connection. We've got the militia boys who stomped me, then we've got practically a direct connection to Owl Creek through the tattoo on Knox's wrist and the mud Jerry identified on his shoes. But then his murder is like a signature for the Russian Mob."

"Except for one aspect," Dom pointed out. "In this instance, the excision of the eyes appears to have been postmortem, while both Trevor and Detective Sochaczewski said they would have expected it to be performed antemortem to create maximum terror and trauma."

"True," I conceded. "But if that's a setup, then that's a pretty elaborate staging for no obvious reason."

"Unless it's just to throw us off," said Katie.

"That's what's worrying me." Most times, if there is a staging, say to make a domestic murder appear to be a burglary-rape that went south, we can tell, since we know a lot more about how things are supposed to look than the average offender. Here, I was picking up no pattern. Which made me wonder if there was actually a pattern I just wasn't seeing. Looking at evidence can be a hall of mirrors. You're never sure if what you're looking at is real or merely the reflection of something you think you've already seen and interpreted.

"Another thing," I continued, "the break-in at Toni's house. It was clearly meant to scare me off the case, just like the pounding I took outside Quantico. But in no way was cutting off the heads of my daughter's Barbie dolls the style of any militia group or anything I would expect from them. It's too subtle."

"I have to agree with that," said Trevor.

"How would they even know Ali had those dolls?" Katie asked.

That question hung uncomfortably in the air. I tasted bile and my throat burned.

"So you think that was done by someone who'd been inside Toni's house or knew your children well enough to know their toys," Jerry said. That was exactly what scared the shit out of me, though I hadn't been emotionally willing to articulate it so bluntly.

I swallowed. "It's like we're purposely being led off in all different directions to obscure the one direction we should be pursuing."

"Whoever it is, is manipulating us, sure," said Katie. "The best ones do that. But it's as if he knows just how we think."

"That, in itself, certainly suggests someone with inside knowledge," said Dom.

I nodded. "Which is all the more reason we've got to keep this quiet. We need to force the issue, then wait and see what happens."

Since Mrs. De Vries's suite had two bedrooms, it seemed a waste not to utilize both rather than having to pay for an extra room. It made the most sense for Katie and me to share the suite/command post. Gentleman of the old school that I am, I gave her the master bedroom and bath. I took the small bedroom and the bathroom on the hall. We put up the other three in the regular part of the hotel. Trevor would stay to work out the telephone link I wanted, and Jerry and Dom would continue going over Knox's apartment for any further trace clues that could send us in a more specific direction.

When the others had gone, Katie and I opened a bottle of Mrs. De Vries's single-malt and sat on the floral-patterned, chintz-covered sofa, two broken wings trying to mend, gazing out at the Manhattan skyline. She stretched her long legs straight out, crossed them at the ankles, then rested them on the inlaid coffee table. "So tell me," she said, "have you thought seriously about anyone since you and Toni split up?"

Was she prospecting? "I know this is going to be bad for my image," I replied honestly, "but I was so overwhelmed between work and what was going on in the family that I didn't have the energy."

"I figured that. Or else you were hiding it pretty well."

How much more was I hiding? I wondered to myself. I let the Scotch trickle over my palate, burning around the base of my tongue. It would be so easy right now, the two of us alone, mellow and unguarded from the booze. Fragments of all sorts of fantasies paraded themselves fleetingly in my mind. So easy and yet so difficult, because once the inhibitions were fully abandoned, even for a moment, they would be impossible to fully recover. And then everything changed, not only for us, but for each of the people I'd made part of my mission. "What about you since Rob left?" I asked, not wanting to abandon the topic completely.

She took another sip, actually more than a sip, and swished the liquor expressively in her mouth. She swallowed, then said, "At first I was too pissed off at men in general to want to do anything. I mean, he really hurt me, walking out the way he did. But after I licked my wounds for a while, I just wanted to get back at him. And the best way to accomplish that seemed to be to go out with every hot, good-looking thing in pants. When, in the fullness of time—big surprise—that exercise ceased to be emotionally fulfilling, I pulled back in. I guess I haven't quite reached the next stage yet: you know, the one where you finally understand who you are, where you've been, and where you want to go in a relationship."

"If you do, you'll have to lead me."

I caught a sparkle in her eyes. "In the meantime, there's always the pistol range when I really need to let off steam. For now, it's just me and my fantasies." I could only speculate what they were, but there was a little electric jolt in wondering if they intersected with any of mine.

The moment passed, at least I thought it had, as Katie stared down into her drink and swirled it in a circular motion. "You've researched and written a lot about fantasy as the key precursor for predatory sex crimes," she said.

"I have indeed."

"So does it follow, do you think, that fantasy is a precursor for wanting sex in general?"

"Probably."

She leaned forward. "What do men fantasize about?"

"You must have some pretty good idea by now," I teased.

"I mean normal men."

"And are you including me in that category?"

"Well . . ." She shrugged and smiled. "You tell me."

Actually, she had just touched on one of the most tantalizing and emotionally thorny issues we deal with: all human behavior is a great continuum, and saint or killer, our feelings all originate in the same place. A healthy, enthusiastic male—or female, for that matter—might take his sex partner aggressively, even roughly, if that's his style, and the act will be symbolic of his great appetite and passion for her. A rapist might take an unwilling victim, threaten her life, forcibly penetrate her, and then beat her just to watch her suffer. We have the same emotions that killers have; we merely act on them differently. A normal person will become angry when someone cuts him off on the highway. A sociopath might become just as angry, but shoot the offender through the head. The acts are completely different, but they are different by *degree*, by where they fall along the continuum.

Katie was right: the act always begins in fantasy. I fantasize about the woman I want also wanting me. The sexual predator fantasizes about forcing the woman he wants to gratify him.

"Or maybe I should ask, *who* do you fantasize about? I'm just curious, that's all," Katie said with theatrical innocence.

"And you are getting at what?" It was as if we were each waiting for the other to stake out the territory.

"I just wanted to see if we were both coming from the same place on this."

"I hope so," I said, waiting anxiously for her next move or response.

She rose and gave me that enigmatic smile of hers that fixed the dimples in her cheeks. "Yeah, something like that." With that, she walked over to the master bedroom. "Nighty night," she said, and closed the door behind her.

I spent the night wondering what was being thought about on the other side of that door.

∘

I didn't see Katie much the next day. After breakfast, she told me she was taking advantage of her time in New York to go shopping. By lunchtime, Trevor came up to the suite and told me the special phone line had been set up. He handed me a small Motorola unit in a hard leather case that would comfortably fit on a belt, in Katie's handbag, or my jacket pocket. Then I got a cab to the CNN office to begin my media blitz.

I was met at the reception desk by a tall, thin woman who ushered me back to the makeup room and did me up herself.

She brought me into the studio during a commercial break, and the floor director set me up behind the news desk with a microphone clipped to my tie and an earphone so I could hear the questions from Steve Phillips, the news anchor in Atlanta. I could see him through a monitor behind the two cameras.

Phillips announced, "As you know, CNN has been following events surrounding the death of FBI director Thomas Boyd. As you may also know, Jake Donovan, the legendary profiler who until his recent retirement from the Bureau was known as the Mindhunter, has been asked by Acting Director Orlando Ravan to carry on an independent investigation. This is Jake's first public appearance since then."

But far from the last, I thought to myself.

"Welcome to the program."

"Thanks for having me, Steve."

"Is it true that you've refused all interviews and public statements until now?"

"That's right."

"Why the change of heart?"

"Because a new element has come up in which the public's help could be vitally important."

"Okay. But let's back up a moment here. Jake, are you yet prepared to say at this point that Judge Boyd committed suicide, as seems to be the case from all indications?"

Somehow, the blackmailing angle had never surfaced. I was amazed there'd been no leaks from the Bureau. "No," I replied. "I think it would be premature, as Sherlock Holmes suggested, to come up with a hypothesis in advance of all the facts."

"Then you are still collecting evidence."

"To be sure. Not necessarily death-scene evidence any longer, but with any equivocal death, there is always an elaborate network of intersecting forces that affected and influenced the individual, and before we can say anything with any certainty, we've got to really understand all of them." *How is that for not saying anything?* I thought to myself.

I could see Phillips struck what must have been his most serious, penetrating expression. "Is there any evidence you've come across to suggest that Judge Boyd's death might not, in fact, be a suicide?"

"Well, Steve, I'm not prepared to say that just yet. But I'd be less than candid if I didn't say that the reason we're still investigating is because there are some elements to the case that are, to say the least, troubling. I am convinced, for example, that there are people out there who have knowledge or information which could help us in completing the puzzle."

"And so that's why you agreed to this interview today?"

"Exactly." I gave my most sincere you-can-sleep-better-at-night-knowing-that-dedicated-upstanding-agents-are-out-there-working-to-protect-you delivery and gazed straight into the camera lens. "I'd like to show your viewers a photograph."

"By all means," Phillips said from Atlanta. The second camera moved in as I held up the close-up of the blond mystery woman's head. I'd had it backed on cardboard for the show.

"From our investigation, we believe that the woman you see in this photograph is a material witness to critical events surrounding the death of FBI director Boyd. Let me emphasize that this individual is not a suspect, but we believe she has important information."

I put on my most concerned face. "But most important, certain facts have come to our attention which make me very, very worried for this woman's safety."

"What do you mean by that?" Phillips pressed. "Do you mean to say that her life might be in danger?"

"That's exactly what I mean. Ma'am, if you're watching this broadcast, or if anyone watching knows her or knows who she is, it's my belief that the people who got you involved in the activity which may have made you a party to Director Boyd's death are now desperate enough to want to silence you."

"That sounds a bit elliptical, Jake. Could you tell us what kind of activity you're talking about?"

"She'll know what I'm talking about." I didn't break eye contact with the camera. "We've set up a special secure line so that you can contact us. You can call any time of day or night and the only ones who will answer are myself or persons working directly for me. Please call. I believe that your life depends on it." I gave the phone number, then repeated it for emphasis.

"You could get a raft of calls," Phillips said.

"We have ways of qualifying callers. And let me say that if anyone calls frivolously, that will be treated the same as phoning in a false fire alarm or making a capricious threat on an airliner. The FBI will take this kind of interference with the investigation very seriously. You will be traced, located, and severely prosecuted." I didn't know if the Bureau would be or not since I hadn't consulted anyone. "Don't ruin your life by calling unless you're the woman we're looking for. But if you are, just remember that we believe you to be in grave danger."

By late afternoon, I had managed to hit all the television networks and had done interviews with the Associated Press and *USA Today*.

Within twenty-four hours, this woman's face would be so widely seen that I was hoping she'd have to turn herself in just to stop curious people from asking if she was the mysterious blonde.

I met Katie back at the Waldorf. We ordered up room service in the suite again and stared at the Motorola cell phone Trevor had given me, waiting in vain for it to ring. Katie had code-named our mysterious blonde Needle. The entire rest of the world represented our haystack.

31

I was awakened by the ringing of my cell phone and could feel those little anxiety bubbles coursing into my system. But by the time I sat up in bed, I realized it was not our new special line I was hearing.

Katie must have gone through the same mental process I did, because she opened the door and came in to my bedroom to listen. Her hair was tangled from sleep and she was in an old gray FBI Academy T-shirt and white string panties. With her hair tangled and the ensemble wrinkled from sleep, she had the look both of a vulnerable innocent and a predatory tigress always ready for the hunt.

Peter Sutherland was on the line.

"What's up?" I asked him. "Any new developments?"

"Only one. *La merde* has hit *le* fan here at Quantico. In fact, I'd say it's all through the air-conditioning ducts at this point. Mrs. Boyd was none too pleased about having her husband publicly associated with a young blonde and made sure the Raven knew her feelings on the matter. And, of course, Harry Gillette's going ape shit." At least Pete was starting off my morning with good news.

Katie saw me smile and mimed a quizzical expression back to me. I held up my hand to indicate it was okay. It was always gratifying to know that somehow you'd ruined the day of a Bureau-crat, but I thought I ought to inquire as to the specifics to determine how far over the line my own ass was hanging. "In re?"

"In re you launching this dragnet for this woman without clearing it with anyone over here."

"Fuck him!" I explained cogently. "I'm supposed to be completely independent."

"You don't have to convince me, but to Harry, *independent* is the 'I-word.' It's a threat to everything he holds dear. He wants you shit-canned from the case."

"What does Neil Burke say?"

"He just tells Harry to handle it."

I didn't know what to make of that. I wondered if Ravan the Raven was playing both sides, using me not for ultimate truth but for his own purposes. All the more reason to keep doing things my own way and make the case. If I was successful, a multitude of sins would be for-given. If I wasn't, I was horse meat anyway, so what the hell was the difference?

"It gets worse, though," Peter reported. "Ted Novello wants you off the case."

"Ted Novello? What does that little pain in the ass have to do with anything now that he's been moved out?"

"Someone must feel sorry for him now that his champion's gone, be-cause he's got Neil's ear, and through Neil, the Raven's, too."

Maybe nothing was going to change after all. It sure would be a pisser if Ted ended up actually gaining by his champion's death.

Pete was equally disgusted. "And now he walks around like one of the disciples after the crucifixion." Then he shifted to a more serious tone. "You think you're onto something with this woman?"

"I hope so. I'm really not sure." I didn't think Pete was the kind to report everything I told him to the Bureau-crats and anyway, I didn't want to put him in the middle in case they pressed him, so I decided against telling him more than I had to. Once this was all over, I could clear it up with him.

"What have you guys come up with?" I asked, trying to shift the focus.

He grunted. "It's pretty much a dead end. My idea for the graveside surveillance went nowhere. Not a peep from anyone. Then, I don't know if you heard, but when they finally read Boyd's will, they realized they'd screwed up. So they had him disinterred and cremated."

"You're joking!"

"His ashes were scattered over the Golden Gate. Sometimes life is stranger than fiction." Pete hesitated a moment. "Look, I don't want to pry or interfere; I understand the logic of this compartmentalization. But if you can't locate this woman—and if she's still alive—you may want to try it again through the Bureau."

"How so?"

"I think your instinct to try to bring her in is good. But if it doesn't pan out, it may be just that she's spooked by this one guy—you—saying, 'Call me and I'll protect you from all the forces of evil.' "

"O ye of little faith!"

"Not me, my man. I'm your greatest fan. But you see what I'm getting at. It's possible that if she felt the entire FBI were behind her, she might be more likely to come forward."

"You may have a point," I conceded.

When we got off the line, I filled Katie in on the conversation, trying not to focus on the diversion she presented. I said I'd be continuing the media blitz one more day in the hope that Needle would still come to ground. Katie would therefore be monitoring the secure phone, and I thought it would be a good idea if she stuck pretty close to me throughout the day. If we hadn't gotten any response by the time I finished the last interview, I'd spell her and take the phone back for the evening.

As I shaved, showered, and then donned one of my special-agent dark suits, I was already trying to come up with a contingency if the mysterious Ms. Needle remained hidden in her haystack.

∘

Katie asked if I minded if she ducked out for the evening after dinner. I said that would be fine with me and resisted the temptation to ask where she was planning to go. I didn't want to seem either controlling or possessive.

"Want to catch dinner first?" she asked.

"Sure. What are you in the mood for?"

"I've got a yen for thick red meat. Meat still attached to the bone that I can rip off with my own teeth."

"As long as Trevor or someone like him hasn't actually gone out and shot the animal for you?"

"Come on, Jake, I'm hungry."

"Okay, then we'll just deal with hunting on a metaphorical level."

"Fine by me. Let's go eat."

"Oo-kay, Agent McManus. Red meat it'll be."

I took her to Gallagher's on West Fifty-second and watched with amazement as she tore into an enormous porterhouse. After dinner, we parted company at the corner of Fifty-second and Broadway. I had the sudden impulse to tell her to be careful walking around New York by herself at night, but I stifled it. Most women would find that kind of admonition touching and considerate. A woman who carries an H&K semiautomatic in her bag and can handily kick the shit out of most men twice her size would find it patronizing. In the end, I said only that I'd be glad to see her when she got back.

I took my time walking back across town. On this lovely, warm night the city was alive with electricity. It was almost possible for me to disappear in these crowds, to lose myself and all of my worries and concerns.

When I finally got back to the Waldorf, I hit the bar, taking a small round table off near the wall, and ordered a margarita.

The first stage of solitary drinking in a public venue brings the sensation of loneliness and self-pity. In my case this transitioned quickly into missing the kids and feeling guilty that I wasn't there for all of their formative moments. The third stage was a kind of mushy sentimentality, and I realized I was really drinking so I wouldn't have to think, so I should just stop thinking and keep on drinking. I would feel the same in the morning no matter what thoughts passed through my mind tonight.

I was actually about to call it a night when a woman in a short black cocktail dress, sparkly dark hose, and narrow spiky heels walked by my table. She glanced over at me, stopped, and then turned to face me directly. She had wavy, dark brown hair that cascaded past her bare shoulders, large brown eyes, and long, full eyelashes that she seemed adept at using to full advantage. I'm not good at guessing women's ages, but I pegged her as late twenties. A sophisticated high twenties by the way she carried herself.

"Excuse me," she said, "but aren't you that Jake Donovan? Didn't I see you on television today?"

"You might have," I said cordially. *And if you happen to know the whereabouts of the blond Ms. Needle, pull up a chair and I'll buy you a drink. In fact, I'll buy you a bottle.*

"Do you mind if I sit down for a minute?"

I gestured her to the empty chair opposite me. I know I'm not alone among men in experiencing the phenomenon that when I'm not even trying, in fact not even thinking about the subject, women seek me out.

"You're the Mindhunter, aren't you?"

"Some call me that."

"I'll bet you've led a fascinating life."

Let's don't go there, I silently pleaded. "And you?"

"Penelope Miller."

And I'll bet people call you Penny.

"People call me Penny."

"You don't say. Care for a drink?"

"Thanks. Whatever you're having."

I could play this like a 1940s film noir, if that's what she wanted, as I waited for her to indicate her intentions. Maybe she was taken with the "glamour" of my image. Maybe she actually found me devastating. Maybe she was buddies with the guys who beat me up. In my business, you reserve judgment until all the behavioral evidence is in.

The waiter brought us a pair of margaritas. Penny leaned in to clink glasses with me and I inhaled her perfume. It had a rich, heavy, musky scent, as if formulated for the express purpose of encouraging human mating habits. Actually, it made me a little dizzy.

"You staying in the hotel?" I asked.

"No, I work around here. Public relations. But that's boring. I'm just fascinated by what you're doing. You've left the FBI, right?"

"Indeed." As a result of Katie's recent reproach, I made a point of noticing her ring finger and found it naked.

"You know, Jake . . . Ah, may I call you Jake?"

"Why not? My soon-to-be ex-wife does."

"You know, Jake," she continued, "I thought you were pretty good-looking on television, but you're even better looking in person."

You should see me when I'm sober, I thought to myself. Opportunities like this did present themselves from time to time when I was on the road for the Bureau, especially in some out-of-the-way town where I had nothing else to do but sip margaritas and think about the latest unsolved murder I was there to analyze. But I'd been legally taken then, so I tended to guiltily fight off the impulse. The few times I didn't, I felt so crummy about it the next morning that I was tempted to call Toni before she left for her office and confess. That's why, when people ask me if those of us in my unit know enough about murder to commit the perfect crime, I say no, because no matter how meticulously we planned the killing itself, something in our postoffense behavior would give us away. In my case, Neil Burke's secretary could hold up one of my travel vouchers and I'd immediately assume I'd done something against the regs that I could be crunched for.

I had no intention of letting my dick rule my brain, at least not until

I found out what was going on, but that didn't mean I couldn't enjoy the scenery along the route. What separates the predator from the rest of us is his unwillingness not to act on his impulses and feelings. But that doesn't mean the rest of us shouldn't try to stay in touch with ours.

One thing led to another, as it often does. I still wasn't sure of Penny's game plan, but decided I could control the situation better in the privacy of the suite. I hoped Katie would stay away long enough for me to figure out what, if anything, was going down.

She wasn't back in the suite yet. I didn't do anything dramatic like order up a bottle of Dom Pérignon for the room. Frankly, I felt that I'd had enough to drink for one night—or an entire week, for that matter—so I'd get by on my scintillating personality.

We were sitting together on the floral sofa. Penny had already taken off her shoes and tucked her legs up under her to "get more comfortable." The heavy scent of her perfume filled the small space between us and aggravated the hangover headache that was just starting to creep into my skull.

"Tell me why you're looking for that woman," Penny said, batting those long brown eyelashes for emphasis.

"Why do you want to know?"

"Just curious," she said with an innocent shrug. She sounded like Katie for a moment.

"Afraid that's not good enough."

She gave a little pout, then tried another tack. "I'll bet she was having an affair with Thomas Boyd, wasn't she?"

Okay, now maybe we were getting somewhere. "Why do you say that?"

She shrugged again. "You want to find her really badly. You say you don't think she killed him. It's the only reason I can think of why you would. Maybe she was blackmailing him or something and that's why he killed himself."

"You'd make a good detective. But that's not why I'm looking for her."

"Then why?"

"I told you: I can't say. Secret government information."

"Oh, pooh," she retorted, and hit me lightly on the shoulder with a chintz pillow. But right after that she relented and seemed to relax again. I could hear the faint whistle as her stockinged legs brushed against each other and noticed the short dress riding provocatively up her thighs and revealing a stocking top held up by a garter strap. I liked that.

"Why don't I help you relax?" she half-whispered.

"What do you have in mind?"

"Well . . ." She leaned in close and wrapped her fingers around the knot in my tie. "We can start with this." Before long, she had pulled the undone tie free of my collar.

She eased backward a little and said, "I don't know how you are, but I can't really chill out until I've got my shoes off." With that she untied my laces and slipped the black wing tips off my feet. Then she started massaging my feet through my black socks. And she was good—my feet started relaxing right away. Too good, I thought, not to have this be a practiced part of her repertoire.

When Penny could tell that my feet felt really loose and relaxed, she moved back up north and started unbuttoning my white shirt. With each button, she'd run her fingers around the hairs on my chest. When she finished the last one, she dabbed at my right nipple with her expressive tongue.

Yes, I confirmed for myself, *very practiced.*

As she finally pulled her tongue away, she turned her body to present me with her back, presumably so I could return the undressing favor. *Okay, let's move on to Act Three.* I reached out to grasp the zipper between her shoulder blades and gently tugged it down toward her waist. She arched her back to help the process along. When the zipper was all the way down, she wriggled out of the dress and stood before me in her black, strapless bra, matching briefs, and garter belt.

Even a garter belt! She dressed for a teenage wet dream.

Speaking of which, I admit I was way out of practice, but I don't think I'd be alone among men in saying that the thrill of the hunt is the best part. This is true whether you're talking about beautiful women or repulsive men. On the professional level, for instance, bringing bad guys to justice is the ultimate satisfaction, but the thrill of the hunt is what keeps the juices flowing and the skills sharp. And by the same token here, if I wasn't being called upon to strategize how to get a new conquest down to her knickers, then a key element was missing for me. That was the one element missing here, the one element Penny hadn't made "realistic" enough for this to ring true.

She pulled up on one of my shoulders to get me to turn over and lie facedown on the sofa. She took a step up and straddled me, coming down just past my waist, on the upper region of my butt. She leaned forward, took one of my shoulder blades in each hand, and started kneading them vigorously. "So tense," she noted as she massaged my upper back. I justified my compliance by telling myself I had to see what she was up to.

She went all over my shoulders, upper arms, and back. When she'd completed a particular section, she'd lean forward again and finish the area with a tongue massage. I hadn't figured out exactly what was wrong with this picture, had only confirmed my initial sense that something was. The funny thing was, when I was a young man in new-agents training, they used to warn us about this kind of thing all the time, yet it had never actually happened to me or anyone else I knew.

Penny climbed off me, then pulled my hand to get me to turn back to a normal sitting position. Well, I could play along while she did my entire body, and I hated to get in the way of her fun, but it was time to assume a more proactive approach.

"Who sent you here?" I said sharply.

She stopped. "I beg your pardon?"

"Beg it all you want. But tell me who sent you here."

She went rigid and some of the color drained from her face. Actually, in the interests of accuracy, some of the color drained from her entire body, changing subtly the contrast between her pale skin and shiny black lingerie.

I sat there staring at her, my arms outstretched on the back of the sofa. I could see that Penny was processing what she was going to say next. I let the silence build in the air. Through my years of experience interrogating suspects, I know how much silence can help the side that can tolerate it the longest.

"What are you accusing me of?" she asked.

"I'm not accusing you of anything. I just asked a question."

"I don't know what you're talking about."

"I think you do." I seized her wrist and bent it down.

"You're hurting me!"

"Unsociable, I know, and I may start hurting you more than that if you don't—"

"I swear to you—"

"Didn't your mommy ever teach you not to lie?" I forced her arm behind her back and her head and shoulder down on the sofa.

"What are you going to do to me?"

This woman was used to being threatened. I released my hold on her. Slowly, she untwisted from the position I'd forced her into and sat on the sofa, trembling.

I kept her stripped to her underwear. This none-too-subtle ploy gave me the interrogation advantage. So having just made her physically uncomfortable, it was time to throw her the emotional lifeline.

"Listen, I'm not going to hurt you, but my instinct and experience tell me that you're caught between two sets of folks who might. I'm guessing that whoever sent you here is more than capable of doing you some serious violence. And if I'm right, then that means the FBI or the cops are capable of making life rough for you if you don't cooperate. Believe it or not, I'm your best alternative." I stepped over to the phone, picked up the receiver. "I'm calling the police."

Her lips quivered; she shuddered. I twisted slowly in the metaphorical wind.

It must have been a good half-minute before she spoke. "J. P. Napoleon," she said at last.

It hit me hard, even though the name had never been far from my consciousness. I thought back to when I'd had the team together in this very room and told them how evidence was going off in too many directions—almost as if it had been orchestrated that way. Napoleon was the one "suspect" whose tentacles could penetrate to all of those far reaches. And then again when I'd met with Richard Royce, I hadn't come away with a strong sense about his group's involvement. Anyway, the militia groups don't use beautiful women against their enemies; it's not their style. But Napoleon might; it would be only one of the weapons in his arensal.

Napoleon would have had a strong reason for wanting the FBI director dead. Boyd had pledged to go after his operations with a vehemence unknown since the days when Bobby Kennedy was attorney general and took off after Jimmy Hoffa and other organized crime figures. Whether Boyd actually thought Napoleon was that worthy a target or merely good headlines was difficult to know. But whatever his motive, it was one of the goals he and I had shared in the Bureau: figure out who Napoleon is and how far his influence spreads. What wasn't difficult to see was that Napoleon must have seen Boyd as a major threat and would have been willing to devote considerable resources to neutralizing him, either by blackmail or murder.

"Did he tell you in person?" Neither I nor anyone else in the FBI even knew what this individual looked like.

"No, he called," Penny said. "Or someone called. Someone always calls. I don't know if it's him or not. I suspect it probably isn't."

I had the blood scent now and wasn't letting go. "Have you ever seen him?"

"In a crowded party in Switzerland once, maybe. We weren't introduced, I just saw a lot of people I knew were important in the company talking to him."

This was the chance. "Would you recognize him?"

"I don't know. Maybe."

I took her by both her bare shoulders. "Think hard!"

She groaned with fear and sniffled back tears.

"How did he know where I'd be?"

"I don't know."

Still holding her, I shook her violently. "You're just not coming up with the right answers, honey!"

"I . . . I saw you on the street in front of the hotel."

Dubious, but I decided for the moment to move on. "*Why* did he send you?"

"I'm not sure."

"To seduce me?"

"Probably."

"What do you mean, probably?"

"He expects me to use my own initiative."

"Expects? So this is part of your job description?"

"Informally, maybe."

"So was this all an act?"

She recoiled as if I'd slapped her. "No. I like you. I feel . . . good . . . around you."

Curiouser and curiouser. Right here in Mrs. De Vries's suite. A paranoid thought struck me. Paranoia or self-preservation—they were pretty much the same in my business. "Are there cameras hidden in here!"

"I don't think so. How would I know? It's your room."

I grabbed her by the arm and forced her gaze. "Tell me! What about recording devices?"

"I told you," she said, wincing from the pain of my grip.

"Then what was the point of this exercise?"

"Just to get to know you," she said, starting to cry. "Then whatever happened, happened."

I heard the tumblers move in the front door. It opened and Katie walked in, carrying the Playbill to *Ragtime*.

"Oh, excuse me," she said. "I see I came in in the middle of something."

The three of us stood there awkwardly for a beat, until Penny suddenly broke free of my grip and ran off to the bathroom, slamming the door behind her. We heard the lock snap into place.

"I am sorry," Katie said, her large eyes not able to fully suppress a look of amusement and, if I interpreted correctly, a little possessive irritation.

"Don't be," I said. "It was all going downhill."

"Then appearances can certainly be deceiving." She paused, then sniffed the air around me. "I've only smelled that perfume once before. On a corpse."

"J. P. Napoleon sent over one of his honey pots to compromise me," I said. "How was your evening?"

"I was going to tell you all about this wonderful musical . . . but let's talk about you."

I filled her in on the evening's events, the seemingly chance meeting with Penny Miller and as much as I could make out about her connection to Napoleon.

"He's the only one with the power, the geographical range, the resources, and the intelligence capability," I told Katie. "Just like in a serial-murder case, this is exactly what we'd expect a sophisticated, organized offender to do—to somehow inject himself into the investigation to gather intelligence about the progress of the case and who the suspects are. Only here, he's powerful enough to do it by proxy and still not let us see him."

Penny had been in the bathroom an awfully long time. I hoped she didn't intend to spend the rest of the night in there. "Do you think we ought to check on her?" I asked.

"Maybe so. Make sure she hasn't gone and slit her wrists."

Oh, Christ, I hadn't thought of that. *You idiot, Donovan! You never leave your suspects alone before they're fully interrogated. You're letting this get out of hand.*

Just as we were about to force open the bathroom door, it opened. But the woman who emerged was not the one I'd seen hurriedly rush away in her underwear not fifteen minutes before. Gone was the wavy, dark brown hair cascading down past her shoulders. Gone were the long, full eyelashes. Gone even were the brown irises at the centers of her expressive eyes. The eyes were now blue, the eyelashes and short-cropped hair were blond. The young woman now wrapped in a white Waldorf-Astoria towel was unmistakably the unknown female we referred to as Needle.

32

Katie gave her the fluffy, white Waldorf robe from the master bathroom, then went to make tea in the kitchenette for everyone.

"Okay," I began, still reeling from this latest revelation, uncomfortably questioning my own powers of observation, "let's get down to basics. Let's start sorting this out. Is your name Penny Miller?"

"No. Wendy Winslow."

"And did Napoleon send you to me or did you come on your own?"

"He *suggested* I get together with you. Or whoever calls me for him suggested it. Not today," she clarified, "but when it first came out you were working on the Boyd investigation."

"So Wendy . . . May I call you Wendy?" I said sarcastically. She nodded her head silently. "Why did he 'suggest' that you should get together with me?"

"That's one of the things I did."

"Be specific." I tried to suppress my anger—both at her and myself for not having been sharper. She was the one we were looking for; I told myself not to blow it here.

"It was the way they did things. They wanted to see how far you'd go, whether we could establish an ongoing relationship."

It sounded like the KGB ploy of compromising high-ranking officials and military personnel into giving out sensitive information without even knowing they'd done so.

I took a step closer to our visitor. "Then you're a hooker? That's what you meant by 'public relations'?"

"No!" Her eyes once more filled with tears.

Katie came back from the kitchenette with the tea. "Calm down. Can't you see she's scared and confused?" She put down the tray and smiled warmly as she handed a cup to Wendy. "You washed off that awful perfume. Good."

"What did you do in this capacity for Napoleon?" I pressed on, trying to separate my fact-finding goal from my sense of vulnerability. First the thugs outside Quantico, now the beautiful woman here in New York. How closely related?

"I guess you'd call it gathering intelligence," Wendy said, finally able to meet my gaze with belligerent eyes.

"Let's call it spying." I raised my hand in a gesture of exasperation. She must have thought I was going to strike her because she cringed.

"She's not going to tell you any more if you threaten her!" Katie snapped. She turned to Wendy with sisterly tenderness, put a hand on her forearm. "He's not going to hurt you."

"We'll see," I muttered.

"Just stop it, Jake! Now . . . why don't we all sit down and you tell us about yourself?" Katie and I had naturally slipped into a good-cop/bad-cop routine.

"Okay, Wendy," I said, "here's the drill. It's very simple: I ask you questions, you answer them, succinctly and to the point. Got it?"

She was whimpering now, having come apart like a pretty little girl who's just realized that this time, her cuteness and charm aren't going to spare her punishment. "On . . . on TV, you said I was in danger, that I should come to you and you'd . . . take care of me. I . . . I thought you'd treat me better than this."

Katie started to speak up, but I silenced her with my upraised hand. "Yeah, well, I'd planned to. Sincerely. But I hadn't figured on you having such a propensity for game-playing. So now we're going to cut the games and do it my way. Then it'll be like I tell my kids: you earn your privileges by your behavior."

"I . . . I don't have to take this," Wendy said sullenly through her tears.

"No, you don't," I responded. "You're free to leave anytime you want."

"But you said I was in danger. Someone might have seen me come here."

"Life is full of tough choices."

"Jake, this is cruel," Katie protested, and went over to put her arm around Wendy's shoulders.

I let her stay there, but continued boring in on the subject. "Have you always lived here?"

"Since after college. U-Conn."

"If I check with the registrar tomorrow and they don't have a listing and transcript for a Wendy Winslow, there's going to be hell to pay."

"I promise," she pleaded.

"Then what?"

"I got a job with Ward and Associates; it's a public relations firm. I got an apartment on the Upper West Side."

"By yourself?"

"Yeah. It was small, but okay."

"And Ward paid you enough to afford to live by yourself in such a trendy neighborhood?"

"I got some local modeling, too. Paid pretty well for the time I had to put into it." That didn't surprise me. She was tall, with a model's face and figure. Undoubtedly, that was one of Ward's key considerations in hiring someone so young and inexperienced.

"And Empire International was one of Ward's clients?" Katie asked.

"Right."

"What did you work on?"

"The main thrust was trying to affect arms export policy on Capitol Hill."

"And that's what you did?" I said.

"Actually, I was assigned to a smaller unit working on Empire's behalf to get the Brady gun bill through Congress."

"Why would an arms dealer want that?" Katie wondered.

"It makes sense," I said. "First, it's good for their public image. Second, it cuts down on the legal competition."

"What are you talking about?" Wendy asked.

"Empire is just the legitimate arm of J. P. Napoleon's, well, empire," Katie explained. "He also happens to be one of the largest regular suppliers of illegal arms to the urban drug wars."

Wendy seemed sad at this, but not surprised. If she worked for Napoleon in any capacity, I reasoned, she couldn't have avoided at least a suspicion of Empire's other activities.

"So how did you become involved with them . . . on this level?" I questioned her.

"I guess the way I looked and, you know, kind of how I carried my-self, I started getting invited to Empire receptions, promotional functions."

She'd be the perfect blond trophy for such occasions, I thought.

"From that, I got requests to meet and escort people Empire considered VIPs when they came to New York."

"Were you paid extra for this?"

"Not officially. From time to time I'd get a gift."

"What kind of gift?"

"Jewelry, mostly—diamonds. Designer clothes sometimes. Plane tickets and hotel vouchers."

"And what was the job description?"

"Oh, fawn over them, make them feel important and comfortable, flirt, come on a little."

"Sleep with them?"

"No!"

"Were you ever told not to?"

"Well, not in so many words. I guess if I had to to get what they wanted . . ."

"And what would that be?"

"Information, attitudes, whatever it was Empire was interested in each one for. I would get debriefed afterward, usually by the same person who'd called to give me the assignment."

"In person or over the phone?"

"Always over the phone. We never met in person."

"This didn't seem odd to you," Katie asked, "that you were never given any names or told anything face-to-face?"

"Well, yeah. But I didn't know what to expect. I understood it was a sensitive sort of business. They'd told me that Mr. Napoleon himself was never seen in public. I was making good money and no one ever asked me to do anything . . . you know . . . really wrong."

Katie glanced at me. "She didn't have any other frame of reference."

"Then, a couple of months ago, it was 'suggested' that I go see this photographer Louis Knox down in Chelsea to audition for a modeling assignment. When I met him, he told me that physical characteristics were very important for this assignment, so I'd have to pose nude so he could gauge my entire body."

"And you agreed to this?" said Katie.

"I asked if the assignment itself involved nude shots. He said some of them would be, yes, and did I have any objection to posing that way. I'd done some lingerie work for a boutique down in the Village and it had turned out pretty well, but I'd never done completely nude. I guess I was kind of afraid of upsetting whoever it was who'd told me to go for this job."

Katie asked, "Were other women 'trying out' the same way?"

"I had that impression, but I never saw anyone else. I was creeped out enough as it was. Then the next day he called and said I'd gotten the job, and to come back the following morning prepared for an all-day shoot."

I wanted to tell her how many lust murder cases I'd handled that had started out with the ruse of a "fashion photographer" inviting a naive, pretty young girl to take some "test shots." But Wendy struck me as being only as naive as she wanted to be.

"He was right," she continued. "It did take all day. There was a man there; Louie called him Bill. I never found out his last name. He was nice enough; that's all I can tell you about him. Louie explained to both of us that we'd be duplicating an 'assignation'—that's what he called it—based on a famous scene."

"Did he have you wear any special clothes?" I asked.

"Yes. He had a dark suit for Bill."

If the plan against Boyd was so elaborate that it involved duplicating photos of him and his wife with specially dressed models, it followed that it would have to be a deep-pockets individual or group with scope, with influence, with financial and intelligence resources. And that paradigm certainly fit J. P. Napoleon.

"Was this suit for Bill more Brooks Brothers or more Armani?" asked Katie.

"Brooks Brothers, definitely."

That squared with Boyd. "And you?"

"A blue knit suit. Conservative compared to what I wear myself. At the beginning of the session we were both fully dressed, and we kind of had to rip each other's clothes off shot by shot."

"Was this all supposed to happen spontaneously?"

"Just the opposite, actually. The camera was on a tripod and Louie was working from a set of prints that he never let us see; he said he didn't want our facial expressions to be influenced. But for each pose he'd come over and physically position us just the way he wanted us." Wendy managed a small laugh. "I have to tell you, it was about as unsexy an experience as you can imagine, even by the end when both of us were stark naked. Louie seemed mainly concerned with getting my head in the right position, which I thought was kind of strange since we were doing a 'sex scene.' " She paused. "By the way, we didn't really 'do it.' And Louie was a gentleman throughout."

Because she and Bill were both just puppets for him. And Knox would have known better than to screw around with someone associated with Napoleon. "Let me make sure I've got this right," I said. "Knox would position both of you the way he wanted, then go back to the camera and snap off a picture?"

"Yeah, except that first he'd take a Polaroid, check it against the shots he was working from, and keep taking Polaroids until he got each pose just the way he wanted. Then he'd snap off a lot of shots with the 35mm camera. Usually eight or ten."

"The contact sheet we saw must have been second generation," I said to Katie, "after he'd selected the image he wanted for each shot." Ironic, I thought, that in Wendy's first nude photo session, it was only her face the photographer was interested in. And the guy Bill wouldn't even rate that. He was merely a stand-in.

"Did you see the finished product?" I asked.

Her voice was stronger, some of the tension gone. She might even have been glad to be telling us her story.

"No. After the session, I asked him if I could have copies of the good prints. He refused, so I asked if I could just come over and see them. He said no to that, too. That's when I got suspicious."

"Of what?" asked Katie.

"I got the impression he was blackmailing someone."

I could feel my pulse. "Why?"

"He was so focused, had to get it just right. And with the secrecy and all the effort and expense he was putting into the shoot, I couldn't figure out any other way he could make money from it."

"Do you think this guy Bill was involved?"

"I don't think so. I don't think he had any idea what was going on."

I said, "Did you confront Knox about what he was doing?"

"I asked him if he was going to doctor the pictures—putting me in with someone else. He told me not to ask questions, I could get hurt. That scared me. I shut up. Was I right? Was he blackmailing someone?" Wendy asked me. I'd become her ally. Katie had been right, as usual. I'd let my anger get to me and I'd begun with the wrong technique.

"That would be a logical conclusion."

"Since you're involved, was this person he was blackmailing the director of the FBI?" Wendy wanted to know.

I was surprised by her perceptivity and reminded myself it wasn't a good idea to underestimate her. "I thought so at first, but with what you've confirmed for me, I don't see how."

"Why don't you ask Louie? Put him through the third degree like you did me."

Katie and I glanced at each other. "Louie Knox was murdered," Katie stated.

Wendy's face went even paler. She made a gasping noise that sounded like "Eeesh."

"It was done rather messily, to make a point."

She shuddered, a whole body spasm of fright. Not an inappropriate reaction. Katie tried to reassure her with a sympathetic smile.

Now we were reading off the same page. I asked Wendy, "How did you know to find me here?"

"I knew you were in New York appearing on television. And I knew you were working for Millicent De Vries."

I was dumbstruck. How the fuck did she know that? Katie's sudden expression was asking the same question. "How did you know that?"

"I was told."

"By who?"

"Same one who told me to go to Louie Knox's studio. On the phone. I've never known his name."

The familiar electric jolt of paranoia, only stronger this time, starting deep in my gut and radiating out in waves until it hit the air. "And that's how you knew to find me here?"

She nodded. "He told me Mrs. De Vries had a suite at the Waldorf Towers. And I knew from a dossier Empire had prepared on you that when you're on the road, you spend time in hotel bars."

The paranoia shimmered along the surface of my skin. So Napoleon was having the same kind of profile material prepared on me that I was doing on him.

As that sank in, Katie took over. "Instead of going through this ruse with the disguise—a good one, by the way—why didn't you just call the number Jake gave in the interviews and show up as yourself?"

"Once my picture was all over television, I was really frightened."

"If you'd called, we would have come to you. You must have realized that."

"I wanted to be able to control the situation, to back out or leave if I wanted." She turned to me. "And I had to get a feeling for you, make sure I trusted you."

"What made you decide you trusted him?" asked Katie.

"Something in his eyes. I can usually tell by that."

Katie smirked. "Would you like to come teach a course at Quantico?"

"So you use this disguise with your, ah . . . professional clients?" I picked up.

"Most of the time. It was safer, cleaner that way. I developed a persona to go with it. Not as shy, more outgoing than I am as myself."

"What about the garter belt?"

Katie looked at me askance, but Wendy smiled. "That was a special touch. I know that guys of your age get turned on by that sort of thing."

My age?

Katie fought back a laugh. "Okay, Jake, so what now?"

"I don't want to go back to my apartment," Wendy said. "Whoever killed Louie Knox could do the same to me. You said yourself I was now in grave danger."

"You'll stay here with us," Katie said. "We'll make sure nothing bad happens. You'll sleep in there with me tonight, and then tomorrow, we'll figure out what to do." That seemed to reassure Wendy somewhat. Katie led her toward the master bedroom. "Come on, you look like you're ready to turn in. I'll get you set up in there."

Meanwhile, I sat there with a Scotch mentally reviewing the through-line of this case. Owl Creek, the militias, the probability that they had been the ones who attacked me—these were all unprovable peripherals at this point. Maybe they were relevant, maybe they weren't. Even the break-in at Toni's house did not fit into any particular slot. But what did we know?

Needle was the woman we had connected to the late Louie Knox, through the contact sheet Paul Sochaczewski had found at the murder scene. Through this same contact sheet, Knox was connected—directly or indirectly—back to Boyd. Since one of the photos from the sheet was found at the house in Sausalito, this was presumptive evidence of a connection to Boyd's death. Needle is revealed to be Wendy Winslow. Wendy is connected—directly or indirectly—to Napoleon through the Empire-

Ward bridge. Is it reasonable to infer, then, that Napoleon is, in fact, tied to Boyd's death? Further, Napoleon apparently knows of the relationship between me and Millicent De Vries. How? And why is it important to him?

I looked down and noticed my glass was already empty.

Katie came out from the bedroom about ten minutes later and closed the door quietly behind her.

"How's she doing?" I asked.

"She'll be okay. I got her washed up and she was off to never-never land. You still drinking?"

I shrugged. "Hair of the dog."

A bottle of Stoli was handy on the top of the bar, so Katie poured for herself. I stayed with the Scotch. I saw her tongue dart tentatively into her glass, stay there a moment to absorb the comforting burn. "Are you as nervous as I am?"

She took me by surprise and a chilly ripple snaked through me. I don't like admitting things like nerves to myself, but she'd called the question. "That I am, Kathleen."

"We've got to be watching our flanks all the time."

"You watch mine and I'll watch yours."

She raised her glass in a salute. "That's what I love about you, Jake: that blithely insouciant wit in the face of danger."

"Hey," I said, returning the salute, "whatever gets you through the night."

"Odd situation we find ourselves in."

"What do you mean?"

"Now we're not only hiding a dead body, but a live one, too. How long are we going to keep Wendy with us?"

"I don't know," I said. "Until we figure out what to do next."

"Do you think it's possible we've overcomplicated this case? I mean, could Louie Knox be our guy and that's as far as it goes—no political overtones, no secret government cabal or any of that conspiracy-nut stuff?"

I nourished my brain with another swallow before I spoke. "It does seem that Knox was the one who was blackmailing Boyd, but I don't think he could have been acting alone. For one thing, Dominic is now convinced Boyd didn't fire the shot himself of his own free will. And Wendy says she was hired by Napoleon."

"True."

"Now let's say for the sake of argument that Knox came to the Sausalito house with the intention of getting some dough out of Boyd, they got into an argument, then what? There was no sign of a struggle. Boyd just let Knox kill him?"

"Okay . . ."

"Then how did a flabby little guy like Knox get a bigger guy in much better condition to swallow his own gun? It doesn't make sense. By himself he couldn't have done it. Someone else must have been there with him."

Katie paced in front of me. "You're right. And the next question is, where would he have gotten the pictures in the first place? I mean the pictures of Tom and Madeline Boyd that he cribbed from. There's another conspiracy element right there."

I had just been considering that very question; it was another of those sudden-cessation-of-ignorance moments. "It was something Ted said about the surveillance camera in Boyd's home in Sausalito when I was out there. Ted said that Boyd wouldn't let it be used because the time that he and Madeline spent out there he wanted to be private and off-limits. When I thought about that, I realized it could imply that when the director was in the Washington area, he knew he couldn't expect the same degree of privacy. Which means, I'll bet there are one or more security cameras in the Chevy Chase house, and they work."

"So the original pictures that Knox shot of Wendy and Bill are based on surveillance shots of the Boyds making love."

"Exactly."

"And how did Knox get access to those photos? Who passed them on? Obviously someone on the inside."

"More to the point," I said, "if Louie Knox was the one blackmailing Thomas Boyd, then who killed him? And why?"

33

As I've said, I'm not a psychic, but I do believe you can train your intu-itive powers to work for you. The ones who claim to be police psychics often just have the ability to pick up on subtle indicators at a crime scene or unusual nuances in the behavior of others. Then they filter these observations through their experience and imagination and come up with their "startling" conclusions.

When I started analyzing crimes and crime scenes as a profiler, I tried to train my subconscious to help me out. Before I went to bed, I'd immerse myself in details of a case, almost willing myself to dream about it. Though a lot of the dream would be weird and/or irrelevant, there'd often be a useful nugget in there, my subconscious mind having filtered out all the garbage and pointed me to the one element I needed to concentrate on. These dreams aren't the flights of fancy you normal-ly think of; they're much more—how can I say it?—procedural, almost waking fantasies. Anyway, toward morning, just before dawn, I had one.

In it, I was going on television, saying I was looking for an individual named J. P. Napoleon, who had information crucial to the solution of Thomas Boyd's death.

I got an anonymous call from someone who told me to wait outside the Waldorf, where I would be picked up. A few minutes later a huge midnight-blue limousine pulled up and the rear door opened. The driver told me to get in. Then he blindfolded me, just as Richard Royce's men had, closed the door, and drove off.

Hours later, it seemed, the car pulled to a stop. But when the blindfold was removed, I was standing in front of Millicent De Vries's mansion in Washington. Mrs. De Vries was waiting for me in the solarium, dressed in tennis whites, with a racket slung over her shoulder, tending her orchids. "But . . . but I came to see Napoleon," I stammered.

She smiled. "Who did you think Napoleon was?"

"I . . . I don't know."

"Where do you think all of my money comes from?"

"I thought it was from the pharmaceutical company."

"That's part of it. Of course, now that it's been combined with Empire, there's even more. Now we're a full-service company."

"I thought you hated that takeover. It's why you wanted me to go after Napoleon for you."

She looked at me with pity, as if I were hopelessly naive. "Think about it, Jake: Didn't any of the details of our arrangement seem unusual or suspicious to you? The several-million-dollar drug-smuggling airplane that I was able to secure with a snap of my fingers? The knowledge of your confidential Flying Squad proposal? The way Ms. Winslow knew to find you at my suite at the Waldorf? My interest in supporting a washed-up, broken-wing FBI agent who can no longer shoot straight, for whom I was willing to write a blank check? Why would I do all that? What did I stand to gain?"

I stood there dumbfounded. Before I could respond, she answered her own question. "You always teach that the most sophisticated criminals will figure out a way to inject themselves into the investigation—to gain the intelligence they need to stay a step ahead. By asking you to 'go after' Napoleon and report back to me, I'd be able to stay that crucial step ahead. What do you think I've been buying? And in my income bracket, this entire operation has been very reasonably priced, considering what I'm getting out of it."

She poured glasses of champagne for both of us, then said, "Now, let's talk about your next assignment."

That was when I woke up, sticking to the sheets by the perspiration that had bathed my body. My head pounded from excessive drinking and my gut felt as if it was about to betray me. Carefully, I sat up, put my legs over the side of the bed, then tentatively tested my stability on my feet. When I was reasonably confident they'd support me, I staggered out of the bedroom and into the hall bathroom, where I stood in front of the sink and splashed cold water on my face.

Man, are you a sight, I told my forbidding reflection. *You got to regroup before the troops see you.*

I was clammy, the entire surface of my skin felt twitchy, and I knew I'd never get back to sleep. So I stripped off my shorts, turned on the shower tap, and stepped in.

But even as I stood there, letting the jets dart into me, I couldn't shut my mind off or turn it away from the message my subconscious had been giving me.

Was I onto something? I'd never fully understood Mrs. De Vries's motivation for funding the Flying Squad, and I'm never comfortable when there's something basic that I don't understand.

Okay, what if Millicent De Vries really was J. P. Napoleon? What if he/she was behind the Boyd murder and that was why she had taken me on? It seemed far-fetched, even crazy, but the things she'd enumerated in my reverie couldn't be completely ignored. I wasn't sure exactly what it was telling me, but at the least, I figured I was warning myself not to place too much trust in anyone at this point.

I called Trevor to the suite to watch over Wendy, then Katie and I paid a visit to her West Side apartment.

As soon as I opened the front door with Wendy's key, it was obvious. The entire place had been ransacked. The upholstered furniture had been slashed and overturned, crockery had been smashed to the floor. We drew our weapons and went through the place. I went to the right, into the bedroom, while Katie went left into the kitchen.

"Kitchen's clear!" she called to me after a few minutes.

"Bedroom's clear!"

She joined me in the bedroom. The double bed had been overturned, the closet and dresser drawers pulled open, and Wendy's dresses and lingerie slashed, ripped, and cut.

"No question they came looking for her after my public announcement," I said.

"And when she wasn't here, they decided to punish her anyway."

"As well as warn her if she ever came back. Just like they tried to warn me by breaking into Toni's house."

"So did we save her or almost get her killed?" Katie wondered out loud.

"I'm not sure," I replied grimly. Occasionally, on certain types of predatory crimes, I've convinced the sister or female friend of a victim to act as "bait" to lure the UNSUB out into the open. This is probably the most difficult and emotionally ravaging type of decision I ever have to make, and even though I've never "lost" one, there hasn't been a single incident where I haven't searched my soul and second-guessed my actions. And I was sure starting to do that here.

34

We decided to say nothing to NYPD about the break-in until we figured out our next move. We had no idea *who* knew *what* through *whom,* and until we did, it would be dangerous to say anything to anyone.

When we got back to the hotel, Wendy and Trevor were finishing up a room-service breakfast. Trevor was almost never too stressed to eat, and it looked as if Wendy was starting to relax a little and had an appetite to show for it. She looked comfortable wearing Katie's gray Academy sweats.

I gave her some time to digest, then told her about what Katie and I had discovered. "But we're going to protect you now," Katie assured her.

Then I brought out the set of photographs of "her" performing sexually with Thomas Boyd. She took in her breath with a clutching sound, and for a moment I was afraid she was choking.

"This is why we had to find you," I explained. "And this is why whoever wrecked your apartment didn't want us to. Now that Knox is dead, you're the most vulnerable link to Thomas Boyd."

Wendy sat slightly hunched forward, with her forearms resting on the tabletop, wringing her hands. "Why don't you take first turn in the bathroom?" Katie said. "I'll get cleaned up after you're through."

"Okay," Wendy replied, and stood up.

"Wendy, does anyone know you came to see me?"

She stopped. "No."

"No one at all? This is very important."

"Well, I was told in a call from Empire to 'look you up,' but it wasn't like I was supposed to come here tonight and report right back . . . you know?"

Katie and I exchanged a look. "Well, the idea that she might decide to freelance was enough to try to deal with her the same as Knox," I said to the other two.

I called Dominic and Jerry up to the suite. It was time for another case consultation meeting.

A common misconception about criminal investigations, encouraged by novels, TV shows, and movies, is that the wily detective is so smart that he can figure out early which set of tracks to follow. In real life, it ain't often that clear-cut. In a real investigation, as often as not, you find yourself embarked on a massive fishing expedition. You keep throwing out your net or line—what we call going proactive—and hope that something will snatch the bait. That's what Peter Sutherland was doing when he recommended that the California police surveil the grave site. And that he happened to be at cross purposes with my team wasn't his fault, or that the initiative went nowhere.

One of the techniques the FBI has developed to manage a case that seems to go all over the place is the visual investigative analysis, or VIA. Essentially, it's a chart that begins from the point the crime is committed and graphically follows every lead in whatever direction it appears to go. When you see all the events, dates, and locations laid out in front of you, it's easier to see what jibes. That way, any overlaps or intersections can actually be appreciated visually. It's proven to be an effective means of stating the all-important *WHY? + HOW? = WHO?* equation.

I had the hotel's business office send me up a large laminated white board and easel and a set of colored erasable marker pens, then drew out the case as a central timeline with the various clue or lead branches radiating off at the appropriate points. For example, at the "Death + 2" day indicator, I had noted the attack on me, its location, and likely involvement of a militia/survivalist group. I backed that up with a notation of the animosity between the FBI and the Wyoming Defenders. On the VIA chart, the Louis Knox murder related directly to the Boyd death because of the contact sheet found on Knox's premises. Knox led to Wendy . . . Wendy led to Napoleon . . . which tied Napoleon back to Knox and, therefore, presumably, to Boyd. I also produced a visually apparent tie-back to the militia thread because of the tattoo and the dirt Jerry found on the work shoes. Not definitive, as I noted, but something that belonged on the chart. A separate line represented the gouging out of Knox's eyes as a potential tie to the Russian Mob.

"Okay, let's focus on the Knox connection," I said, underlining that reference in green. "As Katie said, the faked photos were really well done. Even after she knew it was Wendy's head on Mrs. Boyd's body, she couldn't tell how it was done. But someone else would be able to tell no matter how perfect the match."

"Boyd himself," said Katie.

"Right. Because as soon as he saw the photos, he would know he'd never had sex with this woman, and in all likelihood, he'd recall the actual event when he and Madeline did it in the hallway of their Chevy Chase house."

"So that wouldn't be a very effective way to blackmail him," Jerry offered.

"Congratulations!"

He looked back at me quizzically. "Then what are you saying?"

"That not only don't I think Judge Boyd carried those supposedly compromising photographs out to California with him, I don't think he ever saw them."

"Not even at the murder scene?" asked Dominic.

"Not even at the murder scene. Those photos, or actually that one photo that 'accidentally' fell out of the pack and slipped under the bed, was for the benefit of whoever found him. The burned ones were part of the staging of the crime scene to make us think Boyd had tried to destroy embarrassing evidence. My guess is that after Knox produced that roll of shots, they went through them and chose one for us to see."

I moved farther to the right on the VIA chart. "And as we've shown, through Wendy, we can tie J. P. Napoleon to Knox, which means we can tie him to Boyd."

"Are you saying Napoleon had him killed?" asked Jerry.

"Not necessarily. I don't think we have enough evidence yet to say that. But what we do have is a through-line from evidence found at the murder scene to the individual who produced that evidence to Napoleon, or his henchman, who told Wendy to go for the studio job."

I went back to the top of the chart. "Okay, let's consider our equation. Why? Why would the militia groups want to get rid of Boyd? I think we all know that. No disagreement. But then we get to how. They'd be more likely to try something public and symbolic, something that would get all of their people to rally round. For whatever it's worth, when I confronted Richard Royce, I got the feeling he was telling me the truth, that whatever he thought of Boyd and however outraged they were about Owl Creek, they didn't do it. Besides, I think the plot with the faked photos and the model and all that isn't their style. It's too complicated, not direct enough for them.

"So let's look at the Russian Mob. Again, we have a signature and a motive. The signature is the gouging out of Knox's eyes, and the motive is Boyd's public pledge to crack down on all foreign organized-crime elements. And while La Cosa Nostra has steadily lost power and influence ever since the mid-1980s, these other ethnic organizations are growing, particularly the Russians here in New York."

"What about the how?" Dominic prompted.

"That's where they lose ground," I said. "If they were going to kill Boyd, I don't think they'd do it this way, and I don't think they'd do it in California, where they're still pretty thin. Again, I'd look to see them try something symbolic if they wanted to make a public statement, or else something direct and efficient if they didn't—like an out-and-out assassination. And since this looks as if someone who Boyd knew would have to be involved, I doubt they've got anyone close enough or high enough in the organization to fit the bill."

"Then Napoleon is the through-line," said Katie.

"I think so. We've got motive: he runs a profitable international organization which he knows I was foaming at the mouth to uncover and Boyd wanted desperately to close down. But just as important is the how. This was an elaborate, secretive, and very tricky scenario—Napoleon's style. He doesn't want to make a public statement. He doesn't want to arouse any emotions or rally anyone to his cause. He just wants an adversary out of the way.

"It all fits in with the profile we've come up for him," I continued. "Napoleon is a game-player; that's his signature. His games are deadly, but they're still games. That's the way he operates—by indirection, by masking true goals and motives, by outmaneuvering and compromising his enemies. I could even see him staging certain elements to make us think it was one group or another, or merely to confuse us by combining elements of several different possible killers. And since we know from DEA tip-offs that Napoleon has an elaborate intelligence network in place, it makes sense that he would go about offing Boyd by penetrating the director's own circle."

"How would he have done that?" asked Jerry.

"The most direct and obvious way would have been by offering money, and he'd be in a position to offer gobs of it. It's the same thing as turning guys in the CIA. You start looking into their backgrounds and you find debts, kids who need to go to college, wives with a taste for the good life, things like that. Normally, FBI agents don't have the same kind of wares to sell. But think about it, it doesn't even have to be someone superclose to Boyd. You think about all the agents and support personnel he'd recognize by sight, all the ones who might have some legitimate reason to go to his house, that's a huge population of potential accomplices. And remember, we don't even know who Napoleon is or what he looks like. As with Wendy, it all would have been done through intermediaries—probably intermediaries who never even showed their own faces."

I noticed Jerry doodling idly on his pad. I hoped I wasn't losing him.

"We've got to figure out who those accomplices might be," I went on. "When we do that, we can also determine whether I'm right about Napoleon, and if I am, exactly what his connection might be."

Dominic spoke up. "So how do we find out?"

"It's time to go fishing. First, we move operations back to Washington, where we have more control. Second, we go proactive again and set the mousetraps."

Katie frowned. "And I assume you're talking about using Wendy as the cheese."

"We'll keep her protected in every way," I resolved. "After all those years in the Bureau, I'm not going to lose one now."

Left unsaid, of course, was that old J. P. Napoleon was so slick that we had had to profile behavior and tactics of someone we neither knew, nor could infer, anything about on a personal level. Of course, sometimes you have to figure things out based on the *absence* of evidence. I once profiled a gangland stabbing in a meatpacking plant and determined that the murder weapon, which no one could find, was a stiletto molded out of ice.

I was still coming up against the same frigging brick wall. The scent of Napoleon was all over this thing, and yet he still remained a phantom. Not only did it challenge me, it pissed me off. Somehow, I would get this guy, whomever he—or she—turned out to be.

Jerry doodling idly on his pad.

It hit me. "Jerry, what are you drawing?"

He looked up in surprise. "Huh? Uh . . . actually it's a picture of you, Jake. You don't mind, do you?"

"I want you to make a sketch with Wendy."

"A sketch of Wendy? Sure, if you want."

"No. A sketch *with* Wendy. A composite of J. P. Napoleon."

○

I had Katie stay in the suite's living room to help Wendy relax and keep her calm. Trevor, Dominic, and I cleared out.

Jerry worked with Wendy for about ninety minutes, letting her describe the man she told us about at the reception in Switzerland. Once Jerry had an overall idea of the type she was talking about, he began keying in on the individual components of the face, feature by feature. What were his eyes like? His nose? Mouth? The line of his jaw? What kind of eyebrows? How low did his hairline reach? Did his ears stick out? And on and on.

When Katie called and said they were done, I came back to the suite. Jerry held up his work.

It was a white male in his late fifties, with heavy, dark eyebrows that were set off by his graying hair. The cheekbones were high and prominent, almost feminine. The nose was medium-sized, straight, and slightly pointed. He had a mustache and goatee, carefully trimmed and somewhat darker in color than his hair. And though there's no scientific basis for it, I often think I can tell something about predators, particularly serial sexual predators, by their eyes. In Jerry's composite, this guy had that kind of eyes—dark, cynical, cruel. It may sound like a cliché, but I think it is a cliché because it's become a part of our collective subconscious. Whether or not we understand why or how, we sense evil when it is around us.

I turned to Wendy. "The man you think might be Napoleon: Is this what he looks like?"

She nodded. "As closely as I remember."

"Watching the process between her and Jerry, I'm convinced it's a good composite," Katie said.

"Okay then." It was odd, in a way, finally being able to personify this man, this entity, I'd pursued for so long. On one level, it focused me more, made the goal of getting to him seem more concrete and attainable. On another level, though, particularizing him—if, in fact, this was him—took something away, detracted from the all-encompassing evil he represented to me. Giving this criminal force a face and visual personality diminished him, made him banal. It made him, in some ways, just like the rest of us.

○

On the way out to *The Broken Wing* at JFK, I called Orlando Ravan and requested a meeting at his office with Peter Sutherland and Neil Burke present. Ravan was only too happy to accommodate my request. In fact, he told me to get my ass back and report to him ASAP. Though I hadn't asked for Harry Gillette, I had no doubt Burke would bring him along.

Katie's immediate assignment was to prepare Wendy for her role. It's never an easy decision to involve a civilian in what is essentially an undercover operation, but sometimes there's no practical alternative. In the case of a drug bust, where the civilian is an established druggie or trafficker who you've turned in exchange for immunity or easier treatment, you don't feel so bad about it. When the subject really is an innocent party who's inevitably going to have to be placed in some danger, the responsibility and concern weigh heavily. I think our colleagues in the espionage trade deal with it better emotionally than we do. They consider themselves at war and know that in a war you're going to take casualties. Those of us in law enforcement who deal in high-intensity/low-numbers situations can't stomach those casualties as easily.

Still, that Wendy had so successfully taken on the Penny Miller persona and damn near fooled me meant we had some talent working on our side. Ultimately, it was Katie who convinced her to go along with the plan, and Katie would do something like that if she felt it was the only way to make Wendy safe and eliminate the unknown danger. I just hoped Wendy could rise to the challenge.

Harry Gillette was indeed part of the meeting in Ravan's office, and he didn't do much to hide his utter disdain for me.

"How's it going, Harry? I've missed you," I rode him, but he refused to take the bait. He merely stood next to Neil Burke and glared. Actually, though, he might prove useful, I'd concluded. I wanted what got said here to leak down through the various Bureau channels until it reached my targeted UNSUB or UNSUBs, and the greater the number of participants, the faster that process might move. Especially someone like Harry, who'd do whatever he thought he could to thwart me.

"All right, gentlemen, let's take seats and get started," Ravan said, rapping with his knuckles on his large mahogany desk. "Jake, what is it you want to report?"

Remaining standing while the others sat, I paced back and forth in front of the acting director's desk to make sure I was maintaining his attention. The others would fall into place around him.

"Unfortunately," I began, "my attempt to go through the media to have the woman we've code-named Needle come forward has not been successful."

"It was a ridiculous stunt to pull without letting the Bureau in on it," Gillette said. "Personally, I think it comes damn close to interfering with an investigation."

You want to see interfering with an investigation, you little twerp, I'll show you interfering with an investigation, I thought to myself.

"In retrospect, Harry, it appears you were right. This isn't an exact science. The question before us now, though, is what else to do, since I not only believe this woman's life to be in danger, but believe she may hold the key to whether or not we'll be able to state confidently what really happened to Judge Boyd."

"I'm going to recommend disciplinary action," Gillette huffed.

"Ah, Harry," Peter broke in, "that might be kind of tough. Jake's not in the Bureau anymore."

"I'm sure there are avenues. Neil, I'll look into it and prepare a memo for your consideration."

"Yeah, Harry, you do that," Burke said deadpan.

Then Ravan said, "Jake, do you have any ideas?"

"Well, actually, sir, Peter's the one with the idea. He and I decided that if my technique didn't work, it might be because I don't have the credibility as an individual, the Bureau should try the same thing with a different phone number, and see if she'll bite."

"The only thing is, to pull this off, we'll have to appear to discredit Jake and his investigation in the process," Peter pointed out.

"I'm aware of that," I said. "And I'm willing to take the fall. I think it's that important. Of course, I'd hope you'd 'rehabilitate' me after the case was closed."

Gillette turned up his pudgy little nose and sniffed as if he'd just smelled shit. "Is Jake going to be involved with this phase of the operation?"

"No," Peter answered. "We both believe it would be better policy if he's not."

This seemed to mollify the little turd-head.

Ravan turned to Burke. "Neil, I want you to organize this thing. Get whatever resources you need from Engineering. I'll make sure they know this is highest priority. Mr. Sutherland, I'll expect you to give whatever support's required. And I want to be notified as soon as anything turns up."

"Absolutely," Peter responded. "I'll make some calls from here before we even go back."

As we were walking out, I got Peter alone for a moment. "I trust you'll let me know, too."

"Of course. I just wish there was some way I could let Harry know that I'm letting you know."

I grinned. "Don't worry. He'll suspect it anyway." I hesitated. "There's one more thing you can do, that we don't have to involve the others in."

Pete frowned inquisitively. "What's that?"

"Find out who in the Bureau might have had access to security-camera photos from Boyd's house."

∘

While I was meeting at headquarters, Trevor was scoping out a room we'd rented for Wendy at the Watergate Hotel. Actually, we'd rented three rooms, because we had the adjoining rooms on either side, accessible by connecting doors. Katie wanted to go along to assist, but I needed her to baby-sit Wendy, whom I didn't want in the room until we were ready for her. Instead, we made an exception to our crew noninvolvement policy and brought along Scott, since he would be helpful on the technical requirements of the job. If the suitcases the porters brought up to the rooms seemed unusually heavy, it was because they contained the tools, instruments, and equipment Trevor would need.

The room was traditionally furnished, so a crystal wall sconce turned out to be the perfect location for the tiny fiber-optic video camera that would transmit to our staging room/command center. Trevor mounted two wireless mikes on the underside of picture frames. When he and Scott were finished, they wheeled the luggage into the staging room, then called Katie and told her to bring Wendy over. Katie would be occupying the room on the right.

I wanted everything covered and each potential suspect considered as a possible. So when he left the hotel, Trevor went back home and made a call on our secure cell phone to his one strong contact in the militia/right-wing survivalist movement. This contact was so sensitive that I didn't know his identity and don't to this day. What I did know about the man was that he had been at the heart of the Wyoming Defenders, but had become increasingly uneasy about the talk of assassinating public figures and undermining the federal government. After the publicity over Owl Creek, the man secretly contacted Trevor and told him he thought he could be effective as a contact and source.

And now Trevor told him to get the word out within the movement that the woman who we hoped would be a material witness had come to D.C. to talk to the feds and was being put up in Room 632 of the Watergate Hotel.

That was step one.

For step two, I called Paul Sochaczewski in New York and asked him to use his contacts to get the same word out to the local bosses of the Russian Mob.

Then for step three, I called Emily Jones, a reporter at the *Washington Post* with whom I'd always had a good working relationship. I'd first met her when I was directing the Bureau's hostage negotiations during the National Rifle Association headquarters takeover, which was a controversial and extremely stressful experience for all concerned, and I thought she was very evenhanded. Since then, when I'd had a story I felt I had to get out, either openly or anonymously, I'd often turned to Emily because I knew I could trust her. I told her that the FBI was about to put out a public call for Needle, and that we had reason to be optimistic she would turn up. If she did, I'd give Emily the exclusive on who and where this person was, and I wanted her to be ready to run with the story as soon as it happened. That way, I figured, if neither the militia groups, the Russian Mob, or anyone in the FBI itself took our bait, we'd open up competition to the public at large and see what happened.

It was now a matter of sitting back and enduring the toughest part of any investigation: the wait.

∘

While I waited, I made a run over to Millicent De Vries's house, parking the Aston Martin on the drive.

Frederick escorted me into the sunroom, where Mrs. De Vries was waiting. As usual, she smiled warmly, greeted me, and offered me a glass of wine, which I declined.

"I hope I'm not interrupting anything," I said.

She brushed away the absurd notion with a wave of her hand. "Not at all. But you sounded rather urgent on the phone."

"Well, I've got something you might be interested in."

"I'm interested in whatever you have to show me."

"This, I think, you'll be very interested in."

"And what would that be?" she said with another gracious smile.

"A composite sketch of the man who might be—and I stress *might be*—J. P. Napoleon."

Suddenly, the sunny disposition and diplomatic airs vanished, replaced by determination and riveted concentration. "Let me see it."

I handed her a copy of Jerry's sketch and watched as she took it in.

In all of my years in law enforcement and crime-solving, I had never encountered anyone who actually looked as if he or she had "seen a ghost."

Until now.

Millicent De Vries was pale, almost gray, and her hands were trembling as she said, "This looks like my late husband, Fletcher. Or what Fletcher would look like now—if he were still alive."

35

Now we were back in the Tudor-style library, sitting together on an ancient, rolled-arm, tufted-leather sofa, the great shelves of matched, leather-bound books providing a comforting isolation from the vagaries of the outside world.

"Are you certain?" I asked her.

"No, of course I'm not certain," Mrs. De Vries replied with the first display of brusqueness I'd ever experienced from her. She rose and went over to the desk, where she picked up a silver-framed picture and brought it over. "You tell me."

I took the frame from her and held it in front of me, trying to absorb the image as an entirety before I made a judgment. The man in the photo was much younger and smiling broadly. From the way he was dressed, it looked as if he'd just returned from the boat, the avocation that, shortly after the photo was taken, would cost him his life. The Fletcher De Vries in the picture was clean-shaven, his jawline squarish on the sides but angling down to a pronounced point at the chin.

"Did Fletcher ever have a beard and mustache?" I asked.

"I think for a little while in college. Never since I knew him."

Nevertheless, I had to acknowledge a striking resemblance between the lighthearted young man in the photograph and the eerie, malevolent-looking one in Jerry's sketch. The characteristics that don't change much with age—nose, ears, eyebrows, lower forehead—sure looked as if they could be the same person. The eyes, usually the most telling feature, weren't much help in this case because of the vast difference in expressions. If you could imagine the man in the composite smiling at all, his eyes would take on a malignant, menacing countenance, nothing like the merry and buoyant expression in Fletcher's photo.

But the cheekbones—they were a telling factor. Those high, almost femininely elegant cheekbones. Others could have the same facial structure, of course, but together with all the other elements, I had to agree with Mrs. De Vries that if Fletcher were alive today, he'd probably look just like this.

"Could he be alive today?" I asked.

"He drowned almost twenty years ago."

"Excuse me, Mrs. De Vries, I'm sorry to have to put you through this . . . but are you sure?"

"He went out in a boat from the harbor at Monte Carlo and neither he nor the boat ever came back."

"Was a body found?"

"No. There was an extensive search, but nothing turned up. A mast from the boat—they were almost positive it was from Fletcher's boat—eventually turned up, but that was all." She leaned forward, one hand rubbing the back of the other. "Just what are you trying to tell me, Jake?"

As she leaned forward, I leaned back, crossing my legs to force myself into a more relaxed posture. "I'm not trying to tell you anything. I just wonder if it is remotely possible that Fletcher . . . Ambassador De Vries . . . didn't drown that day."

Instead of responding directly, she rose abruptly and crossed over to the window, staring out at the terraced garden as if she couldn't bear to face anyone at this suddenly private moment.

"I'm sorry about asking you these questions," I continued, talking to her back, "but apparently there was a woman on the boat with him: Elena Farrare. I understand that she wasn't seen again until her remains washed up on shore."

Without turning around, she nodded.

"I know this is very painful, but to your knowledge, were the rumors true about . . . about their involvement?"

"I don't know," she replied softly. "Of course I heard things from time to time . . . not about this woman but some others. I never knew whether they were true."

"Not Ms. Farrare?"

"No. Never. Not until after the accident. But there could have been a completely innocent explanation."

"Yes, of course there could," I said soothingly.

"So without proof, I chose to think the best."

"I understand."

Finally, she turned around. "So . . . where do we go from here?"

Yes, that was the question. It would be easy and tempting to jump to conclusions, but I knew from experience that this could be perilous. Once any investigation goes off on a particular assumption, it's difficult to go back and find your direction.

"I don't have an answer for that yet, Mrs. De Vries. But as soon as I do, I'll let you know."

○

By the next afternoon, the FBI started getting the word out. Not the way I'd done it, through personal interviews—the Bureau culture doesn't put a human face on unless it is absolutely necessary. What they did was release a bulletin with a photograph attached that just about every news organization in the country picked up. Certainly the other groups to whom we'd leaked the conflicting information that Needle was already under FBI control would see these reports. But they would figure it was just part of an FBI plot to keep them away, so if any of them turned out to have a vested interest in the proceedings, they'd be sure to show up.

I decided to give it all a little more time to look legitimate—to up the ass-pucker factor within the Bureau. We'd let the story come out in the next day's papers before we finally dropped the baited hook into the water. Until then, I went home to try to clean up some of the mountains of crap I hadn't been tending to since . . . well, since about the time Toni and I split up.

For a second, I was about to get in my car and go over to visit the kids until I quickly remembered that I had sent them away, that what I'd now gotten myself involved in made it unsafe for them to be around. I'd always been the one out traveling and leaving them at home. Now it was the other way around, and the void was dark and enormous. Was this the way it had been for them each time? How could I have repeatedly made them feel as bad, as lonely, as I was feeling now?

The phone connection wasn't the same, but it was something. I was delighted when Eric answered. "Hey, champ, how you doing?"

"Oh, hi, Dad. It's okay."

"And your sister and mom?"

"They're okay."

"Good. What's going on?"

"Nothing much. Aunt Josephine took us to the pool yesterday."

"How's your swimming?"

"Okay."

He was going through all of the standard, perfunctory responses, the same as if he'd been writing a letter from camp. Kids of that age, boys especially, don't have much to say to their parents. That was why the phone was such a poor substitute for actually being able to see them and hold them.

I wanted to tell him that I now realized how painful it must have been for him and Ali all the times I was away . . . never knowing when I was going to leave and when I'd be back. But that would have been an unfair burden to place on him, merely to relieve the burden of my own. So I just said, as cheerfully as I could, "Is Ali around?"

"Nah. She and Mom and Aunt Josephine went to the mall to go shopping. Sounded too yucky and boring to me."

A clutch of panic gripped me under the breastbone. "Eric, is anyone there with you?"

"No. It's finally quiet around here without all those women talking, talking, talking all the time."

Should I call the police and ask them to send a cruiser? Should I call Peter and take him up on his offer of Bureau surveillance?

Hold on, Donovan, I told myself, *get a grip!* The point of sending them away to Wisconsin was to get them out of harm's way. No one knew where they were. How many times had my kid been alone in the house since he'd been there? Twenty or thirty, probably. I was getting panicky because I happened to know about it. Was he any safer if his sister, mother, or aunt were home? Maybe if Glenn was there, but he worked in town; he was always away during the days. I'd already concluded they were all safer if I didn't alert anyone, even law enforcement contacts, and so I had to live by that decision. And this was another burden it would be criminally unfair to lay on my son.

"Okay, sport," I said. "When they all get home, tell them I called and that I love them."

"Sure thing, Dad. Bye."

I hung up, thinking about a discussion I'd had with Toni in which she'd warned me that I couldn't let my profession and what I'd seen make prisoners and paranoiacs out of my kids. I couldn't go through life, through their lives, with one of them handcuffed to each of my wrists just to make sure they stayed safe. But I was the direct cause of this situation, I reminded myself. It didn't make any difference, though. I couldn't resolve it and this exercise wasn't productive, so I decided to put it out of my mind for the time being. I was unsuccessful in that, too.

In the middle of the afternoon I got a call from Peter. "Just want you to know I'm on top of this, chief."

"You're the chief now," I said. "What've you got?"

"I think I'd rather not take a chance on being overheard. I don't want to drag you all the way down to Quantico. How about if we meet halfway, say at Potomac Mills?"

Potomac Mills is a humongous example of that staple of modern life and commerce known as the discount, or outlet, shopping mall. It's located off I-95 in Dale City, about forty minutes south of Washington and twenty minutes north of Quantico. Not only can you find just about anything you want at the price you want to pay, it is also the largest tourist draw in the state of Virginia, even surpassing Colonial Williamsburg. I've also noticed on my forays to the place with my kids that if this represents America, then America is seriously overweight. Not only that, but dresses to highlight the fact. And as I stood at the Ikea entrance waiting for Peter to show, I noted again how I'd never seen such an expanse of spandex utilized to such unflattering effect. The only way Pete and I would get spotted here is if we seemed too thin.

Peter came over to me with an enigmatic smile, as if he couldn't wait to tell me something closely held, something that other people didn't know but would want to. "So?"

"Well . . ." His tone was almost gossipy. "Turns out that set of pictures of Tom and Madeline Boyd getting it on were famous throughout the director's security detail. Obviously they were supposed to be confidential, but when something that unusual and that juicy comes out, word gets around. It was particularly noteworthy because it was common knowledge with the security folks that the Boyds' relationship was—how shall we say it?—chilly."

"Maybe they were trying to rekindle some of the old fire," I suggested as we strolled. "Those pictures had to have been taken in a hallway."

"Your guess is as good as mine. But it just shows you the way things are compartmented around here. We didn't know about the pictures, so when that one showed up at the death scene, we didn't recognize it. The security people would have recognized it, but they weren't in on the death-scene details."

"What about Hennigan?" I asked. "The agent who found the photo under the bed?"

"He was out of the San Francisco Field Office, so he didn't travel with Boyd. Security was only a temporary duty for him while the director was in the area."

"And Ted Novello didn't know anything about the pictures?"

"Evidently not. Or if he did, he was keeping that information to himself." There was a pause in the conversation while we both let Peter's observation sink in. Then he said, "I wonder what that tells us."

We strolled to a place that sold cinnamon buns, stuffed our faces, and continued our walk. Peter reported, "I talked to everyone I could find in the part of the security section that would have had access to the Boyd photos. Most of them acknowledged having seen them, but of course they swore they'd never shown them to anyone outside the division."

"Everyone?"

"Ah! Everyone but one. One guy—his name is Ron Frishman—disappeared within days of Boyd's death." Peter took a big bite.

I stopped walking. "What do you mean 'disappeared'?"

He swallowed. "Just what I said: disappeared. He doesn't show up for work for a couple of days, his squad supervisor calls repeatedly and gets no answer, a team of agents come to his house, but he's definitely long out of Dodge."

"You know anything more about the guy?"

Peter shook his head. "It's taken me all afternoon to come up with this much."

That had to be the connection to Knox, which meant Frishman was probably Napoleon's way into the Bureau. And if that was true, the odds were he'd disappeared for good. My guess was we'd find out Knox had some casual relationship with Frishman that started out having nothing to do with this "job," but that as soon as Frishman was in a position to do something for him, the relationship quickly got more formal.

"Listen, you've done a great job," I said. "Would you mind if I sent Katie down to Quantico to follow up on him? It could be important."

"Sure, go ahead. I'll provide her whatever covering fire she needs."

I called Katie on her cell phone and explained her assignment.

"Like now?"

"Like now."

"What about Wendy?"

"Is Trevor there?"

"Yeah."

"He'll take care of her. Just get your butt down there." I was sorry I snapped. I guessed it must be the fatigue or the strain of worrying about Wendy's safety catching up with me. We all had to hold it together a while longer.

∘

Katie stopped off at my house on her way back from Quantico, her attitude considerably improved. I knew that if I threw her back into the hunt and she came up with something, that would do the trick. I realized I was really glad to see her.

"I gotta tell you, it felt weird being down there," she related. "I hadn't been since your retirement luncheon, and even there, I felt like a gate-crasher. Anyway, I was able to access Frishman's personnel file and the notations on his background check when he first applied to the Bureau. It seems that he and Louie Knox were in the same unit in the Signal Corps. Frishman didn't get an early out like Knox did. If he had, he probably wouldn't have made the Bureau. But now we've got a solid connection between the two of them."

Then that was it. Those photos went right from FBI security into Louie Knox's studio, for the benefit of the very party or parties, it seemed overwhelmingly likely, who soon thereafter ended his tenure on earth. "So he was the one in a position to pass the photos on to Knox. I wonder if they made any connections with militia types while they were in the army. That would tie in the tattoo on Knox's wrist."

"The FBI's been quietly looking for Frishman," Katie added, "but if he's involved in this, he's probably out of the country by now."

"Or involuntarily gone through a trash compactor somewhere." I put my hand on her upper arm. "This is good work. I'm proud of you."

"Thanks. It's nice to be appreciated for a change. You were just about the only one in the Bureau who ever showed it."

"I tried." I took her hand. "Katie . . ."

"What is it?"

I wasn't sure how to continue, so I said nothing.

She looked at me funny. "Are you okay?"

"Yeah . . . yeah, I'm good. It's just . . . you're very special."

She smiled with pleasure. "To the world in general, or just to you?"

"Well, I can't speak for the world . . ."

"God knows you have in the past."

"Very funny. I'm trying to be serious here. I realize . . . I mean, I've always liked you; you know that. But since we've been together on this thing, I realize how much I . . . treasure you, how I just feel good when you're around. Even when you're cranky like you were this afternoon."

"I wasn't cranky this afternoon," she stated, her eyes bright. "You were."

"Or like right now."

She slugged me on the arm, pulling the force of her punch only at the last instant, saying, "I am not!" with a giggle of protest and that impish grin of hers.

As I gazed at her, all the different images, personas, fragments of memory, scrolled through my mind: the cute, delightful girl with the impish grin; the beautiful professional who dressed to kill; the impatient, petulant child; the meticulous, brilliant profiler and analyst; the elegant, sophisticated woman in the evening gown; the athletic tomboy; the panty-hose calendar model with the endless legs; the world-class marksman who joked about changing her underwear after shooting a bad guy; the kitten and the tigress. And on and on. There were so many Katies and I loved all of them.

"Anyway," I said, "you are very special to me, in all your moods, in all of your 'infinite variety.' "

"I like that phrase. You make it up?"

"No. Shakespeare. *Antony and Cleopatra.* "

"Good enough." She turned herself to me and I could see her eyes were moist and glistening. "You've always been special to me, Jake. Ever since that first profiling class at the Academy when I got a crush on the teacher. You've always been my hero, and in one way or another, I've always loved you. You should know that."

I pulled her close and felt her hands on my back and shoulder. Neither of us said anything. I just savored this moment of tenderness and emotional intimacy, which moments had become all too infrequent. Life is short and uncertain. Sometimes you have to rip down the phony barriers and let those close to you know how you feel. I stood there hugging her and wanted to keep on hugging her, knowing she felt the same way.

What I remember next is more fragments: Katie pulling me to her . . . a kind of electric, magnetic connection between our two bodies . . . pulling at each other's clothing, but only as much as absolutely necessary—her silk skirt pushed up around her waist, her bra unloosed under her unbuttoned blouse, my fly zipped open and belt buckle undone . . . the hard surface of the wall contrasting with the firm but yielding surface of her belly . . . the total domination of her lips, tongue, and teeth. And only after we'd finished in the living room did we manage to stagger into the bedroom, where the exploration began anew.

"Oh, God." She inhaled deeply, trying to catch her breath. "That . . . that was good."

"Fidelity. Bravery. Integrity. You got 'em all, honey," I said as I cuddled her head against my shoulder.

"So do you, babe," she purred, the tigress now contented after a successful hunt. If I could, I'd have stayed like this forever.

36

We stayed that way a long time, naked and totally relaxed, not saying anything, trying to preserve the moment. I stroked her tangled dark chestnut hair with one hand while she held the other against her chest. Then, finally, Katie said softly, "Tell me what you're thinking about."

Strange as it sounds, until that moment, as I reveled in the closeness, in the feel of Katie, I hadn't consciously realized what I *was* thinking about, what was going on in the zone just below the surface. Then as soon as she questioned me, it quickly bubbled up.

"There's something strange about the rumors about Fletcher and Elena Farrare."

She propped herself up on one elbow. "Jake, what are you talking about?"

"It's just too pat, too easy, too convenient for the circumstances."

"Oh. The reason I asked is, I thought maybe you were thinking about . . . us. About where we go from here."

"Well, of course I was," I assured her, touching the side of her cheek, "but . . ."

"I know—you can't completely shut the profiler off. He's always in there with whatever else is going on. I'm just not used to conducting a case consultation conference in . . . well, you know." She was starting to sound like Toni, which was slightly unnerving, but I didn't point that out.

"What I mean is—"

"It's okay. Really. It's just one of the many things I love about you." Again that enigmatic grin she used so effectively to keep others on a slippery footing. She sat up in bed and folded her arms over her bare breasts. "Now, as you were saying . . ."

Was this a test? I wondered. Well, if it was, I am what I am and there's no sense starting off on a new road playing games. I stood up and began pacing around the bed. I often think better on my feet.

"Okay, Katie, so about Fletcher's boat . . ."

"What about it? And by the way, you have a nice ass."

"Thanks. So do you. Now, I find it interesting that Elena's body was found, but Fletcher's never was."

"Lot of water out there."

"Yes, but you've seen enough of this stuff—a floater is a floater, and the coastline is so densely populated around there and the publicity about Fletcher's disappearance was so great that it's strange he never turned up."

"I think I'm going in the same direction as you."

"Right, but follow this, too: I'm thinking Fletcher and Elena were *not* having a liaison."

"Were *not*, you say?"

"I looked into her background a little bit. She was one of those typical beautiful beach bunnies who hung around there in the summer, looking to meet rich and influential men, et cetera, et cetera. My point is that she would have been well-known to the locals, so her having an affair with a wealthy older guy like Fletcher De Vries would have rung absolutely true."

"So you're saying the tryst was a setup, at least on his part."

"Exactly. If he's going to disappear, no one's going to question the fact if he drowns with a beautiful young babe he's not supposed to be with. That's the part everyone's going to talk about, especially when her body is discovered."

Katie pulled her knees to her chest, making her point with her finger in the air. "So Elena was sacrificed to make Fletcher's disappearance look legit."

"We have no proof, of course," I acknowledged, "but that's the way I'm fitting the pieces together."

"And after she's been floating for a while, evidence of foul play—particularly a soft kill like drugs or strangulation—is going to be very difficult to detect, especially since the authorities aren't going to be looking for it." Katie paused as we both considered this, then asked, "Are you ready to go the final step?"

"You mean, is Fletcher De Vries J. P. Napoleon?" She nodded. "I don't know. But what was it that Millicent said was her motivation for backing the Flying Squad?"

"Because Empire had staged a hostile takeover of Shipley Pharmaceuticals."

"And that they seemed to have specialized information to do it. 'They seemed to have a profound inside knowledge of the critical workings and corporate strategies,' Mrs. De Vries told me at her house when she made me the offer. 'It was as if, like the Greeks in the Trojan Horse, they had defeated us from inside.' "

○

As soon as I saw the coverage the morning papers had given to the FBI's announcement, I knew it was time to implement the next phase of the plan. We all assembled at our rooms at the Watergate, where Katie and I played a brief but intense private game with our eyes.

She reported that no one had attempted to contact Wendy, but I figured that could still take some time if the interested parties had to get here from out of town.

I didn't want to make Wendy nervous, so I had Katie stay in the room with her while Trevor, Dominic, Jerry, and I waited next door in the command post. I could monitor Wendy's call over a headset Trevor had rigged up.

Through the room mike, I heard Wendy talking to Katie, getting psyched up to make the call. When she started dialing the advertised number, I shifted over from the room mike to the phone tap.

After two rings, a male voice answered, "FBI. Agent Smith speaking."

Ah, so this is how they're handling it, I thought. This was an old law enforcement ploy, one we happened to share with collection agencies. When the sought-after party calls, whoever is manning the phone at the moment is Smith or Jones or whoever, so that the caller always feels he or she is talking to the same person and won't get into an I'll-call-back-later mode. It also meant that the subject could be handled around the clock, always making her feel she was dealing with the same agent. That was too bad for us, though. It meant we couldn't identify the individual she was talking to.

"Hi, this is Wendy Winslow," she began hesitantly, following a general script just as she and Katie had rehearsed it. "I . . . I think I'm the woman you're looking for."

The voice was without inflection. "Very good, Ms. Winslow. Are you safe where you are now?"

"Yes. Yes, I am." I was sure the FBI computers were already searching for anything they had on her.

"Good. The caller ID says that you're calling from the Watergate Hotel in Washington. Is that correct?"

"Yes, that's correct."

"We'd like to talk to you. Would that be all right?" Good technique, not pushy, not intimidating.

"Yes. That would . . . That would be fine."

"Would you like to meet us somewhere or would you like us to come to you? We'll do whichever you feel most comfortable with."

"I, uh, I think you'd better come here."

"Okay, Ms. Winslow, that's what we'll do. It's now ten twenty-eight by my clock. Does that sound right to you?"

"Wait, let me look at my watch. Yeah, that's about right."

"When would you like us to come by?"

I assumed the conversation would go like this, and I'd built in several hours to let the word leak out inside the Bureau. That way, if there was a mole, we'd have a good chance of the news of Wendy and her whereabouts reaching him.

"How about two o'clock this afternoon?" she said.

"Maybe we should make that a little earlier, just to be on the safe side."

"No. I'm getting my hair done at twelve-thirty. Let's keep it at two." This was a nice little touch that Katie had come up with. It's not uncommon for some women, even when their life may be at risk, to want to look their best before they're seen or talked to. Our consulting shrinks think it has something to do with boosting their confidence, feeling more in control of their environment. And this was something that other FBI agents would know about potential witnesses.

"All right, then, Ms. Winslow. Two o'clock it is." She gave him the room number. "I'll be coming myself," he continued. "There may be others with me, but when your doorbell rings, keep the chain on and ask me for my credentials. I'll pass to you a black leather folder which will have a gold FBI badge on one side and a laminated ID card on the other. If this isn't done, or the name on the card is not Special Agent William Allen Smith, then the individual approaching you is not from the FBI. Close the door immediately and do not admit that person. Then immediately call the number I'm about to give you. Do you understand all that?"

"Yes, I do. Thank you."

He gave her the number. When she hung up, I opened the connecting door and went in. "I hope I was okay," she said.

"You were terrific!" I confirmed. "Now we just wait."

I asked Jerry if he'd take over for Trevor for a while; as a precaution, he and Katie would take turns standing watch in the hallway outside Wendy's door until just before two, at which point we'd pull in the guard and wait for the visitor.

With Wendy "secured" for the interim, Trevor, Dominic, and I went out for food. I knew it might be the last chance we had to eat for quite a while.

37

During lunch, I reviewed our contingency procedures. We would watch and listen through the eavesdropping equipment Trevor had set up in Wendy's room. If the encounter appeared to be legitimate, we'd record it and get Peter to find out the real identity of "Agent Smith." Then I'd call Emily Jones at the *Post* and let her run with the story for publication.

But if anything about Smith seemed suspicious or worrisome, we'd bust through the connecting door with our guns out. Katie would come in from the other side so we could surround them. I didn't want to practice the maneuver with Wendy around, but I was convinced we could handle it. All she had to know was that we were ready for whoever and whatever might walk through that door.

We got back to the rooms and I found Jerry standing in front of the door, just as he was supposed to. "Everything's A-OK on this end."

"I'm glad to hear it," I said, relieved.

"Why did you call me and then hang up? Is everything all right?"

"What are you talking about? I didn't call you."

"You didn't?"

"No." I felt my pulse quicken uncomfortably. "What's this all about?"

"A little while ago, I was standing in the hallway like you told me to and a bellman said he had a call from you that I had to take in the lobby. I was surprised, but he said something like, 'Mr. Donovan says it has to do with Needle and it's urgent.' So I went down to the lobby, but when I picked up the phone, you weren't there."

"Did you get Katie to take over in the hall?"

"No. You said . . . he said you said it was urgent about Needle, so I went right away."

Trevor looked at me ominously. I went into the command center and phoned Katie in the other room. "All quiet on this front," she reported.

"Have you see Wendy?" I asked.

"Still asleep. She didn't even want lunch. I'll give her about ten more minutes and then I'll go in and get her up."

"Get her up now!" I said urgently.

I glanced at my watch. Sixteen minutes before two. If I knew the FBI, they'd be here exactly at the stroke.

The connecting door flew open and Katie raced in, her face white. "She's gone!"

"What!" *You blew it, Donovan! You let up for one fucking moment. You should know you can't let up for any fucking moments!*

"I went in to wake her up and she wasn't there. Her purse is gone, too."

"Any sign of forced entry . . . or anything?"

"No. Nothing at all."

"Fuck!" Trevor exclaimed. "I knew we shouldn't have let her out of sight."

"We had to give her some privacy," Katie protested. "She wasn't our hostage. And Jerry was supposed to be standing guard."

"I was until Jake called me," he said defensively.

"Jake didn't frigging call!" Trevor yelled.

I held up my hand. "This isn't productive. We'll go over all that when we have the luxury. Let's just figure out why she's gone or what made her leave."

"Could this all have been some kind of setup?" Dominic asked tensely. "After all, she did try to fool you once."

Didn't make sense. Her ruse had to do with keeping herself safe, and now we were the ones doing that, or supposed to be doing that. And she wasn't sophisticated enough to have been putting us on about her fear. "I don't think so. Katie would have sensed something by now."

Katie nodded. "I sure would."

"Then someone must have convinced her to leave while Jerry was downstairs," Dominic declared.

"I agree that's the strongest shot. And if so, it would have been either in person or by phone."

"I don't think she would have gone off with anyone who came to the door, unless it was Agent Smith following the procedure he'd outlined," Katie offered.

"Trev," I said, "is the bugging equipment automatic? I mean, is it on all the time?"

"The telephone tap is. But the room audio and video have to be turned on and off. Katie insisted on it, for 'privacy.' " He glared at her; she glared right back.

"Okay. Let's try the phone tap and see if there's anything on it for the last hour and a half."

Trevor went over to the surveillance equipment. He pressed a couple of buttons; the tape whirred backward. "There's something here."

In another couple of seconds the cassette had completely rewound. Trevor pushed the START button.

"Hello?"

"Is this Ms. Wendy Winslow?"

"Who is this please?"

"This is Special Agent William Allen Smith again." It sounded like the same voice, but I couldn't be positive.

"Oh, hi," Wendy said.

"Are you alone?"

"Uh-huh. Is anything wrong?"

"Not really, ma'am. At least nothing we can't take care of. But since I last talked to you, we've had reason to believe that it might not be safe for you in the hotel."

"Are you going to come and get me then?"

"That wouldn't be wise. It would arouse the suspicion of the people around you. And we might not be able to protect you in time before you got hurt. Please trust me on this. We have a lot of experience in these situations."

A tone of panic crept into Wendy's voice. "Then what should I do?"

"Proceed by yourself. Don't alert the people with you. We believe we know who they are and whom they represent. And they may try to harm you. You have a two-minute window to leave your room without being seen. Go as quietly as you can to the entrance of the hotel, take a taxi, and tell the driver to take you to Dumbarton Oaks in Georgetown. It's a historic mansion open to the public. The driver should know where it is, but if he doesn't, it's on the corner of Twenty-ninth and R Streets, about ten minutes by car. Don't go in, but turn right and walk next door into

Montrose Park. Walk in on the path and keep walking until I approach you."

"How will I know it's you?"

"I'm five foot ten, medium build, and short black hair. Gray suit, white shirt, and red tie. But remember, and this is very important: I'll show you my badge and ID card in a black leather folder. If this isn't done, don't talk to the individual and begin walking back toward the street. We'll be there to rescue you and intercept anyone. Do you under-stand?"

"I . . . I think so."

"Good. I'm sorry to have to do it this way, Ms. Winslow, but your safety is very much at stake. Now please leave as soon as you hang up. I don't want you in the building at two."

"Okay, then."

She sounded tentative, but obviously she'd gone. Trevor mashed down the STOP button.

"How could she fall for that?" Katie lamented.

"She's not a professional," I pointed out, "and not really sure who she can trust. When you're disoriented, you tend to believe whoever is the last one who talked to you."

"The guy sounded considerate," Jerry said. "He told her to run away if whoever approached her didn't do exactly what she was told to expect."

"Window dressing to make it sound good," said Katie. "The business about the badge and folder is a standard rap."

"Didn't she realize how dangerous it is?"

"But she's convinced she may be in danger from us, so now she doesn't know what to do. That's what they count on. What's the time stamp on this?" I asked Trevor.

He read off the LED. "One-seventeen."

We all glanced at our watches. Twelve minutes to two. Shit!

"Trevor," I directed, "you come with me. The rest of you stay here in case she comes back."

"I'm going with you!" Katie insisted.

"You're not," I said. "I need someone here who can handle a gun. Keep your cell phone turned on."

She realized the logic of what I was saying.

"You ready?" I said to Trevor.

"Armed and ready."

"Then let's get out of here."

We raced down the fire stairs to the lobby and bolted out the front door. A small queue of people were lined up for taxis. We charged in front of them. "FBI!" I shouted, jumping in a cab. "This is an emergency."

I didn't give the driver time to react. "Get us to Montrose Park on R Street in Georgetown and don't stop for lights!"

We dodged oncoming cars and screeched over curbs. Miraculously, we hadn't encountered any cops. Every second that ticked by made it less likely we would find Wendy, and find her alive. I couldn't believe we'd planned so carefully, then one unexpected element had bowled us over. The idea of losing this witness was overwhelming. The idea of having unwittingly betrayed this human being was devastating. Wendy had trusted us and we had delivered her right into the hands of the enemy.

When we pulled up at the street entrance to the park, I threw a fifty and Trevor and I bounded out of the cab. We both had our guns drawn by the time we'd passed the sidewalk.

Hardly anyone was in the park, which was just what the caller must have counted on. A couple of teenagers were playing Frisbee with their dogs in the far right-hand quadrant, and some older people were sitting peaceably on one of the benches.

"We'd better split up," Trevor said. "I'll go left, you go right."

I wished we'd brought Katie with us. This was a lot of territory for two people to cover. Time was against us. Odds were against us. It was too much. There's no job in which you'd more pray to be able to reverse time than mine.

I made my way into a stand of trees, making sure no one was coming up behind me. I didn't call out Wendy's name for fear of alerting whoever was with her. I decided the most efficient thing to do would be to start at the park's perimeter and work in from there, so I darted from one tree to the next, careful not to make myself a target. I ran as fast as I dared, cursing my street shoes. If I turned an ankle on this rough and uneven terrain, the chase was over. Trevor was an experienced hunter and trained tracker. Maybe he was having better luck.

God, don't let them do anything to her. Just give me the little bit of time I need.

The last time I'd had to run after anyone like this, I recalled, I was chanting the same prayer. A seven-year-old girl had been kidnapped from her bedroom in Portland, Oregon. The ransom note to the parents said she had been buried in a wooden box with enough air and water for two days. As soon as the ransom was paid, I knew, the kidnapper would run and let the little girl die.

It was a complex money drop, in the middle of a state park. The kidnapper obviously knew the area well, and we couldn't get close enough to nab him without tipping him off. By the time we saw any movement, he was tearing out of the woods and we had to tear after him.

Finally, I caught a glimpse of him. He was carrying the stash in a canvas backpack, already on the other side of a stream and heading up the root-covered embankment. He knew the woods, I didn't. There was no way I was going to catch up with him.

That's when I decided I had no choice but to perpetrate my own violation of the Bureau's shoot-to-kill policy. If I killed him, the secret of the victim's hiding place died with him. So I squeezed off a shot that hit him straight in the right upper triceps. In those days, I was a crack shot.

He went down, then immediately tried to get back to his feet. I plunged into the stream, splashily waded across, then scrambled up the embankment and tackled him.

"Get me help!" he gasped, clutching his bloody shoulder.

"Tell me where the girl is!" I screamed back at him.

"Fuck you!"

I knelt down over him and pressed the barrel of my pistol up to his nostril.

"You can't bullshit me. I'm down and unarmed. You can't shoot me in cold blood."

"Now listen, motherfucker, there is no way that girl dies and you live. I am not going back to her parents with that. Just remember, I'll be alive and you'll be dead, so my version stands."

I cocked the trigger, ready to blow his fucking head off when he relented. "Okay, okay."

I kicked him hard in his wounded arm. He let out a howl of agony, but told me where she was. She was weak and hysterical, but alive.

I prayed we'd be as lucky this time. Maybe Trevor had already found her. At the same time, I tried to prepare myself emotionally for what was much more likely.

I came upon a fountain and a small kids' playground with a slide, jungle gym, seesaws, and swings. It was empty. I climbed to the top of the slide, hoping to see something from that height. No one. Inside my head, a clock was ticking off the seconds.

The woods grew thick in the back and my progress was slowed. A thornbush ripped into my sleeve. I felt a gash, saw blood staining my shirt cuff. What if she wasn't in the park anymore? Once they had her and had either established trust or simply blitzed her, they weren't going to hang around here waiting for us. What if they'd killed her on the spot and I came upon her body?

By now I'd worked my way back to the central walkway that bisected the park. Trevor approached from the opposite direction with his gun still drawn, alone. My last tiny hope evaporated. My gut seized; my throat constricted and I was wheezing.

"Nothing?" he asked.

"Not even a trace. You?"

He shook his head.

"Think they've left the park?"

"I don't see evidence of a struggle."

"What now?" I asked.

"Switch sides and cover each other's territory. And call Katie to see if anything's turned up. If real agents have shown up, get them over here. And tell her to get the Park Police helicopter up. It'll be faster than trying to get one in from Quantico."

I thought I heard a rustling sound coming from the extreme rear of the park. Trevor must have heard it, too. "Let's go!" he said sharply.

We took off. The activity was coming from the wooded area behind the playground.

There was what sounded like a woman's stifled scream. *Oh, Jesus.* We eased forward. A maintenance shed was in front of us. Whatever was going on was happening behind it.

"Split up again," Trevor directed. "I'll meet you round back. And remember, if you shoot, shoot to kill."

About five paces before the end of the shed, I flattened myself against the side. Then I inched up to where now I could hear the distinct sounds of struggle.

A woman's voice. "No! Please!"

No time to think, only react. I jumped out from my cover with my gun gripped in front of me with both hands. "Freeze! FBI!"

Wendy Winslow was standing there, a look of terror on her bleeding face. It took me a moment to realize she was again wearing the long, dark wig, the long false eyelashes, and the brown contact lenses. She was trying with both hands to pull an arm from around her neck. The man was holding her, her fingers bloody with defensive wounds, with his service weapon to her head.

The man was Ted Novello.

"Ted!" I shouted.

"Stay back!" he ordered. "Stop where you are and let me explain."

"Let her go!" Trevor called out, racing up from the other side.

"Just wait a minute!" Ted responded.

"Let her go!"

Ted knew enough to turn from one to the other of us so that neither of us had a clear shot without endangering Wendy. With my own aiming problem, I was deathly afraid of having to fire. But then Ted still clutching Wendy directed his weapon at Trevor, and I saw his index finger begin to squeeze the trigger.

An explosive *crack!* rang out, the sound ricocheting off walls and trees and resounding throughout the park. Trevor and I looked at each other dumbfounded. Neither of us had taken a shot. But Ted crumpled to the ground.

I saw a man in a dark suit about thirty feet away in the FBI firing stance. The barrel of his gun was still smoking. And Katie was standing next to him with her own weapon drawn.

38

He'd gotten him with a clean shot, right through the K-5 region as we were all taught to aim for. I could tell from the location of the bullet hole that Ted had died instantly.

The man stood staring ahead, and Trevor came over and took his gun away. He gave it up without a struggle. Wendy, her whole body shaking, hugged me tightly. With his handkerchief open, Trevor approached Ted's body and gingerly picked up his nine millimeter off the ground. Other people were timidly approaching the periphery of where we were to see what was going on.

And that was just what I wanted to know. "What happened?" I asked Katie.

She said, "Jake, this is Special Agent—"

"Smith?"

He was tall and hulking with sandy hair and heavy metal-frame glasses. "That's right. Real name is Emilio Moldea."

"He showed up at the Watergate at two," Katie explained.

"When she told me what had happened, we raced over here."

"We looked for you, Trev, and Wendy. Emilio spotted her first."

"When I saw that Novello was about to kill Trevor and escape with the victim. I had a clear shot, I took it."

I stepped over to where Ted lay, slid my hand into his jacket without disturbing the body, felt around a moment, and then extracted his creds. I opened the black leather folder and showed it to Trevor. The laminated ID card read *Special Agent William Allen Smith.*

I wanted to feel sorry for him, diminished, as I would for any dead person. But my only reaction was to wonder—to wonder whether this event had put the final piece in the puzzle or had prevented us from ever finding that piece, or even recognizing it if we stumbled across it.

Why, Ted? Why? You, who had everything to gain in having Boyd alive and in control? Once I was out of the way, your career, your future, were made. What was going on, what did I miss that made you want to kill your champion or, at least, go along with it?

The Metropolitan Police arrived. One uniform did his best to keep onlookers away while the other, seeing Trevor holding two guns, approached him with his own Glock 17 out.

"Don't even think about it," Trevor said calmly.

"FBI," Moldea announced.

Moldea introduced himself and flashed his creds. "This is your jurisdiction," he conceded to the officer, "but it's our personnel involved in an investigation with national security implications, so I'm taking over. If your captain has any problems, tell him to call the attorney general. Now, can I count on you and your people to keep the scene secured until I can get my people here?"

The cops nodded meekly.

∘

They took us to Orlando Ravan's office: Katie, Trevor, and me, and Special Agent Moldea. Peter Sutherland, Neil Burke, and his harem eunuch Harry were already there waiting for us, with Ellen Clemente, the Bureau's general counsel, sitting right next to Ravan's desk. She didn't look happy. I sensed my life passing before my eyes. Detective John Hayford from Metro Police Homicide arrived to represent the city's interests.

"All right," Ravan the Raven opened, and he didn't look to be having any more fun than Clemente. "This case has become a tar baby, just like I feared it would. Now I want answers from everyone and I want them fast. And nothing we talk about here goes beyond this room without my expressed say-so."

He turned to me like a teacher trying to nail an unprepared student. "We'll start with you. Am I correct that when you came to us with your plan to have the FBI locate the woman code-named Needle, you already had her in your control?"

"That's right, sir." I saw Ellen Clemente writing on her legal pad.

And out of the corner of my eye I noticed Harry Gillette attempting a coronary occlusion.

"So, in effect, you were initiating a sting operation within the Bureau."

"That's not all I was doing, but yes."

Harry's carotid artery was pulsing blue. Maybe it really would rupture. "Outrageous!" he said. "I can think of at least ten rules and regulations Jake's violated! He's been a blue-flamer right from the beginning. I'm sure that's why Judge Boyd got rid of him."

"Harry," I interrupted, "seems to me the question here is, who got rid of Judge Boyd?"

"Okay," Ravan continued. "And was that because you suspected involvement from someone inside?"

"I wasn't sure. But if the death was a murder and not a suicide, the most logical scenario involved Boyd falling prey to someone he trusted." I felt as badly about this as anything—I mean that someone within the Bureau family could find it within himself to betray the code. At least with Ted, we weren't talking about the inner circle, rather a guy who came back for selfish, opportunistic reasons.

"Let's leave that aspect for a moment," said Ravan. "Now, Agent Moldea, what's your role in all this?"

Moldea shifted uncomfortably. "You see, sir, I was duty officer here when the call came in from a woman at the Watergate Hotel who identified herself as Ms. Wendy Winslow. We were using the Smith code, in this case William Allen Smith. I arranged a time to meet with her. Before I left the room, I recorded the call in the log book."

"How many people knew about the Smith code for this operation?" Ravan asked.

"More than a few. This was to be manned around the clock until further notice."

"Then how many sets of William Allen Smith credentials were there?"

"Four," Moldea said. "One for each shift, plus an extra."

"You say that when you arrived at the subject's hotel room at the appointed time, she wasn't there?"

"That's correct. But I was met by Special Agent . . . ah, former special agent McManus, who informed us what she thought had happened, and then together we proceeded to Montrose Park in search of Special Agent Novello. I eventually spotted Ms. Winslow apparently being threatened by him. I ordered him to release her. When he turned his weapon on Mr. Donovan and Mr. Malone, I took the shot."

"Ms. McManus, do you have anything to add to that?" Ravan asked.

"That's pretty much what happened. If I had had the shot, I would have taken it."

Ravan addressed Peter. "Now what's your role in this, Mr. Sutherland?"

"Well . . . ," Peter began slowly, measuring his words, "I was up to speed on what we were trying to do with this operation and was monitoring it from headquarters. I didn't know that Jake . . . Mr. Donovan . . . already had Needle in hand."

"I can confirm that," I said.

"I was in the situation room—this must have been after Emilio received the original call—when Ted Novello came in."

"How did he seem to you?"

"Agitated. Jumpy. I asked him what was wrong. He said nothing, he was fine, but didn't I know that Needle had come to ground. He had seen the log entry and played back the recording of the phone call with her. I told him I did know, and that we were going out to bring her in. He said this was too delicate an operation for that. He'd had the closest personal relationship with the director, he knew things that could qualify her that no one else knew, and so he was going to bring her in himself. I was alarmed. I told him that sounded crazy to me."

It sounded goddamn arrogant to me. As the inside man in the murder plot, Ted apparently thought he could control everything—including the silence of the witness I brought to the surface. And just as I would hope in any proactive strategy to hunt down an UNSUB, this one's sense of his superiority led him right into the trap.

"Agent Moldea," Ravan continued, "were you in the room at the time?"

"No, sir, I wasn't."

"Please continue, Agent Sutherland."

"So he asked me where the extra set of Smith creds was. I told him I didn't know, then he practically ransacked the room until he found them. He shoved them into the pocket of his suit jacket and left."

"What did you do then?"

"I wasn't sure what to do. I thought Ted was acting emotionally rather than rationally. I didn't want to get him in trouble, but I couldn't let him go off like that. So when Moldea came back to the room a few minutes later, I told him about Ted and that he wasn't in a rational frame of mind."

"And I left immediately," Moldea added. "I wanted to get to the Watergate before Novello did."

"Did you didn't inform anyone else? Contact anyone at the Washington Field Office?"

"No, sir. This was a classified operation."

"What about you, Agent Sutherland? Did you contact anyone else?"

"I tried to contact Jake but I couldn't reach him."

I didn't bother glancing over at Harry this time.

"So presumably, Agent Novello had made a call to Ms. Winslow himself, altering the plan?"

"I have no knowledge of that," said Peter.

"That is what we believe happened," Moldea said. "Using a voice-disguising device."

"You next saw him in Montrose Park, where Ms. McManus had directed you?"

"Yes, sir. When we caught up with them, he had a woman with long dark hair in his control."

"Wait a minute," said Ravan. "I thought Needle was blond."

"The dark wig, eyelashes, and brown contact lenses were a disguise she'd used previously," I clarified. "I suspect she must have been wary of the sudden change of plans and used the disguise as a precaution."

Ravan nodded, signaling Moldea to continue.

"So anyway, sir, I saw him take her by the arm and move her to an area behind a maintenance shed. She made sounds of protest, so I got closer, with Ms. McManus behind me. I could see that Novello had his service weapon out and appeared to be trying to place her in a certain position. I shouted out to him and told him to stop. He told me to leave, that he had the situation under control. I told him to release the woman and then we'd sort it out. He replied that there wasn't time; that I had to leave and he would explain it all to me when he returned to headquarters. I told him that wasn't going to happen and shouted for him to release the subject. And . . . you've heard the rest."

Ravan addressed Trevor and me. "Did either of you hear this warning being shouted out?"

"No," I said. "But we were both far away. All we heard was the sound of a commotion or struggle."

"I heard it," said Katie. "It was just the way he said."

"And when you arrived at the scene, Jake, Agent Moldea had just fired."

"Actually, we all must have gotten there around the same time."

Ravan turned to the general counsel. "Ellen, you have anything more?"

"Not for now."

"Okay, then. We've got the outlines of the story." Ravan stood up. "Mr. Moldea, you're on administrative leave with pay pending a final determination, which I hope we can accomplish speedily. I want all of you on standby to me until further notice." Everyone else followed Ravan in getting up. "Jake, will you stay a few minutes afterward," he said.

Again I felt like the errant student. When the others had left, Ravan leaned against the corner of his desk. "Is there anything else I should know?"

"Just between us?"

"I'll be the judge of that," he said sharply.

"Yes, I guess you will." How much to tell him? Which parts of it could still get us in trouble? Well, at least I had to let him know we'd come up with information the Bureau didn't have. Otherwise, there was no rationale or justification for the antics we'd pulled and I knew Ravan wouldn't put himself out as our protector.

"One thing you should know, Mr. Ravan, is that the photo of Judge Boyd and Ms. Winslow is a fake."

That clearly astonished him. "How do you know this?"

"Several ways. But for one, Ms. Winslow doesn't have a birthmark on her ass."

I took the acting director through our process of discovery, treading delicately on how we determined that Mrs. Boyd was endowed with the distinguishing feature.

"You copped a look in a women's locker room?" he said incredulously.

"I didn't. Kathleen McManus did."

I kept reminding him during my narrative that he had instructed me to conduct a completely independent investigation, which I interpreted to mean that I should not share information with anyone whom I did not completely trust. I considered letting him in on the secret of where his predecessor's mortal remains currently resided, but I stopped myself. Brass can only absorb so much news at one time.

Ravan summed up. "Is it your professional opinion that if the facts hold up as we've just heard them, that Ted Novello was implicated in the death of Tom Boyd?"

"It would appear that way."

"What about motive? That's supposed to be your strong suit down in Quantico."

I told him that maybe it had something to do with resenting being perceived as the director's pet. But I cautioned, "We're going to have to go deep and wide into Ted's background before I can give you anything definitive."

"And would our case be closed then and ready for a full report?"

"No, sir. That I don't believe. Because I don't think Ted could have acted alone."

"Do you think he was attempting to blackmail the director?"

"No, I don't think that, either. But Louis Knox may have thought he was, and that Ted was involved. The connection may very well be this Ronald Frishman that no one can find."

"Then find him."

39

There was no way they could keep the Ted Novello business quiet, and the media went crazy with it. The negative publicity was like Owl Creek all over again. Everywhere you looked you'd see accounts of how an FBI special agent who was one of the late director's handpicked favorites had been gunned down by another agent successfully attempting to save the life of a material witness. Moldea and Peter had been forbidden by Ellen Clemente's office from making any statements to the press. And interestingly, much of the previously veiled resentment against Ted at Quantico and headquarters now surfaced, and the papers were full of anonymous statements that had he not been Boyd's brother's best friend in college, he would have remained an obscure field agent in some out-of-the-way posting.

I still couldn't feel sorry for him, and I felt guilty about that. But then, I've never felt sorry for anyone I helped hunt down who'd been executed for murder, and I've never felt sorry for any of the jerks killed by police or their intended victims as they attempted armed robbery. So after some reflection, I realized there was no reason to feel sorry for Ted Novello. Like everyone else, he'd made his choices, he'd betrayed his friend and benefactor. And if he'd made the right ones, he'd still be alive.

Orlando Ravan had directed us to find Ronald Frishman. We were trying, but I knew the people he'd gotten involved with were too efficient not to have used a Jimmy Hoffa–like means of disappearance and disposal. Poor stupid fucker.

OPR, the FBI's Office of Professional Responsibility, the equivalent of an internal affairs division, quickly cleared Moldea after reviewing all the evidence. Then they gave him a citation for outstanding service. My team didn't receive any such honor, but we were lucky, just the same. Orlando Ravan couldn't deny that he'd directed me to conduct an independent investigation and essentially told me to find my own resources to do it. I hadn't told Ravan the details of our grave-robbing exercise and its ramifications. I still didn't think I knew all the important answers, and until I did, I didn't feel safe, I didn't feel my people were safe, and most important, I didn't feel my family was safe.

I told Toni I wanted her and the kids to stay away for a little while longer. I had to insist. Then trying to explain to the kids over the phone why they couldn't come back was even tougher.

I went to see Mrs. De Vries. She received me in the Tudor library, her diplomatically cultivated disposition back to what I had come to expect from her. We sat together, just the two of us, sipping her fine white wine, and she asked me directly, "Now that we've had some time to absorb the possibilities, do you think Fletcher could be J. P. Napoleon?"

I knew what I thought, but before I answered, I said, "What do you think?"

She sighed heavily, but her composure didn't crack. She swirled the wine in her glass, then held it up to the light, as if anything could be seen through if only positioned properly. "I've been trying to think like you and your team, Jake. I ask myself, did he give me any indication before the boating accident? And the answer is no. No matter how much I think about it, how much I try to recall, I can't say that anything stands out."

"No change in behavior that would give you any clue?"

She shook her head. "The only change in behavior I'd ever noted in Fletcher came several years before."

I perked up. "And when was that?"

"When my father passed away. Fletcher grew up without a father—he died when Fletcher was six—and he adored mine. I sometimes thought he'd rather spend time with my father than with me. My father made him president of Shipley Pharmaceuticals. The loss of my father was difficult enough for me and the children. But it was devastating to Fletcher. In some ways, he never recovered. In fact, he stepped down as president shortly before the accident."

"Stepped down or was forced out?"

"Like most things, a matter of interpretation. But I suppose if there was a dimension of Fletcher of which I knew nothing, then I suppose there still could be. What do you think, Jake?"

I told her my theory on the so-called affair with Elena Farrare and reminded her of what she'd told me about the unusual aspects of the hostile takeover by Empire. "I think Mr. De Vries might be Napoleon. But from what you've just told me about his relationship with your father, I think it's also possible he may actually be a pawn or functionary of Napoleon's. If he's not Napoleon himself, then whoever is might represent just the kind of powerful father figure he saw in Mr. Shipley. Either way, I think it likely that Mr. De Vries did not drown in that boating 'accident.' " Our eyes locked for several seconds. "I'm sorry to have to say this to you."

"Sorry to have to say that my well-loved and long-lamented husband is probably still alive. This is indeed an ironic world we live in, Jake, is it not?"

"Indeed it is."

She rose and went to the table to refill our glasses. "You'll still pursue Napoleon?" she said.

"That we will."

∘

Orlando Ravan knew he'd better get to the bottom of this one fast. He ordered a full investigation into Ted Novello's background.

Answers came with stunning speed. Within a week of his death, the Bureau's own forensic accountants discovered that Ted had been incurring mounting debts. No matter how much he made, he seemed to spend more. Maybe it had something to do with his deprived childhood, and maybe it had something to do with his ego. But the fact was, Ted was facing bankruptcy, which is not conducive to advancement in the Federal Bureau of Investigation, even if the director is your champion. If discovered, Boyd would almost certainly have cut him loose, and Ted would have been back investigating jaywalking sprees in the proverbial resident agency in East Kiss My Ass, Nebraska.

Though suddenly, Ted's financial problems had disappeared, and the accountants found more than $2 million in an offshore bank registered in the Cayman Islands. Another bank in Switzerland held almost a million more.

I guess I wasn't surprised. If there is one central motive for crime, it would have to be greed. But what a crummy, tawdry motive it is. Why join the FBI in the first place if money is what you're mainly after? Especially an attorney like Ted.

This was the opening topic as the team met at Katie's house. Wendy was staying with her but did not participate in the meeting. When the time came for her to appear as a witness, I didn't want her memory contaminated or discredited by anything we'd said or speculated about. Unfortunately, this also made it difficult for Katie and me to be alone. What was developing between us would have to wait.

∘

I'd largely discounted the blackmail motive when we realized that Boyd would have known the photos were faked. But Wendy did think Knox was using the photographs for blackmail, and when I'd interviewed Madeline Boyd, I couldn't even get her to look at the picture I'd brought with me. I'd been wondering since then if she'd just been trying to avoid an unpleasant subject or if there was more to it. The only way to know for sure was to ask.

At first I considered taking Katie along, or having her do the interview on her own, figuring a woman-to-woman talk might be less threatening. But we'd "used up" Katie with Mrs. Boyd in the country-club locker room, so it had to be me.

Madeline Boyd was gracious as always when she welcomed me into her house. The first thing I noticed as she took me into the library-den was a television security camera mounted in the hallway near the ceiling.

She poured iced tea, then sat down opposite me in a slightly forward body position that I interpreted to mean she wished to dispense with further pleasantries and get down to business.

"This is very difficult for me," I began.

"Nothing about this entire ordeal has not been difficult, so it's better if you just ask away."

"Okay then. Whether or not you knew at the time, do you now have knowledge if your husband was being blackmailed?"

"I don't."

"You're sure?"

She moved uncomfortably. "I'm sure I don't know if he was. I have no reason to believe so."

"In the weeks or months before his death, to your knowledge did he pay out any large or unusual sums of money?"

"No."

"If there were large sums of money being paid out, would you have known about them?"

"I don't see how or where he could have gotten it." Everything about her told me how difficult it was to talk about private family matters with outsiders. Going through the public scrutiny a figure such as her husband was being subjected to in death must have been agony.

"Could he possibly have accessed any of your personal funds without your knowledge?"

She looked flushed. "He could not have."

"I'm sorry to have to do this to you," I said, opening my briefcase. "I held off as long as I could." I removed a stack of prints from their manila envelope and handed them to her.

She took them from me, scanned the first couple, then put her hand to her chest as if she'd just been shot. "What are . . . ?"

"Not what they appear to be. Forget the woman's face if you can. These are actually photos of you and your husband which we believe to have been taken by a security camera in this house. Is that a fair assessment?"

She made an effort at self-control, then went through the photos methodically. At one point I thought I detected a faint smile.

"Yes," she said at last. Her face was a mass of conflicting and confusing emotions, all the more painful for having to reveal herself in front of me. "That's what they are," she stammered. "But how did this other woman's face end up here?"

"That's part of the crime we're investigating."

"Is that why you were asking me about blackmail?"

I nodded. "I know this is extremely oafish of me, but I have to know the circumstances of these photographs."

She looked off into the middle distance. "We'd been rather aloof from each other for quite some time. We talked about what it would take to get us back together, but we were both so busy and preoccupied nothing seemed to come of it. We knew we wanted to stay together, if only for Jason's sake, but we were the types who had to make appointments with each other to talk about anything substantive.

"Then one Friday afternoon, Jason was off to his grandparents' house for the weekend, I had just gotten back from a charity luncheon in town I'd agreed to speak at, I was about to go upstairs and change, when Tom came home.

" 'What are you doing here this time of day?' I asked him.

" 'To be with you,' he said, 'so let's get started.' With that, he came on to me like we were two schoolkids trying to . . . well, you know.' "

I was touched by her description. It made me think of Boyd in a whole new light.

"If you're willing to mentally transpose my head back onto those pictures, what you see is pretty much what happened." She took a sip of her iced tea. "I only wish it had continued to happen that way."

"Then it didn't?"

"I'm afraid not. After that one lovely weekend of passion and renewal, real life set in and we were back to being distinct and distant individuals. Is that what you wanted to know?"

It was. The one thing I do share with psychiatrists and priests, and psychics, too, is that we are all emotional voyeurs. It's not the prettiest aspect of the job, but it's about the most unavoidable.

"Thank you, Mrs. Boyd," I said as I rose to go. "I hope I won't have to trouble you anymore."

40

The latest of my sudden cessations of ignorance dawned on me in the car driving home. Immediately, I diverted to Katie's house so I'd have someone to debrief with.

She seemed surprised, but quickly wrapped her arms around my neck and pulled me close for a romantic kiss. "I'm so glad to see you," she managed to get out as our tongues played for position.

I hugged her around her trim waist. "Is Wendy here?"

"Upstairs. It'll be okay." She worked her hand inside my shirt.

"Call her. I want her to be in on this."

She removed her hand from my shirt, her tongue from my mouth. "You're joking, right? I don't do threesomes."

"Sorry. It's not that. We need to talk."

Clearly disappointed by the change in mood but just as clearly relieved by my clarification, she went to get Wendy. When they returned, I sat them both in the living room and turned to Wendy. I hadn't wanted to include her in our discussions for fear of influencing her memory, but this overrode the concern. "You said you had the impression that Louie Knox was blackmailing someone with those photos."

"That's right."

"And we just assumed it must be Boyd."

"That's the way the crime scene looked," said Katie.

"Right. But as I said, Tom Boyd would have known they were bogus, and if anyone had tried to publish them, it might have been embarrassing, but it was no scandal. He certainly wouldn't kill himself over it."

"So there wasn't a blackmail attempt?" said Katie.

I took her hand for emphasis. "There was! But it was Louie Knox blackmailing Ted." I waited a moment for this to sink in.

"Okay," I resumed, "follow this: We couldn't come up with a satisfactory motive for Ted killing Boyd. But now we know he's got millions stashed away offshore. So let's say someone paid him to do it. Let's say for the sake of argument that someone is J. P. Napoleon. Ted was one of the few people who could get close enough to the director to pull off this murder. Then the scene was staged to make it look like a blackmailing attempt that Boyd, because of his family-man reputation, couldn't handle. Are you with me so far?"

Both women nodded.

"Clearly, Louie Knox is the one who was hired to create the phony picture left at the scene. We think he got them through Ronald Frishman, but that's not important. He got them somehow; that we know. Boyd didn't have any serious money; Madeline just confirmed that for me. But suddenly, Ted Novello did! Money that we believe was his payoff for the murder. And now he also had a deadly secret to protect."

"A secret to protect and the financial means to pay to keep it protected. Those are certainly the ingredients of blackmail," said Katie. "So Knox got greedy and decided he wanted a little bigger piece of the pie."

"Right. And that's why he got whacked. And again, that crime was staged to make it look like something it wasn't. Whoever killed him assumed NYPD would handle it on their own and conclude it was a Russian Mob hit of a guy who had a shady past to begin with. What they didn't count on was Paul Sochaczewski being such a good detective and calling us in."

"Do you think Ted Novello killed Louie?" Wendy asked.

"Not with his own hands," I said. "I think he reported the blackmail attempts to whoever his masters were, and they took care of it."

Katie began pacing. "And those masters . . ."

"Worked for J. P. Napoleon," I said. "At least that's where the lines intersect. Here's the way I've profiled it: The threat from new FBI director Boyd is real, so the first possibility is that Napoleon decides to try to take him out. Timing is everything, and with the new president in office who doesn't agree with the way Boyd's going after organized crime, the moment may have arrived to let that new president appoint an FBI director more to Napoleon's liking—meaning one who'll leave him and his operation alone. To this end, Napoleon locates a guy who's got something they think they can use against Boyd. Ronald Frishman delivers the goods by way of Louie Knox, who must do specialized work for Napoleon. We can assume that from the fact that Wendy was instructed to go audition for him."

"Okay so far," said Katie.

"Or just as likely, Frishman, on his own entrepreneurial enterprise, sees these photos of the director doing his wife and realizes that he's got something profitable. I don't know—maybe he thinks he can sell them to one of the tabloids. He goes to his old friend Knox, who knows about these things and how to profit from them. Louie sees the photos and realizes that there's something big here, because unlike Ron, he sees them not as an end in themselves but as raw material that can be leveraged into something with much more impact. Through his channels, he gets the word back to Napoleon. They come up with a plan. As I say, I'm not sure which came first—whether Knox is the chicken or the egg—but it doesn't really matter. Either way, now Napoleon has to have a partner, someone who can actually get close enough to Boyd to do the job."

"It could be almost anyone in the Bureau," Katie pointed out.

"Yes, ma'am, but the closer to Boyd, the better. So he starts from the top down. Whoever he picks has to be someone who (a) desperately wants or needs money, more money than he can ever make in the Bureau, and (b) stands to benefit by getting Tom Boyd out of the way."

"We can concede the first part," said Katie. "Ted desperately needed the money. But Boyd's his mentor. He's on the fast career track and with his champion gone . . . well, you see what's happened to him."

"True," I conceded. "But remember, anything that happens now is only temporary since the Raven's just the acting director. Remember how we joked about the fix being in and Ted getting promised the directorship under the new president?"

Katie considered. "Yeah."

"It's a little far-fetched, even for someone as ambitious as Ted. But that doesn't mean the fix wasn't in. All that would have to happen would be for Napoleon to make some sizable contribution to the president's campaign. If Napoleon is Fletcher De Vries, he'd be connected in those circles and he'd know just how to go about it. Then when his man is elected, he suggests the kind of person he thinks might be a good FBI director. The president doesn't have to worry about this, since he can't blast Boyd out of office for a while anyway. But then when Boyd conveniently turns up dead, and with a potential blackmailing scandal surrounding him, it all comes together. And maybe there's a side agreement in place whereby Ted gets made a SAC, or deputy director, or even gets Neil Burke's job. The point is, if you profile a guy like Ted, that's what you come up with. Ted and Boyd weren't asshole buddies; they just used each other for mutually beneficial reasons. But Boyd had integrity and Ted didn't, so when the opportunity comes along for him to advance his career, clean up his debt, and set himself up financially for life, he grabs for the brass ring. The only problem is that Knox knows all about this, so he gets greedy and puts the screws to Ted for some serious dough. Ted, being more sophisticated than Knox, calls his contact in the Napoleon organization, reports that Louie has become a liability, and suggests that he be taken care of. It all fits!"

"But you said that you don't think Ted acted alone in killing Boyd."

"And from the wound evidence, Dominic doesn't think so, either."

"Then was Louie the one who helped Novello kill Boyd?" Wendy asked.

"I don't think so. Because Boyd would have known something was wrong if Ted showed up with someone he'd never seen before. Too, Knox wasn't a physical type and couldn't handle a gun, so he wouldn't have added much muscle for Ted."

Katie stood stock-still. I could see the inspiration in her eyes. "Someone else with the motive, the means, and the access." Then there was a long, painful pause. "You know, you could be describing Pete."

I did but I didn't. I had but I hadn't. Maybe I'd been processing the possibility subconsciously. Maybe that's what my dream of Mrs. De Vries as J. P. Napoleon was really all about. Maybe I couldn't face the possibility that my protégé, my close friend, could be other than what I thought he was and needed him to be.

"It couldn't be Pete." *Because that would mean I've misjudged him all those years. And if I could misjudge Peter, I could misjudge anyone, and then what is the great profiler—the one who sees into men's minds, sometimes into their souls?* "What reason would he have to turn?" I said almost desperately.

"The same ones as Ted," Katie said sternly, "only more so. He knew exactly what he had to gain if Boyd were out of the way."

In our business we all suffer at one time or another from a phenomenon known as linkage blindness. It's the psychological inability either to see that certain elements are related or that certain elements are not. We may not face that a cluster of rapes or murders were perpetrated by the same offender. Or we may insist that they're connected when they're not. It happens both ways. To some extent, we all come up with the answers we seek. Those who believe that all murderers must be "sick" or "crazy" will find abuse or a brain lesion or epilepsy or a childhood injury in the offender, anything that can "explain" why he committed the horrible act he did . . . anything other than it made him feel better and more powerful and more sexually charged than any other thing in his life. Just as those who believe that violent crime grows out of social inequality will throw millions upon millions at social programs because they "know" that is the way to "get at the root of the problem." Just as those who think that crime is always a product of free will and moral choice believe that if we just punish harshly enough, if we lock them all up, or better yet, fry them all, "we'll end violent crime."

But nothing in the realm of human behavior is that simple, and that's why it stung me so to hear what Katie was saying, and what I was thinking myself as she said it.

"He had motive. With Boyd out of the way, he could get the job we all felt was due him. He had the means. He's strong, he's smart, he knows how to use a gun, Boyd knew and trusted him and he could have gotten access to him. And together with Ted, they could have overpowered him and forced him to eat his weapon. Even though Ted never did a profile, he wasn't stupid or unsophisticated, and Pete is an expert. Together, they would have known how to stage the scene so that even someone like you would think it was authentic."

Down to knowing the details, I thought, such as that a suicide would want to be looking out over the bay as the last thing he saw.

I fought to deny what was becoming more and more apparent. "But what about his postoffense behavior?" I protested.

"What about it?" Katie countered. "Maybe he didn't go all to pieces like so many of them do. He's too good, too clever for that. But what has he done? He's continually given you the appearance of cooperation, but essentially he's told you nothing. Whenever you asked him what the unit had come up with, he told you there was no progress, then launched into some Bureau gossip. He's injected himself into the investigation at every possible juncture. And that's some of the key postoffense behavior we expect to see from a sophisticated, organized perp. That's something you taught us all in the basic profiling class. And don't you think it's more than a little coincidental that he was the one who just happened to be in the situation room when Ted came in, that he was the one who sent Emilio Moldea after Ted?"

"There are always coincidences in every case," I said. "You know that."

She regarded me with sad eyes. "I'm really very sorry, Jake."

"I still think you're wrong. But I think I know how to find out."

Katie continued looking at me indulgently. "If it turns out I'm wrong, I'll not only be the first to admit it, I'll crawl into Peter's office on my hands and knees and beg forgiveness."

I went out to the car for my briefcase, then went into Katie's little office, where I dug out my calendar and address book. I carefully studied the calendar since Boyd's death. Every day, trying to recall specifically what I and anyone else I could think of were doing, hour by hour. Then I phoned the Marin County office of the California State Police and gradually worked my way through the organization until I found the captain Peter had spoken to about the grave-site surveillance. His name was Larry Polan.

"Yes, how are you, Jake," he greeted me. "I've heard a lot about you."

"Oh. From who?"

"I see you on the tube all the time. You're famous, you know. But if you're looking for specific names, Peter Sutherland over at Quantico thinks the world of you."

That I couldn't authoritatively say the same about Peter was throwing off my equilibrium. I couldn't *feel* it anymore. I was like a pitcher who's suddenly lost his motion. All through my career, I'd never been plagued by the common occupational hazard of profilers: *What if I'm wrong?* Now it was like learning to ride all over again, concentrating on my balance so hard it was almost impossible to stay focused on the road ahead.

"That's gratifying to hear," I replied. "I think a lot of Pete, too. Your deputy said you'd have been the man who ordered the surveillance at Judge Boyd's grave."

"Yeah, that'd be me."

"Was Peter the one who suggested it to you?"

"Not only did he suggest it, but he said you'd come up with the idea to do it in the first place. Said it came out of your prison-interview research when so many of the killers told you they used to come back to the graves, either to apologize and get right with God, or else to relive the thrill of the kill in their own minds and keep on possessing the mind and body and soul of the victim."

I forced a laugh. "You could teach the course for us."

"I just want you to know that Peter gave you all the credit; didn't claim any of it for himself. Just said he was carrying on your programs and your work."

"That is kind." I was suddenly furious, then tried to check myself. Did I have a right to be? *You suspect, Donovan; you don't know.*

"And I'll tell you something else. The cops who had to sit out there in the boneyard grumbled, but I think we might have come up with someone if Mrs. Boyd hadn't disinterred the body and cremated it."

"Yeah, that threw us kind of a curve. As you might suspect, we're trying to tie up all our loose ends now, so I'd like to get some information from you. It could be immensely helpful."

"Certainly'll do what I can."

"Here's what I need to know: Would there be any kind of daily log or diary or calendar or anywhere you might have written down the exact date that Peter suggested you might want to employ this technique?"

"Date? Well, sure, I think so. It's probably in my personal diary, then we also keep computer logs by the case. If you want I can pull it up."

"I'd really appreciate that."

"Do you want to hang on, or should I call you back?"

"I'll hang on if it's all the same."

"Suit yourself. Won't be but a couple of minutes."

I held my breath while I waited and warred with myself over what I wanted the answer to be.

"Here it is," Captain Polan came back to me. "I've got it on the computerized case log and it's confirmed by my own handwritten note in my diary that I had a conference call scheduled with Peter Sutherland. June sixteenth is the date you're looking for."

"June sixteenth," I repeated. "You're sure about that?"

"Absolutely."

"It couldn't have been a day or two earlier that you two spoke and maybe you didn't get around to recording it in your log until the sixteenth?"

"Nope. It'd be June sixteenth exactly. I'm fastidious about that kind of thing. I've seen too many solid cases go down the toilet because someone was sloppy about recording a date and then some defense attorney can pick your timeline all to pieces."

"Amen to that, Captain. You've been a big help."

"Anytime. Good to talk to you."

I felt as if the wind had suddenly been sucked out of me. Fidelity, bravery, integrity—the oath we all took—what did it mean? With all its faults, with all its bureaucracy, with all its Harry Gillettes, joining the FBI isn't just a job, it's a mind-set, an outlook, a culture. It's the way you see things, and it doesn't have to be spoken, just as every Secret Service agent knows he'll die unquestioningly for a president he may personally despise because that is what you do; that is what you are all about.

June 16. June 16 was the day of my meeting with Peter where I half-jokingly told him about Trevor's desire to dig up Boyd's body so that Dominic could figure out what really killed him. I remembered the date distinctly, because that day an airtel had come in from the New York Field Office saying that a Detective Sochaczewski was looking for me. Peter and I had both wanted to know when it came in and both noted the date: June 16.

If Peter was one of the killers, he couldn't take the chance of letting me get at the body, and he'd do anything to stop me. Including recommending that the cops on the scene monitor the grave site. He told them they might nab the killer that way. But what he knew was that he'd keep me and my team from getting to it, and through a means that I wouldn't be able to complain about because it had been my technique in the first place! A stroke of proactive strategic brilliance.

He'd been a fast thinker, too. As soon as I left his office after suggesting what we might do in the cemetery, he'd picked up the phone and asked Cal State Police to put on a stake-out team. Then later, whenever I brought up the matter, he was prepared to say that he'd already called them before I'd even brought up the matter with him.

So Ted wouldn't have been the only one being blackmailed by Louie Knox for his part in Thomas Boyd's death. Knox must have been going after Peter, too.

If Captain Polan had given me a different date, I could tell Katie her theory was suspect. I could maybe even let Peter off the hook and go back and try to reinterpret the facts. But now I couldn't do that. The date sealed it. Timing is everything.

Even his timing with the Wendy Winslow bring-in was perfect. He and Ted must have arranged to go get Wendy together. Pete must have convinced Ted that Wendy was a threat to them, when in fact she wasn't. She tied the Boyd murder to a conspiracy, but not to them. So when Ted went along, Pete told Emilio Moldea this story about Ted coming into the situation room all wild-eyed, then sent Moldea out to neutralize him. Which, in fact, Special Agent Moldea did when he saw Ted holding Wendy and threatening Trevor. That way, Pete got to eliminate the accomplice who could one day betray him and also laid the responsibility for the Boyd killing right at Ted's feet, all at the same time. I knew Pete's hatred of Ted was real. It was a stunning piece of strategy.

His strategy had been well-planned and well-executed throughout. Peter had never told me anything false; he was too smart for that. He knew I'd see through it if he tried. He just didn't tell me everything that was true, and that's a lot easier to slide by the bullshit detector.

And another thing I decided for myself. I could forgive whoever it was who beat the hell out of me. But if Peter Sutherland turned out to be behind the break-in at Toni's house, what she and the kids went through . . . and then offered to watch the place where I sent them and "protect" them there . . .

I try to be rational about these things, but if that was the case, I'd kill him.

41

The Broken Wings gathered again at Katie's house.

"Who would have thought Pete and Ted could be in anything like this together," she mused. "Or that Ted would be willing to risk his status in the Bureau once Boyd was dead."

"Money is a powerful motivator," Dominic commented. He was certainly right about that. We had files of cases where people had killed, not only business associates and friends, but loved ones and families, for a lot less than Ted and Peter must have gotten.

"But there's just one problem with the scenario," Trevor pointed out. "Pete's got an alibi for the time of the murder. It's already been established that he was on his way to Hawaii by way of Los Angeles."

Katie's large hunter eyes brightened. "Not necessarily. I've checked into it. Unlike a lot of the agents, Jake had a great relationship with the support staff at Quantico, and it's amazing what a little goodwill can do for you."

Trevor frowned. "What are you talking about?"

"Normally, the Quantico travel office makes reservations for you when you're on official business. But if it's a last-minute thing, as this trip apparently was, sometimes the only way to get it done in time is to make the reservations yourself, charge the plane, rental car, and hotel to your own credit card, then get reimbursed in the next cycle. None of us like that because it means we're always out of pocket, but that's the way it is.

"Anyway, Pete made his own plane reservations and put on his itinerary that he was taking a United flight out of Dulles that connected to Honolulu through LAX. But I traced down the ticket number and what he really did was connect on United through SFO."

"Would he have had time to get up to Sausalito, take part in the murder, then get back to San Francisco International in time to catch the plane?"

I listened attentively to the discussion, saying little. In the unit I always wanted my people to make their own evaluations without my influence, and listening to them also helped me check my own conclusions. Now I was doing the same thing, only hoping desperately that one of my new people would say something to jar the pattern that had formed around Peter.

"He'd have time if he was organized and had help," Katie answered. "There was about a two-hour layover."

"How did they get around?" Jerry asked. "Did they have a Bureau car?"

"According to the records, Boyd was picked up in a Bureau car at the airport and Ted rode with him. So the two most likely scenarios are that Pete rented a car at the airport and drove himself up and back, or that Ted went out and rented a car after being dropped off at his hotel, picked Peter up at the airport, and then dropped him back again afterward."

I added, "Or that Peter rented a car, drove up to the scene, and then let Ted drive him back and hold on to the car so it wouldn't look suspicious that it was returned so quickly."

"Whoever did what," Jerry pointed out, "we have to assume they did it with phony names and credit cards."

"That's not difficult for an FBI agent," Trevor commented.

"We've got to find out," I said. Despite the timing on Peter's request to Captain Polan, I couldn't hand Orlando Ravan a complete case until we had some hard forensic evidence to back that up.

"Jerry," I said, "if we could actually locate that vehicle, what are the chances you could still find something in it that would tie the offenders physically to the crime scene?"

He seemed to inflate with pride. "The chances are excellent. You know the theory of transfer. It would be very difficult for a perpetrator to leave the scene without taking something with him."

"Even after the car's been turned over to different renters and cleaned up each time?" Katie asked.

"Doesn't matter. Something will remain and we can find it. For instance, we could do trace-metal tests on the steering wheel. Material is often embedded in a steering wheel from the hands or sleeves of the perp, and it doesn't matter whether he was wearing gloves or not. And that broken lamp you mentioned by the bed? I can almost guarantee there will be microscopic glass fragments in that car. They're very difficult to get rid of."

Jerry had a point. One day a couple of years ago when I was driving on I-95 down to Quantico, something shattered one of the side windows of my Land Rover. Professional paranoid that I have to be, I thought it was a bullet and veered sharply to evade more of them, but it turned out to be a rock kicked up by a dump truck at a roadside construction site. At any rate, though I had the window immediately replaced and the Rover thoroughly cleaned, I'm still finding little pieces of glass. I could imagine how much more difficult to get rid of they'd be when, as Jerry suggested, they're microscopic.

"Okay," I resolved, "we've got to find that rental car." I directed my next query to Katie. "Think we can?"

She shrugged. "It's probably doable, but it's gonna take a lot of manpower. We'd have to go through every rental agency and check out every record for that day, flag the possibles, go to the locations, interview the counter clerks to see if they recall guys matching either Ted's or Peter's description, then have the company trace and retrieve the vehicle, and let Jerry and Dominic go over it. That's something the San Francisco Field Office would be much better set up to do than we would."

"But we can't turn it over to them," I ruled. "Can we do it ourselves?"

"Give me as many warm bodies as you can."

"Take all of them in this room but mine. I raise too many red flags if I'm recognized. Ravan would be forced to shut us down then. He'd have no choice."

It was settled. Katie, Trevor, Dominic, and Jerry would fly out to San Francisco the next morning on a commercial flight. If anyone recognized *The Broken Wing* on a tarmac out there, it might attract the kind of attention I didn't want. Katie and Trevor could teach the other two how to search, and Katie would coordinate the entire effort.

"Get a good night's sleep everyone," I said. "It's going to be lonely without you all."

I waited until the others had left before I said my own good-byes to Katie. "I'm really going to miss you, even for a couple of days."

"I'm going to miss you, too. What about me are you going to miss most?" I loved that naughty, playful look in her eyes.

"Hard to say."

"Well, then!" She broke free of my hold, reached under the hem of her short denim jumper, and tantalizingly removed her pale blue bikini panties. She was so sexily smooth, so graceful, I could almost swear she had experience with this particular move. With one hand, she deftly crumpled them into a little ball, then stuffed them into my shirt pocket, where I caught a whiff of her scent on the cotton. "For when you really miss me," she explained, kissing me quickly on the lips, then darting her tongue briefly between them. Katie knew how to control a situation.

"Ah, would you like my Jockey shorts in return?"

"That's okay," she said, and gave me a playful but forceful slap on the butt that let me know she intended to continue controlling the situation. "Remember what you taught us—women aren't generally fetishists."

We walked the final few steps to the door, far enough to transition back into a serious mood. "Are you okay with this trip?" I asked her.

She nodded and kissed me again. "I'm always up for a hunt!"

"Good luck," I replied, and went out into the night.

∘

I tried to keep myself busy while the rest of my team was away. But I couldn't stop thinking of how this would all have to end. I didn't know how it would play out, but the two participants would be Peter Sutherland and me. After that happened, I would set the Bureau's accountants looking into Pete's offshore holdings. They would probably be sizable, just like Ted's. With luck, one of the team would find us the "smoking gun." Although a part of me hoped they came up with nothing.

In spite of the mounting evidence, that part of me just couldn't believe it. Maybe I was being selfish: I couldn't accept that I might have been so wrong. *What do I do now? How do you recover from that?* I asked myself.

The biggest blow of all came the next day when I went up to headquarters with authorization from Orlando Ravan to go through Thomas Boyd's private files. I didn't expect to find any blockbusters because Ravan had surveyed them himself in the days after the death. But Ravan hadn't been an investigator for many years, he'd had a lot of other things on his mind at the time, and he could easily have missed something subtle.

Modest man that he is, Ravan had not moved into Boyd's office, so I had the room all to myself. It was the first time I'd ever been in there alone. Ravan was right; there was nothing that would even remotely tie in. But for me, there was a megablockbuster, one that shut my breathing off and made my chest ache.

There was a confidential memo from Peter to Judge Boyd, about me. Ever since I'd returned from my convalescent leave resulting from the Black Diamond case, he said, I was not the same—my judgment was clouded, et cetera, et cetera. He felt the need, too, to call Boyd's attention to my last firearms qualification. The tremor had not gone away, and if I ever had to shoot in the line of duty, I could put my own life and the lives of my people and the public in jeopardy. Peter knew, he said, that the director, much as he respected me, would not want to take a chance on putting the Bureau in such a position.

So that was what had prompted Boyd to boot me out. Right here in Peter Sutherland's own words. I couldn't contain my rage. I wanted him right here in front of me. I wanted to grab him, I wanted . . . I didn't know what I wanted.

You lying, betraying fuck! Is that what they teach at Yale Law School—to rat out your friends for the sake of your own advancement? Well, Boyd had fucked him pretty good in return, passing him over in favor of Ted as my replacement. Maybe there is a little justice in the world.

But not if Tom Boyd had to die for it.

The other critical document I found was dated about two weeks later. It was a short letter from Boyd, marked CONFIDENTIAL, to the directors of both the Drug Enforcement Administration and the U.S. Customs Service. It began, "As we discussed by telephone, please make the above-captioned impounded aircraft available to the De Vries Foundation for the express purpose agreed upon."

He was talking about *The Broken Wing.*

The evidence was right here: at the same time Boyd had tossed me out of the Bureau, he'd arranged this for me. He'd essentially made the Flying Squad happen. He'd collaborated with Mrs. De Vries. And I'd accused the guy of having no sense of irony!

Was it just to give me something to do? Or was it because he wanted to get J. P. Napoleon as much as she did and thought this was the most effective way to do it? Either way, the inescapable fact was that he considered me the best one to do it.

My world was reeling now. Not only Peter Sutherland, was it possible I'd misjudged Thomas Boyd, too? Was I no longer capable of determining who was for me and who was against me? Had I finally ventured so far into the hall of mirrors that I could no longer distinguish the reality from the reflection?

The more I thought about it, the more incapacitated I felt. I had to stop; that was all there was to it. I had to stop seething, stop brooding about this and just move forward. If I didn't keep moving forward at this point, I knew I'd be swallowed up by this.

As soon as I finished up in Boyd's office, I drove straight to Mrs. De Vries's house. It was the first time I'd shown up there without an announcement or summons.

Frederick answered the door and led me into the sunroom. She joined me there.

"Jake," she said as she swept into the room. "What a pleasant surprise. Won't you sit down."

This time, I didn't accept her invitation. "Tell me how you came to sponsor the Flying Squad."

"I think you know the story," she said innocently.

"The real story." I told her about the Boyd letter.

"Does that negate the validity of the Flying Squad? Does the fact of an agreement between Tom Boyd and myself corrupt it in the Mindhunter's own mind? I took you for a more sophisticated thinker than that."

"Just tell me the story."

She sighed. "You know, of course, of my foundation's work in support of justice and law enforcement."

I nodded.

"And through that, I've developed a close and trusting relationship with each FBI director in turn. Shortly before I first contacted you, I got a call from Tom Boyd saying he was reluctantly having to let you go. He was sincere about this. He told me that he considered you such a critical asset to the FBI that he had been trying to figure out a way that he could continue to utilize your service and talents."

She walked over to the orchid tray and clipped several stems for the arrangement she was working on. "Then he told me about your proposal for the Flying Squad. He said it had never had a chance within the Bureau, but if it was done properly as an independent enterprise, he thought it would become the next great advance in the field you've pioneered. He knew of my personal animosity toward Empire and said we could both use this vehicle—and your talents—to try to identify him and then penetrate his organization. If my foundation would be willing to sponsor the project, Tom said he would secure an airplane and use the director's confidential discretionary funds to have it outfitted according to your proposal."

I was right. Whether the personal motivations turned out to be God and country or love and money, the effect was the same.

"And how do you feel about this, now that we suspect your husband may be . . . is probably still alive?"

Her eyes flashed with steely resolve. "No different!"

"Why didn't you tell me any of this arrangement before?"

"Tom didn't want me to. He felt that if you thought he was behind the plan, you'd either think he had an ulterior motive or that he was offering you charity. Either way, he felt that if you knew, you wouldn't have accepted."

"Did Orlando Ravan know? Was he part of the plan?"

"Of course he was." I felt the jolt of another synapse. I had been a pawn in this big picture every bit as much as Louie Knox, as Ronald Frishman, as Wendy Winslow.

"How fitting that the first mission of the Flying Squad turned out to be the solution to Thomas Boyd's murder," Mrs. De Vries said as she trimmed a white orchid and methodically threaded its stem through the buttonhole of my lapel. "From wherever he is now, Jake, he's counting on you."

Actually, I knew where he was, I almost told her. At least the part you could still see.

42

"You want the good news first or the bad news first?" Katie asked on the phone.

"Good news first. Let's not take a chance on my mental state."

"Okay, the good news is that I think, at long last, we've identified the rental agency, the location, and the car."

"Sensational!"

"It's opposite of the way we thought it might have happened. From what we've determined from both the records and interviews, a man matching Ted's description rented a Buick Skylark from Budget at a downtown location, and a man matching Pete's description returned it to SFO two days later. Which means that Ted must have picked up Pete at the airport, driven him up to Boyd's house, they did the murder, then Pete dropped Ted off somewhere, drove back to the airport, parked the car in a lot so it didn't raise any questions bringing it back so quickly, then turned it in on the return trip from Hawaii. Pete's luggage would have been checked through from Dulles straight to Honolulu, so he would have been able to walk onto the plane without wasting time at check-in."

"Makes sense," I said.

"I want you to know what a terrific job everyone did out here," Katie added. "They've practically been working around the clock."

"So what's the bad news?"

"The car in question was in a wreck about a week ago, totaled, and no one has a clue where it is now."

"Shit! Shit and a half!" *Fucking coincidence again. And it always seems to go against you, never for you. How's that for coincidence!*

"Best guess is it went to a scrap heap and may even be one of those cute little metal cubes by now. Sorry."

I didn't say anything for a long time.

"Are you still there?" Katie asked.

"Yeah." But my mind was elsewhere now, evaluating the possibilities. Without that car, we wouldn't have the forensic evidence I knew would be crucial.

"So what do you want us to do? Should we come home?"

"No. Stay out there. I'm flying out on *The Broken Wing*. I'll meet you all there."

"What's your strategy?"

It was the oldest strategy there was: when you aren't holding the high cards, bluff.

∘

Several years ago, my unit consulted on the case of a political assassin, white supremacist, and serial killer who cut a deadly path across the United States. He targeted interracial couples, whom he would shoot from a sniper's position. He was finally apprehended in Florida and we were called in by the Tampa Field Office. The SAC wanted to know what the best way to interrogate him would be, the best shot of getting something out of him.

I studied the subject's background and discovered that he had a fear of being out of control, not uncommon in serial predators. This could work to our advantage, I thought, because the man had been extradited back to Utah to stand trial for one of the murders, and Tampa was tasked with bringing him back.

Many control freaks have a latent fear of flying, since flying is one of the ultimate you're-not-in-control situations. I recommended that instead of returning the prisoner to Utah through the normal means, the SAC assign his best, most skillful interrogator to take him back in a small, chartered plane. My thinking was that the smaller plane (a) would be a bumpier, more knuckle-gripping ride; (b) would take a lot longer than a standard jet; and (c) would give the special agent and the subject a lot of time together, which, I hoped, would be conducive to having the subject open up.

That's the way it happened. The two of them developed something of a relationship, and every time the small plane hit a pocket of turbulence, the subject would open up a little bit more. The agent stroked the subject's ego and talked about his place in history and, as soon as the time seemed right, turned on a cassette recorder and advised the guy of his rights. The perp continued talking freely, and by the time they were within a half hour of landing, the agent felt the guy was ready to spill.

To up the ass-pucker factor, the agent had the pilot fly over the easily recognizable Utah State Penitentiary, and as they did, the agent pointed out that this was where Gary Gilmore had faced the firing squad, and where four bullets had pulverized his heart. If the perp was found guilty and sentenced to death here, he might expect a similar fate in this very building. At that point, the man was ready to deal. It's just a question of pressing the right stress buttons.

That was my plan with Peter.

Katie couldn't get me the conclusive piece of physical evidence, so if Peter really was one of the killers, I needed a confession.

I had Scott Kenworthy ready *The Broken Wing*, then I called Peter and invited him to take a trip with me out to San Francisco.

"What's up?" he asked.

"I've got something you ought to see. I think it might finally crack this case. But I want it kept confidential."

I don't think Pete suspected anything, but even if he had, it wouldn't have mattered. He had to come.

∘

The flight would give us the time alone. I arranged with Trevor to have him and Katie meet the plane in San Francisco and to come well armed, in case I had a prisoner to turn over. And my agenda for the flight itself was straightforward: present Peter with all the evidence, see how he reacted, and if that reaction was the one I imagined, then try to coax a confession out of him.

Was it foolhardy to go *mano a mano* with him at twenty thousand feet? Maybe, but no more so than being locked in a penitentiary conference room for five hours with a lifer big enough and mean enough to twist my head off and leave it on the table for the guards to find, and with no real incentive not to. There was no way I was going to get a confession with anyone else around. But alone with Peter, I could offer him some face-saving scenario that would at least *explain* why he had done the deed. He would know this strategy, he would have used it himself during interrogations, but if he thought it was the best way out, he might grab for it like a lifeline.

Only the four of us would be on the plane—the two pilots, him, and me—during a flight that would take more than five hours. I trusted my interrogation skills to be able to get a confession out of him if I could just establish the proper frame of reference, and if I had the right visual aids on board to do just that.

Once we were airborne, I took him on a brief tour of the facilities. When we got to the galley, I asked him if he wanted anything to drink and produced bottles of Scotch, bourbon, vodka, and gin. I thought if I could get him drinking, it might lower his inhibitions. He settled for a Coke.

I noticed Pete do a double take. "Umm, Jake, do you know you've got a cat on this plane?"

"Oh, yeah," I said nonchalantly. "That's J. Edgar. He was a stowaway. Katie insisted on keeping him. Myself, I don't much care for cats."

"I'm kind of neutral about them."

"Wait till we hit some turbulence that upsets the litter box. You might change your mind."

I let some time pass while we talked casually and enjoyed the comforts of *The Broken Wing*'s main cabin. Then I was ready to make my move.

"First, let me give you some background," I said. "I think I can show who was behind Ted."

"Great. If we can just nail that down, we can wrap this up. Not just for the Bureau and the public, but for each of us, too."

Something like that, I thought. I brought him into the conference room. "Sit down. Let me lay this out for you." I took the white-board VIA chart, which had been lying face-in against the bulkhead, and propped it up on the table.

His eyes went wide. Good. It was important for me to control his reactions. "I didn't realize you'd done a VIA."

"Thanks." I traced the connections for him, through Louie Knox and up through Wendy Winslow, which was where we could tie in Napoleon. I kept watching Peter, but he followed what I was telling him with calm interest.

"If you look at the way this develops," I said, using my pen to follow the various lines on the chart, "you'll see that both the militias and the

Russian Mob drop out. The only through-line is J. P. Napoleon." Again, I waited for a reaction.

He seemed delighted at the news. "I think you're right. I think you've got it. I mean, he had to be a suspect all along, but you've connected the dots."

I tried not to give any visual clues of my own. "I'm glad you agree." I opened my briefcase, took out a copy of Jerry's composite photo. I slid it across the table to Peter. "Ever see this guy before?"

There it was! A brief flicker in the eyes, a dart of fear, passing instantly, but I caught it before it did and imprinted the reaction on my mind.

"Who is it?" he asked cautiously.

"We believe it to be J. P. Napoleon!" I said triumphantly.

"Where . . . how did you get it?"

"Needle believes she met him at a reception in Switzerland."

His mind was churning, just as it must have been the afternoon when I mentioned digging up Boyd's grave. "You think Napoleon would let someone like her get that close to him?"

"Why not? It's not as if the police are going to be able to circulate the composite and have someone call in."

"Maybe it's not Napoleon," Peter offered. "Maybe it's someone Napoleon uses as an intermediary instead of personal contact."

"That's possible, too. What makes you say that?"

Again, slightly off guard, but a quick recovery. "Huh? I don't know, it just seems logical that he'd keep that buffer."

I nodded emphatically. "Okay, good. I knew the two of us could make some progress if we had a chance to put our heads together. Now, if this individual is a go-between rather than Napoleon himself, he'd have to be someone Napoleon trusted implicitly, someone close enough that he didn't feel threatened having this guy know all his secrets."

"Okay . . . ," Peter said tentatively.

"So I think what we're saying is that the man in this sketch could easily have been the one Ted and his accomplice would have met with."

"Accomplice?" Peter repeated, a few drops of perspiration forming on his forehead. The next indicator would probably be the shallow, accelerated breathing.

"Right," I said, maintaining control. "See, the thing that still nags at me is, I just don't think Ted acted alone at the murder scene."

"You don't?"

I shook my head. "How's he gonna make Boyd eat lead if it's him by himself, even if he has a gun of his own. I can't make a one-man scenario work out no matter how I bend it."

It was subtle, but I thought I detected a wariness creeping into his affect. "Any ideas?"

"I keep asking myself, who had the means and who had the motive?" I let a long pause hang in the air. "Who stood to gain directly by Tom Boyd's death?"

Peter chuckled and leaned back in his chair. "Well, I'm the only one I can think of who's gained so far!"

I chuckled along with him.

"You don't think it was Moldea, do you?" he asked. "You know, that he set Ted up to take the whole rap?"

"It's possible, but I think it's someone with a closer connection. Not as close as Ted, necessarily, but close."

"What about motive?"

We were dancing around the perimeter, each one carefully watching the other's steps. Now it was time to offer my face-saving scenario. "There may have been some money involved, like there was with Ted, but I don't think that was the prime motivation. The way I profile him, he's a guy who's under enormous personal pressure, but who honestly disagrees with Boyd's approach and thinks he's got to get rid of him for the overall good of the Bureau. The way Brutus and the other senators felt they had to kill Caesar for the good of Rome. Whatever selfish reasons Ted may have had, I think the guy who worked with him was not by nature a criminal and did what he did out of conscience."

I was straining to keep the calmness in my voice. This airplane, this tube of steel flying from one coast to the other, had become the entire world. The only thing that mattered was what happened right here.

"You may be right," said Pete. "I hadn't really thought about that possibility."

I leaned in toward him. "Think about it now, you'll see what I mean. And what about access? We know Ted was in San Francisco at the time, but who else could have been there?"

He regarded me carefully. Too carefully. "And have you come up with anything?"

"Funny thing is, the only other one we can place in San Francisco so far is you."

"Me?" He laughed out loud. "I was en route to Hawaii."

"Through San Francisco International."

I had him. Everything up until now had been sparring, supposition, what-if scenarios. Now he was on record with an out-and-out, provable lie.

"No. Through Los Angeles."

"Are you sure? We traced your reservation file through the airline's computer system. They have you routed through SFO."

"I don't know why," he said, suddenly serious. "I'll have to check on that."

"Good idea. Let me know what you come up with."

Suddenly there was an uncomfortable silence, which I let play.

I had a case once in rural Georgia in which a twelve-year-old girl was abducted, raped, and murdered and her body found in a clearing in the woods. The medical examiner determined that she died of blunt-force trauma to the head, and the apparent murder weapon was a rock about a foot long with bloodstains on it found at the scene. From the scene, I could tell it wasn't a planned crime, but rather one that spontaneously presented itself. And since the victim's coat was placed over her head, I concluded that the UNSUB did not feel good about the crime. The police came up with a suspect who fit my profile, and they asked me to interrogate him. I knew a confession would be tough—Georgia is a death-penalty state. So I had them place the rock on the table in front of us. I didn't say anything about it, I just let it sit there upping his asshole pucker factor. As soon as he saw it, the guy started sweating. He couldn't keep his eyes off it. The rock had not been part of any public account, so it would have meaning only to the actual killer. After a couple of hours, I offered him a face-saving scenario in which I suggested the little girl might have come on to him, then threatened to tell when he responded. Of course, I felt no such thing had happened, but it was a lifeline the guy went for. He's currently on death row awaiting execution. And whenever I use this case in one of my lectures to law enforcement personnel, I remind them, "Everybody has a rock."

Now I was ready to show Peter his.

I stood up. "Come with me. Let me show you something." I led him back to the lab, turned on the light, and closed the door behind us.

"This is quite a setup you have here," he said with forced cheerfulness. "Is this the evidence you wanted to show me?"

"Yeah. Wait till you see it!" I positioned him on the other side of the dissecting table so there'd be room to maneuver around the tight

312 o **John Douglas and Mark Olshaker**

quarters, then unlatched the handle on the stainless-steel Mobil-Mort refrigeration unit, opened the door, and slid the gurney about halfway out.

Pete blinked calmly, as if his eyes weren't quite registering. Then those same eyes practically bugged out of his head. "What the hell . . . ?"

"Look familiar?"

"It's . . ."

"You got it!"

"But where did you . . . ? He was . . . He was cremated."

"Actually"—I stretched the word out for maximum drama—"he wasn't. Because, you see, we have him right here."

He turned on me and his eyes grew cold and narrow. "What's this all about, Jake?"

"I was concerned that the medical examination hadn't given us all the information we needed. So I decided we'd better dig him up and find out for ourselves. Didn't I mention it to you? I know I did. Wait a minute! It was . . . I know, it was June sixteenth. That's right, I'm sure of it: June sixteenth." That ought to be puckering up his asshole right tight.

There is a steady deterioration, a progressive decompensation, you can track during an interrogation when the subject knows you know. But a ritual must still be followed, a mating dance of sorts. "Are you suggesting . . . ?"

And the dance must proceed according to its own pace and meter. I turned on him, suddenly explosive. "I don't have to suggest, Pete. You gave yourself away. You betrayed the badge: the fidelity, the bravery, the integrity. But I think you know all that."

No matter how much he knows, no matter how sophisticated he is, the look of a cornered man is always the same. "I swear, Jake, I don't know what you're talking about."

"I'm talking about you killing Thomas Boyd."

"*Ted Novello* killed Thomas Boyd!"

"With your help. That was really clever: using as an accomplice a man everyone thought you hated. And you know what? I believe you did hate him. You just happened to have a mutuality of interests. But hating him made it all the easier emotionally when it was time to cut him loose . . . in fact, when it was time to silence him for good."

"That's insane!"

"That would be a possible defense." This is exactly what an innocent man is supposed to say when accused of murder; a guilty one will try to come up with some excuse or alternative explanation, whereas an innocent one won't—he'll just say the whole thing is crazy. And ordinarily, I'd place a lot of weight on this kind of response. But this was a special case, because Peter knew as well as I did what the appropriate response was supposed to be.

"It was clever." I let my voice calm down. "You knew Boyd's death scene would attract police brass like flies to shit. They'd help you cover your evidence by obliterating hair and fiber evidence. The best part was staging it as a suicide. Dispose of the murder weapon? You figured out a way that you wouldn't have to worry about that. No problem with ballistics. You could leave the fucking weapon out in the open."

"I see what's going on," Peter said, his eyes narrowed. "You killed Boyd, didn't you?" He was losing it. That was the kind of response I'd expect from a sophisticated, disorganized perpetrator.

"You know I didn't."

"You've got the best revenge motive of anyone. Boyd destroyed your career. And the great Jake Donovan couldn't let anyone do that to him."

"Sorry, Pete. It doesn't fly."

"The really creative part was involving Ted. See, I never would have figured the two of you could work together on anything. You've got me in an awkward position here, Jake, but I'm going to have to arrest you for the murder of Thomas Boyd. Let's make this as easy as we can."

I didn't know whether to laugh at his desperation or tear his throat out in rage. Instead of either, I continued methodically laying out the case, just as I would have to a task force of local cops. I told him that Dominic had determined Boyd's teeth chipped inward, and my own analysis was that it would have taken two large men with guns to overpower Boyd and force the gun into his mouth. I told him about the minute glass fragments we'd found on the body.

"Katie was able to locate your rental car, and we not only found matching fragments, but also a paint chip with a partial print that matches one of your own prints on file. That ought to be enough for a probable-cause warrant to search your house, where Jerry Carruthers would fully expect to find fiber and other trace material connecting you directly to the crime scene."

"You can't prove anything by that."

"Oh, but we can. Jerry is very, very good." Peter was an expert behaviorist, but wouldn't necessarily be up on the latest lab techniques. That's what I was counting on.

He gripped the side of the dissecting table until his fingers started to turn white. He was going through the transition. We were nearing the endgame.

"How could you betray us?" I challenged. "What made you slip over to the other side?"

He just stood there trembling, glancing down at the body of his victim. His rock. "I didn't go to the other side," he said finally. "He did. It had to happen. For the good of the Bureau. Just like you said. It had to be done because of what he did to you."

Now it didn't matter anymore. Now the rage was all spilling out. How could he have done this to his leader? How could he have done this to me, who trusted him, who believed in him, who was taken in by him. "Don't give me that bullshit! I know how you set me up. I saw the memo. So where's your loot stashed away? Grand Cayman? Switzerland? The accountants were really amazing on Ted's case. Or is yours all just stuffed in your mattress? Well, if it is, the search warrant will uncover it."

"Let's try to be reasonable."

Okay, I thought, trying to contain myself, I could work with this. Once he broke, he'd become more pliable, even cooperative.

"I'm a reasonable man," I answered. "What do you have in mind?"

"This can work out for both of us." He was talking rapidly, in quick bursts between gasps for air. "I can get you money, enough to be comfortable the rest of your life. Hell, with Boyd gone and Ravan impressed with you, we can probably get you your old job back."

"I don't want it back, though the money sounds attractive." I turned as cold as he was. "Whose money is it?"

"Who cares?"

"I care. It's Napoleon's, isn't it? He was the one who came to you with the Boyd fuck pictures, right?"

"Well, not him personally," Peter corrected me. "No one gets to see the Great Oz in person. Not even me. That's how I knew your composite wasn't him. I recognized your guy. Napoleon, I've never met."

"And did you know that 'my guy' is actually Fletcher De Vries?"

"He told me," Peter said, as if condescending to confide in a much slower friend who's only just caught on to the joke.

"And he would have been the one who relayed your ideas, your own proactive strategies, up to Napoleon himself," I accused. "You knew which buttons to press and when to press them. It would have been you who suggested he arrange for the guys dressed like militia types to try to scare me away and, at the same time, lead us off to the Wyoming Defenders."

"It's not exactly off track," Peter said tauntingly. "Who do you think supplies their weapons and ammo? Why do you think they use such old-fashioned bullets—the same kind that killed Tom Boyd? Because Napoleon sells them cheap, that's why!"

And how deep was Peter in all this? Like Brutus, had he killed his Caesar as a misguided matter of principle, he and Napoleon using each other for their own purposes? Or had he always been a mole, a traitor in our midst? This would be my first question at the interrogation. But first, I had some personal scores to settle.

"When your militia goons didn't scare me off, you got someone to break into Toni's house and cut off the heads of Ali's dolls, figuring that would really scare the shit out of me. Well, you know something, it did."

"I was trying to protect you. I was trying to keep you out of it. It wasn't your fight anymore."

I was still in a white rage. I couldn't let the bastard get away with this, even if he was going to spend the rest of his life in the slammer. "That's what your thugs were saying while they kicked the shit out of me. Sorry, Pete, it's crap. By the way, I was impressed that you guys managed to get that tattoo on Louie Knox's wrist so fast. Very nice touch. Very subtle. Oh, and the dirt on his shoes: the pièce de résistance! It made me divert all the way to Wyoming."

I drew my gun. "I assume you're carrying. Give it to me."

Peter reached into his jacket. "Here. I'm sorry it worked out this way."

"Me, too," I said, as sincere as I had ever been. I came around the table and stuck out my hand to receive his weapon.

He slid open the drawer closest to him, and when I saw his hand again, it was gripping a scalpel. Without warning, he kicked my gun out of my hand and lunged at me. I pulled back. Quickly reholstering his gun, he reached in and grabbed another scalpel, then charged around the table toward me.

Reflexively, I jumped and grabbed hold of the steel light bar bolted to the ceiling, swung my body weight forward, and kicked him in the chest. He staggered backward, but didn't relinquish the two blades.

As soon as he scrambled to his feet, I used my advantage to kick him down again, but he seized one of my ankles and plunged a scalpel high into my leg above the knee.

A jolt of pain shot through me and I felt the wound go wet. I let go of the light bar and frantically pulled away from him, using my fall for momentum. I hit hard on the floor, but rushed to my feet in spite of the pain before he could lunge at me again.

I made a feint forward, then when he went for me, I quickly snapped back, dropped down, and scrambled under the dissecting table, gripped both his ankles, and heaved. Pete came down solidly on his tailbone, uttering a grunt of pain and dropping the scalpels. I reached for them and was able to grab one before he secured the other. I freed myself from the uprights of the table and backed out of his reach. I thought of trying to grab for my gun on the floor, but in these close quarters, there was just as much chance he'd wrestle it from me.

Now we were evenly armed, and in such a tight enclosure, there was little room for retreat. It's a principle of knife-fighting that you're going to get cut, and the winner is the one who gets cut less seriously. I took the offensive again and went for his solar plexus.

Just as I caught him, he pulled to the side, leaving a thin bloody trail across the front of his shirt. But he'd managed to avoid my deep thrust, and he came around and plunged his own scalpel into my right arm.

"Motherfucker!" I screamed. The pain was unbearable. He pulled the knife out again, and it was all I could do to jerk away from him before he could plunge it into my chest.

Peter got bold and climbed up on the table, jumping down on me. I only had a few feet to back up, so I couldn't completely avoid him. This time he got me in my left forearm. But when you're that close with a knife, you're going to end up trading jabs, and I stuck my scalpel into his gut, just above the waist.

He yelled in agony and rage, but as soon as I saw the blood pattern, I could tell I hadn't scored a serious blow. It had only gone into fat and muscle. If I could just get my arm back around, though, before he got out of the way . . .

The floor fell out from under us. We must have hit an air pocket. We both struggled for purchase as the two scalpels clattered and then slid under the sink. Now we were both bleeding and unarmed. Peter still had his gun, but it wasn't any use here. The military hand-to-hand adage about running from a knife but charging a gun is true. This close, he couldn't have hit me, and if he tried, the bullet would have hit the fuselage wall.

I head-butted him in the chest, stunning him long enough so I could get back on my feet. He came after me, throwing a roundhouse with his right at my head. I ducked and sent an uppercut into his jaw. I know he saw stars at that one, but he came back with a solid punch to my chin that threw me back against the wall of metal cabinets, grabbed me around the neck with both hands, and squeezed, pressing both thumbs deep into my neck just above the larynx. We'd both seen enough strangulations to know that if he could keep up this level of pressure, I'd pass out.

I didn't know how much longer I could survive this. I wasn't losing serious blood from my wounds, but they were increasingly painful and robbing me of energy. Another couple of minutes and the bleeding would become a factor. I felt my heart pounding at hundreds of beats a minute. My hands were trembling. I couldn't rip his hands off my neck.

I heard an earsplitting screech and felt the grip on my neck loosen. J. Edgar had jumped onto Peter's face. I hadn't even realized he was in the room. Peter let go of me and tried to pull the beast off. The cat screeched again and scampered away. But he'd given me the break I needed.

I stepped forward and kicked Peter in the groin. He doubled over and I jumped on him and bit him in the neck. He struggled to shake me off, and I landed on the floor squarely on my shoulder. He kicked me in the face, then before I could recover or respond, scurried to the door, wrestled open the sliding handle, and ran out.

Fuck! I pulled myself to my feet, still reeling, and snatched up my gun and followed after him. I could feel my sock wet with blood.

By the time I got out into the corridor, he was disappearing into the conference room.

I chased him, but by now he was into the main cabin. I had to catch him before . . .

He was into the cockpit. I heard clamor from behind the swinging cockpit door. I raced through it.

I saw Scott, a look of panic on his face. Completely unnatural for him and not the expression you want to see from your pilot. My eyes darted over to the second seat, where Trish was trembling in terror with the barrel of Peter's Sig pressed tightly against her temple.

I pulled out my own gun and sprang into the firing stance. "Drop it!" I yelled.

"You seem to be forgetting that even though we're both armed, I have the advantage," he explained with mock patience, the palpable tension raising the level of his voice at least half an octave. "The force of my bullet will be absorbed by this young lady's skull and brain. Unless you hit me squarely from where you're standing, your bullet will go into the fuselage and cripple the plane. And we all know about your inability to shoot straight, Jake. It was the reason you had to leave the Bureau. Remember?"

You saw to that, didn't you, Peter? You made sure Boyd had what he needed on me even without Owl Creek. You made sure everyone had what they needed on everyone else. That was your special gift, your special service to all of us. Wasn't it, Peter? Wasn't it?

I glanced around the cockpit, trying to figure out my next move. I'd taken the precaution of filling my gun with light-load, frangible Glaser safety slugs, and I assumed Peter was using something similar. But even so, his evaluation was absolutely on the nose.

"Descend to a lower altitude!" Peter ordered Scott.

"Why?"

"Just do it!" Peter barked, and Scott complied. I felt my ears clog up painfully as we lost height. I hoped I wasn't blacking out.

What's he trying to do? I wondered. *Is he planning to bail out and escape? To crash the plane?*

"Throw down your gun!" Peter directed me. "It isn't doing you any good anyway."

He might have been right, but it was the last move I intended to make.

"Throw it down or the copilot here becomes a very messy cleanup."

"You can't do that!" I was getting light-headed from the bleeding and pain and tried to keep myself focused. As a hostage negotiator, you always look for some common ground, even if it's no more than a square inch. "She's completely innocent. Ted and Knox were involved, and you had your own reasons for killing Boyd. But you've never killed an innocent person, you've worked your whole career to put away the people who do. I can't believe you're going to start now."

"You forced me into it," he said distractedly.

There was no time left. We were plummeting dangerously low. I needed him to focus. "There must have been something real between us," I pleaded. "This isn't the Peter Sutherland I've known all these years. Let me talk to that one. I'm sure I can still reason with him."

This seemed to get to him, and I desperately watched his face for a sign. "I'm sorry," he finally declared. "I hate doing this. Unlike the people we hunt, I get no pleasure or satisfaction from it. I did what I had to do. And I'm doing it now. That's the way it's got to be. If you don't drop your gun, she gets it."

This was when I lost hope. He had become irrational under the stress and threat, and any further reasoning would be impossible. The key decision anyone running a hostage siege has to make is when a peaceful resolution is no longer realistic and force is the only means left. It is a searing, sobering moment, and I thought through the scenario to assure myself we'd reached it here.

I tried to think clearly. To get out of this now, Peter would have to kill me, he'd have to kill Trish, and then once the plane was landed, he'd have to kill Scott. And if he did kill Trish, I knew Scott wouldn't follow his instructions. He'd crash the plane himself before he did.

Peter was decompensating quickly. He was sweating profusely, his eyes wild and frantic. He'd ordered Scott to descend, maybe so he could see the ground and bail out before the plane crashed. I've known other desperate hijackers to try just that. Or maybe he was planning on going down in the plane with the rest of us.

All of this took a second to figure through. I held myself rigidly in my firing stance.

"Drop the gun!" Peter ordered again. "I'm going to give you about two more seconds, and then I'm going to kill her."

In the first of those two seconds, I calculated that I had one chance, and that was instant incapacitation that would not produce a jerking reflex that could make his gun go off. From how Peter was facing me, that meant a shot between the nose and the upper lip, directly into the medulla oblongata. Trevor could do this easily; he had at Owl Creek. I wasn't that good. But right now, I had to be.

I tried to control the shaking of my hand, made worse by the pounding I'd already taken and the blood I'd lost. I adjusted my aim to the left, as if I were trying to shoot just clear of his shoulder and instead take out the upper window panel behind him. *Isn't this what Katie told you*, I recalled, *overcorrect to the opposite side?*

In the remaining second, I steadily and evenly squeezed the trigger. A burst of fire shot out of the barrel, and almost simultaneously Peter's head exploded, sending bone and brain fragments all over the cockpit.

The wall of the plane behind him remained intact.

His body collapsed; Trish's body went limp.

With my hand shaking uncontrollably, I handed my gun to Scott, then made my way back to the lavatory to be sick.

43

The rest of the Broken Wings were there to meet the plane when it landed at San Francisco International, and before long Orlando Ravan and Neil Burke arrived on the director's Gulfstream. Harry Gillette was not with them.

As soon as she saw me, Katie ran up and hugged me. And then she did something uncharacteristic: she started to cry. She refused to leave my side.

The plane was now a crime scene, and Douglas Steinberg, the SAC of the San Francisco Field Office, assumed personal control. There would be no replay of the fiasco at the Boyd scene. A phalanx of airport security and California State Police kept the army of reporters and media trucks a reasonable distance away.

They took Scott, Trish, and me to the airport police office. When my wounds had been tended to, I gave my statement, the first of many I knew I would be asked for in the weeks and months to come.

Once some of the hoopla had died down, Orlando Ravan pulled me and Katie into a vacant office. She was now clutching J. Edgar tightly in her arms. I couldn't complain. He was the real hero.

"You have my thanks, Jake," Ravan said. "And I'm sure the nation's, too. You've done a hell of a job. All of you."

"Thank you," I replied. "I kind of feel as if we didn't have any real choice."

A rare smile formed on the Raven's lips. "You didn't," he replied. "But now that this is over, is there anything I can do for you?"

I thought a moment. "I'm sure there'll be quite a few once I stop to think about it. But for the time being, I'd really appreciate it if you could . . . ah . . . take the director's body off our hands. I was beginning to think I'd never get rid of it."

"Consider it done," he said as he left the room.

Then I turned to Katie, took her by both shoulders, and pulled her close. "I would, however, be willing to discuss what *you* can do for me!"

∘

Ronald Frishman was never located. As the official investigation drew to a close, the biggest disappointment for me was that with both Ted and Peter dead, we had no way of determining how long either of them had been involved with the Napoleon organization. I was particularly plagued by the ambiguity over Peter, and whether he'd been a covert operative all or part of the time he'd been with my unit. Had any cases been affected because of this possible corruption, or had he been approached and compromised only recently? I would probably never know.

Millicent De Vries threw a great party for us at her house. The whole team showed up, and Toni, Ali, and Eric, too. Both kids seemed the same, as if they'd been through nothing more than a summer vacation. The night I had had to race over to Toni's house seemed forgotten. Eric flirted with Katie, and at one point I noticed her and Toni off together on a bench in the garden, deep in conversation. I don't know what they were talking about, but at the end of it, they leaned in toward each other, hugged, and kissed. I never asked what was exchanged between them, and neither woman volunteered the information, but it made me feel good to see this.

Toward the end of the evening, I found myself alone with Mrs. De Vries on the balcony overlooking the park.

"I guess we've both had to reevaluate who we've trusted in our lives." I had noted that since my last visit, all photos of Fletcher had been removed.

"I guess we have," I responded. "I hope you're dealing with it better than I am."

"I don't know about that, Jake." She smiled wistfully. "I take it you no longer think Fletcher is Napoleon." Katie had begun digging into Fletcher's background and the circumstances surrounding his disappearance. I found it interesting that it occurred about six months after articles of incorporation for a domestic subsidiary of Empire International were filed in Delaware.

"It still wouldn't surprise me if he was Napoleon," I told our hostess and sponsor. "Just as the guard at the gate of the Emerald City turned out to be the Wizard of Oz himself, we're dealing with someone smart enough not to reveal himself to any but his closest and most trusted associates. The man Wendy identified, the man Peter took his orders from, could have been Napoleon without Peter ever knowing it."

She looked off toward the tree line. "And this is the man I loved."

"We're going to find out for sure . . . if you still want us to."

Mrs. De Vries put a hand on my shoulder in comradeship. "I do. But knowing you as I do now, I have a feeling you'd keep trying to find out with or without me."

I smiled. "You're probably right."

∘

With all the media coverage and the key role that Orlando Ravan had played in authorizing our successful independent investigation, the president succumbed to reason and appointed Ravan permanent director of the FBI.

I was going to call and congratulate him as soon as I heard the news, but he got to me first, about six-thirty in the morning. I wondered how he knew I was at Katie's house.

"How are you, sir?" I asked, cradling the receiver against my bare shoulder. Behind me, Katie was up on her knees on the bed, grazing her bare chest teasingly across my back, making it difficult to concentrate on the call.

We exchanged congrats, how-are-you's, and other pleasantries for a minute or two, and then Ravan said, "You sound busy."

"Nothing that can't wait," I assured him, grinning at Katie, who was sitting behind me on the bed.

She slapped my shoulder hard enough to be heard at the other end of the line.

"Anyway," he said, "I'll make this brief. I'm undertaking my own reorganization of the Bureau, and I'd like to offer you and your team a contract."

"A contract?"

"That's right. You'll take on special assignments for me whenever I feel it's warranted. You'll all keep your pensions, and we'll maintain your airplane and equipment, share your salaries and expenses with the De Vries Foundation, and loan you out to other law enforcement agencies when the need arises. You'll be given federal special-agent credentials and full authorizations. And as before, you'll report directly to me. How does that sound?"

An easy decision. "Sounds pretty good."

"Good. Then we've got ourselves a deal."

"Well?" Katie said when I hung up the phone. "What did he say?"

"He said he wants you and me to start spending more quality time together going forward."

She regarded me coolly. "Is that exactly what he said?"

I embraced her with the fierce delight of the hunter. "I'd say we're about to find out."